TO THE RIVER

Why would you risk your life and
all that you love for a stranger?

HUGO DE BURGH

Afterword by
MAX HASTINGS

T

Copyright © 2024 Hugo de Burgh

The moral right of the author has been asserted.

Apart from any fair dealing for the purposes of research or private study, or criticism or review, as permitted under the Copyright, Designs and Patents Act 1988, this publication may only be reproduced, stored or transmitted, in any form or by any means, with the prior permission in writing of the publishers, or in the case of reprographic reproduction in accordance with the terms of licences issued by the Copyright Licensing Agency. Enquiries concerning reproduction outside those terms should be sent to the publishers.

This is a work of fiction. Names, characters, businesses, places, events and incidents are either the products of the author's imagination or used in a fictitious manner. Any resemblance to actual persons, living or dead, or actual events is purely coincidental.

Troubador Publishing Ltd
Unit E2 Airfield Business Park,
Harrison Road, Market Harborough,
Leicestershire LE16 7UL
Tel: 0116 279 2299
Email: books@troubador.co.uk
Web: www.troubador.co.uk

ISBN 978 1 805142 48 5

British Library Cataloguing in Publication Data.
A catalogue record for this book is available from the British Library.

Printed and bound in Great Britain by 4edge Limited
Typeset in 10.5pt Minion Pro by Troubador Publishing Ltd, Leicester, UK

Any profits from the sale of this novel will go to the
Monte San Martino Trust, charity no. 1113897

'*In quelle giornate, in quel momento di crisi profonda delle strutture dello Stato, rinacque l'Italia vera. Fece il suo ingresso in scena il popolo italiano, con la sua antica civiltà, con la sua grande umanità.*'

'In those days, at the very moment when the state disintegrated, the real Italy was reborn. The Italian people entered the arena, with their ancient civility, with their great humanity.'

Carlo Azeglio Ciampi,
Sulmona,
17th July, 2001

From the blog of the Monte San Martino Trust, London, 15th February, 2003

Gerald FitzGerald, the oldest surviving prisoner of PG500, flew to Rome last week to take part in an anti-war march, which turned out to be the biggest ever, of three million people. Some of our members, sons and daughters of fellow escapees Anthony Lange, Stuart Goode and Ian Albion joined him. With a speech given in Italian, Gerald said that it was only right that this demonstration should be in Italy, where war had devastated the lives of ordinary people, who had nevertheless proved more willing to sacrifice themselves to succour refugees than in any other occupied country. He spoke of "altruism", the "extraordinary bravery of ordinary people". He spoke of the suffering of so many, including the woman who had done so much to save him and hundreds of his comrades, and whose son Geraldo and granddaughter Lucia had joined the march that day. Gerald was overcome by his memories but was supported by several of our members. Gerald will be 100 this year.

PART ONE

STRANGERS AT THE DOOR

THE FIRST CHOICE

Not one door was open: every window was shuttered tight. This was a street of merchant palaces with high iron-grilled windows, mighty carriageway portals and dwarf-sized wickets, all clenched shut by the heavy iron bars within.

The white sun weighed down on the woman in black as she walked briskly down via Mazzini. The heat of the flagstones reached up through her soles. She was slender, veiled with a mantilla, holding a black parasol in her right hand. Hanging by a string from her left was a basket of those almond biscuits for which the convent of Palma is famous, and there was a black canvas sack over her shoulder.

She turned into via Cavour which, like via Mazzini before it, was another street of palaces, quite deserted, except that crouching down by one of the massive doorways was a small boy, whimpering.

How strange. He's only about six. Wearing short trousers with braces and a clean white shirt. Riva Lucia's eyes took in the eerie emptiness of the centre of Palma. Then she brought to mind the orphans for whom she had been made to care in her few days at the convent, cleaning them, helping them to feed themselves, combing the girls' hair, putting her arms around them when they cried for mamma. *I'll never forget those children, their pain, their grief.* She stopped by the doorway and glanced down, pulling back her veil so that the child might see her face.

'What's up, *giovanotto*, young man?' *He is very blond, ash blond, not one of us. And how blue those eyes!*

He stared at her. She crouched down to be on his level. He cringed back, as if trying to disappear into the wall.

Just as she put out her hand to touch him, there was a screech of rusty hinges and the wicket opened. She held back. Stepping over the sill was a black riding boot, then a pair of grey breeches with a black double stripe. Then, stooping to get through the wicket came a lanky, athletic man in the black shirt and fez of the fascist militia. Lucia had seen these fezzes on the heads of lads in the square of her hometown, lounging by the office of the party, smirking at the women going in and out of the shops, bawling the fascist song *giovinezza!* at the top of their voices. She noticed a white scar on his jaw and thought he looked familiar, but perhaps it was the uniform. She had never allowed her eyes to meet those of these men. *Mamma calls them "thugs" and even* Dottoressa *Foschini dismisses them as "roughs".* She wouldn't allow her girls in the Young Italians even to speak to them.

The boy winced and Lucia rose quickly.

'You still here?'

In that empty street, the militiaman's voice sounded like the echo in a deep cave; he glanced down at the cowering child.

Lucia asked, 'What's the matter with him?'

The militiaman was out on the street now, and Lucia saw that he had a dagger at his belt, leather pouches and a gun slung over his shoulder. He was not menacing; more showing off, she sensed. He looked her over, her mourning skirt and black shirt. As he stared into her eyes, she pulled the veil back over her face.

'He's a yid. They picked up his parents and sisters a couple of hours ago. I'm just here sealing the apartment. I told him to get lost.'

The blackshirt turned to the boy: 'What's your name? *Deine name?*'

The boy whispered: 'Heinz.'

Looking back at Lucia, the blackshirt spoke straight at her, for in her astonishment she had forgotten to avoid his eyes. 'There. He's called Eye-Enz. He's on the list but was out playing with some other boys somewhere, so we didn't catch him. When he came back, his parents had been taken and I was doing the inventory.'

Lucia asked, 'What's that name?'

'Eye-Enz.'

'God protect us. A heathen name. There's no saint called "Eye-Enz".'

Blackshirt grinned and scratched a red spot on his neck. As he did, so Lucia noticed that his front teeth were stained yellow. She thought them repulsive.

'You're from Ginestra, aren't you? Live in the square?'

Lucia was taken aback. *So that's why he's familiar. Dio, what does he want from me?* Ignoring his impertinence, she asked, 'Where are his parents?'

'They'll be at the station. They take them direct.'

Lucia turned to the boy, giving him what she hoped was a comforting smile. 'Shall I take you to the station? I'm going there myself. And we can find your parents.'

The boy seemed to understand, for he nodded and rose.

The militiaman looked at her levelly, as if trying to work out if she was stupid or naïve. 'You won't get to the station, *Signorina*. When they are loading up the prisoners, there's a cordon all round.'

The boy moved close to her. Lucia put out her hand and he took it.

'Well, maybe they'll allow me to put him in their carriage.'

The militiaman gave a brusque snort of a laugh. 'Carriage! They go in cattle trucks! If you hand him over to them, he might as well be dead. His parents won't thank you. They must be praying that he won't be found.'

He glanced around as if to check that there was nobody nearby to hear his claims.

She didn't understand. 'What do you mean?'

He looked back at her. '*Signorina*, these poor wretches are off to the east. Those that survive the journey die on arrival.'

'What do you mean? Why?'

'Why? Why? Why ask "Why"?' he muttered, shaking his head as if in despair at the woman's stupidity. 'They are better off than the ones who land in Trieste. They must wish they had killed themselves before.'

She watched him shrug, showing that, after all, it was nothing to do with him; he had somewhere to get to. *Like me, got to get on.* He peered down to take a part-smoked cigarette out of his breast pocket, put it in his mouth, and glanced at her again. *I'm rather bemused – I've no idea what he's talking about. Why doesn't he light the cigarette?*

'Take him away, *Signorina*. Take him to Ginestra.'

He really is one of those militiamen I must have passed in town so often and he recognises me. Is it because of this that he is asking me?

'But I can't, I…'

Suddenly angry, he almost shouted, 'For God's sake, woman, save his life. Go on. Get a move on, otherwise I'll have to hand him over.'

Bewildered, hardly believing what the militiaman was saying, Lucia turned, taking the boy's hand, in the direction in which she had been going. He rose, his stiff movements more like a toy than a real child.

Now, the militiaman really did shout. 'No, woman! Are you an idiot? Not that way, unless you want a beating or a bullet.'

She stopped and stared at him, astonished. *Nobody has ever spoken to me like that. Or shouted at me so rudely. But I don't think he's a bad man. Just… not like us.*

Seeing he had her attention, the militiaman gave her clear instructions. 'Get out of town as fast as possible, through via Garibaldi. And here,' he took out a small tin from his ammunition pouch, 'this is black gun grease. Plaster his hair with it. Any fool can see he's a foreigner.'

He put the tin in the hand she unthinkingly outstretched.

'Now go, quickly. If they find you helping him, they'll kill you right away.' He appraised her up and down. 'Or worse.'

She stared at him, flinched at his insinuation.

The militiaman pulled the wicket closed and started rapidly down the street in the direction of the station.

Lucia found the militiaman baffling, but the vehemence in his voice resonated with her and, galvanised by the sense of peril the man had conveyed, Lucia tugged at the boy's arm and started to run back in the direction of the convent.

As she turned into Vicolo Ferragli, the long street that boasted two churches as well as the convent in which she has just spent a few tranquil days, she saw men with guns further down. They were erecting a barrier, cutting the street in half. She stopped, gazing at the convent wall and the big, juicy lemons that cascaded over it with their dark green leaves. Both convent and fruit were beyond the soldiers and their barrier.

The boy looked up at her, as if confused by her hesitation, and she noted again his ash-gold hair and shuddered. Yanking his arm, she turned back and took the road that led south and, eventually, to Ginestra and home. He allowed her to pull him, as wordless and unresisting as a doll.

WHAT THE CARTER SAID

On the outskirts of Palma, Lucia hesitated. When she looked right and left to see whether she had been followed, the child holding her hand gazed up at her, perhaps trying to gauge her thoughts. With a tug, she set off, left the road and struck out across the fields in the general direction of home.

'We can rejoin the road later when we're far from the soldiers, and maybe find a farmer going in our direction.' She addressed the child without being sure how much he understood. He said nothing.

The boy was watching the ground beneath his sandals, whereas Lucia looked up at her world; at the vines crisscrossing the undulating hills, heavy with soon-to-be-ripe grapes. The dry soil. Occasional patches of beans, tomatoes and turnips. Tobacco fields every so often and maize, close to ripening. One or two walnut trees were near the road, and almost all the scattered houses had a few jet-black cypress trees alongside.

He followed her glance into the sky but his cobalt eyes quickly averted from the sun, which was bright like snow. The heat pressed down, a sheet of hot steel. There was a slight hum in the air as if of cicadas. No wind.

Hardly two kilometres had gone by before he started to resist her pulling. Every so often she had to turn, crouch down and cajole him, stroking his head and smiling into his taut face. They were already well beyond the town. The last street had petered into a pitted track and they were now walking with the railway line on their left and the metaled road on the right, a few hundred metres away.

For a time, the railway line was contiguous with the road that they had left. She glanced at the dusty tarmac, as hot as the rail tracks. There was no sound except for that low hum of summer, punctuated by the occasional swish or crackle as her shoes, or the boy's sandals, crushed a desiccated weed or broken twig.

He was faltering. Used to walking long distances and with loads on her head, Lucia had not thought of how this might challenge a small boy – a city-bred boy, by the look of him.

She stumbled across an irrigation ditch with a little brackish water that had survived under the shade of some broom and stopped, climbing down into the hollow and the patch of shade. The boy followed and they both sat. She immediately felt a wave of drowsiness and lay back. She slept for perhaps five minutes before waking urgently and looking round for the child.

He was by the puddle, floating dry leaves in it, talking to himself in something like the language that brother-in-law Salvatore used to speak with his wife. One word she made out, repeated often: "*mutti*". Then sometimes he would cry out what sounded like a prayer: "*oma*".

At first, her instinct was to tell him to stop playing in the water, lest he dirty himself, but the pity she felt held her tongue and instead she watched him. She saw that his short trousers were of leather and his somehow so clean shirt of quality cotton. *He has a good mother*, she thought, *very proud of her little son*. After a while, she said, 'We must go,' and used his peculiar name. 'Eye-enz, we must go.' The boy did not demur. *He trusts me*, she thought.

The road from Palma to Ginestra and beyond did have at least one other traveller. Gino, a small, yellowing and unshaven man with the wide brim of his straw hat shading him, was slumped on the driving bench of a cart. His old donkey Benito plodded slowly onwards, rocking Gino from side to side. Flies buzzed around Benito's sticky eyes, poorly protected with scuffed leather eyeshades, stolen many years before from a landlord's stable. In the distance, Gino could make out two moving figures. He squinted: it was a woman and a boy. It passed through his mind that they must be in trouble, running over there. These days there were so many in trouble. He guessed where they would arrive beside the road and decided to make for the place.

Lucia and Heinz were climbing back up onto the railway embankment. Lucia pulled Heinz up to walk on the even surface of the track with its wooden sleepers. Such was the heat that the excrement from the train latrines, which could make the lines revolting, was dried up and rendered so odourless that even the flies ignored it.

After their rest, the boy seemed happy, jumping from sleeper to sleeper and even laughing. Lucia stepped gingerly between them.

As the line entered a plantation of apricot trees, it became cooler and she walked faster. She began to sense a low noise ahead. The sound became louder and more distinct as they went deeper into the trees: moaning, groaning and wailing.

Heinz, absorbed in his jumping, hadn't noticed. Lucia stopped to listen. Ahead, she saw the railway line divided, the straight line continuing but a spur going off to the left. She could not go forward without exposing them to the left, where the noise suggested there must be many people. So she gestured the boy to be quiet and led him into the scrub that hid the spur.

Through the branches she saw train carriages parked in the siding. She could hear a steam engine chuntering, smoke gushed above the trees beyond.

Barely a hundred metres ahead were groups of foreign-looking soldiers; well-fed, sun-pink youths squatting, standing or sprawled on the ground, laughing and joshing. Lucia stopped immediately, crouched down, jerking the boy towards her.

Lucia did not connect what was before her with the warnings of the militiaman, but she shuddered just at the sight of men in uniform, with their guns and helmets and leather straps.

She crawled forward in the bushes parallel to the line until she had a clear view of the whole train and her heart beat faster as she realised where the cries were coming from.

So far, she had only taken in a few coaches. She now realised that the middle of the train comprised slatted cattle trucks. The gaps between the slats were big enough for her to see living creatures packed tight inside. She could only be sure that they were humans, because many arms flailed outside as the inmates begged for water.

A man in top boots was amusing himself, strutting along the wagon, striking the arms with a leather whip, which resulted in screams and their rapid withdrawal. Apparently tiring of his fun, he strolled to the last carriage, where some soldiers were leaning out of the windows jawing with their pals who were lying, legs spread wide, by the side of the track or drinking from a water urn. He stood looking at them, his whip now thrust into his belt, and put his hands up to his face to pull his eyes into slits, put out his tongue and then, laughing at his own wit, walked away.

Lucia understood nothing, but the blackshirt might have been able to explain to her what she was witnessing. The first carriages contained Germans of the 71st Infantry Division, entrained for the Balkans; the cattle trucks were for prisoners, probably destined for Poland; the last wagon held another kind of soldier, "foreign volunteers" from the Russian empire. Who could know where they were going?

As she watched, two men in the last carriage – slight teenagers really – dropped down from the carriage door, laid their helmets, rifles and packs on the ground, and walked along the train holding only their canteens of water. Lucia saw that, although wearing the same boots and jackets as the pink-faced boys, these two were dark, with narrow eyes and black hair. When they reached the cattle trucks, desperate screams intensified: the two passed their canteens through the gaps.

From the other end of the train, a big soldier with a cane shouted at them angrily and then, running up, smashed the cane down on the boys' heads, afterwards turning it on their faces and bodies. They ducked and weaved. When he stopped, they stood trembling before him, with blood on their lips and running down their faces.

As he bellowed at them, Lucia stared, pulling Heinz closer into her side. *Who are these people? Orientals? It's a mystery.* Other lads, lolling on the banks, gawped as the two boys slunk away. She heard the clatter of a canteen being pushed back out of the truck and falling to the ground. The officer turned on his heel and strode back up to the coaches gaily, slapping his cane against his gleaming calf.

A strident whistle was followed by several hoots of the steam engine. As Lucia and the child watched, the troops hurried aboard, but the two naughty boys, gripping their helmets and packs, were ordered onto the running board, presumably as a punishment. Lucia realised that Heinz had not noticed the prisoners; he was spellbound by the man with the cane, who strolled the length of the train, now with a red pennant in his hand. She drew Heinz further back among the trees. When the train lurched into motion, the man with the pennant strode beside the last open door, looked up, gripped the handrail and, putting one boot onto the step, pulled himself up in an elegant movement. Lucia noticed for the first time that attached to his boots were *those metal goads that landowners wear when riding – spurs?*

Although Lucia and Heinz were hidden to the first carriages, as the train moved off some of the prisoners saw them and called out for water. Lest she be discovered by the soldiers, she pulled Heinz back even deeper into the bushes.

She folded him into her and they waited, staring at the scene before them, trembling with fear and hoping that the boy would not imagine that his parents were among those prisoners. But the boy's view was different to hers: he was wide-eyed at the men with guns.

Once the train had puffed back onto the main line and off into the distance, Lucia remembered the black grease and tried to rub it into the boy's hair as he stared at her, but he tossed his head away. Afraid that he might make a noise of complaint, she desisted, cleaning her hand on her handkerchief. She and the boy rose and headed for the road.

Having correctly estimated where the woman and boy would come out, Gino stopped Benito where rails met road and gave him water from a tattered leather gourd.

As Lucia came out from the trees, she caught sight of the cart and halted. She did not know the carter but she saw that he was a local person, not a foreigner. The boy, grasping her hand, stopped too. He looked into her face, asking without speaking.

The carter raised his head and watched her as she approached, the boy now holding onto her dress with both hands.

'*Signora*, where are you going?'

'Ginestra.'

'So am I.' It wasn't true.

Lucia did not ask for a lift but the request was on her face.

'Come up and sit with me, *Signora*. The boy can get in the cart.'

She hesitated. Her need was great, but alone, with a strange man? She looked at the child, squatting on the ground, now tired and probably hungry. She had eaten milk, bread and cheese this morning, but what had he eaten? Maybe nothing. She remembered the convent biscuits and realised that she had lost her basket somewhere. Before she could work out whether to go back for it, the carter made his offer.

'Come, get on. I'll take you to Ginestra. The outskirts at least.'

What can I do? I have to trust him; after all, he's one of us. She smiled to herself. A few hours ago, all people outside the family or our farms were *forestieri*, outsiders. Now an old carter, by the look of him just a second-hand dealer, is "one of us". *What is happening to me?*

Mute, Lucia helped the boy up. He peered over the edge and smiled. He stroked the straw with his hand, then tumbled in. Soon he snuggled down, curling up as if to sleep. The sun beat down on his hot cheeks, and he tried to shade himself with his hands. Lucia took off her mantilla and laid it over his face. He slept.

A flick of the lash and Benito started, snorted and stumbled off. For a few minutes, neither spoke. Then, Gino asked: 'Who is the boy?'

She found herself lying easily. 'He's my cousin.'

'No doubt, but he's a foreigner, isn't he?'

'No, his family is in Palma, they are coming –'

'*Signora* you don't need to hide from me. I have taken *clandestini* into the hills from Palma. And other places.'

He went on, 'They come from everywhere, these poor creatures. Alto Adige, Slovenia, Friuli, Savoy. All round this area, these people are hiding in cellars, working on the farms, knitting clothes… they call them the *clandestini*. This is the war.'

Lucia said nothing. *This is not my business. My man has been killed. That is all I need to know. Other people have their suffering, but what does any of that have to do with me?*

She glanced into the back of the cart. The boy was motionless. *He is so lovely.* She looked at his little form tenderly for perhaps a minute. Then she said, 'His parents have been taken away. I don't know why. Somewhere has to be found for him, I suppose.' She thought of confiding what the Blackshirt had said, but thought better of it.

As Benito jerked them along the rutted road, Gino talked about himself. 'I'm returning home. That linen press in the back is going from old Signora Fiore to the priest's house. I do these jobs between market days. Keeps me in touch with what's going on.'

He glanced at her widow's weeds. *From her looks, she's about 20, maybe younger. The Ginestra girls marry in their teens.* 'Your menfolk are in the army, Signora?'

'My husband was killed in Sicily on the 10th of July. Six weeks.'

'I am sorry. He must have been very young. And you not long married.'

She did not look at him, stared ahead.

Gino shook his head in wonder. 'Poor lady. May God watch over you.'

She retorted: 'What God!'

His expression, when he looked at her, was pure compassion. After a pause, he asked, 'You are Bregante Salvatore's sister-in-law?'

She was not surprised. Bregante was a well-known man in this area, factor to the counts of Ginestra. *Is that what I am?* she asked herself. *A sister-in-law, a childless widow, living by the favour of my Domenico's family?* 'Yes.'

'Bregante the factor had a foreign wife, I believe.'

'Yes, from the north, where Bregante was working. But she speaks our language. Did speak. She's dead now, poor creature.'

Gino glanced at her to see whether the young widow crossed herself. She did not. 'Yes, I heard. When Palma hospital was bombed. By the Americans.'

Less a clip-clop and more a rasp-rasp, the mule dragged the cart along the potholed road. The old junk dealer and Lucia sat staring before them at the dusty path ahead. A few kilometres went by before they spoke again, and it was Gino who brought up the topic that had not been raised, at least out loud.

'Keep him at home. That's all you can do. If the devils have taken his people, you are all he has left.' He turned and looked hard at Lucia. 'It is insane, and we don't understand it, but these devils live to kill. Keep him at home.'

'I can't. I stay with my mother-in-law and her eldest son. And this child doesn't even speak like us. He has a foreign name, "Eye-en-ze".'

'He'll learn our language quickly. Children always do. Give him a Christian name. Enrico will do. Only call him Enrico. And tell him not to open his mouth before strangers. Until he speaks as we do.'

Lucia wondered at the assurance of this man, merely a carter with bad breath and ragged trousers, advising her how to do things that had been unimaginable just a few hours before.

After a while, Gino took up the conversation again: 'Won't your mother-in-law be happy to have a boy?'

'So many people come to our house. To pay their dues or discuss them. She'll be afraid of people saying bad things.' She blushed as she said it and finished lamely: 'Another mouth to feed.'

'Then you must take him to Dottoressa Foschini, the schoolteacher. Do you know her?'

'Of course, my teacher.' Lucia spoke with pride. Few girls continued through to *Liceo Classico*. Few had been the apple of their teacher's eye, as she had been. 'I can't speak with her about this. Impossible. She is very law abiding. And her son is fighting with the army in Ucraina.' She added, 'It's in Russia.'

'Nevertheless, she knows all about the *clandestini* in Ginestra. Take him at night. She will find the boy a home.'

Dottoressa Foschini had been her classics mistress, and Lucia was astonished to hear of her doing anything that was untoward, underhand. Could it possibly be true that the *dottoressa* was helping outlaws against the regulations of the state? Lucia visited the old lady several times a week, helping her, who now spent most of her time in a wheelchair, and she wondered why she had never heard of this. Was the *dottoressa* ashamed to tell her? Lucia was – for the moment – slow at understanding the stakes.

'I think I'd better give him to the priest.'

'Father Filipović?'

'Yes. He can probably settle the child in some orphanage; priests can be useful sometimes.'

'No.' Gino's tone was unexpectedly sharp. 'Whatever you do, don't do that.'

She looked mystified, but Gino did not elaborate.

'I can make his hair dark,' she said, as if to fill the space. 'Someone gave me some oil.'

Gino thumbed behind his back in the direction of the boy. 'Do it.'

Lucia prised open the lid, hesitated, then twisted herself round so that she could smear Heinz's hair with the black grease. He did not wake, even when she riffled his hair to impregnate it further. After that, she saw that her handiwork had made Heinz's hair more or less like the gleaming locks of one of those seasonal labourers from the south. His pink skin would darken. Gino shoved a cotton cloth at her and she wiped her hands.

When the carter next spoke, he was even more mysterious. He talked of compassion. This perplexed her.

'Young lady, compassion brings many different kinds of people together. Some people who are forever talking about charity are absent when that is needed. But others, even those who thought that they were above the troubles of their neighbours, suddenly find that their hearts move them.'

Again, Lucia glanced back at the sleeping child. *I must find a compassionate person to look after this child*, she thought. *The carter is right. But first we'd better get home safely.*

STRANGE MEETING

The walled hamlet of Greppo is a *frazione* of the township of Ginestra and lies a few kilometres out, on the unmetalled road that eventually connects Ginestra with a tributary of the Puricelli autostrada. In August 1943, Greppo was the home of five families, including that of Lucia's late husband. Much to Gino's inconvenience, he skirted Ginestra and dropped off his passengers on the road for Greppo. Should they enter Ginestra, whether on a cart or on foot, the child's existence would be known by everyone within a few hours.

Anyone travelling that road from Ginestra to Greppo passed both the cemetery and the new prison camp, although the camp was reached by a drive separating it from the road and therefore from the thoughts of passers-by. It was late afternoon and Lucia knew that she would probably find her mother-in-law and, quite probably, her brother-in-law, there at the cemetery, which they visited at this time each day.

Bregante Domenico's grave had been made ready in case his body could be found and brought home. At present, there was only a wooden cross over the place; tacked onto it was an enamelled photograph of the laughing, curly-headed boy whom Maria bore and Lucia married. The mason had not yet completed the marble monument, although the deposit had been paid, up front, in olive oil.

As Lucia made for the all-too-familiar spot, so did others, with very different agendas. From the other direction, approaching the cemetery up the incline, was a curious group. There was a mule, carrying a man, flies buzzing around both. Leading the mule by a rope tied to its bit was one of two soldiers; the other dragged his scuffed boots some metres behind. They were both stocky, black-haired men with the walnut faces of deep southerners and a slow, bent, gait.

By contrast, the rider was slim and held himself erect. The first thing noticeable about him, which marked him out as a foreigner, even more than his Nordic features, was that he wore a turban. His skin was dark from the sun and his moustache stood out almost white against his face. His eyes were barely more than slits as he shielded them from the sun; when he glanced down, they could be seen to be clear blue.

On his torso was a patched, stained and sun-bleached bush shirt with some metal badges glinting on his shoulders. Its collar was turned up to protect his neck from burning. He stared ahead, his thick thighs in corduroy breeches gripping the animal, for there were no stirrups. One hand was on the pommel of the mule's saddle, the other balancing a rifle crosswise. An observant witness would have realised that one of the guards had no weapon but was instead carrying a pair of crude crutches on his back. The rider lurched from side to side with the mule's rocking gait. His right lower leg was in a plaster cast. A spare riding boot was slung over his shoulder on a hempen twine.

There was a contemptuous expression on the face of Gerald FitzGerald, an American-born Irishman serving in Britain's Indian army, as he looked down on the guards beside him. Their helmets were swinging from their belts; one had a dirty white kerchief tied round his head to protect him from sunstroke, the other a cap folded from newspaper. They repeatedly wiped their oozing faces with their cuffs, which were dark with grime.

The clop-clop of the mule's metaled hooves was muffled by the soft soil unless they scraped on a stone; the walkers' boots were almost silent.

Over to the left, and despite the heat, was the shadow-like figure of a running woman and a child flitting between light and shade in the distance, bounding in the same direction, veering down towards the turning in the road ahead.

The guard with the rifle shifted its strap from shoulder to shoulder every ten minutes or so, his lips grumbling as he eased an ache. His companion had some hill flowers wilting out of the unbuttoned upper pocket of his tunic. Not one word was uttered.

What lay beyond the turning was obscured by a clump of cypresses. Here stood the walls of the cemetery, with its panoply of tombstones and family mausoleums, sorrowing angels and soaring crucifixes, all hemmed in by a square of high ramparts breached only by a wrought-iron gate. Once the soldiers reached the bend, they would see not only the cemetery, but, in the far distance, the tall fences and corrugated roofs of the prison camp. As they did so, Maria was on her knees beside the memorial to her son. There were freshly-laid paper flowers.

Maria – Signora Bregante to her daughter-in-law and most of the community of Ginestra and the surrounding farms – was dressed entirely in black and with a black headscarf. She was weeping. As she did every day.

After completing her prayers and crossing herself, Signora Bregante rose and pulled open the rusted iron gate of the cemetery, which rasped as she did so, and walked out to the hard earth road, carrying her string bag.

She reached the road, her head bowed as if she were repeating her prayers to herself. Then, alerted by the tinkling sound of hoof on pebble, above the low hum of insects, she looked towards a cloud of dust about half a mile in the distance, where the road disappeared downwards. Step by heavy step, coming over the rise, was a mule, bearing an upright rider; with it, two men walked.

At the very moment that she saw the group, and before she had had time to decide what it might mean, her attention was arrested by the voice of her daughter-in-law, flushed from running, her shoes covered with dust and her dress torn. Without a headscarf in this weather! Holding onto her hand was a small, fresh-faced boy with horribly greasy black hair.

'God protect us! What? What is happening? Lucia?'

Breathing heavily, Lucia looked up the hill before speaking, then, pointing to the boy, said, 'I shall put him in the cemetery then come back.'

The older woman stood open-mouthed as Lucia pushed the child through the iron gate. She glanced back up the road. The three men and the mule would be upon them in a few moments.

Lucia hurried back out of the cemetery. Answering her mother-in-law's unasked question, she spoke rapidly: 'It's a foreign child. Without parents. Salvatore will speak to him in his language. I thought he would be here with you.'

'Language? Foreigner?' A shiver of fear ran through Maria. She seized the young widow's wrist as she seemed to move off. 'What have you done, Lucia? Have you stolen a child?'

There was no time for the two women to understand each other. 'Holy Father, look!'

Maria's face turned towards the mule, rider and two soldiers. Her daughter-in-law followed her gaze. They stood still, the older woman kneading her string bag with jerky, nervous movements.

The group came closer and halted by the two women, who drew themselves up. The older woman stepped forward, holding out her bag like a market stallholder selling vegetables.

Lucia tried to slip behind her mother-in-law and would not meet the sheep's eyes of the two guards. Maria spoke first. 'What are you up to, boys? Sit down and have a rest, you're worn out.'

The first soldier pointedly addressed the younger woman: '*Salve, Signorina bellissima.*'

Lucia, with a hauteur invisible until that moment, retorted, 'I am not *signorina*, I am *signora*.'

With a leer, the first soldier whispered, 'Sorry.'

The second soldier answered the older woman, as he sank down on the ground. 'Good idea, *auntie*. What joy! We'll rest a bit.'

The Romeo too plumped himself down, dumping his helmet and kit. Lucia was not afraid of the two slovenly foot guards; they were just country boys, brazen because they were dressed up to look like soldiers. But for the stiff figure on the mule, she felt instant revulsion.

The foreigner had a manner about him that made her think of that booted and spurred train marshal strutting along the railway track. She shivered and forced herself to avert her eyes.

Maria, producing bread, sausage and tomatoes from her string bag, offered them food. 'Have something to eat.'

The second soldier reached out for a tomato. 'With pleasure.'

Maria asked: 'And who's the gentleman up there?'

'A *pezzo grosso*, important bloke.' The guard indicated his own blank shoulder straps with the fingers holding the half-eaten tomato, and Maria glanced up at the metal badges on the prisoner's shoulders. They meant nothing to her.

'He's a prisoner. He's an *Inglese* colonel. We're taking him to the camp.'

'*Povero passerotto*. Poor sparrow. He needs food too, tell him to sit with us.'

The guards used gestures to suggest that the rider should dismount and join them, but he stared ahead, not acknowledging the invitation.

Maria gave a motherly smile. 'Proud, these soldiers. Now, how did you get such an easy job, looking after one nice handsome prisoner? The men from our village are all on the front line. My sister's son is having to fight, *povereto*, poor creature, she waits trembling for news every day. I hope he will be courageous and desert.'

The second soldier swallowed a piece of bread, then remarked laconically: 'He will be shot if he deserts.'

'Mary Mother of God! Do they shoot people who desert?'

'Of course.'

'Worse than savages. We need men on the farm.' She waved at the land: 'All this work – all this and only old people in our village. The boys who aren't dying in battles have been taken to build walls for the war, or else they are hiding in the hills.'

The second soldier, shrugging his shoulders, spoke. 'What can we do? *Insomma*! So there we are!'

The first soldier resumed his attempts to get Lucia's attention, adopting a more respectful tone: 'And you, *Signorina*, do you have brothers fighting?'

'I told you, I am *signora*.'

'Excuse me,' he grinned.

Maria crossed herself. 'My son, her husband, was killed two months ago in Sicily. My brother was killed in North Africa last year.'

'I am sorry.' His attitude changed to commiseration, and he too crossed himself. 'Those damned *Inglesi!*'

The second soldier. 'That damned Mussolini!'

In the silence that followed, Lucia recalled, yet again, the moment she had learnt of her man's killing. The Station Sergeant who had come to inform her had told Lucia that it was the *Inglesi* who killed him. At the time, it didn't matter. English, Germans, Americans: they were all the same thing. But now she remembered. The killer could even have been this man. Had the soldier not said he was an American? She made herself glance back up at the face of the enemy. She hated this man as much as she did those on the rail track earlier. Their glances met. She saw a thin, supercilious, smile. She thought, *he knows my bitterness and he gloats. Uniforms make men brutes.*

Lucia said quietly to Maria, '*Signora*, I am off. I must speak to your son.'

'But don't let him get involved!'

Lucia turned to go. 'I won't.'

The soldier looked up, disappointed. 'She's leaving?'

Maria replied, with an ingratiating smile, 'She has my grandchildren to look after.'

They watched Lucia, the form of her back revealed by the blouse that was more close-fitting than usual in the countryside. Nothing needed to be said.

Maria distracted them: 'You are taking the gentleman to the camp?'

'Yes, *Signora*. PG500. We picked him up from the station. He came from a hospital at Lucca.'

'Why does he wear a hat like a magician?'

The soldier shrugged: '*Bo!*' It was too hot for thought.

Maria glanced up the road from which the soldiers had come and pointed at another cloud of dust ascending above the rise. It grew bigger and a Volkswagen jeep emerged. Dust seemed to explode around it as it ground towards the little group. They made out a driver and another uniformed man in the front seats, both wearing goggles and coated with grit.

At this sight, the two guards hastily pulled the mule to the side of the narrow road to let the car pass. The prisoner had to grip tight to prevent himself from falling as the mule stumbled sideways. The two guards' demeanour became frightened, obsequious. They even put on their helmets, which were burning to the touch. Maria packed away the foodstuffs. The jeep slowed down and stopped alongside the group.

The two guards shouldered their rifles and stood to attention, ill at ease, shabby.

It was clearly an important person who swung out of the jeep. Spry, in his late twenties at first glance, he was very like the prisoner in his Scandinavian looks, though comparatively lightly tanned. He wore riding breeches and top boots, which shone beneath a faint film of grime. A leather belt with a silver buckle drew in his tunic, emphasising a slender waist and broad shoulders. There was a pistol holster on his left hip.

The German ignored the Italians, looking only at the man on the mule and addressing him in confident Oxford English, with a very slight accent, an elongation of the vowels:

'What do we have here? Good afternoon, Colonel.'

'Good afternoon.'

'I am Fröhlich, Major. May I have the honour of your name?'

'FitzGerald, Lt Colonel. Major Fröhlich is a tank commander, I see.'

Looking up at the rider, the German smiled to know that FitzGerald could read his uniform.

'These… fellows… are taking you to the PG500, Colonel?'

He gestured at the guards without looking at them.

'Yes.'

'Well, allow me to give you a lift in my car, Sir. With your gammy leg,' he nodded towards the rider's right leg, looked very pleased with himself as he used this expression, 'you will be more comfy.'

He paused so that the prisoner could take in his excellent English, then added: 'We will make a short stop en route, where my men are making an operation. But that should not delay you much.'

He turned to the two Italians and, speaking German, ordered:

'Help the Colonel down. Into my car.'

FitzGerald slid off the mule, putting one hand on the shoulder of the nearest Italian guard that he then patted by way of thanks, as one might reward a dog. The other handed him his crutches. The woman watched.

As FitzGerald approached the jeep, he noticed the badge painted on the door, a skeleton key, but showed nothing of the astonishment he felt as he climbed into the back seat. Fröhlich joined him, taking in the faded medal ribbons above his prisoner's left pocket.

'Colonel, your medals. May I congratulate you and ask you where and when?'

'In North Africa, Major Fröhlich. When we chased you out of Alamein.'

Fröhlich laughed. 'We did a lot of chasing you before then! And will again!'

'And you wear the Iron Cross. Was that awarded here in Italy?'

'No, in Ukraine. At Kharkov. We come here for rest and recreation.' He laughed, enthusiastic and childlike.

FitzGerald gave a more measured, older man's, smile. His eyes were watchful.

The prisoner's former escorts stood to attention in their uncouth fashion and the mule snapped some dead flowers from one soldier's pocket, dousing him with saliva in the process. As the jeep moved off, FitzGerald glimpsed the peasant woman's eyes following it and her lips moving noiselessly in prayer. The two officers sat side by side in the back, laughing. Brothers in arms.

GREPPO

As she stumbled up the rocky path to the great gate of Greppo, pulling the dusty child, Lucia decided to put the experiences of the last few hours behind her.

I'll leave Greppo and return to Mamma. I'll study daily for the teaching concorso, *competition, with Dottoressa Foschini. After all, for a professional, I'm young, which is what people said when Domenico asked to marry me.* She looked over her shoulder at the child. *I must find him a family. Will we have to pay for someone to take him?* Her thoughts drifted to supporting the child through school. *Could I earn enough for him to be educated properly?* Then she shook herself. *Don't be silly Lucia, don't complicate life. Someone else will do that.*

Greppo, home to her husband's family, was one of the many fortified hilltop villages of the area. From a distance, it looked like a castle, with its high walls and their arrow-slit windows and its massive gateway. Approached by a rough stony road, little more than a path fit for mules and wheelbarrows, the gateway opened onto a cobbled piazza with houses, all built into the medieval walls surrounding it. There was a very tiny chapel, visited by the priest from Ginestra only for weddings, baptisms and funerals, and a communal hall for *feste*, celebrations. On the other side of Greppo there was a postern, hidden from view by the lean-to extending the factor's house, mainly used by the factor himself as he went, unnoticed, to his store nearby or further, to the outlying farms. Over the roof tiles and walls, vines and bougainvillea cascaded, and round the base of each home were tubs of scarlet geraniums. The scent of smoky jasmine clotted the nostrils of anyone who passed by.

Twenty minutes or so after leaving the cemetery, as Lucia and the boy panted up to the open gate of Greppo, another shock awaited her. She was halted by the sight and sound of a crowd of people surrounded by soldiers. There was wailing and arguing and the raucous sound of orders in a foreign language.

For a moment, she just stood and stared. She had seen herself, after escaping from what was happening to Palma, as getting back to the dull peace of Greppo. Here she was, but, even if the houses and cobbles and the people were as before, it was utterly unfamiliar in spirit. Shock had followed shock this day, and there were more shocks to come.

A few soldiers had collected the neighbours into a group of thirty or so, old and young, male and female. Lucia sensed funk as women sobbed, children wailed, old men cursed.

She was about to turn away when a soldier came up behind her and, wordlessly, used his rifle to prod her and Heinz towards the mêlée. In it she spied her brother-in-law Salvatore, one arm around Bisnonna, the other hand holding little Ebbo's, who held Chiara's. For the sake of the child gripping her own hand, Lucia quelled the foreboding that rippled through her and lifted her head to alert her brother-in-law to her presence.

Salvatore glanced behind, saw her and looked at her companion, all without changing his expression. Lucia started to push through the press towards him just as the soldiers shouted at them and drove the lamenting gaggle back through the same gate, veering down a track which would take them to the Corvo family's farm.

Surrounded by the old and the very young, Lucia had no

time to think but emulated her brother-in-law, comforting and consoling their desperate neighbours. When she reached Bregante, Lucia took one of the two youngsters off his hands. They looked at Heinz and then at Lucia.

Before they could say anything, she replied to their unasked questions:

'I brought your little cousin Enrico back from Palma to stay with us.' She smiled down at Heinz. 'You three will enjoy playing together.'

An old man beside Bregante stumbled and Bregante, releasing his charges, pulled him up, patted his trembling shoulder and then turned back to help Bisnonna negotiate the slippery stones of the downhill path.

A woman's voice called out a prayer loudly; soon everyone joined in.

'*Áve María, grátia pléna,*
Dóminus técum.
Benedícta tū in muliéribus,
et benedíctus frúctus véntris túi, Iésus.'

Matteo, the simple-minded uncle who kept the gate, tripped and fell. A teenage Adonis in a helmet, a look of self-importance spoiling his angelic features, kicked him, bellowing: '*Aufsetehen! Aufteshen!* Get up! Up!' Lucia released the two children and moved to pull up Matteo, then rushed to rejoin the group before the soldier could chase them.

Are we to be killed? Is this why they look at us like this? She found herself asking a question that, just a few hours before, would never have occurred to her. She was astonished to be asking it. For the first time in her life, she felt fear; fear at being at the mercy of something so malevolent. Yet whereas fear made the others weep and howl, Lucia felt alerted, a new intensity flowing through her. Without moving her head, her eyes looked to right and left, trying to find some opening, some possibility of escape or, at least, appeal.

PROFESSIONALS

While the families of Greppo were being herded towards Corvo's farm, the two enemies were enjoying a civilised conversation in the back of Fröhlich's jeep. 'We,' said Fröhlich with boyish ardour, 'are pacifying Eastern Europe and, *Gott mit uns*, the Slavs too, and should by rights be allies with the Irish, in the pursuit of a better world and the dissemination of universal values.' He explained to FitzGerald that once the war was over, he would retire to France to make new translations of Beowulf and the Nibelungen poems, which originated from his very own hometown. He asked the prisoner whether he had a favourite poet.

Amused by Fröhlich's enthusiasm, FitzGerald revealed his liking for the Latin poets, especially Virgil's "Georgics", his copy of which had been lost after capture. Fröhlich promised to see if he could buy a copy and have it delivered to PG500.

Descending from a long line of Irish soldiers, Gerald FitzGerald had been born on his grandfather's Californian ranch. His father, of whom they said "he could never miss out on any war", had been killed in South Africa, as a volunteer in what he saw as a fight against slavery. His wife's attitude to his chivalry is not recorded. Their son, Gerald, served in the US army, resigning in 1939 to wangle his way into a British Indian Army unit operating in France and North Africa. Like his father, he had taken no notice of his wife's views. He left her, dissatisfied with a woman who wanted to narrow down his life to her version of domestic bliss, when he dreamt of fighting for liberty and democracy throughout the world. By the time of his capture in Tunisia in early 1943, FitzGerald had reached the rank of Lt Colonel and been twice decorated.

FitzGerald thought of himself as a real soldier. 'The Indian army attracts adventurers and men who love soldiering rather than climbing up the greasy pole.'

Fröhlich too was confident of his superiority. 'In Germany, the aristocrats in the army officer corps are more concerned about playing the role of the cavalier. We SS just get on with the job. No romantic equivocations stop us serving the people.'

FitzGerald looked out at the countryside. In the distant fields crawled small, dark men and white buffaloes; women in headscarves move among the vines. *These are the people we have come to free*, he thought. *And I am fraternising with the enemy.*

Fröhlich stared straight ahead, then interrupted FitzGerald's reverie.

'I commiserate with you as a fellow professional. I would not like to be taken prisoner. You have lost your command: your career is finished. We soldiers do not like to be prevented from doing our duty.'

FitzGerald knew he was being teased. 'I fully intend to resume my command again. When I get back to the lines.'

Fröhlich was delighted at his reply 'You won't, Colonel; we shall see to that. Although I am sure you will consider it your duty to try.'

FitzGerald laughed back at the challenge. 'As would you!' He added: 'Every man is ashamed of being a prisoner. My duty is to be killing you instead of sitting in your car.'

The German chuckled. 'Well, I am glad you are sitting in my car!'

LUNCH AT CORVO'S FARM

The jeep carrying the two warriors was making for a typical stone Umbrian farmhouse. Across the yard were parked military vehicles bearing black, white-fringed crosses on the sides. Soldiers, their rifles stacked like wigwams by the vehicles and under guard, were going in and out of the house, carrying out hams, sacks of dried mushrooms, chestnuts, grain, cheese and wine towards the parked trucks. One had a piglet on a lead.

A table and chairs had been set up in the shade under some vines, and food and a *fiasco*, a green wine bottle with a bulbous bottom and straw covering, placed on the clean check cloth, though nobody was sitting there. There was a noise of shouting and laughter as the German boys dug out some new edible.

A sergeant major, sporting a field cap that made him look as if he were involved in some country sport, stood in the centre, directing. Behind him, the six members of the Corvo family, two of them small children, were hanging from the eaves. The stools on which they once stood were overturned below them. Nobody paid attention to the dead, who, like strings of onions, swung gently.

Not far away, and guarded by a boy who gazed longingly at his mates having such fun looting the house, was a living family, the adults in rumpled city clothes. A fair-haired man in a suit, in his late thirties, held the hand of a younger woman, presumably his wife, in a flowered dress, his other hand in that of a daughter aged around 12. There were two more flaxen-haired children, twin boys of about eight wearing lederhosen over white shirts, their chubby legs salmon-coloured from running about in the sun, identical walking boots and green stockings on their feet. The females had been weeping and all looked tense and bewildered. Beside them were some suitcases.

Someone shouted at the sergeant major.

'Company Sergeant Major, the boss is here!'

Striding into vision came Fröhlich, with FitzGerald swinging along behind on his crutches.

Out of the house ran a teenager with a lieutenant's epaulettes, who saluted Fröhlich by flinging his arm into the air: '*Heil* Hitler!' He then gestured to the meal laid out on the table and announced something, unintelligible to FitzGerald.

Fröhlich, courtly and polite, introduced the lieutenant to his prisoner. 'Here is our guest today, Colonel FitzGerald of the Imperial Indian Army, who is on his way to PG500.'

The lieutenant clicked heels and bowed to FitzGerald, 'Reichenau, 1st Panzer.' FitzGerald nodded without expression.

'How's your English, Reichenau? Tell the Colonel what you are doing!'

'Yes, Sir.' Reichenau bowed rapidly to his superior, turned to FitzGerald and spoke in accented English. 'My Sir Colonel! Italian peasants hiding enemy agents are. Our intelligence discovers this and we found the agents,' he gestures to the cowering family, 'who have arrested been.'

'I see.' FitzGerald took in the family, whom he recognised immediately as townspeople and central Europeans. But his glance moved to the dead hanging from the eaves.

'And who are they?'

Reichenau replied quickly, 'They are the guilty ones. They help the enemy agents. According to law their lives and property are finished and we make punishment immediate, to show to the local peoples. My soldiers are now to bring the local peoples to show them.'

FitzGerald was no longer the conversationalist. The camaraderie had gone. He emphasised his words. 'The guilty ones.'

Fröhlich butted in. 'They are just collateral damage. Some people do not understand the rules of alliance. And peasants are really irrational; the only way they can be taught a lesson is by strictness.'

FitzGerald was calm, though his words were accusing. 'Kill as many Italian soldiers as you can. But these ragamuffins? What purpose is served? Do your men get pleasure from hanging children?'

Fröhlich was mildly indignant at the idea. 'Certainly not, we do not get pleasure from it. It is very unfortunate, and I dislike it very much. My soldiers find it difficult to do, but they must carry out their orders. The criminals must know what happens when they break the law.'

FitzGerald remained expressionless.

At that moment, there was a commotion and all turned to see a group of about thirty or so peasants – women, children and elderly – being pushed and prodded along towards the farmyard by half a dozen soldiers. One old man was protesting his love for Germany but all he got for trying to ingratiate himself was a bash in the face from the barrel of a weapon. Blood flooded from his nose, through his fingers as his hands rose to ward off another blow. Two women were crying that they had babies to care for. A boy stumbled and was kicked back up again. The baby in the arms of a woman screamed and the nearest soldier shouted that he would hit the child if it didn't stop howling. The mother, terrified, put her hand over its mouth.

As the shambling group arrived at the farm from where FitzGerald watched, impassive. When they were positioned in front of the dead bodies of their neighbours, a great cry resounded. Several women screamed. Others fell to their knees. FitzGerald realised they thought they were going to be killed, but he doubted this would happen – at least, not in his presence.

The young lieutenant saluted Fröhlich: 'Would you like to address them, Sir? There is a factor who speaks German and can translate.'

'Yes. Where is this factor?'

Fröhlich liked to make speeches. He knew he was good at it. He inspired his men, who might die for him and would certainly kill for him. He excited women and adolescents, whose hearts throbbed at his voice. He knew he terrified the Italians, over whom he ruled.

Bregante Salvatore stepped out from the group. As he did so, the hubbub quelled, perhaps because he showed no fear. He was a striking man in his thirties, dressed similarly to the other peasants, but neater and in better-quality cloth. He halted in front of Fröhlich, inclining his head.

Fröhlich addressed him as an inferior: '*Wie heißt du?*'

'Bregante Salvatore, *hochgeborn*.' Bregante used the term of obeisance he had learnt in the north, 'of noble birth'.

'Don't call me *hochgeborn*! I am not a nobleman. We national socialists are revolutionaries.'

'Yes, Sir.'

'And why do you speak the language of Herman?'

FitzGerald, leaning his weight on his crutches, his bad leg lifted, noticed that Bregante was momentarily confused.

'As a boy I worked in Alto Adige.'

'What is Al-to Ad-igi?' Fröhlich deliberately mispronounced the name. 'You mean Südtirol?'

'Yes indeed, Sir, Südtirol. I worked for Freiherr zu Wolkenstein.'

'So, you may be a little bit civilised!' He laughed. 'Right, follow me and translate what I say.'

FitzGerald observed that, as the German started to speak, the faces of the peasants looked towards him in dread. Aside from Bregante, there was no man who looked under eighty. The grandfathers were lined and sun-darkened, as were the older women. Among the younger women was one who stood out for her intelligent expression and fine features. She had been at the cemetery – or someone very like her had been. Around her, all were breathing heavily, but she was smiling reassuringly at a little girl who clung on to her left hand. There was a small boy on her right, gripping her hand with both of his.

Around that woman were others, her neighbours presumably, either keening and crossing themselves rapidly and repeatedly, or praying, slowly and deliberately. The children stared, stunned. A woman got down on her knees to a soldier but was hauled up. As FitzGerald observed, Lucia glanced in his direction and for a second their eyes met.

Lucia's heart was heaving, though not now, to her own surprise, with fear or even sorrow, but with fury. *Since I moved to Greppo, I saw the Corvos almost every day, at least waving to them as they trudged to the fields. I was in the same year at primary school as Carlo. He so hated sitting at a desk. As soon as he could write a little, he left. When Carlo was 17, he brought me that stoat he had trapped, as a present, and I laughed at him.*

Carlo had a club foot that had saved him from being called up. Signora Corvo stopped praying for its healing and instead paid for a mass to thank God for his munificence. The two little brothers were born so late and so unexpected. Signor *Corvo was so thrilled to have boys rather than girls, who need a dowry, but I think* Signora *Corvo had wanted a daughter's companionship. She feared that no decent girl would marry her crippled eldest.*

She left behind a basket last time she brought eggs. I meant to return it. How frightened poor little Angelo and Vittorio must have been. And did the children die before their mother? Lucia's face was suddenly awash with tears and, for the first time, she shook.

Heinz was staring up into her face, as if trying to gauge what she was going to do next, what she was thinking. She pulled herself together, pressed his hands and smiled down at him. *When he smiles back at me, it is hard not to cry.*

As Fröhlich started to speak, Lucia saw that officer prisoner, the one with the broken leg, watching. *They're all the same*, she said to herself. *They are not each other's enemies. They are all our enemies.*

'Peasants! Italian citizens! My soldiers and I are assisting the Italian government in its heroic resistance against American capitalism, English imperialism and Jewish Bolshevism! Today you can see the punishment for traitors! These people harboured enemies and have received the punishment ordered by the supreme commander in Italy, Field Marshall Rommel! To make it quite clear – if you help runaway prisoners or enemy agents, not only will your homes be destroyed, but your entire family will be executed. This is the law!'

As Bregante finished his interpretation, Lucia's anger boiled over. *These generals and their filthy laws*, she thought. She forgot the children beside her, let go of Heinz's hand and, raising both fists, cried out, 'Law of savages! How can you kill children!'

The nearest soldier thrust his way through the group towards her, his weapon in his left hand, his right grabbing at her, yanking at her so that she was wrenched out of the crowd, from which a great cry went up.

As she straightened, he slapped her hard across the face. He turned to look at his commander questioningly.

Lucia swayed, stunned, a red weal on her cheek. All of a sudden, the wailing stopped and everybody, soldiers and peasants, watched the man, who decided who lived and who died, considering her.

Before that man could speak, in the hush, FitzGerald's drawl could be heard, loud enough for all to hear, 'Really, Fröhlich, it is not very chivalrous to hit ladies.'

It was not clear from his expression whether he was making a cutting joke or trying to speak up for the woman. It came to Lucia that she might be pushed over to the execution ground at any moment and killed.

Fröhlich turned towards FitzGerald, laughing cheerily as if he'd made a witticism: 'You are a true English gentleman, Colonel.' He ordered the soldier. 'There is no need to hit the woman, Junker.' Lucia remained impassive as the man came to attention and bellowed, 'Yes, Sir!'

Lucia could see that Fröhlich's body language was respectful towards FitzGerald, by contrast to his strutting before her people. He seemed about to speak when Lucia lost control and, as if uttering an incontrovertible truth, shouted: 'You devil. You are the devil!'

Urgently, Bregante called out: 'Stop it. It's no good. You'll only cause more suffering.'

He turned to Fröhlich, who was looking at Lucia with a sardonic smile: 'Please excuse her, Sir; her husband has just been killed fighting in Sicily. She is very emotional, *commossa*.'

A soldier who had moved towards Bregante, menacing with his weapon, stopped as his commander spoke.

'Oh really, killed how?'

'Fighting beside the Hermann Göring division.'

Bregante looked as if he hoped the German would be impressed, but Fröhlich snickered, making another sally in English and glancing at FitzGerald as he did so. 'Oh well, that's one less impediment for the Göring division!'

Reichenau obediently laughed. Fröhlich flicked his hand in Bregante's direction and the nearest soldier shoved the factor back into the crowd.

FitzGerald knew his approbation was sought but did not collaborate. He looked straight at the factor, his head bowed, and the now-silent Lucia. FitzGerald then realised that Fröhlich was continuing to address him in his comradely way.

'Women yell, that's what they do.' He shrugged. 'If it means she stops the men doing idiotic things, that's fine. Let her howl and all her menfolk will do what we say. All Italians are cowards. They must be taught lessons.'

FitzGerald was enigmatic: 'She's only an Italian.'

A look of gratitude appeared on Fröhlich's face. 'Exactly, but it goes against our grain. I do keep reminding my lads that we are soldiers first and gentlemen second. We must harden our hearts. Rock hard.'

'Quite so. They must be rock hard.'

Fröhlich continued, 'We do not do these things for career advancing, let alone pleasure. We act purely for the cause. Tomorrow belongs to the pure. And the pure must be above sentimentality.'

FitzGerald's reaction was deadpan. 'I am sure that it is important to be pure.' Around them, peasants stared, mystified, observed by their guards. Even the babies were silent.

'Our supreme commander, *Reichsführer* Himmler, enjoins us to harden our hearts and steel ourselves not to weaken whilst remaining a decent person.'

'I am sure that Mr Himmler is an ideal role model. He has steeled himself not to weaken, so many times.'

Fröhlich missed the sarcasm and went on playing the gallant host. FitzGerald saw that he was oblivious to his, FitzGerald's, mood.

'Now, Colonel, my men have prepared a cold collation for us.' He indicated, with a sweep of the arm like the major-domo of a grand hotel, towards the table under a canopy of unripe grapes and leaves. 'Please do me the honour of sitting down in these pretty surroundings under the Mediterranean vines!'

'Thank you, Major Fröhlich, but I prefer not to. I will wait here until it is convenient for you to send me to PG500.' FitzGerald put a shimmer of distaste into his voice.

Fröhlich was surprised. 'You should not be so fastidious. In the last war, British and Germans feasted together at Christmas. And I wager,' again he seemed very pleased at his command of English, 'that they did not have food as tasty as we have today!'

'It's not Christmas.'

Fröhlich laughed gaily. 'Oh, you English, so droll! But, please, you are my guest.'

'No!' This time FitzGerald made his revulsion evident.

The smile fled from Fröhlich's face. Ignoring FitzGerald, he turned away towards the table and snapped his fingers at the young lieutenant.

'Reichenau, sit down!'

The lieutenant moved fast to sit at the table, taking off his cap and putting it beside the setting that had been laid for their guest.

Fröhlich sat and, as he did so, commanded: 'Wine, Reichenau!'

'Yes, Sir.' He poured.

As if to spell out his indifference to FitzGerald, Fröhlich put his own cap beside the lieutenant's and compared them. FitzGerald remained standing as before, on his crutches, impassive.

Fröhlich pointed out the slight variations in the headgear to his assistant. 'I like your *schiffchen M38*. It retains the elegance of the *schirmmütze*, but without the decorative chin strap or embroidered badges. It is suitable for the field but more obviously an officer's headgear than the *knautschmütze* or the original *schiffchen*.'

Lieutenant Reichenau nodded sagely. 'They vary according to maker, Sir.'

Fitzgerald could see the same conversation taking place in his mess. He had brother soldiers to whom their badges and accoutrements mattered very much. There were others who thought most about the technology, vehicles, guns, planes or binoculars. Each group shared a kind of familial language.

'Hugo Boss is the best, both for quality and elegance. It's the Porsche of uniforms. Without Daimler-Benz, we couldn't travel to war, and without Hugo Boss, we wouldn't be dressed for it! We must look, as well as be, efficient. Naturally!'

The lieutenant agreed. 'We have the best designers and organisers in the world, Sir.'

FitzGerald was listening. *Some of our lads are just the same. But we don't turn our men into savages. Why do they?* Fitzgerald was jerked out of musing as he heard Fröhlich shout, 'Company Sergeant Major!'

All of a sudden, Fröhlich had noticed that the crowd of Italian spectators was watching him at lunch.

'Yes, Sir?'

'Get rid of all those gawping Italians!'

'You mean…' The sergeant major drew his finger across his throat.

'No, no, send them home. Frighten them. Make them run, but don't harm them. They must tell all their neighbours that they can survive if they do as they are told. And get the Jews into the truck. How many Jews are there?'

'*Funf stuck*. Five objects.'

As he turned away, Fröhlich called out:

'Bring me the factor.'

Bregante stood bareheaded before Fröhlich, bowed in obedience, his fingers on the rim of his hat.

Fröhlich: 'You, as the factor, are known to everybody. A leader. With local charisma.'

'Yes, Sir.'

'You will pass the orders of my sergeant major to the farmers. We want food and wine. But the first thing you will do is make sure that all the peasants around here know very clearly that aid to any enemies is punishable by death. You have seen that we dispense justice effectively.' He nodded towards the hanging bodies. 'Do you understand? Here there is the rule of law!'

Bregante, with neither emotion nor a hint of obedience, replied: 'Yes, *Herr* Major. The rule of law.'

'And because you speak German and are almost civilised,' here he smiled at his own wit, 'we will hold you particularly responsible. I am going to stay in this zone for a long time and I will know all about you. Do you know who I am?'

'No, Sir.'

'I command 1st Panzer and we are here to stiffen the resolve of you Italians to work with us in uniting Europe. In this province, I rule. Your farms, your factories, your banks, your hospitals, your police. Your lives. I decide everything.'

Fröhlich looked into Bregante's eyes. 'There are several thousand prisoners in this region, as well as Jews in hiding. Not one will get away while I am here. Got it? You're the one who worked for Wolkenstein, aren't you? What did you say your name was?'

'Bregante Salvatore, Sir.'

'You are my messenger. And you will report to my man about the good behaviour of this area. He will tell you how to communicate regularly with him. Now go.'

FitzGerald saw him turn away from the bowing factor and clink glasses with the lieutenant. The sergeant major returned. 'And the Englishman, Sir?'

'Get him to the camp. Fast. And make sure he knows that if any of his men hide in the villages, we will execute every man, woman and child in those villages.'

'Yes, Sir.'

The Jews were being prodded towards the trucks. As they moved, one of the children dropped a rag doll onto which he had been holding. As his mother bent to retrieve it, the soldier kicked it well out of the way. The child cried out and the mother gave the soldier a look of incomprehension.

'Why?'

The man shrugged. 'Here, there is no why!'

A COUP D'ÉTAT

Before reaching the Greppo turning, on the road from Ginestra, well past the convent with its church attached, was a driveway lined by cypresses. This led to a compound surrounded by several kilometres of barbed wire, the outer perimeter of the prison camp, *Prigione di Guerra 500*.

Within was a line of wooden sheds with tin roofs, each holding about forty men. The floor space was taken up by three-tiered wooden bunks, arranged in long rows close together so that the passages between them were too narrow for two men to pass without standing sideways. There were no mattresses, only two thin blankets for each man. The light was perpetual.

There was a mess hut in which the prisoners ate. Areas for primitive ablutions and latrines were off to one side.

"The field" was a large area in which the prisoners would muster for roll call. Surrounding the field was a high palisade of tangled barbed wire, six feet thick at the base. Some yards to the front of this was a tripwire, beyond which any prisoner would be shot by the sentries. The stretch of ground between the two barriers was grass, undisturbed by human feet.

Beyond the first palisade was another, and beyond that was a high wall with spikes and more barbed wire to the height of thirty feet. At regular intervals along the walls were observation towers with three men, equipped with searchlights and a machine gun. The whole camp was illuminated after dark. When local people looked out of their windows at night, they shuddered at the eerie sight of a bluish white circle of light, as if some elfish coven were joining wands.

The prisoners who were captured in desert clothing had, once these disintegrated, been issued with blue serge uniforms from one of the Balkan countries. There was a mixture of costumes, but all prisoners wore a large red diamond on the back of the jacket, the seat of trousers and the knees.

Sentries strolled back and forth.

Only minutes after the events at the Corvo farm, the camp had been stirred by the arrival of a notorious officer who had peremptorily staged a coup d'état and taken over as camp leader. The event had been sudden and swift. It was remembered, for many years thereafter, like this:

A game of football was taking place. The men were mostly bearded or just unshaven. Some of the spectators had long hair. They were lounging and there was nothing military in the atmosphere.

A cry was heard. 'There is a new chap!' The footballers paid no attention but most of the spectators rose and sauntered away towards the main gate of the camp, where a curious sight greeted them. Just outside the gates, visible through the wire mesh, a man in a British desert uniform, but sporting a turban with a scarlet hackle aloft, was astride a mule. He was a fit, sunburnt man, with an air of command about him. He was taking a rifle off his saddle to hand back to a guard, who was holding up a pair of crude crutches to him in exchange.

A prisoner rose and shielded his eyes from the sun so he could better see the arrival. 'It's Colonel Fitz! Bloody hell, he's carrying the guard's rifle!'

Another: 'Gallowglass FitzGerald? Yankee FitzGerald?'

Under the eyes of the camp's sergeant major, the rider gingerly placed a crutch on the ground, then, rejecting an arm offered by the soldier holding the reins of the mule, swung down on one crutch and one booted leg. The prisoner unclipped his kitbag from the saddle and slung it over his shoulder. He thanked the escort, slapping him on his upper arm like a team captain. Once on the ground, his movements were brisk, authoritative.

Now on both crutches, he swung towards the gate and the guards standing by jumped to open it.

'Yes, it's Gallowglass FitzGerald. Who'd imagine him being a prisoner? He'll be out as soon as Bob's your uncle.'

'Balls. With that leg, he hasn't a chance. Look, here comes the SBO.'

The camp leader, or Senior British officer (SBO), was well turned out, with a crisp shirt and shorts ironed by batman Baker from Dorking, a contrast to the majority of the ragamuffins who hung around the inner gate to see the new arrival. A few shouts from the football game were all that broke the silence; the young men here just stared, as if at a catafalque.

Although he had the sartorial advantage and bearing of a man on parade, SBO Marsh had none of the presence of the equally tall man who swung in on his crutches. Stopping as if to invite Marsh to come towards him, FitzGerald threw his kitbag at a random prisoner, who caught it. That gesture broke the silence and the surrounding men started to clap and cheer. Nobody quite knew why, except that it was a gesture of welcome to a man with a reputation for leadership and daring.

FitzGerald allowed a slight smile to acknowledge the applause, which quietened as Brigadier Marsh approached and gave a salute which he ended rather lamely, as if he had had second thoughts just as his hand rose. FitzGerald, both hands once more engaged with his crutches, did not salute.

'It's FitzGerald, isn't it?'

'Yes. Marsh?'

'Yes. Welcome to PG500. Sent you up from Bari, have they?'
'No, Lucca. From the hospital.'
'What happened to your leg?'
'I slipped on some rifle butts. Some Italians wanted to prove that they knew how to use their weapons.'
'Uncomfortable, I bet. We heard you got in a bit of bother with some fascist general. Come and sit down.'

The story going round PG500 was that FitzGerald, then at a transit camp near Bari, had complained about the gratuitous shooting by an inspecting general of two prisoners who had tried to escape. For his pains, FitzGerald had been beaten by some of the guards. Afterwards, he had been taken to the prison hospital, where the Italian medic had identified, among the bruises and bloody scrapes, a fractured tibia, or what FitzGerald called a broken leg. That was more or less accurate. A competent and considerate man, Major Sciplino provided a plaster cast and warned his patient that his calf would take six to eight weeks to heal; thereafter, he would need to exercise it gently for a further month before it regained full strength. When FitzGerald showed his irritation at this prognosis and predicted that he, a British officer, would not need to dally as long as a mere Italian, Major Sciplino attempted to mollify him by saying that, as he was astonishingly fit and highly motivated, he might recover sooner.

FitzGerald made it clear that he intended to get back to his unit at the first opportunity and kill as many Italians as he could. Major Sciplino tried to calm him by lending him his Petrarch. Nevertheless, the good doctor feared that, no matter how expert the care he provided was, even if it were to the standard of the treatment given to the grandest general, no matter that he initiated conversations on the classics, which FitzGerald obviously enjoyed, he would not succeed in reducing that man's contempt and loathing for his compatriots.

The two British officers started moving towards the huts, the subaltern with the kitbag following.

'I expect you'd like a drink. We're quite well stocked here. Some of the boys make gin out of something filthy. And we get a wine allowance.'

'I'd prefer to meet the escape committee right away. Now that Musso is in irons and our lads are pushing up the boot, Italy will surrender any moment. We must get out before the Huns take over.'

Marsh stopped and grinned in FitzGerald's face. 'No escape committee here, Fitz. We've orders from London not to let anybody get away. We wait until our forces have reached us. You haven't heard the stay-put order?'

Pensive, FitzGerald examined Marsh. 'I have just had the honour of meeting the German commander in this area, Marsh. This afternoon I saw his men hanging women and children that he considers to be collaborators. And he is rounding up Jews to be sent to Germany. I am quite sure he has every intention of rounding up you and every man jack here.'

Marsh looked impatient, as if FitzGerald's information was irrelevant. 'Orders, FitzGerald, orders. Even if the Italians scarper, I'll keep the gates closed and the chaps in.'

FitzGerald then gave one of his charming, disingenuous smiles, which those who had worked with him knew was a sign that the gloves were off. 'Marsh. I am not a soldier that I may grow fat waiting to be rescued. I don't obey stupid orders. Stay here if you want to revel in Poland's labour camps. If you ever get home, you can report me for disobedience. Meanwhile, everybody else will leave this camp when I say so. I will address the men in an hour.'

Marsh was riled, but attempted indifference. 'FitzGerald, I am the SBO. Here I am in charge and I have told the men that, if the Italians scarper, I will post our own guards to keep them in. I'll court martial anybody who tries to leave.'

FitzGerald laughed. He just stopped himself saying 'you fool' but it could be seen on his face. 'I have seniority.' He tapped the bar of medal ribbons on his chest.

The two men had not noticed that a crowd of prisoners had

gathered around them as they talked.

FitzGerald glanced to his right and left to find a great many men – mainly in their early twenties or even younger – following the conversation, or simply enjoying the spectacle of two senior officers disputing in public.

He raised his voice. 'Escapers, behind me. Stayers, behind Brigadier Marsh. Move!'

Shuffling and pushing, the men shifted around until there were perhaps as many as two hundred behind FitzGerald, leaving a forlorn group of less than ten facing him from behind the brigadier.

Someone whispered loudly so that he could be heard by his mates. 'Look at his gongs. Crikey. This bloke's a real soldier.'

Another added, 'He'll get us out.'

Not all agreed. 'Who the hell wants to get out? Here we're safe.'

FitzGerald fixed an intimidating stare on Marsh's face and gave another of his smiles. 'That's settled then, Marsh. We'll meet in your office in forty-five minutes. Make it happen.' Flinging his right crutch forward, he swung past the brigadier and made for the huts. Several prisoners hurried to keep up with him, keen to bask in his authority.

HEINZ IN GREPPO

Fröhlich achieved his objective of causing panic among the villagers of Greppo and all hamlets nearby. Everybody swore that they would never do as the poor Corvos had done – risk their all for strangers – no matter how desperate. The one other family who had a lone Jewish orphan hiding with them made her keep out of sight and told their neighbours that she had left. Bregante forbade Lucia to bring the little foreign boy into the house. He even refused to speak with him, to see whether they spoke the same language. With the devils so close, they would be asking for trouble. Lucia did not argue but instead insisted that the boy should be hidden in the nearest of the grain stores that were scattered over the fields. These were reached through the postern that adjoined Bregante's house and made it possible for her to come and go without being seen by the other villagers.

Leaving him there, she assured the quivering child that she would return with food very soon. As she did so, closing the postern behind her, it was to discover that he had followed her and smuggled himself into a bramble, yards from the walls, from which he could see the door of Bregante's house.

They walked back to the grain store together. She had found

him woollens and warm food, for even in August, the middle of the night could be cold. She stayed with him as he ate, with his left hand in hers, so that, after he had gobbled his food and lain back, unable to extricate herself without alerting him, she too fell asleep.

Later, she woke and found that she and the boy were covered by a tarpaulin; she smiled to realise that Bregante must have come to check on them. She felt the boy curled up against her. She hugged him; he slept on. She felt the outline of his form and pictured his little nose, his long eyelashes, saw his freckles. Who could want to destroy this life? Why were men so wicked? She touched his other fist and his hand opened in his sleep and took hold of her wrist.

The next day, with the boy once again having followed her and hid in the bramble, Lucia told her mother-in-law that she would go to Ginestra and discuss with her own mother what to do with the child. She did not suggest bringing the boy into the house, nor did her mother-in-law.

As they spoke, standing outside the house beside the open postern, she could feel the boy's eyes on her, as if he could understand that she was talking about him, or about leaving him. Her mother-in-law followed her glance and caught sight of him. To Lucia's surprise she called to him – '*E, ragazzo* come, come!' – and, when he hesitatingly arrived, embraced him. He escaped and instead hugged Lucia, not letting her go, continuing to hold onto her dress as she returned to the parlour, where she talked with the other woman, moving between table and stove as she prepared the meal. She did not prevent him but modified and slowed her movements so that he could follow her close, round the table or over to the hearth, always holding a clump of her cotton dress in his fist.

The factor returned from town to take a dish of *minestra* before going up the hill to visit one of his employer's farms. He ignored the child but, this time, he made no objection when Lucia asked him to speak his dead wife's language to the boy, to explain that she would be going away for a few hours but would be back that very day.

His words were spoken kindly. The boy nodded as if in agreement, but Lucia saw anguish in his eyes. His hand had to be prised from her dress and, as she left the house, he made as if to set off with her. Outside the walls, she turned.

'You stay here with the others, Eye-enz – Enrico. I shall come back.'

There was no expression on his face. He remained on the spot as she started off, watching her, then, when she had disappeared, sat down and crossed his bare legs, waiting.

WITH MOTHER

Ginestra is below Greppo, from which the small 15th century township, built around a moated fortress, could be watched. The architectural and natural beauties of Italy are so profuse, that what would be a treasure elsewhere in Europe was nothing special for Umbria. There was a piazza in front of the fortress, with shops, houses and a colonnaded market. The church was, naturally, elegant and contained some notable paintings from the 17th century.

At first, Ginestra's inhabitants had experienced the war through their sons and fathers and brothers, who were away being heroic, according to the wireless or the occasional newsreel shown in the piazza on a Friday night, in outlandish places such as Greece and Russia, Poland and the Balkans. It was not until Domenico was killed in Sicily on 10th July that the inhabitants of Ginestra took on board that the war was edging closer to them.

There had been some early warnings, though. At the start of 1943, a prison camp had been erected a few kilometres outside Ginestra and quite near to Greppo. This had been a benefit to the town, since the camp bought supplies from the local farmers, bakers and pasta makers. Locals had been employed for its erection. The camp had been designated PG500 and manned by category-three soldiers, mostly older, married men who were not given to carousing or causing disturbances when off-duty, although they did patronise the *enoteca*.

Ginestra's elite was charmed by the commandant, Colonel Vicere, formerly of the crack Bersaglieri regiment. He had been called out of retirement. Not only was he a suitable dinner party guest, but he was apolitical, a monarchist who hankered for pre-fascist days, and ensured that the several temporary officers and elderly NCOs administering PG500 were like-minded.

The fortress was also the office of the *podestà*, mayor, because its owner was the largest landowner and, some years before, that landowner had been recommended as *podestà* by a relative who was well in with the party. Don Maurizio Sanvitale, Count of Ginestra, was no fascist, but he was no active opponent either. He was connected with many other landowning families; he was married to an American whose own network had been thought, by Rome, in the days before Italy and the USA became enemies, to be potentially useful.

Opposite the Sanvitale fortress, where there had, not long before, been a cake shop, was the HQ of the local MVSN, the fascist militia. Two guards with black shirts, black fezzes and grey puttees would swagger backwards and forwards outside with their hands on their daggers. The wall had pencilled on it:

CREDERE OBBEDIRE COMBATTERE!
BELIEVE! OBEY! FIGHT!

On the corner, in a medieval tower that had once had a connection with the main church, was the *carabinieri* station. Above the door was the royal flag and coat of arms. There stood guard a *carabiniere* in a grey-green uniform, black leather gaiters and the distinctive "Napoleon" bicorn.

On the walls of the little ochre and tangerine houses around the square before the fortress had been stencilled several other slogans:

IL DUCE HA SEMPRE RAGIONE!
THE LEADER IS ALWAYS RIGHT!
MEGLIO UN GIORNO DI LEONE CHE LA VITA DI PECORA!
BETTER ONE DAY AS A LION THAN A LIFETIME AS A SHEEP!

Lucia paid no more attention to these exhortations than anybody else, especially now that Mussolini had been dismissed and the more informed citizens assumed that before long, the king, who had taken over the government once again, would make peace with everybody and stop the fighting. Lucia's mind was on her own future and her mother's.

It had been intended that as soon as she might be with child, Domenico and Lucia would, in Greppo, move two doors away from the family home, into a smaller house also owned by the Bregantes.

Domenico had been due to manage the Bregante family farm, enabling Salvatore to concentrate on his important job of factoring for Don Maurizio. With Domenico looking after the family business, Salvatore would also have taken over management of the count's home farm, as was the count's desire, so that he could get on with his technical innovations.

These thoughts flitted through Lucia's mind as she climbed the narrow stone stairs, worn into soup dishes by centuries of residents. The tiny medieval home contained a cooker in the corridor, off of which there was a privy (though without drainage), and which lead into the one room. The room was divided into two parts – at one end was a big bed and at the other was a table. On one side of the table was the sewing machine while the other was the place where Lucia used to study her Greek and Latin. Of her books there now remained only a worn classical concordance, a gift from her teacher.

Her mother was knitting, or rather had risen from her knitting at the sound of her daughter's step, and held needles and part of a shawl in her hands as Lucia entered the room.

Through the back window, which looked out onto the little square of San Michele, a dog was yapping.

After Domenico had passed away, had Lucia been pregnant, Lucia would have remained at Greppo and Signora Riva would have joined her to keep house for them and share care of the child. Together they would have become adjuncts to the Bregante household and, perhaps, in time, Lucia might have married her brother-in-law. Alas, Lucia was not with child, and Signora Riva's life had retained its old rhythm, with the grim difference that Lucia was not at home.

After embracing her daughter, Signora Riva sat back down in her big old basket chair. She breathed heavily. In contrast to her daughter, she was fat. Not because she was lazy, far from it. But she had worked sixteen to eighteen sedentary hours a day, knitting and sewing, sewing and knitting, and now found moving her legs painful. When she had prepared food for Lucia, the meat, fish, fresh vegetables and fruit had always been for her child. She insisted. The mothers of Umbria are indulgent in many things, but not over diet. If little Lucia did not eat her designated portion, her mother's anger was severe. Lucia ate. And Signora Riva? When her daughter tried to share her food with her mother, the reply was always that mother preferred pasta with a little scraping of cheese and a drop of oil. That continued year in, year out.

Seeing Lucia so wan in the weeks after Domenico's death, even fearing for her daughter's sanity, Signora Riva had accompanied her to Palma and left her to drink in the fatalism and calmness of the convent at which her elder sister was Mother Superior. And, perhaps rendered defenceless in her grief, Lucia had agreed.

Now, she asked Lucia how she had got on in Palma. Her daughter replied: 'Auntie is very kind. We talked at great deal. The music is beautiful and the sisters were very good to me.'

'And?'

'I won't go back there. I shall stay with you and study to become a teacher as the *dottoressa* and you both wanted.'

Despite her inability to believe, Lucia had used her time in the convent well. Her grief still clawed inside her, but no longer overcame her will to live. She had begun to resign herself to the end of her childhood dreams. *I will never have the family that Domenico and I planned. I will not try to pretend the dream without him by staying with the Bregantes. I will become the modern, independent, woman that the dottoressa always advocated.*

When Lucia declared this to her mother, Signora Riva was glad that at least her daughter had found a route out of sorrow and would not bury herself in the world of her dead husband, as the country people expected her to do, to become devoted to widowhood and remorse.

Lucia, however, had not yet factored in the ways in which the world had changed for her in twenty-four hours. She still thought that the great transformation had been Domenico's death and that her response must be, admittedly with difficulty, resumption of the life she would have pursued had there been no Domenico. She had yet to react to the apocalyptic force on her of what she had witnessed the day before, or to adjust to her already adjusted plans.

'I must tell you about something else, Mamma.'

Signora Riva listened to Lucia's recounting of how she found the boy and took him to Greppo.

'The Bregantes are afraid. They want me to take him away. They are not pushing me, but they talk of the danger to Salvatore's children.'

Signora Riva pursed her lips. She sighed long and gloomily. Lucia looked sharply at her mother.

'This boy – what do you call him? Enrico? This Enrico has lost the most important person in the world. He is alone. This child has lost his all; she who gave him life, who gave him everything. Such loneliness is terrifying.' She paused for a moment, then gave her daughter a look of such sadness that Lucia found herself shuddering.

'His heart is crying out in the emptiness and silence.'

'Yes. So I must find him a home. Perhaps your priest will suggest something.'

Lucia sat down on the stool beside her mother's armchair, the stool on which her mother would, late at night, place a glass of draught wine and a slice of grey bread before bed.

'This child has nobody, if what the militiaman says be true. Except you. You are his mother now, unless you give him away. But you can't do that without making him desolate a second time.'

'I can't keep him. He would be another mouth to feed for you and me.'

'Stay with the Bregantes.'

'And condemn myself to being the widow of Greppo for the rest of my life, for a foreign boy? Anyway, Salvatore won't let him in the house.' This was no longer quite true.

'He is a good man. Wait a while. He'll come round. And, after all, yours is the only family into which the boy can easily be at home. Bregante's children speak the foreign language of their mother. And so does Bregante himself. You can say this boy is from his wife's family.'

'But there are the neighbours. They know. They will know, as soon as they see the boy go outside to play with Chiara and Ebbo. We all saw what the devils did to the Corvos and we became mice, reeking of fear and submission.'

'There are no evil people in Greppo and the Bregantes have no enemies there. Don't be afraid.' Signora Riva pulled her daughter down beside her and her head into her apron, which covered her copious bosom. For a moment or two they just stayed like that, the daughter's face muffled in her mother, whose arms encased her.

'But, Mamma, if I stay in Greppo to look after this child, I will never do the *concorso*.'

'Perhaps.'

'There is no perhaps!' Lucia abruptly stood up and faced her mother, almost petulant. 'The only way I can study for the *concorso* is if I stay here with you and see *dottoressa* every day. You know that. The child cannot live here. If I am to mother him I cannot do the *concorso*. I will not give up my future –'

'For his future? That is what we women always do, Lucia my love. This is why there are a few good men in the world. Because we loved them more than we loved ourselves.'

'No! There is a third way.' Lucia told herself: *Mamma is imposing on me. It's like a priest's homilies to befog trustful women.* Her mother looked askance, but Lucia did not want to share with her mother what she had learnt about Dottoressa Foschini hiding people. *That is my way out*, she thought. *This child must join the other clandestines.*

RETURN OF A HERO

The next day, Lucia called on her former teacher.

Over the colonnaded market were several houses, reached by broad, shallow steps upwards of the back of the colonnade. One of these houses had a ramp up the left side of the steps, pinned to the stone wall. It belonged to the Foschini family who, for several generations, had been Palma's drapers until Pier Francesco Foschini, the designated heir shortly before WW1, decided that he preferred to be a pianist and poet and would return to the old family home in Ginestra. It had been from Ginestra that his forbears had long ago set out to make their name in the business community of Palma and the surrounding province.

Foschini had married a woman from an academic, and thus impoverished, family, who believed that to be a schoolteacher was the highest calling. Foschini himself died before he had earned anything from his creative endeavours, leaving his wife to bring up their son, Alessandro, on her miniscule teacher's salary and the remains of the Foschini patrimony.

Captain Alessandro Foschini had been away for two years, the latter part of which had been spent first in a military hospital in Kyiv and then a convalescent centre in Sonnenstein, in which he had recovered from multiple blast injuries and the amputation of his left arm. Three days earlier, Alessandro had sent a message from Bolzano to say that he hoped to arrive this very day. Bianca, the dottoressa's housekeeper, had been sent out early to buy fresh pasta and fresh bread and, if she could get it, fresh meat too. A message went to Lucia who, before her marriage, had often helped her teacher, asking her to replace Bianca that day and help her rise, wash and dress. Dottoressa Foschini wanted Lucia to ensure that Bianca had made every part of the house, especially Alessandro's room, as clean as a new pin.

Though in a wheelchair, paralysed from the waist down, Dottoressa Foschini had survived poliomyelitis to continue teaching classics at the *Liceo* Benvenuto Cellini di Palma. For this reason, and the fact that she was a widow, her only child could have avoided military service. Unlike the peasants, with their dread of losing their children in pointless wars of which they knew nothing, neither mother nor son had sought this privilege. They were modern, believers in the revolution, believers in the war against communism and in the *Duce*, who would lead Italy to the promised land. Family interests and personal predilections – all were to be sacrificed to the cause, to public service, to the building of the new world.

Lucia had prepared chamomile tea. Now she was sitting on one of the dark, heavy mahogany armchairs in the *dottoressa's salotto*. Above her, on the wall, there was an oil painting of Rome's Pantheon. On the grand piano, in silver frames, were photographs of grandparents and of *Signora* Foschini with her classes. There were diplomas too, on the walls; her degree certificate and that of her son's.

The large portrait photograph of a young man of about 19 in the uniform of the university militia at La Sapienza, Rome, was naturally of Alessandro, the last Foschini. Beside it was a photograph of the march past of that university militia, with the *Duce* taking the salute. Alessandro was the standard bearer, holding aloft a black pennant edged with gold lace, with the device, embroidered with gold wire, of an eagle, book and rifle in its centre. Also on the wall were parchments denoting Alessandro's award for fencing and his commission into the army.

Lucia sat opposite her mentor, holding her saucer with her left hand and the handle of the porcelain cup in her right, as she told *Dottoressa* Foschini her tale of finding Enrico. She described the behaviour of the militiaman, the flight from Palma, the scene at the railway siding and the help and advice given her by the carter. She withheld her mother's opinions.

To Lucia's surprise, the *dottoressa* made no comment about the militiaman's behaviour, the flight or even the prisoners on the train. 'So Gino told you that I am on the ladies' committee? He's a naughty boy.'

Lucia could not see the old carter as a naughty boy and did not respond.

'Now you know what we do here. I have not involved you in the work because you have your own troubles. But that's not the only reason. The older ladies and the plump matrons draw no attention from those who might be looking for signs of forbidden activity. And with many refugees hidden in the castle, in the church, in the cellars of shops, there is always food to be carried, the doctor to be called, people to be moved… and the most beautiful girl in Ginestra attracts attention, as she always has done.' She flashed an admiring look at her protégée.

Lucia looked down at the floor and blushed, as she always did when she was admired.

Dottoressa Foschini cherished the familiar reaction and, seeing it, felt her passion for this child surge. She thought back to her failure to support Lucia when the Bregante parents had tried to forbid their son from marrying her, two years before. The Bregantes had looked down upon the Riva girl as a stray without a dowry or any useful connections. By contrast, Dottoressa Foschini had thought the Bregante boy not good enough for her star pupil and was so distressed at the idea of Lucia being thrown away on a peasant that she had even told *Signora* Bregante that she was doing the right thing in preventing an engagement.

Later, when she understood the couple's devotion, *Signora* Foschini had been filled with remorse. She had begged Lucia to come to see her and wept with her, ashamed at her own snobbery. The academic in her classified people according to their affinity with Italy's poets, painters and philosophers, but the political activist she also was had faith in the people, and it was this faith which won. She had, then, in her most executive manner, met with the countess of Ginestra – referred to universally as Donna Chiara – and formed an alliance to influence the Bregantes to accept Lucia.

This was not difficult. The American woman who had married Don Maurizio of Ginestra had notoriously liberal ideas and cared little for the social distinctions that put Lucia beyond the pale for such a rising family as the Bregantes. In addition, not only was her husband Bregante Salvatore's employer, she had also got to know Lucia and had come to see her as an intellectual equal, unlike anybody else in Ginestra bar *Dottoressa* Foschini herself, the physician, the pharmacist, an erudite Sicilian, and her own husband.

In her last year at the *liceo*, Lucia had worked for the countess with research for her book on life in medieval Palma. Although Donna Chiara had never overtly criticised the party, Lucia had noticed how she regretted the war and closed the window as soon as the blackshirts in the piazza below started singing "*giovinezza*". To Lucia, the American, with her knowledge of the world outside Ginestra, Umbria and Italy, made her feel that not only she, but even her wise teacher, were benighted, their education limited to a *piccolo mondo antico,* an outmoded little world. Yet, the Countess loved Italians, as well as their civilisation, and Lucia loved her for the generosity and respect with which she treated people of every kind. Trust and affection had developed between the two women, though they were so different in age, background and prospects.

Now *Dottoressa* Foschini said to herself that she must hide nothing. Taking on Heinz, Lucia had, unwittingly, already involved herself in "the work".

'You must keep the boy. Persuade Bregante. Greppo is out of the way, less likely to be investigated than Ginestra. You are the only person this child knows. I cannot thrust him into a family terrified for their own survival or let him join a group of children as an outsider. And does not Bregante speak German? There is nowhere better for this one to go.'

Mamma tells me the child needs my love. Dottoressa *suggests that there is no alternative. It is as if they colluded against me. But this is not my destiny*, she told herself.

'He would be happy with you. We can teach him to look after you.'

'My dearest child, have pity. Holed up in a flat with an old cripple? You can give him work to do on the farm, he can play with your niece and nephew...'

Lamely she brought up the *concorso*, but the *dottoressa* was almost dismissive. Her insistence that they must, together, put first the needs of those who had fled to Ginestra, mortified Lucia. This did not register on her face, but consumed her nevertheless: *how can I choose for myself alone?* Dottoressa, *like Mamma, asks me to consider what is the point of a career in a collapsing world. Yes, it is collapsing.* She thought back to the soldiers in Palma, the brutes on the train. *At the last trump, how could I say that I preferred studying my books while others are being tormented?*

Lucia continued to fight, though. 'Then I shall give him to Father Filipović.'

'Never. Don't let that man near your little boy! Ever! Promise me!'

Lucia knew that her teacher loathed the way the priests indoctrinated children with what she called their "claptrap" about hellfire, virginity, afterlife and so on, but she was surprised at the vehemence of her reply.

There was no time for further response, for just then they heard the door being opened downstairs. The Heinz conundrum was suspended.

'Lucia, quick, go to greet him!' Lucia rose swiftly and made for the door. 'Wait! Tell Sandro nothing of this.'

Below, *Signora* Foschini's soldier son had let himself in, with difficulty. He had lost his left arm and had to put down his kitbag in order to rummage about in it for his key. Once the door was open, he was in the tiny hallway, big enough only for two people to stand before heading upstairs.

Foschini Alessandro, the gallant in the photo, now in his late twenties, was dressed in his now rather scuffed service dress of an officer of Alpini, with green collar flashes and green piping on epaulettes and cuffs bearing the three gold wire bars of a captain. There were some medal ribbons over his left pocket, including the blue and white of the Cross of Valour, and pinned to that pocket was the Russian Front badge with its crossed sabres. The famous foreign decoration at his neck, the Iron Cross, in its "knight's" version, had drawn much attention on his journey from Germany to home. Some fellow travellers had made a tsk-tsk when they recognised the silver wound badge and the German Cross in Gold on his tunic's right pocket, another award for courage.

His empty left sleeve hung by his side and he had a red and raw scar all down his left cheek.

Foschini Alessandro picked up the kitbag. As Lucia ran down the stairs, he turned and gave a schoolboy's joyous smile, dropping the bag again in order to put out his good arm to embrace her.

Long lashes, smooth skin, full lips. These things about Lucia had not changed. Though there was a certain tiredness in her expression, where there had been perpetual gaiety before. 'Lucia, how wonderful to see you! So you are still seeing Mamma?'

After the hurried embrace, they faced each other, very close in the tiny vestibule, consciously not touching, both happy but in some manner restrained. She did not divulge that she had helped his mother wash and dress and spoke lamely: 'We meet to talk about books.'

'I am so sad to hear about Domenico.' He bowed his head, though only slightly, for they were very close.

She continued to search his face; otherwise how could she have failed to see his empty sleeve? He put his remaining hand on her upper arm in a gesture of solidarity.

'To lose Domenico so soon. Unimaginable. And such a good, kind man. I am so sorry.' His sorrow was real. He felt tears coming to his eyes: tears for Domenico, tears for Lucia, tears for the awfulness of this war, for which he and Domenico had volunteered.

They remained mute. Then, after a minute, she looked down, her face set as if controlling herself. She pointed at his tunic.

'What medals you have!'

Abruptly she drew back with shock as she took in that empty sleeve.

'Oh Mother of God, your arm! Oh Sandrino,' she used his childhood name, 'Sandrino, Sandrino.' Without thinking, she threw her arms around him and put her head on his shoulder and stroked his hair like a lover, choking, groaning.

He stood straight. 'Didn't Mamma tell you?'

She lifted her head and moved backwards, letting her arm drop and wiping her eyes. 'Yes, but seeing you is much worse. She will be horrified. She has been praying for you every day.'

It crossed Alessandro's mind that his mother never prayed. Never had prayed, anyway. So much was changing. 'I'll go to her.'

He made as if to touch her hand, but now she shrank from him. *Revulsion at my deformity,* he wondered, *or fear of being intimate?*

NEWS FROM UKRAINE

Lucia left mother and son together after a few moments. Dottoressa Foschini did not notice her leave, so besotted was she with her son. She had never revealed to her friends and neighbours anything but absolute confidence in his survival and the victory of the cause. Yet the news from families in the province who had lost their brothers and husbands along the River Don, in battles at Kharkov, intelligence that seeped down in the whispers and gestures of mothers and lovers, had filled her with foreboding. Although she had never admitted to herself that he might die, neither had she fully believed that he might live.

Now, so great was her relief that she hardly registered his wounded face or lost arm until he took off his tunic; then she wept and he comforted her. After school, when he had left provincial and parochial Ginestra to study law at La Sapienza, she had been so proud of his every achievement; when he was commissioned as the standard bearer of the university militia, she willingly spent a huge sum on his parade uniform and, as his awards accumulated, sewed them onto his dove-grey tunic herself. When Napoleon sneered that men will fight long and hard for a piece of coloured ribbon, he omitted something: they will fight long and hard for a piece of coloured ribbon to give to their mothers.

Bianca had prepared a full meal of *ribollita*, beef, mushrooms, salad and even a *zuppa Inglese*. They talked of the other boys who had left for the war, of their distant relatives, and of the leak in the roof that had been repaired at great cost in Alessandro's absence. He put his mother to bed and then he himself lay down. Before he could take off his boots or undo his jacket, he was asleep on his boyhood bed, safe at last.

The following morning, Alessandro and his mother talked and talked, but this time they touched on different things. He stood by the bookshelf, beside which there was the portrait of Gentile. She looked up at him from her wheelchair.

'Why didn't you come home directly? Did you really need to go to Salò before coming home?'

'Those who have remained loyal to the *Duce* are regrouping in Salò. I get the impression that they expect the *Duce* to join them. I wanted to tell the *Duce*, or someone close to him, about what is happening in the east. I was received by Graziani.'

'You met the marshal!' His mother's eyes shone. 'Did you remind him that you received the standard from the *Duce*'s hands at the university that day?'

Her son ignored her question. 'I was with him for just a few minutes. He said that he wished he had more soldiers such as we Alpini. But Graziani is a cruel man. No-one will willingly fight for him. Gentile says –'

'Oh, you met Gentile too!'

'Gentile invited me to tea. He says that the *Duce* will save Italy from destruction by the Germans and save our lads in the east from liquidation.' As if a new thought had come to him, he changed his tone and asked: 'Do people here know that the Germans are slaughtering thousands of Italian soldiers in the Greek islands?'

Seeing his mother's astonished face, Alessandro did not wait for a reply. 'Our leaders realise that if they don't make a show of keeping Italy on the German side, they will do in Italy what they have done in Poland.'

'What do you mean? They are harming our boys?'

Alessandro sat down and held his head in his hands, spoke to the floor under his mother's rapt gaze.

'It's not our boys that need talking about. Italians are being killed, yes. Less than ten percent of we Alpini have survived. But they died fighting bravely for a cause about which they were misled. What our allies continue to do all over Poland and Ukraine is much worse than war. Thousands, hundreds of thousands, are being murdered. They are clearing all the villages, butchering everybody to give land and property to Germans. Those they do not kill are to be slaves, worked to death in factories and on farms. It's not just the military. Every German businessman is joining in to get free labour, whom they treat like trash, killing them when, due to malnutrition and maltreatment, they are too sick to work.'

'It's not possible!'

He ignored her protestations, driving on as if he had been longing to talk about these things. 'I have passed... through hamlets where there are piles of bodies of women and children. Every day. Sometimes they drive these poor creatures beside huge pits and machine gun them in groups so that the dead and half-dead fall on top of each other.' He raised his head and gazed into space. 'I can smell them still, kilometres and kilometres of butchered people. That smell. It's in my clothes, my skin.'

His mother's face became white and strained. 'God help us that we are allied with such people. Does the *Duce* know?'

'I tried to tell Graziani, but he said I was to speak with Gentile. He is the president of the Royal Academy now. So I showed him the photographs I took. I told him everything.'

Dottoressa Foschini, as a high-minded student at Pavia in the early years of the century, when very few women attended university, had been drawn to the rational and progressive propositions of fascism, when she compared them to the corrupt chaos of liberal politics. Tucked away in a peaceful part of Italy, detached from political extremes, she had been wilfully ignorant of the violence of fascist *squadristi* elsewhere in Italy. Until refugees found their way to Palma, she had given no thought to the race laws. The declaration of war in 1940 had worried her, but her son and her son's friends' enthusiastic embrace of the "crusade against communism" mollified her. It was not until she had been confronted by the victims of Mussolini's follies in the shape of real fathers, mothers and children, terrified, dispossessed and hounded for their lives, that she had begun to see what had become of the movement she had served.

Donna Chiara Sanvitale, originally Clare Jefferson, had approached *Dottoressa* Foschini when the first refugees had arrived to ensure that the *dottoressa* would not interfere. Far from interfering, when she met those desperate creatures, the *dottoressa* wanted to help. Not for one moment did she think that obedience to the authorities should trump human sympathy.

'Oh, how I wish Gentile could run the country. He is our only hope. What did he say?'

'He said the *Duce* knows. Knows about the barbarities. In Poland, they started by killing all the educated people they could find – the graduates, priests, officers, musicians, writers and artists. Then they blew up the buildings. All to obliterate Polish culture. The Poles are all to be slaves. Gentile fears that they will obliterate Italy too, unless the *Duce* can get them to treat us as allies still.'

Crossing herself, she said, 'God help us all. At least we are innocent.'

Alessandro was surprised to see his mother cross herself; it was something she had never done in all his life.

'We, innocent? We have been murdering thousands in Slovenia. Roatta has copied the Germans, starved people to death and exterminated dozens of villages.'

Alessandro rose from his chair without warning, strode the three meters across the room and back and there and back again. ''I joined the army to liberate the east from communism, but find that we are as evil as Lenin's butchers.

'We were so sure of ourselves, so proud of the party. We were going to overcome self-serving individualism, greedy capitalism and the corrupt political classes. We'd abolish the church and all its mumbo jumbo about a life after death that hoodwinked the poor into enduring exploitation by the feudal landowners and the moneylenders. Bah!'

His mother sat gazing at her boy, trying to absorb the momentous changes that his words reflected. She recalled his earlier vehemence; how he and his friends at university had worshipped the heroic leader, thronged to his marching bands. She had been carried along by their youthful energy and idealism, suppressing her reservations as those of a mere female. They had longed for self-sacrifice, even martyrdom, and shouted in unison for the great one to whom they might dedicate their lives. And what had it all come to?

Her boy was staring at the photograph of his friends in the university militia. 'We mobilised ordinary men to do terrible things. And because we made sacred tenets of obedience, faith, unreason – just like the church we professed to despise – then people who had been brought up addicted to faith believed in us and did what we told them.'

She waited for more, but he sat staring at the floor, tears dropping onto the tiles.

'How will it all end, Sandrino? Even an old woman in a wheelchair can see that Germany can't fight on four fronts, in a war that has stirred up all Europe.'

As if to himself, Alessandro mumbled: 'I'll not go back to fight with the Germans.'

'Thank God. *Bello mio*, give me your hand.' As she said it, she remembered, and she too began to weep.

Her son came towards her, squatted beside her wheel and gave her his one hand. 'I have told my comrades. Hide. Wait.'

'I want you to settle down here and forget the war. Surely after your wounds and medals you cannot be expected to go back?'

Alessandro gave a scornful laugh. His mother changed the subject.

'You know Lucia was always my favourite pupil. I was so proud of her. I wept when she said she would marry Domenico.'

'I know. But Domenico was a good boy.'

'But a peasant!'

There was a knock on the door. Lucia, had returned and let herself in downstairs. She told herself that she was coming to finalise the matter of Heinz. She had explained to Bregante that Captain Foschini had arrived before they had reached a conclusion as to what to do with him. Bregante understood. The return of the *dottoressa*'s son was an event that put all else in the shade.

'Forgive me, *Signora*, but I wanted to see if you need anything.'

'Oh Lucia! It is so lovely to have you both here!'

The younger people looked uncomfortable and there was a heavy silence.

Trying to find something to deflect the conversation, Alessandro's eye was arrested by an unfamiliar book on the piano. He picked it up and turned the pages. It was the Hebrew Bible.

'Mother – why have you got this Jewish book here?'

Momentarily frightened, *Dottoressa* Foschini did not reply but stared at her son as if trying to work out what to say.

Lucia thought quickly. It was a moment of choice. She did not ask herself what to say: the subliminal cogitations of the last forty-eight hours; the nightmares and the recollected and digested words of her mother and teacher; all these interventions in her life, shuffled and reshuffled in her mind, resulting in her making a choice as fast as light. She joined "the work".

'I am sorry, I left it behind. My studies.'

'You?!' He almost shouted at Lucia.

She blanched at his tone. He went on, in the voice of an interrogator, 'Are you hiding a Jew?'

Silence. She seemed tongue-tied,

Dottoressa Foschini gave a sigh: 'No, my son. It is I. I am hiding four Jews. A Dr Behrens, Mrs Behrens and two children. He is a dentist from Trieste. But Lucia is not involved. She is just trying to protect me by claiming that book.'

'My God! They will kill you both. Why, for Heaven's sake? Mamma, how can you?!'

'How can we not?' Lucia looked straight at him.

Alessandro turned back to Lucia, aghast. Nowhere in Ukraine had he seen a soul who put out a hand to the condemned. Neither he, nor his comrades, the nurses, journalists, cooks or doctors thronging behind the troops; nobody had raised a voice, still less the German civilians, who swarmed over purloined homes and looted possessions.

Now that Signora Foschini had learnt from her son what her ladies committee was really pitted against, there was a new urgency, a renewed vigour in her manner. From an importuning mother she turned back into the youth leader, the form mistress. Ignoring her son, she spoke directly to her pupil in a tone of authority.

'Lucia, I will talk with my Sandro later. Meanwhile, I want you to do something for me. The commandant of PG500 believes that the Germans intend to take over the prison camp and I am concerned that, to avoid this, the prisoners will get out and may try to hide in the town. That will be disastrous for the refugees, because if the devils search the town looking for *Inglesi*, they will find all our poor little outcasts. I want you to go and talk with the prisoners, persuade them not to risk the lives of the refugees. To make another plan.'

'Me? Why me, *Dottoressa*? I am not worthy.'

'You can do it with your brother-in-law. He has always avoided anything to do with the refugees, perhaps because his wife was German, but alas she has passed. And he too should be eager to stop the prisoners trying to hide in Ginestra. Find a solution with him.'

'How many prisoners are there?'

'Six hundred.'

'Six hundred!' Lucia found it difficult to think that her teacher could imagine her having an impact on such an army. Foreign men, too.

As Lucia left to return to Greppo, she had not said whether she would obey her teacher, but she had not refused. The ask hung heavy on her. She now understood the dangers of crossing the devils. It had dawned on her, not only what was at stake for little Heinz, but what was at stake for those who helped him, let alone helped six hundred of the devils' enemies. Six hundred! Let them rot, she decided. *They shouldn't be here in my home. Who invited them? But* Dottoressa *is not asking me to help them, not like Heinz; only to keep them out of Ginestra. But why me? What can I do that others cannot do better?*

Even as she thought in this way, a new idea started to take possession of her. *These are the men who killed my Domenico. If I helped them, would I not be showing them the superiority of charity over violence? If they give up violence because I forgive them, rescue them from their enemies, would Domenico's death not mean something? Bah! I am thinking like a Christian, just trying to justify my actions as sacrifice.* The beginnings of tears came to her eyes as she pictured Domenico, now in his soldier's clothes, in a prison like the one near home. *Each of those men has a mother and a woman like me, longing to know that he still exists.*

That night, Alessandro at last turned in, as fortunate children do, undressing in his boyhood room with its model ships and lead soldiers, school textbooks and a portrait of the *Duce,* who had beguiled him to dedicate his life to a great cause. Wearing pyjamas, soft pyjamas, for the first time for as long as he could remember, Sandro Foschini marvelled that his mother, even without seeing the horrors of the Eastern Front, had felt a higher kind of loyalty. He pulled open the bedclothes, paused and reached up for the portrait of Mussolini. He detached it from the wall and slid it under the bed, face down.

PG500

As the war ground on, the highly educated men who commanded the regiments, brigades, divisions and armies of the Third Reich, unlike Captain Foschini, rarely questioned the modern superstitions with which they had been galvanised to fight, even when it was apparent that they would be defeated. Why did they, almost all brought up with the injunction to love their neighbours as themselves, not have the courage to stop the carnage? They abandoned the moral scruples recited at their Sunday schools, the humanity modelled on their mothers' laps, gladly accepting in quittance more pips on their epaulettes, the estates of Polish nobles and the apartments of murdered Jews, looted artworks and pretty medals. Their acolytes, such as Joachim Fröhlich, effectively *gauleiter*, viceroy, of the Palma region, pressed on. Fröhlich exhorted his men – whom he believed he loved – to ever greater efforts to achieve death or mutilation, causing so much collateral damage along the way.

With their customary insouciance towards the doings of lesser breeds, the young men from the English-speaking world took little interest in the affairs of the country in which they found themselves prisoners. They had been cheered by news of the July invasion of Sicily, promptly predicting the imminent surrender of Italy and withdrawal of the Nazis. The more informed realised that the democracies were not likely to hurry north up Italy and that Nazi troops were pouring down southwards to repel them.

Unlike the unkempt, lackadaisical youths hanging around the camp on his arrival, the three watching their commanding officer's face on the first morning after his coup d'état were alert and, insofar as it was possible, well turned out. Though their uniforms were bleached by the sun and repaired by hand, they at least had the trappings of soldiers, with clean and pressed clothes.

Lange was an architecture student with a prematurely wise face and cautious expression. Albion was a captain at 24 and had two military crosses for bravery. And there was 'Commie' Goode, who had found himself a library of Italian poetry and plays, though nobody could understand from where. Son of the schoolmaster of Edzell, Goode was a gaunt, incisive man who, aged 28, already spoke Russian, German and Italian. He retained his Brechin accent, so the other prisoners dubbed him 'jock', when they didn't call him 'commie', and pretended they couldn't understand him. Whenever he had a chance, Goode chatted with Italians. No sooner did FitzGerald seize the role of SBO than he discovered Goode and appointed him his aide.

FitzGerald was standing by a silk paratrooper map of central and southern Italy, pinned onto the wall. He used a cane to pinpoint on the map. Gone was the ironical, drawling style he had employed in speaking with the Germans; now, he spoke with authority.

'Since Mussolini was dismissed from government, following our invasion of Sicily, it has been generally expected that Italy will surrender to the Allies.'

Goode was eager to share his ideas. 'Mussolini's war has always been unpopular, especially south of Florence and even more in the deep south and Sicily where all the fighting is taking place. Italy will split, with the south rising against the fascists and the north supporting the Germans.'

Lange, taking off his spectacles, asked one of his careful

questions in his faint Edinburgh accent. 'Do you consider it likely that Alex will land near Rome and even in the north, Sir?'

General Alexander, commanding two field armies in Italy, was another Irishman.

'I doubt it. Alex will not rush to fight our way up Italy. The whole point of our attack is to tie up as many Huns as possible for as long as possible. To divert resources away from Russia and France. The Huns won't make it easy. They've got to stop us getting near Austria and the Balkans.'

Goode noted, thinking of those now at risk of being transported to Germany, or even the soon-to-be-frozen wastes of Ukraine, 'There may be as many as 100,000 of us prisoners of war.'

FitzGerald: 'When Italy surrenders, the Huns will take over the camps. Although they have form in massacring prisoners, those are Russians and Poles, not Anglos. In my estimation, it is more likely that they will transport us to the east with a view of working us to death.'

He looked round the group.

'You may be pleased to know that I do not intend to let this happen.'

Albion, quiet and unemotional, remarked, 'Praise be, Sir. The ayes have it.'

Goode was always the activist, his thin body pulsing with enthusiasm. 'We can overcome the guards.'

Albion smiled happily, 'A piece of cake.'

Fitzgerald ignored them. 'If you do as I say, you'll be disobeying orders. London has in its wisdom decreed that all prisoners of war should stay put and await liberation by our armies as they fight their way up Italy.'

Lange adopted a sardonic look. 'German hotels are going to be worse than this. Even our least enthusiastic lads would rather take their chance in the hills than accept the Huns' invitation.'

'Quite so. So, I intend to disobey the stay-put order and get out as soon as feasible. Any comments so far?'

Lange: 'How, Sir? Do we fight the guards?'

'Getting out should be a breeze. When Italy surrenders, the guards will go home to their mammas. We can just march out. But the problem is, what then?'

Goode was thoughtful. 'Personally, I think the Italians will help us, because it was only the city mobs who howled for war. The proletariat has no interest in Mussolini's wars.'

'That's your hunch, but we don't know for sure. We can't rely on Italian sympathy, although we can rely on their cowardice. Helping us'd be cupboard love, anyway; they'd be ready to stab us in the back if the war started going better for the Huns.'

Lange: 'Sir, with respect, we are in enemy territory, without food or proper clothing for autumn or winter, without arms or Allies. Only if we make friends with local Eyeties –'

FitzGerald cut him off. 'The Italians are just benighted serfs, cringing to any authority, without any initiative. We Brits and Yanks are descended from people who made their own freedom. We're a match for any of them.'

Albion was confident. 'We're a battalion strong. We can overcome the Eyeties, take their arms and set up our own HQ in the hills.'

Lange: 'And when the Germans come for us with tanks and proper weapons?'

Goode: 'There are *bande*. Units of partisans.'

Albion: 'But what's a gang of Eyeties worth? And without serious arms.'

FitzGerald: 'Quite. My preference too is for establishing a guerrilla army to fight behind enemy lines, but I must be realistic. In hostile country, with no supplies, the Huns would make mincemeat of us.' He saw in his head the key stencilled on that jeep but did not tell his team of its significance.

Lange. 'So, the best we can do is to get through the lines and re-join our units in the south?'

Winding up discussion, FitzGerald's tone became decisive.

'There are several options and it's probably best our lads scatter in all possible directions. There's north to Switzerland. If you go through Milan, there's an organisation to hide you and supply guides to get you over the Alps. If you go eastwards to the coast, to be picked up by our navy, there is an SAS detachment in situ ready to help. You get straight back to Britain. Those who go west should aim for Rome, where there's an escape organisation run from the Vatican by a priest called O'Flaherty. I'm going south to rejoin my own outfit. Each route has its particular challenges, and the boys will have to decide each for himself.'

'We will march out formed as a German battalion, such that the Huns' air reconnaissance will take us for their own. We will park up nearby until they have given up looking for us. Thereafter, we will break up into parties of two or three and scatter along as many different routes as possible.'

The audacity of their commander's plan struck all three silent for a moment. They watched their leader as if they sought to absorb his bravado.

'Six hundred chaps is a lot to hide in a cupboard, Sir.' Albion received a nod in response, from which he could see that the boss was not going to be daunted by such a practical consideration.

Lange: 'March out as a battalion? But Sir, are you assuming we will have overwhelmed the guards first?'

FitzGerald: 'It's more likely they'll have run away as soon as Italy surrenders. They ran away on the desert when they were supposed to be fighting, after all…'

Goode added, 'Sir, I would tackle the commandant. I can't believe he'll want to go along with the Nazis. His ADC Basili speaks fluent English and can't abide them.'

'Has anyone here any experience of him?'

Albion nodded. 'He's elderly, Sir. A retired gent. Very polite and elegant. Speaks good French. Oh,' he added, 'never carries any weapon except his dress sword.'

Everybody guffawed.

'Splendid! I will tell him that as soon as the Italians change sides, or surrender, or stop fighting or whatever, I want him to remove the guards and let us take over the camp. And that he is not to liaise with the Huns to give us up.'

Lange was sceptical. 'And if he won't play ball, Sir?'

'On first meetings, we will just be very polite and friendly. But when the surrender is announced, we will see him again – just Goode and I, because this will now be the way we do things – and we will overpower him and his ADC and force them to obey us. If the commandant doesn't carry a weapon but his ADC does, Goode needs to get the number two's pistol while I neutralise the commandant. Are you confident that you know what to do?'

Goode: 'I have some judo, Sir.'

FitzGerald: 'Chinese wrestling?'

Goode: 'Japanese, Sir.'

FitzGerald: 'Show me.'

Goode did a tackle on Albion and rendered him defenceless.

FitzGerald chuckled. 'Very good.'

Albion, slyly: 'And you, Sir?'

'I am rather crude. I just break a chap's neck.' He shot out his hand and shammed the crushing of Albion's windpipe.

They all liked that.

FitzGerald: 'Now let's get down to the more difficult bit – after we get out. As long as we move fast, two to three hundred small parties will be impossible for the Germans to round up, although they might get a few. Every pair or threesome can decide for itself where to go. And some may hide up in the hills.'

Goode: 'You, Sir?'

FitzGerald: 'To the river. The Biferno. Rommel will making that his line of defence in the east. Alex will smash him there and I want to join my lads and share the smashing. As soon as I bloody well can, with this rotten leg.' He swatted his left leg with his cane.

Albion whistled, 'To the river. Not easy, Sir.'

FitzGerald agreed. 'No, and that's why I'm letting everybody decide his own route.'

Goode was still for fighting. 'Or whether to stay and nip the Huns in the rear?'

Lange did not give his colonel the opportunity to reply. 'And we live off the land?'

FitzGerald: 'Steal food, warn the Italians that if they betray us then revenge will follow when the Allies arrive. Threaten them and you will be alright. They are only Italians, after all.'

Albion: 'The Huns have to stand behind them with tommy guns or they will all do a runner.'

Except Goode, they all chortled.

FitzGerald: 'That's why we don't have to fear them turning us over to the Huns. They know that sooner or later we'll be in charge here and they had better treat us well. You can offer them a letter, a reference, that they can show any of our units who pass this way.'

Lange was concerned. 'Our chaps aren't yet fit enough for a lot of clambering over hills. And they have no maps or compasses.'

'That's why I've appointed you three as company commanders. You have, at most, a few weeks to get the men fit. Turn them back into soldiers. Enthuse them for returning to the fight. No more beards, long hair or slouching. Mr Goode, you speak Italian, I understand?'

'Yes, Sir. Though my Italian is rather academic. I am better at Dante and Petrarch than at daily conversation.'

FitzGerald jeered. 'Forget the poets. Every man here must learn enough Italian to get around, within ten days. Enough Italian to get directions, demand food, threaten reprisals.'

Goode: 'Yes, Sir.'

FitzGerald: 'And you, Albion. Football is not enough. I want running, walking and PE for everybody, to get them fit. All day.'

Albion said, eagerly, 'Sir!'

FitzGerald: 'Lange, you are i/c Red Cross parcels. I want you to start building up a stock of vittels for every team. As to changes of clothing, we need to do a deal one of the leading guards. Suggestions?'

Albion: 'There's that Captain Basili. The ADC. Worked in Slough before the war.'

They all grinned.

FitzGerald: 'You know him?'

Albion: 'I liaised with him on the SBO's account. He's as good an egg as we've got.'

FitzGerald: 'Then tell him what we need. Report back tomorrow after rollcall. Alright lads?'

All: 'Aye aye, Cap'n!'

FitzGerald: 'Dismiss.'

THE FACTOR'S HOME

Like every man and woman all over Europe who followed what news and rumour they could get, Bregante sensed that Germany was in the process of being vanquished. He compared notes with his employer, or his employer's wife, every morning at 08:00, at their customary management meetings, which had turned into exchanges of information about the war.

Don Maurizio knew quicker than anyone else in the area what was going on due to his varied sources of information. His wife listened to the BBC, risking execution, and talked with Dottoressa Foschini, who had her sources through the party; he himself played scopa with the physician, a secret adherent of Kropotkin's anarchism, who was nevertheless connected with most leftist circles in the province. From time to time, Don Maurizio would meet the Vacca family – fellow landowners who could pass him insights from the Vatican. Bregante reported to him what the peasants had seen and on the activities of 1st Panzer in the vicinity. The Station Sergeant kept an eye on the blackshirts and regularly took a coffee with Don Maurizio. And now the count had the perspective of Captain Foschini.

Relieved that Mussolini had been sacked, Don Maurizio was

sure that the Nazi adventure, too, was over. But as, unlike the Italians, the Germans would not admit that the curtain was down, they would still have to tread carefully.

This was brought home to him that morning, when Bregante warned him that Donna Chiara was taking a great risk in harbouring fugitives and in their own home too. He described the fate of the Corvo family and the treatment of their neighbours, who were forced to witness the atrocity. He told him how his sister-in-law had come across a parked train on a siding near the Palma junction, a dozen cattle trucks stuffed with pitiful human beings crying out for water.

'*Eccelenza*, if we cross these devils, our people will be treated like that. The devils have no heart. Warn Her Excellency, Sir, and forgive me.'

'Turiddu, I value all you say.' Don Maurizio was the only person who called Bregante by the Sicilian form of his name. They were both inordinately proud of their Sicilian connections. 'My dear Turriddu,' his tone was despondent, 'I shall talk with the countess. And we shall see.'

'Thank you, Eccelenza,' Bregante said with a slight bow. Then, Don Maurizio summarised the news he had.

After Bregante had been briefed by his employer, he spent the morning trying to grasp the news' implications while he checked on the refurbishment of some cottages on the outskirts of Ginestra. At each of the homes he passed, he stopped and handed a leaflet to whoever was the acting head of household, explaining its content while watching it being carefully placed, according to his advice, in a prominent position in the living room. Having warned all the nearby families of what they risked if they upset the devils, he then walked back towards Greppo for lunch. He would arrive just after the departure of an unwelcome visitor.

Greppo had only one street and it was quite short. At the end furthest from the gate of Greppo was the Bregante house, entered by a low door outside of which was a bench and two or three oil containers: large green glass flagons with straw cosies. Inside, the room was dominated by the range; hams, garlic, onions and strings of chilies hung from the rafters.

Lucia was working on the lentil stew that had been interrupted by the visit of the officer from PG500. The glass from which he had drunk Bregante's wine remained on the table, a pink sediment in the bottom. A platter sat beside it with a few crumbs of bread and cheese.

There had been consternation when a uniformed man on a bicycle arrived sweating at the great gate of Greppo. Women had fled into the houses, children hid behind the big pots of geraniums and two old men sat outside their doors, tense. They had been reassured when they found they could understand Captain Basili's speech – he, being from Lazio, could barely understand theirs – and when he asked for the Bregante house. The news flew to Bregante Maria, who immediately assumed him to be a suitor for her daughter-in-law and made ready to repel him with harsh words as the first bout in a negotiation. In the event, he had indeed wished to speak to Signora Lucia, but out of hearing of her mother-in-law, though of course not out of sight. Yet he did not give the impression of having conjugal intentions.

Captain Basili had now gone, racing down the hill on his rusty black bicycle, clouds of dust billowing around him. Lucia had returned to her duties and reassured her mother-in-law that the officer was bringing them nothing useful, after which Bregante Maria lost interest in the visit of the man she had first described as "*bell uomo*", a "handsome man", and then, after his mission appeared to be so pointless, as "*quell fesso*", "that idiot".

As Bregante arrived home, Lucia was pulled away from the big bowl of stew by the two children. Now she was sitting on the lowest step of the stair, reading to them. Enrico snuggled up shyly beside her; she put her left arm around him and pulled him closer. Their *bisnonna*, great grandmother, sat in a rocking chair, knitting a shawl very slowly, so that the clicks of her needles sounded like the steps of a wounded cricket.

Bregante was holding a bundle of leaflets. His two children jumped up and ran to their father, Chiara grabbing at the leaflets, which he relinquished to her with a smile, while Ebbo put his arms around his father's leg as if to root him to the spot. The father picked up his son and kissed him. Enrico crouched next to Lucia, watching Bregante embrace his children.

Bisnonna was grumpy. 'She's reading to them again. Poems. What's the point? You can't eat with poems. And there is so much to be done in the house…'

Bregante just smiled, so she opened a new topic. 'A man has been seeking her out, an officer. She gave him wine and cheese.' Bregante was startled, seeing the evidence on the table before him. Bisnonna was content at his reaction. 'You must stop these visits. We will get a bad reputation.'

'Yes Nonna,' he spoke in a tone of finality, which she always understood to be telling her to stop talking. She saw from his look that he did not want to speak with her, but to Lucia. *He must sow her field before more unsuitable men come sniffing. She isn't perfect, too headstrong. And all those stupid books. But men lust after her and* – Bisnonna took in her daughter-in-law's hips yet again – *she could produce plenty of children. Salvatore had better get on with it. Hump her before that foreign captain.* And with that, Bisnonna started the slow ascent to her sleeping quarters, ready to refuse the meal a few times before finally conceding that she would preside over the younger people as usual.

Lucia had ignored Bisnonna. She looked up from her reading and, pointing to the papers in his hand, asked, 'What are those?'

Bregante turned to his little ones. 'Children. Go outside and play. I will come soon.' To Heinz: 'You too, Enrico. Chiara, take Enrico to play.'

The silent boy looked quickly at Lucia, as if seeking reassurance. She smiled encouragingly and nodded. She sighed with relief when he turned towards Chiara.

Chiara took Heinz by the hand and pranced out into the street to join her brother, already shouting greetings to some other boys near the gate.

'Leaflets. From the Germans. I've been going round the neighbourhood, telling people about the killing of the Corvo family. Warning them not to shelter people.'

'Don't you think they know already?'

'But they are still taking the risk.'

'Won't you?'

'No. I shan't get you and our children and neighbours killed because they look after others who won't be killed themselves.'

Lucia was about to remind him that he was already sheltering a fugitive but remained silent. She got up and returned to the kitchen table, where she began kneading pasta.

Before long, she was flattening it to cover the tabletop like a cloth. She reached for a knife and started cutting strips of tagliatelle.

Looking at the plate and the sediment in the lone wine glass on the table, Bregante questioned, 'Are you not going to tell me about that visitor?'

'What do you want to know?'

'Bisnonna thinks he wants to court you.'

Lucia laughed. She cut six more strips, then said, 'He wants you and me to find somewhere for the prisoners to hide. He doesn't know the area at all, so he needs advice for when they get out.'

'What? The camp officer will help them?'

'Yes. He says that the devils are coming to take all these prisoners away, maybe kill them. He wants to help them run away. And he asks for our advice.'

'My advice is that he clear off, he and all his kind.'

Bregante moved towards the table at which Lucia worked. Lucia did not reply.

Bregante looked at her hard. 'The Corvos died, but the Jews were not even hurt. They were just taken away.'

Lucia remained silent and got on with cutting pasta, making

neat, slender lines. She hung each one on a frame, where they joined hundreds of others to dry.

Bregante went on: 'I know they are not treated very gently. But they are not killed. They are resettled north of Trieste. Or maybe Poland.'

Lucia gave her brother-in-law a look as if to say, *do you really believe that?*

'Donna Chiara is taking a great risk by hiding refugees. Not just for her, but everybody. You are putting us in danger with this boy Enrico. You should send him away.'

He waited for a response, but Lucia just continued slicing pasta.

He went on: 'Before, I thought they just helped people who fled the bombing. But they have some Jews. This is foolhardy. They will bring destruction on many other people. Is Enrico a Jew?'

'How should I know?'

Bregante hesitated. This was not a topic to be discussed with a young woman. But he was anxious: 'You washed him. His body. '

'So?'

'Jewish boys have an operation that makes them... different.' Bregante blushed.

'Yesterday I washed some poor little mites in the fortress. They aren't Jews, and Enrico is different from them. If that is what makes him a Jew, then, yes, he's a Jew.'

'My God.' He could not restrain himself from crying out loud. 'This is mad.'

Lucia looked up. 'Do you want to divide the Jews from the non-Jews and tell the Jews to go away? Most of the people looked after in the fortress are families fleeing the starving cities or the bombing. I have been told that some are Jews. Dottoressa Foschini is housing a family of Jews herself, a dentist from Trieste. There are also Germans and Americans in the fortress. All need help.'

'My God!' he swore again. 'Deserters! They're just as dangerous as Jews. Why get involved? When did you think you had to mix up with politics, with city people's battles?'

'Well, soon there are going to be lots more. Basili says that all the prisoners at the camp need help. There are six hundred of them.'

'Six hundred! Look, Lucia, they will just be put back in prison. Or taken north. We will all die if the devils find out you helped them.'

He came closer, took her forearm and looked closely into her face. She lowered her eyes.

'Lucia. You are my brother's wife and now the mother of my children. Please put our family first. Think of my brother, your husband, would he want you to do this? Have you forgotten Domenico so quickly?'

At the mention of Domenico's name, a look of anguish crossed Lucia's face – anguish and shock, shock that he could have questioned her feelings for Domenico.

Bregante dropped his hold and stepped back. He looked ashamed. 'Forgive me, Lucia. I'm sorry. Forgive me.' His eyes looked pleadingly at her.

Lucia was immobile, looking ahead as if addressing someone far away. 'Grief does not have to be seen to be real. Do not imagine I do not think of your brother every day. When you, his brother, walk, I see his gait. When I pass the tree under which we sat, I see his smile. His voice follows me as I go down the stairs. If I see a washing line, I can smell his vest. As I doze, I think of him, remembering putting my hand up to touch his cheek and murmuring to him to place his arm around me.'

She looked round as if looking for somebody, then her eyes alighted on Bregante and she spoke more prosaically. 'He was so embarrassed when Lucia, so much younger and a female, helped him with his maths homework! He did not understand what I saw in him. That modesty was him to a tee. Your brother.'

'I know. I'm sorry for what I said. Forgive me.'

She moved over to the large photograph of Domenico, smiling gaily, on the wall. 'I think I have worked out what I am going to do without my Domenico.' She looked back at her brother-in-law.

'Salvatò, you and I both love Domenico. It is because of what happened to him that I want to help these people. My beautiful man – your brother – has gone, but there are thousands of Domenicos, hungry and afraid, being hunted in the hills and valleys.'

'But –' Bregante was not permitted to continue.

'You're right, I never thought about these things before. Not until I understood what had happened to Enrico. And I did not even understand that until I saw the Corvos killed. I never imagined people could do such things. Such cruelty. Such meanness.'

She paused, turning to look at her brother-in-law: '*Carissimo fratello*, think a moment. These poor creatures are outcasts, far from their mothers and sisters, with no food and no roof under which to shelter. Wicked men are searching for them with guns and dogs. Will you really have our people turn them away to starve in the mountains?'

Bregante looked down. He was not convinced but would not argue with her again, less still bring up his brother: 'I understand. If they ask, I'll give food and send them on their way. If they don't ask, I will not seek them out.'

Silence. Then he looked up and spoke with more decision. 'I am the factor. People look to me for leadership. I must not lead them to their destruction. I will take the devils' leaflets round the area, warning people not to help fugitives. I will tell them that I personally will not put our community at risk.' Then he suddenly remembered: 'But I myself am now sheltering a hunted creature.' He put his palms over his face and made a keening sound. 'Mother of God!'

Lucia remained silent. She went back to hanging the pasta strips from the rack, which she would haul back up to the ceiling. Chiara came in stroking a baby rabbit. Behind her, Heinz crept forward, shyly, as if not wanting to intrude yet not knowing where else to go. He gazed at the rabbit and its twitching ears. Bregante bent down and stroked the side of Enrico's face and smiled at him.

Bisnonna was beseeched to come downstairs, Ebbo came

in from the yard, the children washed their hands and they all sat down for their midday meal. Lucia and Bregante were dour, exchanging only essential words. The children, after rapturing over the rabbit at first, had now placed it in an empty earthenware jar with some vegetables. They barely spoke, eyeing their father. Bisnonna and Nonna discussed the visitor and speculated on his intentions, though disappointed by the silence of the man of the house and the daughter-in-law.

The meal finished more quickly than usual, without stories or talk of neighbours. Lucia tidied the kitchen, hung up the ladle and put away the forks, washed her hands and took off her apron. Arrested on the bottom step, Bregante watched her, his eyes taking in her lithe figure, her tossing back her hair. Then he climbed the stairs.

Once he had gone upstairs and the children were playing happily with their neighbours, Heinz shyly mimicking all that Ebbo did, Lucia slipped on her walking shoes and left Greppo by the postern, heading for PG500.

THE COMMANDANT

At the desk of the camp commandant sat a slender man in his early sixties with the wistful face of a pre-Raphaelite Psyche. Vicere Eugenio, elegant in his gilt-buttoned, tailored tunic of pre-war vintage, was white-haired but had an alert posture and a witty look. In the corner of the room, his dress sword with its gold knot hung on a hook, below his *Bersaglieri vaira* headgear with its long peacock feathers.

He was cocking his ear as Captain Basili reported goings on among the prisoners. Basili, a chubby and officious-looking man in his thirties, sporting a neat tunic without a belt, trousers instead of breeches and long boots, rather as if it were a business suit, summarised.

'Sir, this new commanding officer has turned them back into soldiers, soldiers with purpose. They are getting fit, repairing boots and clothes, learning Italian.' His hand occasionally stroked the bulge of his right pocket, under which was a holster, clipped to his trouser belt.

Hearing a rap on the door, the commandant turned away, called out, '*Venite ragazzi*! Come in, lads!' Goode, waiting outside behind FitzGerald, noticed his 'R' *rovescio*, or guttural R, generally affected by the Italian gentry.

The orderly opened the door and called in 'the senior prisoner, Sir.'

Vicere rose as FitzGerald came in sideways, due to his crutches and the narrow doorway. Goode followed with two armed guards. Captain Basili gestured for the guards to leave.

The commandant spoke in fluent, though accented, English. 'Come in, dear Colonel FitzGerald. We have been looking forward to seeing you.' He gestured at his assistant. 'You know Basili? And this is?'

'Mr Goode, who practices Italian with Captain Basili.'

The older man nodded to Goode with a fatherly smile. 'Ah yes, you are the one teaching your men Italian! I am told you arrived here already speaking our language.'

FitzGerald's tone was mocking. 'The men all think we will soon be allies and so it will be useful.'

'Do sit down, gentlemen.' The commandant gestured to two worn leather armchairs before his desk. They hesitated, but Vicere sat and they slowly followed. Basili remained standing.

Colonel Vicere had not noticed FitzGerald's tone. 'The language of poets, painters and philosophers! Refined Europeans have studied Italian for centuries, as indeed do the enlightened Americans.'

FitzGerald: 'It surprises us that we should be enemies.'

'Naturally we should be allies. My family come from Benevento, of the kingdom of the two Sicilies. For a long period, your great Lord Nelson was our grand admiral. And two of our prime ministers were Englishmen. We shared a need to resist the expansionist ambitions of the French and Germans, their dream of subjugating all Europe. *Tempora mutantur, et nos mutamur in illis.*'

FitzGerald translated. 'The times change, and we change with them.'

Vicere was delighted: 'Colonel FitzGerald!'

FitzGerald gave a cool smile.

'So, some Americans are still marinated in European culture. My governess was English. *This blessed plot, this England.* Ah, how happy I was to go to Stratford-upon-Avon many years ago and drink in the bard's air…' He was about to go on, but noticing Fitzgerald's impatience, or disinterest in their conversation, cut himself short. 'Colonel, please excuse me, I'm gossiping on like an old lady. What can I do for you?'

FitzGerald cut to the chase as all Anglos are supposed to do, in the minds of more discursive people. 'Colonel Vicere, your government is likely to break with the Germans soon and make peace with the democracies. We all know it. What will you do here at PG500?'

'My responsibility, my dear FitzGerald, is to look after you boys, keep you as safe as is possible. Like you I am a soldier so I will obey orders. I anticipate that orders from Rome will be to not permit the Germans to take you. *Ob has causas*, for these reaons, I will defend the camp against them. In such circumstances, I want to have prisoners with whom I can collaborate; the situation may be dire. I might need to arm you. In this case, I need to be sure of your reliability.'

'But, Colonel, is it realistic for you to seek to protect us from the Germans? Your men here are not the crack troops you used to command and they are poorly equipped for fighting 1st Panzer. Even if you armed all my men, we would have a hard job of holding them back. They won't care how many they kill.'

The Italian made a shrugging, fatalistic gesture. 'Yes. And you will still be taken.'

'So instead of fighting, I should like you to turn a blind eye if we leave before the Germans arrive.'

The Italian looked relieved. 'This is also occurring to me. But to take all six hundred men out of the camp and hide them in the town or the hill farms is impossible.'

'It must be possible. We want to get back to fighting and have no intention of being taken away by the Germans for the duration. There is no alternative.'

'But if you leave, the Germans will find you all and, in the process, probably shoot a good number of your youngsters. Then what would I say to their mothers?'

There was a pause in the conversation while FitzGerald and Goode digested this reference to their mothers. Again, Fitzgerald looked amused, even nonplussed.

Vicere continued. 'If you are determined to go, I shall put you in touch with those who are already looking after fugitives in the area. But I must warn you that they are concerned that, in helping you, they will not only call down punishment on the community, but also draw the attention to the hundred or more refugees already being hidden around the town. So, they beg you to consider that. To listen to the ladies committee.'

'The ladies committee?' FitzGerald was incredulous.

'Yes, Colonel. Most of the men are conscripted to Russia, or in hiding to avoid that. Or dead. So the women are –'

Goode interrupted. 'Sir, excuse me. A hundred refugees hiding here?'

'I believe there are even more. Escapees from slavery, Jews, deserters from the German armies, boys avoiding draft, refugees from bombed towns… there is every kind of desperate person.'

FitzGerald shot an irritated look at Goode, then went on. 'We will organise ourselves. All we want from you is your assurance that you will not impede our leaving the camp as soon as there is an armistice.'

'Think carefully, Colonel. You cannot get far away. The German units are very close; the local commander is coming here tomorrow to check out the camp and, doubtless, to give me his orders.'

All present considered this for a short interval. Then Vicere continued. 'I have sent out cyclists to gather information about German movements. If they leave the autostrada and cross the bridge, heading here, the lookout will inform me.'

Goode butted in again. 'Excuse me Sir, but this will give us not much head start–'

FitzGerald cut him off. 'We'll leave well before the Germans get going.' He then leant forward, looking carefully at the commandant.

'You can hide a whole army in plain sight as long as you do it somewhere the enemy will overlook. So, we will decant our men from the camp to somewhere very close – too close for the Huns to bother to search – and wait for them to go far away. With your permission, Commandant, we will go out and take a shufti.'

Vicere looked mystified for a moment, then, having worked out his meaning, went on: 'You can go out and reconnoitre, but I advise you to go with a local person. Captain Basili will arrange an introduction to the ladies' committee.'

FitzGerald was dismissive. 'We don't need help.' He laughed again. 'Certainly not from a ladies committee. I will go out today.'

Vicere smiled indulgently at Fitzgerald's forcefulness. 'You English are so direct! But I insist that you go with a local person. I shall introduce you. If it is to be today, then today it is.'

Not long thereafter, Riva Lucia was admitted into the commandant's office so that he might introduce her as a guide and interpreter for the limping colonel and his assistant. Vicere and Basili then left so that they would not know their prisoners' plans.

Neither Lucia nor FitzGerald showed any sign of recognition. Beside these tall and bulky men in their uniforms, which gave presence to any wearer, Lucia looked slight, diffident and easy to override. But for her expression, she could have been any young unmarried country girl. She wore her habitual long black dress and a black headscarf.

To FitzGerald, the idea that a young woman – a young Italian woman too – could be of any practical use was anathema. He had put the incident at the farm to the back of his mind and did not immediately connect this chit of a girl with that day. She was just another contemptible Italian, like the commandant, who could so easily be got round. At the same time, Lucia saw these Englishmen or Americans – or whatever they were – as arrogant invaders who had murdered her husband. Distaste was immediate and mutual, yet both suppressed their reactions out of necessity.

FitzGerald announced that he wanted his men hidden for several days, and a false trail laid so that the Germans would think they had got far away. Lucia replied that it was in no-one's interest that the men hide in the town, where they would be found, and she had other proposals. Knowing that this was what FitzGerald really wanted, Goode would have closed the deal there and then, but FitzGerald claimed that his men must be lodged in the town. Lucia explained the dangers. Goode interpreted when Lucia's English fell short. FitzGerald shrugged.

Lucia hid her anger. 'If you hide where I propose, I will find food and drink for your men and then show them which direction to go.' Donna Chiara had told her to offer food, but now she regretted it. It was going to be difficult to find food for six hundred; it would stretch the generosity of the local people. She thought it such a great gesture that the foreigners would be grateful.

FitzGerald expressed not a scintilla of recognition that she might be offering something he and his men greatly needed and, moreover, at great sacrifice. He demanded more. 'And clothes. I want six hundred men dressed in civilian clothes.'

'For so many, it's not easy,' she said.

'Then we stay in the town until you clothe us.'

Lucia stared at the soldier, his chin high, looking down on her without the slightest warmth or appreciation, and loathed him. Only mindfulness of her mission held back a retort that would have put paid to everything. *Donna Chiara and Dottoressa Foschini both rely on me getting these things right. So do the children and the expectant mothers and the querulous old and Dr Behrens and his family from Trieste; they need for me to button up. That they may live, I must humour this arrogant brute.* Lucia did not imagine that FitzGerald too might see himself as fighting for the survival of his charges, and in a malevolent land.

'Colonel, I have already found a place and discussed it with Captain Basili. Now I can show you.'

'The clothes?'

Lucia bit her lip in frustration. At the Corvo farm, she had learnt self-control under extreme provocation.

'By the time you leave I shall have found them.' *I am lying. I am only telling them this to get their cooperation. Or can I really do anything, anything at all, if it is needed enough?*

HEROES

The following day, Alessandro Foschini heard from his mother that the local German commander would visit PG500 on 4th September and that, as it was important in the circumstances to get the measure of this man, Donna Chiara and her factor would be present. He also received a message from Lucia, asking him to meet the German commander and to try to understand the man's intentions.

As he was letting himself out, he found Father Filipović on the doorstep. A large, well-built and fleshy man, he had slightly orange fair hair which made him stand out. He was a Croat from Friuli, brought in as assistant priest before Don Carmelo had passed away.

Filipović was enthusiastic, embracing Foschini and calling him 'hero'. Before the war, Alessandro had been very impressed by a priest so different from the indulgent Father Carmelo. This, younger, one was strict in all his observances and judgments. He had talked at length to, though not convinced, Alessandro's mother about the harmony of faith and fascism. His soutane, elegantly tailored with a high collar and moiré sash, swished like whiplash as he strode through Ginestra. He would visit families whose adolescent sons he would urge to prayer and martial sports, reminding them of their obligations to God, the saints' days and penitence, and that doubt was a sin.

'My dear Alessandro, congratulations on your sacrifices in the great crusade against Bolshevism.' Father Filipović put his hands on Alessandro's shoulders, looking straight at him such that Alessandro thought he would be enfolded in his arms. Rapidly, before the priest could make that move, the captain asked: 'Has anybody else returned from the Eastern Front?' He wanted to know whether the priest had heard, perhaps from confessions, what was going on. 'What have the mothers and sisters of my comrades said?'

The priest's face changed from joyful to serious in an instant. 'They worry. They are sad for the many deaths in Ukraine, in Russia, but I assure them that their men are heroes, crusaders for a better world. You can't make an omelette without breaking eggs. Many people suffer and die, sacrificing themselves, following the example of our Lord and the martyrs.'

Foschini stared at the black cassock before him, the priest with the diagonal strip of cream linen at his throat, his silky biretta. Through his mind were going pictures of naked, screaming mothers holding children tight to their breasts while being whipped and gouged along forest paths to those pits, where…

He wanted to vomit. A sour, putrid something seemed to be rising in his throat. He wanted to kick the priest, but the lessons he had learned with the Germans held him back. He sensed the fierceness of the man before him and knew, instinctively, that he should not reveal his doubts. He managed to control himself, with great effort, and spoke in an almost normal voice.

'Father, we must continue our conversation another time. I'll be late.'

As he strode away, Father Filipović watched him. The priest shook his head as if in sorrow and returned to his Perpetua for breakfast, then to his study and a forthcoming catechism class.

A few hours later, and while Captain Foschini was kicking up dust on his march to PG500, Colonel Vicere, Bregante and Donna Chiara Sanvitale stood outside the gates of PG500. The Daimler belonging to the countess was parked nearby, the chauffeur, in his blue uniform with two rows of silver buttons bearing the Sanvitale arms, dozed against the steering wheel.

'Officially, this German unit is based at Ginestra, but the commander moves them around the countryside regularly and never comes into Ginestra. I imagine that he suspects that the town is too easy a target from the air and, anyway, doesn't want his boys becoming too comfortable in a town with girls and wine!'

The voice was that of the camp commandant, who was stylish in well-cut dove grey. The graceful lady to whom he spoke wore a two-piece cream outfit and matching hat. Although in her late thirties, the American woman looked ten years younger, with cheerful smiles and rapid movements, her close-fitting suit showing off the figure of a tennis player. Vicere flattered her with his glances. They looked well matched, as if about to pirouette down Milan's fashionable Via Montenapoleone together, not wait outside this dingy camp for some Nazi overseer.

'My dear countess, how beautiful you are as always!'

'Nonsense, Colonel, only less drab than your guards.'

Beside these two, Bregante stood out. Though as tall as they, his shoulders were broad, his face tanned and his wrists and hands big and calloused. Standing slightly apart, he was playing the part of the reverent factotum.

'The prisoners are behaving better now.' Vicere was responding to an earlier enquiry; Donna Chiara had been concerned at the wretched condition of the men, a topic of general gossip in Ginestra. 'A new senior prisoner came and took command the day of the Corvo murders. Indeed, he witnessed those murders.'

Bregante, listening, realised that he had seen this *Inglese*.

'The men now all shave and have cut their hair. There is drill and sports and PE every day. Drunkards are punished and it is not permitted to rile the guards. This FitzGerald does not allow swearing, fines them for dirty words! We may soon be able to let some of them out on work parties.'

'Does the new senior prisoner request this, Sir?' Bregante was interested: there was a dearth of labour in the area for the forthcoming harvests.

Vicere turned, surprised, to the factor. 'His aide-de-camp speaks some Italian and has communicated this to my assistant, Basili.'

At that moment, two German military vehicles drew up, led by a staff car, containing Fröhlich and an Italian officer wearing the black fez of the militia.

Fröhlich leaped out, fit as Mercury and handsome as Adonis, and approached the group. He stopped before Donna Chiara, clicked his heels, made the 'German salute' with a '*Heil* Hitler!' He ignored Vicere, who saluted, but, to his evident discomfort, received no response. There was no sign of the ingratiating charm that Fröhlich had exhibited with FitzGerald.

Fröhlich declaimed: 'Fröhlich, major, 1st Panzer. Am I right in guessing that madame is the mayor?'

The countess, in Italian with a slight New England accent, concurred. 'Almost, Mr Fröhlich; I am the wife of the mayor.'

Fröhlich, in English now, 'I am honoured to meet you, my lady.'

The wearer of the fez, a well-fed consul of militia in his mid-thirties, also in long boots and riding breeches, made the fascist salute in a stately, rather than military, manner and then bowed slowly, brushing his lips over the countess' hand.

'How exquisite you are today, dear Donna Chiara!'

'Don Carlo, don't exaggerate.' She gave him a facetious grin. As the younger son of a landowner a few miles south, Don Carlo Vacca was well known to her. She turned to the German.

'Your English is excellent, Mr Fröhlich. How so?'

'I spent a year at Westminster School in London, Madam. And you, why is your English so good? Is it because you are an American?'

'I have for many years been proud to be an Italian. Mr Fröhlich, what is your role here? Why are you wanting to inspect us? We are delighted to meet you, but are not sure why you and your troops are here, so far from the front.'

'Very simple, Countess. I am here to assist the government of Italy to keep order and, in particular, to ensure that terrorists and bandits are dealt with according to law. I want the camp commander' – here he acknowledged Vicere for the first time, with a nod in his direction – 'to know that no prisoners are to escape. Anyone found helping the enemy will be executed. On my orders, your factor here' – he indicated Bregante – 'will be warning all your peasants.'

Bregante, without averting his gaze from Fröhlich's face, saw that Foschini, in uniform, was striding up the road towards them. The countess did not miss the annoyance that, very briefly, crossed Bregante's face.

She continued: 'I thought, Mr Fröhlich, that we were allies, not a subject people.'

'Naturally, Countess, but there are rules for the alliance. You have to understand that to create a new and better world, we have to have order. The rule of law.'

'But we do not want a new world, Mr Fröhlich. We like the world as it is.'

'That is because you are a reactionary, Madam, of the old ruling class.'

Donna Chiara smiled because she thought the German was being humorous, but his face remained serious. *How boring political men are.* She removed her smile, gave a small sigh and replied, 'That's as maybe, Mr Fröhlich. But if you go around shooting us, you will lose what support you have. By menacing people, you make enemies of the population. You should win their hearts, not make adversaries of them.'

'I disagree. Italians are cowards, mother lovers. A thousand years of Jesus worshipping have cut the balls off them. Please excuse my rough soldier's expressions, Countess. If Italians know that they will suffer when they disobey, but be rewarded if they turn the enemies in, they will do what we say.'

At that moment, Foschini arrived, trim in a clean uniform. Fröhlich and Don Carlo both stared at Foschini, clearly mesmerised by the German Cross in Gold on his tunic and the Knight's Cross at his neck. The countess and Bregante could not help but see the young captain's missing arm.

He took Donna Chiara's hand and bowed. '*Contessa*.' His obeisance was somewhere between Don Carlo's operatic version and the military edition offered by Fröhlich, to whom he then turned. 'I am Foschini, 3rd Alpine Division.'

The German's manner instantly became deferential. 'I am honoured to meet you, Sir. We have all heard of 3rd Alpine's achievements at Nikolayevka.'

Foschini, taking in the cursive 'Adolf Hitler' embroidered above the German's cuff, waved away the compliment with another. '1st Panzer is renowned all over Europe.'

Donna Chiara had known the young captain as a teenager, to her a more important fact than his political affiliation. 'Captain Foschini, I am glad to see you back safely. We were very sorry about your injuries. Your mother told us about your wounds. This is Colonel Vicere, commandant of the prison camp.'

The older man clicked his heels. 'Vicere Eugenio, Bersaglieri, retired.'

'Honoured, Sir.'

As the two Italian soldiers made polite conversation, Fröhlich stood unnoticed, momentarily silenced, gaping still at Foschini's medals.

A car drove up and parked beside the jeep. Out stepped a German officer carrying a large camera, who sidled up beside Fröhlich and spoke quietly in his ear. After inclining his head to listen, Fröhlich straightened up and turned to the mayor. 'Please excuse me, Countess, a man from "Signal", our most important periodical, wants to take a photograph of me with Captain Foschini for a feature. Captain Foschini is a hero with our troops in the east. Please, Foschini, let us have the photo together...'

Alessandro demurred. 'It's you he wants, Fröhlich, not an Italian with one arm.'

'Not at all. You are the hero. Please do me the honour.'

Ignoring the mayor and commandant, Fröhlich put his arm round Foschini's shoulder and guided him towards the photographer hovering a few metres away, checking out backgrounds for his composition.

'I am so very pleased to meet an Italian hero who has shown such valour in fighting for the New Order. We now have Spaniards, Frenchmen, Norwegians, Swedes all fighting for a united Europe under German leadership. Together, Europe can never be defeated by the decadent democracies or the Slav beasts.'

Foschini was perfunctory. 'Ah yes.'

The "Signal" photographer took many pictures of Fröhlich and Foschini side by side. He adjusted the two men's stances to ensure that Foschini's German decorations were very evident. They were made to be arm in arm; to shake hands; to salute each other with the Roman salute; to place arms around each other's waists. After several minutes of varying poses and shots, Foschini made to leave, but Fröhlich insisted on having more.

'Please, Fröhlich, they don't need me; you are the person that "Signal" wants to feature, not some unknown Italian on leave.'

'Don't be modest! You are a hero. Few Germans even have your combination of medals!'

Fröhlich pulled Foschini back into the frame.

Not long after, the meeting broke up. Vicere offered a tour of the camp to the German, but he declined and left. The countess' chauffeur drove her back to the Fortress and Bregante plodded over to Greppo.

Foschini joined the elderly commandant in his office to gauge his view as to what should be done with the prisoners in the weeks ahead. He had promised his mother that he would try to get on with the old man. Having had to accept that he could do nothing to curtail his mother's leadership of "The Work", he now reckoned he was in for a penny, in for a pound, or as he put it to himself, *quando si è in ballo, bisogna ballare* when in the dance, you have to dance. Lucia's involvement had clinched it. He, too, would take part. She wanted him to get to know the German area commander, which is why he had gone along with the photographic session, though his heart had sunk at the thought that he might be seen embracing an SS officer, already notorious among the soldiery for his violence in Ukraine, on every newsstand in occupied Europe.

Now he was to make an ally of Vicere.

The commandant was only too keen to talk: 'Do you think you can talk to this German fellow, make him turn a blind eye to our refugees, if only to save himself from revenge after Germany's defeat? After all, he is not important enough to be one of the bought.' Vicere was referring to the common knowledge that Hitler bought his general's complaisance with gifts of property and cash.

Foschini could see that the old man belonged to a different world, had no experience of ideological soldiers. Foschini had. 'No, he'll do what he believes in until the very end. He will press on and exhort his men to ever greater efforts. They will follow. Perhaps I can persuade him not to destroy Ginestra, but I could only do that by showing him that to do so would be counter to his objectives. No other appeal can succeed with these believers.'

The discussion had drifted off into the histories so enjoyed by the old colonel, when an orderly entered with the message that the parish priest had called to see the Commandant. Foschini looked enquiringly at the Colonel.

'Father Filipović. Confessions. Mass each week. He has found some Catholics among the prisoners. He says he is converting others.' He shrugged. 'Who knows?'

Both men rose at the same moment and the commandant accompanied his guest out of the office.

Alessandro Foschini, hero of Hitler's Ukrainian war, was going to betray his comrades.

WHAT THE FACTOR FOUND

A few days later, Bregante pushed open the door of his barn, just outside the wall of Greppo and on the slope close to their house. It was a store in which his mule could be housed in winter and where dogs and cats sheltered when giving birth. Bales of straw were piled high along one end with farm tools: shovels, hoes, forks of many different sizes; a sledgehammer and a mallet, trowels and axes. It was the inheritance of generations.

As he entered the barn, which was lit only by the doorway and a small, dirty skylight in the roof, he saw that the straw bales had been rearranged. He was so surprised that he immediately forgot what he had come for and stepped over to that side of the room. Gingerly, he pulled out a bale, then another and another, shifting them to one side to reveal a space created by the rearrangement. There was neither animal nor human there, but piles of clothing. And dozens – perhaps hundreds – of worn army water bottles. And a box of penknives and table knives.

He picked up a bottle, a knife and an old kitbag and then put them back, mystified. When he realised that these were supplies to give to people hiding out in the hills, he quickly made the sign against the evil eye. Not knowing what else to do, he replaced the straw bales, quickly, as if soldiers were knocking at the door.

Sweating, Bregante dusted off the straw that had caught on his shirt and trousers and left the barn.

Coming towards him was Lucia, carrying a pile of carefully-folded clothes; grey trousers and blue jackets, topped by a moth-eaten greatcoat.

He stopped in front of her, barring her way, angry. 'I found your store.'

She looked into his eyes defiantly. He was conscious of his weight and strength as he looked down upon her.

At a loss for what to say, he put out his hand and felt the cloth of the greatcoat. 'Your refugees don't need such warm things.'

'These are not for the people in the town. They are for the prisoners. Most will head for the mountains. The nights will soon be cold and Foschini says they may have to stay in the mountains through the winter.'

'Ah.'

'My mother has contacted the family in Abruzzo. To help.'

It was bad enough that she was collecting clothing for the *clandestini*. The second surprise was that these things were destined for those several hundred prisoners. The third was that Foschini was working with Lucia.

Bregante was, despite an unorthodox marriage, traditional. His Sicilian genes made him particularly conservative in family matters. As Lucia's brother-in-law, he was her protector; moreover, she, aunt by marriage, was standing in as mother to his children. She was a defenceless young woman, and alluring too; if truth be told, he thought of himself, now that his brother was gone, as her proprietor. He knew better than to express these thoughts aloud.

Instead, he asked: 'Your mother's family?'

'We work together.'

'They are helping you with… these people?'

'Yes. We have found somewhere for them to head to when they first leave the camp. They can spend a few nights in the open but they must quickly take refuge in people's homes. They will need food. And they can't all go in the same direction.'

'You mean all six hundred of them?'

'Yes. I showed the English leaders a hiding place big enough for all of them.' She hesitated. 'The Rovacchia.'

The choice was a good one. The Rovacchia was a dry riverbed, canopied by trees and walled in by mighty shrubs so that it would be invisible from the air. It was several kilometres long, which had pleased the arrogant *Inglese*, who wanted his men spread out. It could not be approached, or seen, from the road, though care would need to be taken that the passage of so many men along the fields' edges would not leave a trail visible from the air.

'But that is a mere half kilometre from the camp! And so near our neighbours' farms! The devils will find them immediately.'

'No. The devils will learn that the prisoners left in twos and threes the previous night and that they are headed east, for the coast. Even if they don't believe that they're going east, they will know that the walkers have done eight or ten hours marching by the time the Germans start looking, so they will send their planes and their search parties far from the camp.'

Bregante looked at his younger brother's wife with wonder. Whose voice was this? Who told her that an east exists? That men can march for eight hours and how far they can get in the time? How to deceive and how to cajole? He tried to sound reasonable, but there was an edge of resentment in his tone. 'And when they find nobody, they will come back and ransack Ginestra.'

'Foschini has arranged a diversion. There will be a partisan attack near Terrazza. That will be more serious to deal with than rounding up prisoners.'

Foschini. It was Foschini. One of those who had brought this hell of war down upon them. Bregante could no longer disguise his hostility. 'So, you sacrifice Terrazza to save the *Inglesi*?'

'Foschini promises no-one will be killed. Actually, what they are doing is breaking into a boot factory – where the Nazis get their boots repaired and replaced – to steal as many as they can, but they'll be noisy and carry on long enough for the devils to be called, then disappear when our "friends" arrive. I have been promised that nobody will be killed.'

The idea was ingenious, two birds with one stone, but Bregante ignored the last aspiration. 'The devils kill ten for every one of them killed.'

'Foschini says that they stick to rules. If none of them die, they will kill none of us.'

'You believe that? I hope Foschini has planned this well. I don't understand why he is risking so much for foreign soldiers, the very men that killed my brother. Enemies he himself has been fighting! Foschini!'

Bregante looked at Lucia with a hardened expression. Surely this was her weak spot? How could she put her own family and friends, her own hometown, at risk for a bunch of foreign killers? And why was she trusting Foschini, a fascist and an officer?

'Salvatò,' she implored, 'they are in peril. *Dottoressa* says that we must do for them what we would want others to do for our sons, brothers, lovers – in Russia, Africa, wherever they have been sent. We women are enemies only of war itself.'

'So, you are *their* mother, now?' Perhaps regretting his tone, Bregante became more matter of fact in his speech. 'The camp leader, that man who wears the cloth on his head, the devils know him well. We saw them together when he made Mr Fröhlich very angry. He won't be allowed to get away. They are not forgiving.'

He went on, 'They are martinets, these devils; I know, I worked for them. All their passion is in hate for those who cross them.' An idea came to him. 'If you let them get that camp leader, they may be appeased. And forget the others. After all, they have plenty to do.'

She did not care about the fate of FitzGerald in particular. But, she mused, recalling the sight of him sparring with Fröhlich, if it is true that the devils remember him, then he is a liability. That, I need to know.

PART TWO

FLIGHT AND WAR IN THE APENNINES

IT'S A LONG WAY TO TIPPERARY

On the afternoon of the 8th September 1943, FitzGerald and his staff were called by the operator of the camp's clandestine wireless to listen to the BBC. What they heard was being announced simultaneously on Italian wireless. Up and down Italy, thousands heard an announcement upon which all would react differently and which each would retransmit differently:

Italy has signed an unconditional armistice with the Allies. The surrender was signed five days ago in secret by a representative of Marshal Pietro Badoglio, Italy's prime minister since the downfall of Benito Mussolini in July.

As FitzGerald rose, the younger men all looked at him expectantly.

'Goode,' he said, and Goode got up, followed by Lange and Albion, 'go and tell the commandant that we are moving out. Lange, have the men form up by company and in German formation as prepared.'

Lange beamed. 'So, Sir, we are taking the Italian lady's advice and going to her site?'

'I wouldn't put it quite like that. I chose the bund, even if she found it.'

There was shouting outside. The four men all cocked their ears to listen. Tumult.

FitzGerald continued, 'And you, Albion. Activate the stores plan.'

His glance swept over the three excited, flushed faces. 'We're off, boys! Back to war! Let's go!'

Just outside the gates through which the prisoners hoped soon to leave stood the commandant, his aide Captain Basili and Riva Lucia, holding a bicycle and with a small boy holding her other hand.

Lucia saw FitzGerald lead several young men out into the hubbub of the parade ground. Prisoners and guards were pulling open the gates. Sentries were embracing each other, shouting: 'No war! Peace! War finished!' Not waiting for orders, guards were climbing down from their watchtowers. Prisoners were running back to where they had stored their kit and others were already forming up on the parade ground. Some put on clothes as they ran; others did up bootlaces or tied parcels as soon as they arrived at their place. Deep voices were singing.

Colonel Vicere turned to Lucia. 'Signora, I fear that we Italians have not really understood the situation. We think the war has ended. For many, it may be just beginning.'

Lucia pondered his words and watched the prisoners.

FitzGerald was picking up his pack, launching it onto his back, then taking up his crutches. She heard him ask, 'What's that song?'

Lange was all bounce. '"Kiss Me Goodnight Sergeant Major", Sir. The Italians think we're all perverts, so the boys sing it to frighten them.'

FitzGerald shrugged. Near the gate, and at the very front of the column, a table had been placed, with a chair beside it to act as a step. He was amused: the Italians had erected a saluting dais! Vicere could be seen by the great gates, arranging a few of his men in a guard of honour. That Italian girl was standing by, holding a small boy by the hand. The men were in ranks. Now they were singing "It's A Long Way to Tipperary".

As the last of them fell in, FitzGerald stumbled as he climbed onto the dais and righted himself with a crutch, ignoring Goode and Lange starting towards him, below. Everybody fell silent. All were watching him. FitzGerald looked down with a supercilious fatherliness on the guard of honour, small men in baggy uniforms holding outdated rifles. Vicere, crisp and polished, seemed to belong in a ballroom.

FitzGerald glanced over his platoons to check that everything was in order. He nodded to Lange, the parade commander, who gave the order.

'Parade, parade, shun!'

The men came to attention in one crash. Many of those whose regulation boots had disintegrated had pilfered their metalled studs and attached them to the soles of their clogs or plimsolls.

FitzGerald, from above, called, 'At ease.' The ranks on ranks relaxed, though only with the regulation step; their boyish, excited faces looked up at him. 'Lads, we're on our way. We will be snoozing in a snug wee glory hole until the Huns have given up searching for us. And they will give up because we've arranged a little shindig for them. It'll keep them busy while we get away... More briefing when we get to the bund.'

As he spoke, there flashed into FitzGerald's mind the thought of another six hundred, whose deaths were immortalised in a great poem, and he shuddered as if someone had walked over his grave. Just as he was to inspire his men, it came to him that he had never asked himself whether he was condemning them to death more surely than transportation to Poland would. He swatted the thought from his mind and displayed the boldness expected of a leader.

'Today, now, we will move smartly and fast to avoid detection. The Huns are very close, but we will outwit them. Then it'll be each man to find his own way back to the fight. I'm booking a bar for our reunion at Christmas – in Piccadilly!'

There were cheers. Somebody bellowed: 'Three cheers for Gallowglass!' and before he could stop them, there was a roar of "hip hip hooray", repeated louder each time by six hundred young throats.

Lucia watched the scene of tribal enthusiasm with incredulity.

When the cheering had died down, FitzGerald signalled to Lange, who roared, 'Battalion, battalion! Shun!' Another great crash across the square as the men came to attention. 'Right turn.'

FitzGerald saw how well they did it, having been drilled back into soldierly mode by Lange in short order. Men like to be commanded, commandeered, he reflected. But only by those whose authority they recognise and respect.

'By the right, quick march!'

FitzGerald saluted as the first platoon passed. They were whistling "Colonel Bogey", marching at a fast clip. As they came to the end of the tune, they started singing the dirty version. FitzGerald gave a slight smile.

'Hitler, he only has one ball,
Goering, has two but very small,
Himmler, is very sim'lar,
But Goebbels has no balls at all!'

As the last company passed by, FitzGerald descended the dais and shook hands with Vicere.

FitzGerald: 'Thank you Colonel. Will you, too, leave now?'

'No, I shall remain behind. Otherwise, the Germans will take revenge on the town. They will have to blame someone.' He turned to indicate Lucia. 'Signora Riva will accompany you to the Rovacchia.'

FitzGerald shot him a quizzical glance, then swung out, followed by Goode and Lange.

Lucia lifted Enrico into the seat that Bregante had constructed on the back of her bicycle, once it had become clear that being separated from Lucia caused the child anguish that no words could assuage. As she climbed onto her saddle, intending to ride to the head of the column to check that they knew where they were going, and to warn everybody to go single file down the track that lead from road to Rovacchia, she heard FitzGerald talking. 'Unusual man, that. Peacock but prepared to sacrifice himself. I feel rather cheated. Instead of us having prevailed over him, it seems he has saved us!'

Lange: 'Maybe he'll make his peace with the Huns.'

'Doubt it, he knows what he is in for.' With that, FitzGerald put forward his right crutch and swung away after his men. The guards had gone too, some leaving their rifles and helmets lying on the ground.

Colonel Vicere now stood alone. He saluted FitzGerald and Goode as they passed through the gates of PG500 for what they believed would be the last time.

Lucia had achieved her objective of persuading the prisoners to avoid the town, and she was confident of Alessandro doing his best to disorient the Germans. She stood astride her bicycle with Enrico's fist grasping the back of her dress, and watched FitzGerald lurching along on his crutches, the junior who carried his bag pacing himself beside him. She knew that there might be many more challenges to come. Hiding the chief prisoner would be difficult; he couldn't get far, not yet.

At least the other men could scatter over hundreds of miles within a few days and she knew that if the peasants had food, they would share it.

There were bandits in the hills who would take them on, but should they join these so-called partisans in order to eat, they'd be back to violence. To Lucia, this was the worst outcome; that the men to whom she had shown a way out of war should be clawed back in for survival.

Mere days earlier, Lucia would have shrugged off these problems as belonging to someone else, but already, unthinkingly, she assumed the men to be her responsibility. For a moment the German commander came to mind and she shivered at the thought that he might blame her brother-in-law for the disappearance of the prisoners. If so, she guessed what punishment he would exact.

Lucia put her right clog on the pedal and pushed down. She rode quickly, knowing that once she left the metalled section of the road, it would be almost impossible to overtake the marching column. As she passed them, her dress flying about her, many of the men waved and beamed and called out. A week ago, she would have lowered her head and blushed, but today she waved back and smiled a smile of triumph.

HIDDEN

Late on 8th September 1943, six hundred prisoners were secreted in the long hollow, shaded and hidden from the air by the overhanging trees. There they waited and talked quietly. From time to time there was a laugh, or a rather-too-loud voice mentioned some famous cricketing moment, competition on the Curragh, commentary on Aberdeenshire scones or Cornish pasties, Welsh sheep cheese, Twickenham or fishing on the Trent. Many became soft-eyed as they fantasised about getting home soon. Others were dozing.

Very early the next morning, as light revealed the contours of the sleeping men and the sun warmed them, preparing them for the fierce heat ahead, local people, some loaded with baskets or pots on their heads, passed by the Rovacchia with bread fresh from the bakers. They came with hoes over their shoulders and bread and olives and cheese and water hidden in bags, in groups pretending to be on their way to the fields. They would drop their bags into a designated part of the ditch and continue on their way. Lucia remained out of sight, watching them. Trusting only herself to flit between the drop-off and the Rovacchia, Lucia ferried the bags two at a time, with Enrico tugging at the small ones. Once they had a large pile, she distributed water, bread, grapes and hard, dry chunks of Parmesan cheese to a queue of hungry, sleepy, men.

The more awake soldiers nudged each other and stared at her. They had all heard that the colonel and Goode had done a recce with this filly, who'd found them the bund.

'Lucky bugger, old Gallowglass. Look at her! Bloody gorgeous!'

Lucia pretended to be unaware of the thrill she caused. As FitzGerald hobbled over to her, she merely remarked, 'Colonel, the townspeople have brought food. Clothes later.'

FitzGerald and his staff stood in a detached group. Goode had waylaid some of the people who had come up the road with supplies and returned with intelligence: 'There's every possibility of a major insurrection against the Nazis and their allies, Sir. A few of our lads providing backbone to each of the partisan formations could cause havoc among the enemy.'

FitzGerald could see from the excited eyes of the other two young men that this was their dream, too. Another couple of his best subalterns, Craig and Wheeler, were listening, seeming to approve Goode's enthusiasm.

FitzGerald had to be careful not to alienate his followers by squashing their ardour; to appear to them as Marsh had appeared to him.

'I won't organise a formation myself: to operate in hostile territory is not possible without major backup. My job's to get back to my own outfit as soon as possible. But any of you who can find existing operations to join are free to do so – if they are trustworthy, or remotely competent. As you suggest, our military training may be useful.'

To avoid further discussion, he looked towards Lucia, who had been handing out food from the baskets. Until now Lucia had separated herself and sat down a few yards away. 'I'd best thank the lady,' he remarked to the young men, moving over to join her.

'Very helpful, your people, Mrs Bregante.'

'My name is Riva, Colonel. We do not give up our names when we marry.'

'I apologise. I don't know your local customs.'

'You don't like us, Mr FitzGerald, do you?'

FitzGerald, with a slightly patronising smile, said, 'My experience of Italians has not been good.'

'How?'

'I faced them in the Western Desert, North Africa. They surrendered at the first opportunity and let the Germans do the fighting.'

'How wonderful! How brave of them!'

FitzGerald, uncomprehending, hostile, said, 'I'm sorry?'

'It takes more courage to refuse to fight than to fight. Even when you know that fighting is wrong.'

'Soldiers who don't fight are not much admired. We usually call them cowards.'

In silence, Lucia looked away.

FitzGerald reflected that he was not behaving as a gentleman should, particularly as she was a young widow. *The excessive warmth of their family relationships feminises Italian men*, he thought, *but that is not her fault.* 'I am sorry to hear that you have lost your husband, Mrs Riva.'

Looking at him with undisguised disgust, she threw back, 'That particular "coward" was killed on the first day he went into battle, by you people.'

'I am sorry. It must be very hard.'

There was no response from Lucia; she simply stared into the treetops.

'I hear that he won a medal for valour.'

Again, no reaction from Lucia.

'You must be very proud of him.'

Lucia's anger flamed up. 'Proud? No. He was a fool. He was a fool to go and fight. He should have deserted. He should not have left me.'

She looked away. Tears crept down her face; she brushed them away.

FitzGerald watched her, daunted.

Lucia went on: 'A brave man does not abandon his family, his wife, his home, to fight stupid wars for brutes and idiots. His duty is to look after those who love him, not enjoy himself playing the hero.'

'I am sure that he thought he was defending you.'

Again, there was no response.

FitzGerald tried another tack. 'Italy should never have joined with Germany. Now we will liberate you.'

Lucia turned on FitzGerald a look of hate. 'What is this Italy? This Germany? All rubbish. There are only families and villages. People. You men talk about liberating: we women expect rape. You men talk of your mission: we women see the loss of our breadwinners. You men talk of changing the world: we women see homes burnt and children weeping. I don't know anything about politics. All I know is that war is always wrong. And all suffer, not just the soldiers, so that politicians can have sport.'

'If we don't stand up to the Nazis, they will cause even more suffering.'

'You are a soldier. War is your life.'

'No, keeping the peace and stopping the hooligans is my life.'

'Your men call you "Gallowglass FitzGerald". I understand that means a warrior who fights anywhere, for anything. So don't suggest you are just *Ghino di Tacco*, Robin Hood.'

FitzGerald gave a wry smile. 'I didn't know that this nickname had got out among the civilian population! But I suppose it's rather a good thing, if it means people do what I want.'

'Yes, they will be afraid of you because you are good at killing. What kind of a human being is that? '

'Sometimes killing is justified, Mrs Riva.' *I shall not dismiss this insolent female's opinions outright. She's put herself in danger to help us. But I can't let our honour be besmirched.* 'We're Irish. My family has produced soldiers for generations. That and a spot of horse breeding. From boyhood, I thought it was the noblest profession. I'm older now and I think it's just an unfortunately necessary profession. I'd left the army before the war and was happy breeding horses in California. Yet when I saw that Britain was standing alone against the barbarians, Nazism and communism allied against her but Uncle Sam not helping, I had to join the Brits. You know they held out for two years before the big boys came on side, the Russians and the US.'

'All men who want to fight have a good excuse. It's Italy or the *Duce* or – what did you say? Liberty? – or some other fantasy. But it's really just power they want; liberty for themselves, to impose on others.'

'For hundreds of years, the Brits have stopped dictators who wanted to hold Europe in their fists. Spanish fanatics, French tyrants, German brutes. Although I am Irish, I have to admit this.'

Lucia's knowledge of history since the death of Constantine the Great was hazy. 'Well, that's your excuse. My brother-in-law Bregante will do nothing for any of you. Like most of us, he was against the Germans before his wife was killed, but now he just hates you all.'

'How did his wife die?'

'Because she was to have a crosswise birth, the doctor recommended she go to the Palma hospital to have her child. When she was there, the hospital was bombed by your people.'

'Very bad.'

'He now has two children and a sick mother to care for.'

FitzGerald found that he did not have the vocabulary with which to respond to such suffering and he felt, momentarily, ashamed.

'You help him?'

'Of course.'

Surely, he abruptly questioned himself, *she can't know that my regiment was the first to engage in Sicily, and therefore the first to kill Italian defenders like her husband? No, it can't be.*

Lucia was stung by the man's boorish superiority. She was sure he despised her and was only polite because he needed her help, even if he would never admit it.

That instant, motor engines could be heard on the road, several hundred metres away. There was an immediate silence on the Bund, with its hundreds of soldiers frozen into immobility, staring at the direction of the noise.

THE WAY OUT

While six hundred men were hiding in the Rovacchia, Major Fröhlich had discovered that PG500 was empty, but been persuaded by Captain Foschini that there was nothing to be gained from searching in the town because all entrances had been guarded by militia and ransacking the town would be an unprofitable distraction. Fröhlich assuaged his anger by berating Vicere, letting his men bash him about a bit and dispatching him to a concentration camp in Germany. Fröhlich's presence near the town did not stop Lucia supplying her charges with food. While she was doing that, Bregante had stopped his old schoolfriend Giulio, now in the forestry militia, from turning in two deserters from the Germans, Kalmyk teenagers. He did so simply because it seemed to him so unjust that pressganged children, uncomprehending of the war they had been pushed into, ignorant even of where they were, should die so casually. Giulio grumbled that he needed the reward of 1,000 *lire* each. To the militiaman's surprise, Bregante compensated him with 1,000 for both. As he promised to set the two curious youths up as shepherds, far up in the hills, he rued his own inability to stick to his guns and resist involvement in the war.

At first light on 10th September in the Rovacchia, every fugitive received some kind of bag or haversack to replace any military-looking one. Packed into them was the contents of the Red Cross parcels – tins of cocoa, porridge oats, bars of chocolate, biscuits, packets of tea and coffee – plus anything left over from the peasants' donations, including cheese and the coarse grey bread of the area.

Locals arrived with curious-looking garments that were divided up among the platoons, whose commanders lay them out in a long row, like a shop counter.

Lucia stood behind FitzGerald, watching the men joking and joshing in their new clothing. So unworried, these *Inglesi*, laughing at themselves and each other as they tried on bits of peasant clothing, bumptious as if setting out on some school hike. *Six hundred of them, out of the war. They will live because our people will care for them. Perhaps some of these boys will stay on the farms and replace the disappeared, those thousands who have been sucked away by the war machine and are suffering God only knows where.* As she watched them, the boys grinned at her; some doffed their peasant caps. She waved back.

Now that the German search parties appeared to have gone elsewhere, FitzGerald started to release the men. He spaced the walkers, telling some to stay a night or two locally to let others get away.

FitzGerald himself planned to remain behind because of his bad leg. He shook each man by the hand.

'Good luck Craig. Wheeler. Godfrey. Lange. See you in Piccadilly.'

Lange was always cautious: 'So far so good. It's the beginning of the end, Sir!'

'More like "the end of the beginning". We are now at large in the land of our enemies, hunted and at their mercy. Or are they at our mercy? You've got to keep the upper hand with the Italians, Lange, get them to fear you more than they fear the Huns. Good luck.'

'Thank you, Sir.' Lange left, heading north.

FitzGerald turned to Lucia. 'We'll be lucky if half of them make it, Mrs Riva. Between starvation, winter and the German rewards, they have some formidable foes.'

'You decided to push them out of the camp, Colonel. It might have been less dangerous for everybody if you had made them stay.'

As when they had talked of her husband, FitzGerald suppressed his anger, though now with greater difficulty. He was not used to being spoken to in such a manner by someone so young and female – and so socially inferior. He responded in officialese.

'It is our duty to get back to fighting, Mrs Riva, as soon as possible. The battle for democracy and freedom is not yet won.'

Lucia looked at him as if he were a child talking nonsense.

FitzGerald said nothing but looked smug. *I will not waste time remonstrating with an emotional woman. I am magnanimous, as I should be, given the death of her husband and her sister-in-law too. Hysteria is an expected reaction by females to such situations.*

Lucia, on the other hand, felt exhilarated to find herself talking back to the foreign soldier. All her plans had succeeded. The *Inglesi* were doing what she had organised. She had taken them out of the war, even if their commander was himself determined to get back to it. Nevertheless, even he, for all his bravado and arrogance, relied upon her. So it was she who spoke next.

'What are you going to do, Colonel, with your bad leg? Hop your way to the battlefield?'

FitzGerald gave her a frigid look. 'Goode and I will stay here until the bloody leg works properly. Shouldn't be long.'

'I have made arrangements for you, Colonel, if you can bear to take help from cowardly Italians.' She pointed to a boy who looked about 10. 'This little coward is Aldo. He'll take you to my brother-in-law's farm. Or not actually to the farm, but a shepherd bothy, twenty minutes' walk from it.'

FitzGerald hesitated.

'I know that you don't want to be dependent upon us, Colonel, but in your present condition, you are best advised to let us shelter you.'

Goode had been listening. 'Sir, I think she has a point. We are in unfamiliar territory and they know what they're doing.'

FitzGerald was chastened. 'Very well, *Signora*, I will follow your advice. Thank you.'

'We don't need to meet again, Colonel; Aldo will look after you. I am sure you will get back to your army and kill plenty more people. Whomsoever they are. Goodbye.'

FitzGerald saluted her without speaking and she left. He smiled ruefully to Goode. 'Looks as if the decision-maker is now this chit of an Eyetie girl!'

Goode laughed. 'No, Sir, I think she's just a special adviser, local operative. And you couldn't have a prettier one.'

'Not relevant! Can't have you youngsters fraternising with the enemy. Now, where's this boy scout she's given us?' He snapped his fingers at Aldo, who was squatting under a tree: 'Hey, boy, do you speak English?'

DINNER AT THE BREGANTES

What was it that changed Bregante's mind? When he realised that he himself did not have the heart to turn away the little playmate that Lucia had brought for Ebbo? When he saw how the countess had defied the threats of the occupiers and continued to add to her number of refugees? When he learned of the bravery of the old colonel at the camp? When he came to terms with Lucia's resolve, not only to advise the prisoners in PG500 but also to equip them and set them on their ways, all six hundred of them? When he understood that those prominent people in his own community, even the Foschinis, were complicit? Once he had felt pity for those two lost boys and given them back their lives without considering the risks? Regardless of what moved him, when Lucia told him that she needed to hide the lame soldier nearby because he could not walk far, he agreed.

'Let the limping foreigner stay in our bothy. It's far from the roads but near enough for him with his bad leg.'

He instructed the boy Aldo and relieved her from having to attend to FitzGerald and Goode, who remained in the Rovacchia until every other man had left.

With Aldo in the lead on the short walk from the Rovacchia

in the direction of Greppo, FitzGerald and Goode soon found themselves in front of a brushwood store next to a ruined mill. It was a small stone bothy, like a windowless cottage, once used for shelter by shepherds who stay out in the fields during winter. There was brushwood, that could not be stuffed in, piled all round. One bale was pulled out to show a narrow tunnel. FitzGerald and Goode crawled through into the darkness and sat on a layer of some soft, fragrant substance; refuse from the mill.

For a long day they lay there and imagined search parties combing the surroundings. The main force of Germans may have been distracted, but either they had left some guards behind or the militia was doing the job for them, for the crack of hand grenades echoed through the valley. There was an occasional burst of gunfire.

At last, someone unplugged the tunnel and they heard Aldo's voice calling softly. They emerged into a dark and moonless night, surprisingly cold after the heat of the day and by comparison with the packed and airless dormitories of the camp.

Aldo had come to lead them further away to another bothy that had been prepared for them. A log glowed in the middle of the stone floor. Smoke filled the room and hung a couple of feet from the floor. Early chestnuts were spread to dry on canes that made the ceiling between the beams. There was bread, cheese, fruit and red wine. They tended the fire, roasted chestnuts, drank wine and talked.

During the following day, no-one disturbed them. Sleep became a stupefying escape from consciousness, from which they were distracted only by mice squeaking round their food.

The boy came again. They had lost track of time. He said: 'Come, you will eat with Bregante tonight.'

'Germans have gone?'

'The factor says yes.'

The chaos of arrival had been so great that they had barely noticed the surroundings of the bothy. The path ran down with a rush of water beside it. The evening was utterly quiet except for their boots ringing out on the path. Looking up, they could see the deeper black of the hillsides against the dark of the sky. There were a few stars between the clouds. The path began to widen. They could hear a river ahead. A white strip became the main road. They walked, watching for the sight of Greppo rising up, black, before them, one or two flickering lights in the murk.

At the postern, Bregante was waiting and welcomed them with a serious face and an inclination of the head. As all three met the cobbled street, FitzGerald was startled to see, by the light of an oil lamp, two strangely oriental-looking boys in German uniform.

'Who the hell are those two?'

Bregante was laconic. 'Chinese, something like that. Orientals, anyway. They were German "volunteers". Now they are prisoners. Tomorrow they will be shepherds.' FitzGerald said nothing but wondered at the presence of the enemy, even prisoners.

They entered the house. There Bregante's mother and three children were making *capelletti* and *tortellini*, slicing ham Bregante had smoked, pummelling home-grown tomatoes into *sugo*, pouring out red wine from the Greppo wine harvest of last year, adding oil from their own grove to the *sugo*. This area had not yet been looted.

FitzGerald and Goode drank wine and Goode cut bread into chunks when he was ordered.

Lucia brought in the two sheepish "Chinese". They sat in a corner on stools.

She addressed him, 'Mr FitzGerald, why are you doing nothing? In this family, everybody works! Please take over the tomatoes, make them into *sugo*.'

FitzGerald obeyed and started pounding the cooked tomatoes in the pot. Lucia came over and threw in basil, meeting his eyes with a derisive smile as she did so.

'You need an Italian name, Colonel. We will now call you Fizzi.'

With that, she left the room.

Bregante looked uncomfortable. 'Forgive my sister-in-Law, Colonel, she means well.'

'Mr Bregante, I have nothing to forgive her for. Are all Italian women as forceful as she?'

Bregante grinned: 'She who rocks the cradle rules the world, and nowhere more than in my country, you know.'

'I was sorry to hear of your brother.'

'Thank you.' He crossed himself. 'And now Signora Lucia treats my children as if she were their mother. We are all one family. A united family.'

'Yes, I can see that. I thought before that she was your wife.'

Bregante flushed: 'She has taken my wife's place. But as a mother, you understand. She is my children's aunt.'

When Lucia returned, they all sat down to eat at the massive deal table.

Bisnonna, great-grandmother's, rheumy eyes were on Goode. 'Where do you come from? '

'Scotland.'

'Is that near here?'

'It's a long way away.'

'Near Africa then?'

'No, not near Africa. '

'But my daughter-in-law said you came from Africa.'

'Yes, we were fighting there.'

'Why do people fight in Africa?'

'There's always fighting in Africa.'

'You should've seen our pots and pans before the *Duce* took them to make shells. All copper. And my wedding ring. I had to give it for a war in Abyssinia. Where is Abyssinia?'

'In Africa.'

'*Mamma mia*, always Africa. Are they Christians in Africa?'

'Some people are, some aren't.'

'How do you know?'

'I've been there.'

'Fighting?'

'Yes.'

'Fighting the Africans?'
'No, the Italians.'
'Why the Italians?'
'Because we are at war.'
'There shouldn't be any wars.'

Later, Bisnonna wobbled over to FitzGerald and sat heavily down next to him, carrying her spoon and bowl. He braced himself to try to understand her. In the event, she spoke very simple phrases. 'Did you eat well?'

'Very well, thank you,' FitzGerald replied.

'In England you eat five times a day.'

'Who said so?'

'The *Duce*.'

'It's not true.'

'Do you hear that, Salvatò? I always said the *Duce* told us a pack of lies.'

Turning back to FitzGerald, she continued: 'You sell your wives.'

'No, but we can divorce them.'

'That's what we need, divorce.' Turning to her grandson, she opined: 'Do you hear Salvatò? Divorce! But the damn priests won't let us.'

Salvatore and the children played music and sang, and Lucia and the little girls danced. FitzGerald sang "Greensleeves" in a baritone. Goode sang "Marie's Wedding".

FitzGerald addressed Lucia. 'I thought your brother-in-law wouldn't take sides.'

'When he is faced with real people and their needs he decides he can no longer be just a bystander. But he is not helping you because you are allies, but because you are poor souls in distress,' Lucia answered.

'I can't say I think of myself as a poor soul in distress.'

Lucia laughed at him. 'No, you think of yourself as a warrior. But it is always good, even for warriors, to learn how they are seen by others.'

THE WINE SHOP

There were no streetlamps; only the moon cast a bluish glow on the rooftops and cobbles of Ginestra. A few shafts of light from beneath the door of the *enoteca*. Much laughing and shouting from within, in German. Fröhlich's troops drinking, unwinding after operations to the north.

The only Italians, apart from the proprietor and waitress, were two blackshirts who looked ill at ease. Those militiamen knew that the Germans here were members of the 1st SS Panzer, which had just been massacring Italian soldiers who had thought that the war was over in Parma, Cremona and Piacenza.

Fröhlich entered the *enoteca*. He stood just inside the door. Many of the men rose, holding up their glasses. All cheered. Then someone started singing the "Panzerlied" and, in a flash, every German had risen and was singing it and facing Fröhlich as if in homage. Their commander gave a slight, proud smile. The waitress, an elderly lady with a blonde wig, cocked her head and gazed admiringly at the big, bovine boys as they belted out their anthem:

'*Ob's stürmt oder schneit,*
Ob die Sonne uns lacht,

Der Tag glühend heiß,
Oder eiskalt die Nacht
Bestaubt sind die Gesichter
Doch froh Ist unser Sinn Ist unser Sinn,
Es braust unser Panzer Im Sturmwind dahin.
Mit donnernden Motoren Geschwind wie der Blitz Dem Feinde entgegen,
Im Panzer geschützt Voraus den Kameraden,
Im Kampf steh'n wir allein Steh'n wir allein,
So stoßen wir tief,
In die feindlichen Reihn.'

'[Whether storm or snow or in sun's laughing light,
In day's scorching heat or in bitter cold night,
Our faces covered with dust.
But our hearts fill with joy, yes, with joy are filled.
Our panzers like whirlwinds advance in the field.
With thundering engine and lightning-fast speed,
We charge toward the front on our steel-sided steed,
And leading on our comrades, push deep into the enemy ranks]

From behind Fröhlich, Foschini entered. As the singing came to an end, Fröhlich shouted: 'Good lads! *Heil* Hitler.'

A tumultuous answering yell: '*Heil* Hitler!'

Fröhlich noticed Foschini, who had come to stand beside him, and glanced again at his medals. He put a hand on Foschini's shoulder and made to leave with him. Then he turned back and called out:

'Enjoy! Drink! Drink! Brotherhood, drink!'

Immediately the boys took up that song. 'Lassen sie sorgen zu haus Leave your troubles at home...' Fröhlich and Foschini exited to stand in the street and the clamour from the wine bar in the background faded as the door closed.

Fröhlich's expression instantly transformed into one that was hard and accusatory. He jabbed a finger towards the Italian.

'Foschini, only one of the prisoners has been found!'

'What? Only one? But there were several hundred. It's impossible.' Foschini was genuinely shocked that one had been found. 'Where did you find the one?'

"I went to the hospital to meet the colonel with the broken leg and instead there was a dressmaker! A man called Newby!' Amazingly to Foschini, Fröhlich laughed. 'He sits in bed writing a book! Truly the English are mad.'

He turned, thought better of it and, taking a piece of paper out of his pocket, shoved it under Foschini's nose. 'A letter to tell us that the factor organised everything'. He sneered. 'How Italian. The writer wants to shop the factor. The factor must have deceived me. Instead of warning the peasants, he probably recruited.' He refolded the paper and slipped it back into his pocket.

'You mean Bregante?'

He shrugged dismissively. 'I will hang him.'

Alessandro had known the Bregante brothers all his life. To hear Salvatore consigned to death was not like a reference to some random foreign soldier. He clenched his hands.

'Why?'

'Why? You ask me why? I gave him the task of ensuring that no-one help these scum. Yet everyone has got away. This they could not do without local contrivance. Traitors. Greedy people taking bribes. Subversives.'

'But he may have tried. And what is the point of killing more people?'

'He disobeyed the rules.'

'Perhaps he acted out of pity. It's a Christian virtue.' As he spoke, Alessandro knew he was being stupid.

Fröhlich was infuriated. He turned upon the Italian, a rabid preacher. 'Foschini, you are a fascist. You know Christianity must be extirpated. As the *reichsführer* says, we live in an era of the ultimate conflict with Christianity. We are progressive. Enlightened.'

There was a pause. Foschini looked down, unwilling to meet

Fröhlich's eyes, though not for the reason Fröhlich imagined.

'Captain Foschini, don't let me think that such a fine soldier as you could defend these people. It is only because of your word that I have not raided Ginestra. Because you have been awarded our highest decorations!' Fröhlich stopped a moment, waiting for Foschini to look back at him, then, with finality, stated, 'I will have him hanged according to law.'

Foschini controlled himself and turned a bland look on him: 'Of course, Fröhlich. We can disagree about how to do our duty. But we are both quite clear as to what our duty is. And my compatriots will support you if you treat them well.'

Fröhlich, sceptical but keeping it to himself: 'My men will find them. And I will find that Indian colonel.' With a '*Heil* Hitler' he left.

Foschini gave the fascist salute vaguely, not as precisely as he would have done before mobilisation, then hastened round the corner where there was a fruiterer. Though shuttered, it was always guarded by a young boy who slept on a truckle tucked against the shutters. Tonight, such a boy was sitting on the edge of his truckle, ready for errands.

'Aldo. *Carissimo*. Come here.' With his hand on the boy's neck in an affectionate embrace, he bent down and whispered in his ear. The eager, excited face gaped at his hero's. As he turned to go, Foschini hissed: 'Whatever happens, the devils must not see you. And tell the Bregantes to go *now*. Not one minute must be wasted.'

The boy turned, then Foschini grasped his shoulder to hold him back. 'Wait! If anybody stops you –' and now he took something out of the left pocket of his tunic – 'say that you are taking this to Lucia Riva from a...'

The boy had a grin of admiration and complicity as he said, 'Lover?'

Alessandro swallowed hard. 'Yes.' He passed him a little silk purse embroidered with cranes. 'Now go.'

The boy ran, his pale legs under his shorts seeming, in the

gloom, to flash like the spokes of car wheels.

Foschini stood still and pondered for a moment. *If Fröhlich finds they've all gone, he will suspect me. Still, as long as he doesn't find Aldo, he will not be certain. But I must be more careful now.*

There came into his mind his university mentor, the man who had done most to engage Alessandro's emotions with the cause and make him feel that faith and obedience are the greatest virtues. Alessandro was quite sure that his mentor would remain loyal even after total defeat. *Is it a weakness in me that I abandon the cause to which my mentor holds fast? Why can he believe, but not I? Perhaps there is a genetic predisposition to faith, a kind of personality that fears uncertainty, flexibility? That wants to give up its own power of reasoning and doubting, to obey some external authority?* Savonarola *was as like that as* Torquemada. *So is* Fröhlich. *I am not, though I tried to be.*

Back at home, he merely told his mother, 'I will not be far away, but you can say that I am reporting to Graziani for duty.' He slipped out of the house in the middle of the night, avoiding the one road block that remained manned.

FLIGHT

FitzGerald heard a rustling, like a small animal in the brushwood. He tensed for a moment, then before he could rise, a shadow fell across the room and a face appeared. It was Lucia, her voice hoarse and panting. 'You must move, the devils are coming. Coming to Greppo.' The words exploded from her lips in short, sharp sentences.

The two men scrambled up and yanked on their boots.

'We go to the *capanna*. It belongs to my cousin, the woman who gave you the blanket. Hurry, hurry. Give me the blankets, give me the bag. Let's go.'

Outside it was eerie, the trees and hedges and distant hills all emerging from deepest black to charcoal grey. In the distance were pinpoints of light – Greppo. They headed down a path in the opposite direction.

Then Lucia was moving off across the stubble, the two men as close on her heels as they could, what with Goode carrying FitzGerald's kit and he swinging along with crutches. *He's like Long John Silver*, Goode thought, the colonel's hands gripping the crutches, his eyes scouring the ground.

They followed Lucia, running at a tangent. FitzGerald could move fast on level ground, but on a field it was laborious to tug his crutches out of the earth. Lucia held back, tried to help FitzGerald over a stile, but he ignored her and struggled over. He was already sweating. They passed through some trees, over a stream, and then they had placed a thick row of poplars between them and the path.

An oxcart, with Gino leading it, was waiting for them. Lucia breathed a sigh of relief that, so far, everything had gone right.

To Goode, she commanded, 'Quick, into the cart with him.' She indicated FitzGerald. 'Signor Goode, cover him with hay.'

FitzGerald hated to be the casualty. 'What of the children, your brother's family?'

'Gone into the hills. Now it is you we move.'

With Goode and the old man walking beside the cart, it rocked slowly along. There were no springs, so it lurched with each rut and clod, and FitzGerald gritted his teeth to prevent himself crying out at the pain that travelled up his spine at each motion.

Cocks were crowing in a ragged chorus as the light came; then the crimson dawn; then the first peasants arrived in the fields. Among them were even girls and small boys turning, or rather chopping up, the earth with *zappe*, small spades.

They could hear, far away, another cart clattering down a rutted lane.

As the light revealed it, peasants straightened themselves and watched the unusual group. Some shouted a question or two at Lucia's receding back but she answered sharply, in no mood for conversation.

Goode asked. 'Will they tell the Germans?'

'Do you not yet know what kind of people we are? How can you ask such a question?'

Conversation soon ceased. The heat, a heavy, suffocating heat, became unbearable to Goode and FitzGerald. Gino had foreseen that and brought several gourds of water from his well. By midday, they had travelled for seven hours and stopped to eat a piece of bread and cheese, fill up the gourds from a stream and sleep for ten minutes. Then they continued, without a word exchanged.

Many hours later, as the sky darkened and the moon rose in a sky suffused by pink, they were on a narrow path and glimpsed a tall, double-storey, rectangular-shaped building, half-hidden behind large oaks on the right. Lucia came to a stop beside an oak, the trunk of which had a broad splash of whitewash near its base.

'The *capanna*, here it is.' She pointed to an opening in the ground. That was the name she gave to the shelter.

They went down some broken steps and found themselves in a small concrete cave about two metres deep. It contained a single small bench, one fair-sized stone, and some straw on the unpaved, beaten-earth floor. Here and there, water had welled up out of the earth and the straw was saturated. There was a hole in the middle of the floor, apparently to let the water out as soon as it rose too high in the shelter.

Lucia picked up a bristle broom from the corner, rejected Goode's attempt to take it and started sweeping. She motioned them into a corner.

There was the rattle of machine guns from far away, elongated by distance and followed by echoes, airy and remote, flying back from the peaks. One, two, three bursts.

Lucia tensed. 'They're at it here. What's going on? Haven't they had enough?'

FitzGerald and Goode squatted down. Goode got out a dirty copy of Dante's "Inferno" and FitzGerald his King James' Bible. Light slid through the entrance and the slits at ground level.

'Can they be still combing the mountains? They are supposed to be fighting our armies, yet they still have time and energy to search for unarmed fugitives!'

FitzGerald asked himself whether any of his men were in danger, but when he spoke he was ruminating over the enemy's motives. 'Obedience and order end in themselves. Why to obey doesn't matter; if they obey, they belong. The Germans never question. Trains are commandeered to transport harmless victims hundreds of miles to eastern Europe because it's in the plan, yet I bet their generals can't get transport for their troops. It is because of this mentality that they'll lose the war.'

Lucia retorted, 'Not until they've butchered half the world.'

Lucia finished tidying and spoke again as she wiped her hands. 'You men are all the same: you want to fight to show off, to prove that you are not held back by your mother's softness. That is what war is all about. Perhaps in the past it was about grabbing food and women, but now you and your generals just want to lord it over them and their generals.'

'No, Mrs Riva, you're wrong. At least, in our case you are wrong. We came here to save you from barbarians. We think of ourselves as Romans, marching out from the capitol to guide the nations, impose the rule of law and wage war until the haughty are brought low.'

Lucia laughed. 'You think of yourselves like that, stealing Virgil's words? Well, I will answer you with the words of another thinker, an *Inglese*.

"Every man, is accompanied by a miasma of comforting convictions, which move with him like flies on a summer day." You have brought your flies with you to my home where they had long ago been superseded. Please look around you and consider this.'

Goode had the answer to most of the issues of life in his Marxist convictions, so he watched the exchange with detached amusement. FitzGerald was irritated but knew better than to contradict his host and guide. Before he could respond, Lucia added: 'I'm going.' And then, in tones that seemed condescending to FitzGerald,

'The people here are defending you. Do not fear.'

FitzGerald looked blank. 'Thank you, Signora.'

Lucia acknowledged him with a nod, turned and went.

Both men slept uncounted hours, then woke to the noise of shuffling feet and the sight of three branches being placed crosswise over the aperture, to be followed soon by more foliage. FitzGerald rose, went and put his head through it. A woman was coming down the path with massive twigs and shrubs in her arms.

'Who are you? What are you doing, *Signora*?'

'I am just covering up the opening so that no-one can see it.' She bent down to deposit her burden, pointing at the tree with the mark: 'The whitewash on the trunk is a signpost to the shelter. It will have to be taken off.'

Later, two children came, one bent almost double under a huge bale of straw, the other struggling to hold a pile of folded grey-green blankets.

Goode pulled aside the covering of vegetation and the two children stumbled down the steps and dumped their loads.

'We are Gina and Francesco. I am the oldest. We are seven children; I am nine years. My brother is nearly seven.'

'But I am braver!' Francesco was impish.

'Stupider!' his sister interjected. 'Mamma was so cross with you.'

FitzGerald smiled at the two children: 'Why? Why was your mamma cross?'

The girl was fast with her reply: 'He stole these blankets from the Germans. Mamma says if the Germans knew they would kill him. And everybody else. '

The boy drew himself up proudly and bowed deeply.

'My goodness me.' FitzGerald and Goode looked anew at the now evidently unused blankets.

The two children, having told their story, got to work. They shook the bales out, spread the straw thick over the ground, paying special attention to where the water had percolated through.

'That's better, now you won't get wet.'

When the children had gone, they worked on their Italian, or rather, composed conversations in Italian to help FitzGerald improve his grammar and extend his vocabulary.

He had, in a few days, mastered the basics about food, water, shelter and danger and, to his teacher's satisfaction, had moved on to attempting discussions about philosophy and history. An

Italian might well have not understood much of what FitzGerald said, but under constant correction from Goode, he would soon be able to converse with Italians about the things they thought worth discussing.

As the light died, the two men wound down, covered themselves with the stolen blankets and ate the last of their rations before sleep overcame them once more.

A FARM

It was afternoon when FitzGerald woke. As the day had heated up, he had thrown off the blankets in his sleep. Now he lay on the straw, breathing in its sickly-sweet smell.

He had never been one for lying in bed. His mind alert, his throat thirsty, he reached for his crutches and heaved himself up. As he did so, Goode woke and blinked.

'Morning, Chief.'

'Good afternoon, Goode. At least, I think it is afternoon. I'm going to go out and see if I can find some breakfast.'

'Oh yes, Sir.' Goode scrambled up, the blankets flopping around him.

'We'll make our beds first, Goode.'

'Oh yes, Sir!' The younger man bent to pick up a blanket and FitzGerald added: 'Don't forget the hospital corners, Goode.'

'Hospital...' As Goode turned, he realised that FitzGerald was laughing at him and shrugged.

'Need a nurse for that, Sir!'

'I could easily use a couple of nurses,' was FitzGerald's laconic reply, then he looked back in Goode's direction: 'I suppose that, as a son of the Free Kirk, you are disgusted?'

Goode did look disapproving. 'While on the revolutionary road, Sir, yes.' They both laughed, at themselves and at the other.

After moving the brush and branches carefully, they looked around. Silence. FitzGerald and Goode re-covered the entrance behind them and set off down a little path that appeared to bypass the *capanna*.

Disorientated as they were, they both realised that the day was drawing in on a landscape cloudy and damp, unexpected after the heat of the previous days. They had slept as prisoners do, for, when malnourished or deprived of stimulation, human beings sleep or feign sleep by instinct, conserving energy or recovering from stress. Both had run and walked hard the days before and had done so after months of relative inaction, especially FitzGerald, following several weeks in a prison hospital and a diet with little protein.

As they set out, there was a sudden rainstorm and thunder growled; black clouds darkened the sky. They came to the precincts of a home already soaked. It was part house, part rock, seemingly built against or into the hillside. It was so small that the cowshed, which had a hayloft over it, seemed bigger than the house itself. Every few seconds, the house and its outbuildings were illuminated by lightning, so they looked as if they were coated with silver.

The buildings were roofed with stone slabs and, down towards the eaves, these great tiles, now glittering wet, had rocks on top to stop the wind ripping them off. Smoke and sparks were streaming from the chimney, made from little piles of stones with a flat piece laid on top. Water sluiced down onto the mire, which was churning under the battering of the rain.

Before they had even entered the yard, yellow-fanged dogs appeared in a frenzy, and rushed, yapping, to and fro, saliva dripping from their mouths and water from scabby backs.

Goode shuddered.

FitzGerald stood his ground: the dogs could not get near. He pointed. 'Look – they can't touch us.'

Their collars were attached to a cord going up to a slip ring on the wire, strung between the eaves of the house and a pole in the corner of the yard.

The geese by the pond were unmoved by the noise, waddling up and down as if all was normal; ducks stirred in the shadows. Somewhere nearby, a donkey brayed. Some chestnut trees overlooked the yard and there were beehives a short way off.

By skirting round the dogs' circumference, FitzGerald realised they could get to the byre.

The door was closed but, through cracks and holes, faint pinpricks of light shone out.

FitzGerald pushed open the door and went in. There was a sweet warm smell of fodder and animals and the light of a lantern was casting huge, distorted shadows of the creatures, which he could not yet see, on the whitewashed wall in front of him. For a second, FitzGerald imagined he might encounter a minotaur from the sound of the heavy hooves rustling the straw.

There was the sound of milk spurting into a pail. Once the door had closed behind them, the noise of the storm faded into the background.

A small man appeared from behind one of the great looming beasts, which were to the left of the doorway. He had a toothbrush moustache, wispy hair from under his cap, a week's bristle on his face and although, as he was to tell FitzGerald later, he was only 32, he looked almost old enough to be the Irishman's father. His clothing was more a patchwork quilt than a suit.

FitzGerald was tall and imposing on his crutches. Goode stood behind him, just in case anybody might take advantage.

FitzGerald's voice was commanding: 'We'd like some water. We are British officers.'

The man looked up at him, silent, quizzically.

'No,' he said, 'no water.'

FitzGerald felt his anger rise. He had said "water" because he was ashamed to ask for food. But he expected to be obeyed by these wretched peasants. He was about to say that the bloody peasant had better help, when the little man raised his cap to scratch his head and said, in a deadpan voice, 'No. You cannot have water, but you may eat. And drink wine. We will soon have our dinner. I will tell the woman to feed two more. Come.'

As he took them across the yard, the dogs were silent. He opened the door and let them in, then disappeared.

They found themselves in a house of quite a different order to Bregante's home; much further from modernity, it seemed to Goode as if they were entering the primaeval cave.

At one end, there was a fire of dry brushwood that sent slithers of flame up round the pot, a copper pot on a long chain, slithers which subsided quickly into a bed of hot ash, grey with a glowing heart. The fire was kept burning by one end of the branch of a tree in it; the other end stuck out into the room. The floor was stone-flagged. The furniture was home-made.

There was nobody.

Goode looked around. 'The others must be working in the fields.'

In one corner was water, which must have been carried from the well in pitchers, for drinking or washing. From the ceiling, away from the mice, hung a salami, a home-cured crude ham and a lump of tallow for greasing boots. Very little light entered the one window; there was a carbide lamp hissing gently over the table.

An elderly housewife, in a long dress of dark brown and a headscarf, holding a large squash, stumbled in unsteadily and stopped short, seeming shocked to see them, just stared. She waited for him to speak. Goode, for some reason, was tongue-tied; perhaps, he thought after, from shame.

FitzGerald stepped forward: 'Excuse me, *signora*, we are *Inglesi*. Escaped prisoners.'

She looked him up and down, then beckoned him to come closer. Finally, she spoke: 'Alright. We'll eat soon. Have a rest now. Come.'

FitzGerald and Goode glanced at each other. The woman

picked up a candle and lit it with flint. Then, with gestures, she encouraged them to follow her as she moved towards the stairs.

She took them up stone stairs and showed them into a room with a bed so big that it took up almost the whole room, leaving only a slim corridor around it. Once they had sat, sheepish, on the edge of the bed, she returned downstairs; they could hear her moving about, the clang of a ladle on a pot as she started cooking.

They took off their boots and Goode pulled out his grubby copy of Dante's "Inferno" and laid it on the shelf, next to a plaster Madonna. About to lie down, they heard the clatter of new arrivals, and Goode went back to the top of the stairs to observe. He saw a younger woman coming in with her two children.

Reassured by the domestic scene below, they both lay down. Goode, the moment his head touched the pillow, fell into a deep sleep yet again. FitzGerald laid his head as near as possible to the window, stretched over for Goode's copy of "Inferno", looked for the passage to which Goode had introduced him earlier, and read:

Si ch'a bene serar m'era cagione... l'ora del tempo e la dolce stagione. So that the hour of the day and the sweet season… moved me to good hope.

After some thirty or forty minutes, he was suddenly aware of being watched and sat up. Two teenage girls were gazing at him from the doorway. When he saw them, they giggled and winked in a kind of pantomime flirtation.

One of them, who looked the eldest, asked: 'What are you reading?'

FitzGerald explained: 'Dante's "Inferno".'

'Oh yes, Dante is the greatest person that ever lived.'

FitzGerald found himself nodding, which seemed to exhilarate the girls.

'Will you read something to us? It must be nice to be able to read.'

A shout came from downstairs; the girls looked round quickly and then disappeared in a flash.

The noise from downstairs grew. Now there was a hubbub. He

prodded Goode awake, looked carefully out of the window, to work out an escape route, and gestured him to look downstairs.

Carefully, Goode tiptoed down and found that the room was full and preparations were being made for a meal: he worked out that the old woman must be their host's mother; a patriarch in his eighties or more was surely his father; then there were two daughters and, because she was physically so unlike the others, he assumed a daughter-in-law; there were several girls just arriving, in their teens, assorted small children, and a maiden aunt. He made his presence known and the old man bowed to him: 'Ah, Sir, you are welcome. My wife tells me that you *Inglesi* gentlemen have honoured us with a visit.' He gestured to the table. 'Please come and eat.'

'Thank you, Sir.' Seeing that FitzGerald had climbed down after him, Goode introduced him. FitzGerald, tall and authoritative despite his crutches, was greeted with admiration. The patriarch bowed to FitzGerald; FitzGerald, hesitating only a millisecond, bowed back.

The small silent man was the only male between eight and eighty. Goode asked him politely how he might address him, and he replied with one word, 'Zanoni,' not pausing as he cut bread, holding the big flat loaf to his chest and slicing wedges from it with his clasp knife.

The woman they had first met was his mother. When she heard their names, she tried them out in her mouth several times: 'Fizzerra, Fitserra. Ood, Oood.' Then she laughed and said she would call them "*Inglese* Man" and "*Inglese* Boy".

Goode had it on the tip of his tongue to say that he was a Scot and FitzGerald was Irish, or Irish-American, but FitzGerald thought to himself that they were all the same to their hosts, so could see no point of mentioning it. He raised an eyebrow at Goode, who had clearly just had the same thought.

The men sat first and Signora Zanoni poured polenta, like golden lava, onto the table, scattering a few odds and ends such as tomato and scraps of meat on top. Then everybody gathered around the table and set about digging in with a fork apiece, eating their way to the middle.

As soon as they had eaten all they could, the children ran about and shouted and giggled and pinched their elders. No adult remonstrated them but, if a child hove in view, smiled and stroked them. An older girl, aged about 13, sat at the table demurely, her eyes following the other children's antics wistfully. *She is expected to act like a peasant wife*, FitzGerald thought. Lucia came to mind. Was she, too, condemned to the same fate? He saw her as she had been in their brief conversations in the Rovacchia, when he had attributed her with options more ambitious than those of a mere peasant.

The wine was harsh. Following the meal, there was a handful of nuts and some medlars. As they finished eating, the fire died. The old man and the women went out one by one to relieve themselves in the byre.

They returned and one of the women topped up the wine. The old man asked, 'Are you Christians?'

FitzGerald allowed Goode to answer. 'No.'

'Do you believe in God?'

'No.'

'Do you hear that, Maria? Educated men, and they don't believe in God.'

His daughter, Maria, intervened. 'Maybe that's their custom.'

The old man sounded crotchety. 'I always told you there was no God.'

FitzGerald was careful not to offend the patriarch, who he assumed was the most important person there. 'I think we should keep an open mind. There may be a God, there may not be. We don't have to decide; his existence or lack thereof makes no difference to our lives.'

The patriarch looked intently at FitzGerald, absorbing this novel idea. Then he addressed him directly.

'Why don't the Allies bomb the Vatican?'

'Why should they?'

'Well. They'd get rid of the priests. We won't have another chance like this.'

Nobody followed up. The old man looked down and gazed into his wine, morose.

After a few moments, he spoke in a grumbling tone. 'Before you came here, we were unlucky. La Riva gives all our neighbours at least one lost youth to join the family, but not we. Now we too are blessed. So please, raise your glasses and drink our poor wine! To peace, and the hope that you will soon be home with your mothers again!'

Goode addressed the old man as he had heard his family do. 'Grandfather, who is the Riva you mention?'

FitzGerald was irritated by Goode. Grandfather! Was he going native? Instead of trying to ingratiate himself by adopting their ways, he should remain detached, English. *But of course, he is not English. He is a Scot. I'm not English either. Yet I know how to behave like an Englishman. Goode doesn't.*

'Riva Lucia? The young widow from Ginestra.'

So Lucia had brought them to her relatives, or at least to her relatives' community. FitzGerald remarked. 'She helped us get away from the camp.'

Maria added: 'Her mother's family are from these parts. They sent her away when she was with child –'

'Bah!' The old man suddenly spat out in irritation. He changed the subject: 'What's that message La Riva sent us? Tell these *Inglesi*.'

'You tell them.'

'Yes. I shall. La Riva sent her boy over. So that we can tell you.'

Goode said, 'She couldn't know that we would meet you.'

The old man opened his mouth in a big laugh. He had three teeth only, all very yellow.

'Never mind. What she knows she knows. And you must be told that that devil Mussolini has escaped from prison!'

FitzGerald cursed inwardly. Goode exclaimed: 'Musso escaped!'

'Yes. And there will be more war. Why, I don't know. But that is what the boy said. To tell you. And that you must be more careful. Do not go back to the shelter, stay with us but stay in the house all day tomorrow because it is Sunday and we will have visitors and one of them might fancy the 5,000 *lire* reward for denouncing you.'

FitzGerald was startled. 'They have offered a reward? Then we must go, leave immediately.' As the old man did not react, not seem to understand, FitzGerald turned to Goode to ask him to use his better Italian to explain. He rose, as if to leave at that moment.

Maria remonstrated. 'If La Riva says you are safe here, then you are safe. She knows the situation more than you and we do.' Perhaps she thought she had gained two strapping men who might be useful on the farm, at least once FitzGerald's foot was healed.

Again, that Riva girl. For a moment, before he recovered his cool, FitzGerald was stabbed with resentment at the mention of her name. It reminded him that he was in the hands of others, and Italians too.

Goode appeared to have sensed that. 'Do you ever feel, Sir, that we are enmeshed in a web being spun by that widow?'

FitzGerald grunted, rather than spoke, what seemed to be an affirmation. *There is something spooky about the way this woman has a hand in our every move,* he thought, but he did not share his thought.

IN THE EARLY HOURS

At nightfall, the temperature outside dropped to twelve or fourteen degrees, so that even in that crowded cave, the chill was felt. Little by little, the mothers and babies disappeared and finally only the old people were left with their guests. FitzGerald and Goode had intended to disregard instructions and return to the shelter, but the rain was heavy and Maria insisted that they would lose the way.

To clinch the argument, *Signor* Zanoni made his only contribution to it. 'Signora is right.' FitzGerald and Goode were to sleep in the big matrimonial bed upstairs.

The bedposts were tall and white and ghostly-looking in the light of the single candle with which Signor Zanoni led the way back into the bedroom. There was now a great lump in the middle of the bed, as if one of the larger children had curled up inside. Seeing their surprise, Signor Zanoni commented, 'It's the priest.'

Before they had time to react, he threw back the bed cover to reveal a brazier warming the sheets. He took it out and placed it in the corner of the room.

Just before he gave in to sleep, FitzGerald mused that he and Goode were slumbering like babies, most of the day and night. *Will my brain atrophy? My limbs seize up?* Beside him, the younger man had again fallen asleep the moment he drew the covers over himself. FitzGerald knew that he would follow him in seconds, lured by the warmth of the bed, of his own clothes, which he had not taken off since leaving the prison camp, the air warmed by the brazier and the heat of their two well-fed bodies. He began to dream, in that haze that precedes slumber, of his parents, childhood friends and events that had no connection with his life today, as either fugitive or soldier. *I abandoned my wife, not compulsorily, like these young mothers' men. How terrible it will be for them if their men never return, or return crippled. My Annie has options, an American; she can manage her own destiny if she choose. She never evinced the intensity of my* máthair, *so like these Italian peasants, in their reticence and dignity.* He visualised Lucia and wondered where she might be. *I must apologise to her. For not understanding.* And then he thought of the insulting terms he had allowed the men to use about Italians, "Wop" and "Eyetie" and blushed. With this thought, FitzGerald fell into a deep sleep.

He sat up sharply as he felt a hand on his shoulder. In the faint light afforded by a stray cast of moonlight through the shutters, he could make out the face of Maria, whispering, 'Be careful. There are Germans here. They got lost, they are not looking for you. Do not be afraid. Just be quiet and stay in bed, pretend to sleep if they come upstairs.'

LUCIA AND THE PATRIOTS

Lucia planned to get the lame colonel and Goode further south and out of the clutches of the revengeful devil commander, whose attention Alessandro had temporarily deflected. This meant transport, at a time when any non-military vehicle on the road would *darebbe nel'occhio*; stand out a mile. There were only two categories of civilian who could drive without arousing suspicion: pharmacists and medical personnel. The local physician was from Milan, was thought to mix in communist circles, whereas the pharmacist was a Sicilian, fellow bibliophile and associate of the count. Using her borrowed status, that of amanuensis and friend to the countess, she headed for the pharmacist's villa, outside Ginestra, on her bicycle.

Foschini had gone to ground there. The Station Sergeant had driven him and, greeted by the grave Sicilian and his twelve-year-old son, accepted a glass of wine. The three men were sitting together under the vines which shaded the pharmacist's veranda. Now that the "youngster", for that was what the Station Sergeant called Alessandro, had revealed himself to be pragmatic, as they saw it, the pharmacist and the Station Sergeant drew him, metaphorically, to their bosoms. They discussed openly among themselves the escape of the *Inglesi* and how to deal with the Germans. The two older men were survivors, not fighters. To survive, you often needed to be an actor, to lull a fascist or communist into believing you are one of them, when all the time you were serving a higher kind of loyalty; to family, but also to virtue. The pharmacist was a master at this, never denying the Germans anything he could provide, while making, for the child refugees in the fortress and the Jews and other outcasts, whatever medicines were needed.

It was by chance that Lucia, with Enrico on the back of her bicycle, called to see the pharmacist when he was entertaining both confederates. As she approached the villa, she saw that the Station Sergeant's vehicle, with its bombardier badge, stood before the front door. It brought back a multitude of memories, but one in particular. 10th July: she could never forget the exact day. She had not even known that there was fighting in Sicily, where her Domenico was. She had been complacent that he had not followed other local men to Africa, or Russia, faraway. *No harm can come to him in Sicily*, she'd thought; home of his ancestors, which she pictured as it had been when it was the richest jewel in the Roman Empire, colonnaded temples soaring atop the mountains, amphitheatres showing those Greek plays to multitudes. *Not that Domenico would have thought much about that*, she smiled fondly as she pictured him in his smart new outfit, his forage cap rakish on the back of his head, him hanging on her words, docile, as she advised him what not to miss of Sicily's glories, his eyes on her showing so clearly his wonder that this girl, with all her beauty and wisdom, was his.

It was the duty of the Station Sergeant of carabinieri to inform the families of the area of their loved ones' glorious deaths in battle. He was a kindly man, who clutched his hand to his heart as if in shock when, one morning in his office, he read the name on the order paper. In his early fifties, with a drooping grey moustache and a face lined like creased canvas, he wore the ribbons of the Great War over his left pocket. He knew the young bride, had smiled at her wave every weekday as she tripped to school, or slid past him on her way up to Dottoressa Foschini's home. The stages in her life had gone so fast for the Station Sergeant, reminding him of his own mortality. Even after her marriage, the lovely girl, now walking with the slower gait and dignified mien of a married woman, would stop if he were outside the station to ask after his wife and children.

The Station Sergeant knew how difficult it had been for the waif – even so special a waif, whose glance made everyone happy – to be united with that fine Bregante boy and when, one evening in the guardroom, the corporal had come in with the news that the engagement had been announced, the Station Sergeant had opened another bottle and all the lads had toasted the factor's son and the loveliest filly in all of Ginestra.

So, on that awful day, he had first broken the news to Signora Riva and then driven her up to Greppo in the unit's SPA AS.37.

Lucia was in the square, hugging Chiara. Chiara had been excluded by the boys from some game or other and wanted sympathy. Lucia heard the sound of the car stopping outside the gate, but it had not registered to her, until she saw her mother and the Station Sergeant enter through the gate.

Lucia's mother found the cobbles difficult to traverse and the Station Sergeant, his grey-green bicorn in his left hand, supported her with his right arm. Lucia pictured him again now. Without that hat of authority, she had noted how old he was, for his head had just wisps of grey hair that the breeze was wafting around his spotted pate. But what struck her most and told her immediately that they had come on some terrible mission was that the old man was weeping. Great tears were coursing down the Station Sergeant's leathery cheeks and when she saw those tears, she sank to her knees, grasping Chiara to her so tightly that the child gasped. She cried out in anguish: 'He's been wounded! He's been wounded!'

Her mother struggled to run over the shiny cobbles, slipping and stumbling, holding tight to the weeping man lumbering beside her, her own eyes now blinded with tears, and the two old people sank down beside the young woman and put their arms around her so that Chiara screamed and slid out from them. But Lucia did not heed the child, only looked into their two faces, begging them to agree with her and repeating, again and again: 'He's been wounded, he's been wounded! Where? His foot? His arm? Where, where?'.

Little over two months later, outside the pharmacist's house, Lucia steadied herself with her hand on the bonnet of that familiar vehicle, while Enrico stared through its windows. *Domenico and I married. Then he left me. Fate put this child in my hands. The* dottoressa *gave me responsibility for all those people, those men. To stop me going mad after losing Domenico? Now I am like a travelling pedlar, going up and down the countryside, a woman without modesty, even calling on men as if I myself were a man. Oh God, Domenico, what has become of me?* Enrico was running his finger along the car door, checking the dust that it collected, drawing rings in it.

At that moment, the pharmacist had got up from his chair on the veranda behind his house because his little son had come up and whispered in his ear that there was boy touching the Station Sergeant's car. He recognised Lucia, knew her story and adopted the tones of sympathy and affection appropriate to her situation.

'My dear *signora*, welcome. It is always so good to see you! And what a handsome boy!' He patted Enrico's head; his now dark brown hair had been cut back and felt and looked like velvet.

As soon as he appeared, Lucia was all feminine bashfulness, accepting gracefully the courtesies of the other two men, who rose, with downcast eyes as she was led onto the veranda. She was gratified to find that they treated her as a married lady, bowing over her hand and brushing it ever so slightly with their lips. She allowed them to start with pleasantries and direct the discussion to the exigencies of the moment, making her suggestions tentatively, glancing from time to time into Alessandro's eyes to see if they met with his approval.

The two boys ran off to visit the family goats when the discussion of public affairs recommenced, with Lucia, now seemingly an honorary man, an equal. In the north, there were young Jews hiding in the mountains, swooping down from time to time to destroy a militia post or an ammunition dump. An Italian had flown in from the USA to coordinate partisan activities with the democracies' armies in the south. Nearer home, there was a *banda* whose commissar, Neri, had returned to Italy from Moscow. Some officers had kept small numbers of their troops together in the hills and were believed to be waiting for orders from the king. Alessandro would seek out whichever unit could best utilise his expertise. The older men joined with Lucia in trying to dissuade him. 'You can do more good here,' they claimed. 'Wait for the democracies to push the Nazis back into Austria, mitigate the damage being done here.'

As to her request for transport, they were decisive. Neither the Station Sergeant nor the pharmacist would risk their cars to transport fugitives, but they knew of a physician who was already doing so, a Dr Scotti. The pharmacist called Scotti using cryptic phrases to communicate his needs. To listeners, he and Dr Scotti would have seemed to be having a recondite argument about botany and herbal medicines, but arrangements were actually being agreed over the future movements of an *Inglese* colonel and his assistant.

Lucia's network was expanding; the risks too.

UNWELCOME VISITORS

Goode was alert, he swung his feet onto the floor. As FitzGerald thrust their packs under the bed and felt around for any other trace of their foreignness, Goode tiptoed downstairs, to see unseen.

German soldiers were in the kitchen, maps spread out on the table at which he and FitzGerald had so recently eaten. A plump German captain, a pink-faced young lieutenant and a grey-haired sergeant major were bent over the table, discussing their route with the patriarch, who was in his nightshirt. Two other soldiers stood between their officers and the door. Of the children, there was only a little boy and a girl of about nine huddling with their mother, one of Maria's daughters, wearing an old coat over her nightdress, standing in a corner.

Above, FitzGerald peered between the slats of the shutters to see more Germans below, smoking around the doorstep.

He slid into another room in which he could hear breathing of several people still asleep – *the young, they can sleep through anything* – and gently opened that shutter the width of a finger. More Germans were lolling against the wall. When he returned, Goode was getting back into bed, curling up to appear shorter. FitzGerald did the same.

Goode hissed: 'Light blue piping, supply troops. Like our Service Corps.'

'That's a relief,' was FitzGerald's reply. Not for the first time, he was glad that Goode was an Intelligence officer.

Below, Maria and one of her daughters were now chatting to the young lieutenant who spoke Italian, while the other soldiers were all taking a glass of wine. They were friendly. The captain had a placid face, like that of an office clerk or parish priest; the sergeant major, with his weathered cheeks and rough hands, looked like a gardener or farm foreman.

The room was filled with that very distinctive smell of damp uniforms and equipment, sweat and cordite, that every soldier recognises as he returns to barracks or enters a quartermaster's store.

The chatty lieutenant, his eyes scanning the room for anything out of place, noticed FitzGerald's boots drying by the fire. He addressed the peasant nearest to him, Maria's daughter.

'Whose boots are these?'

'My husband's.'

'Where is he?'

For a moment, she was going to tell the truth, that her husband was in the army in the east, but then she realised that the Germans would almost certainly search the house for the owner of the boots. She trembled, as she replied, 'Asleep.' Then, as if to explain why he had not come down, 'very tired'.

'Tell him to get down here. I want to know how he got English boots.'

Realising that her daughter was almost paralysed with fear, Maria distracted the lieutenant by responding for her, with a smile, 'I shall wake him.' She started upstairs.

There, she found her two *Inglesi* feigning sleep in the dark. Fearing that she might be followed upstairs, she quickly directed herself at Goode.

'You are my daughter's husband. They have seen your boots.

Do you understand?' Goode nodded. He rose, stripped off his army socks and followed her downstairs in bare feet.

The lieutenant seemed not to notice what to the old patriarch was obvious: this man coming down into the room neither had the jib of, nor held himself like, a farmer. But the old man could also see that his own of perception of difference, of distance, was not the German's, who demanded of the foreigner, fiercely and in bad Italian: 'Where did you get these boots?'

Goode tried to imitate the dialect Italian that he had been hearing all around him. Aware that his intonation was markedly Scots, he said as little as possible, playing a tongue-tied peasant: 'Englishman dead. I take his boots.'

The lieutenant, turning to his brother officers, showing off his translation skills, announced that, 'He says he stole them from a dead Britisher. A likely story!' He turned towards the mother holding her children in the corner and addressed the boy. 'This is not your father, true?'

The little boy was frozen with terror but his quick-witted sister detached herself from her mother, rushed over, put her arms round Goode's thigh and looked up into his face.

'*Abbraciami*, Papa! Give me a hug!'

Goode lifted the girl into his arms and kissed her lightly on the forehead. The Germans all laughed.

The young lieutenant looked sceptical but, as if to forestall him prolonging the investigation, the sergeant major turned to the captain. '*Herr* Hauptman, we're wasting time. We must be going.'

Putting down his glass, the captain agreed with the older man, 'Yes, of course.' To the lieutenant, he said, '*Leutnant* Milch! Let's go.' He clicked his heels and bobbed his head to the patriarch, to Goode. '*Grazie Signori.*' He bowed to Maria. '*Grazie Signora. Arrivederci!*'

Shouts of command rang out and there was the shuffle of soldiers' feet and the clinking of equipment and weapons beyond the door, where the family stood to bid their visitors farewell.

Goode returned upstairs, sweat trickling down his back.

Outside, trucks started up and roared into life, corporals bawled and others cursed. He and FitzGerald gathered up their kit and, as the last vehicle rumbled away, clambered downstairs.

Maria, coming back in, was shocked: 'Where are you going?'

'We are leaving. It's too dangerous to be here.'

'No! The Germans will not be back. And it is the middle of the night, it's cold.'

'We can go back to the *capanna*.' FitzGerald looked into her eyes as if truly comprehending her for the first time. 'Your courage and goodness are beyond rubies. You are heroes.'

The housewife ignored this: 'Well, at least you must have more warm clothes.' She raised the lid of the great coffer beside where she stood and pulled out some woollens, thrusting them into Goode's hands.

They left. Into the wilderness once more.

DAYTIME

FitzGerald and Goode slept the next few hours in the *capanna*. As they were preparing to leave, Signora Zanoni arrived with hot milk and bread; just as important, she had in her apron pocket a rough map, penned on grey paper, which she said had come from Riva Lucia by the hand of a small boy.

After seeing that it gave them a route up into the hills, FitzGerald and Goode set off. With Goode carrying his kit, FitzGerald could now move at a reasonable speed on paths not too rocky or churned. Goode sauntered behind him so that his chief set the pace. Sometimes he would sing Scots songs; "Marie's Wedding" and "Twa Knights" were repeated again and again. Sometimes he'd initiate a conversation, but there was little response from FitzGerald, who needed to put all his efforts into keeping up the pace, and all his concentration on the path ahead, dim in the dawn light.

FitzGerald looked up at a cloudless blue sky and thought back to the slights that Lucia had aimed at him. At the time, he had merely reacted with irritation, but he now recognised that she had hit home, made him question himself and his motivations. *Why did I do what my father did? He left his wife and family to go on a crusade.* The Riva woman would have called that "poppycock", or whatever is the Italian equivalent.

FitzGerald forced himself to acknowledge that he had used a similar claim to justify his own desertion of Annie and his child. *Yes, I'd been fed up with a wife who wanted to narrow life down to her version of family meals, reproduction and home improvements. I must admit that it was this that had been behind my going to war, as much as my ideals.*

Riva saw through me, ridiculed me for thinking I might make a difference, that my choices might have meaning. Had this been my father's folly too? Rather than being an exercise in free will, a demonstration of individuality and prowess, was I, the son, simply following the genetic plan inherited from my father? And, God help me, from my grandfather as well? What drove me to do as they did? He came to no conclusion, but glanced behind from time to time at Goode, propelled by his belief in revolution, and asked himself how two men could be doing the same thing for such different reasons.

In the distance were carts pulled by white oxen, usually in pairs, which moved so slowly they seemed hardly alive at all. From afar there were the cries of a farmer exhorting his steed to greater efforts, the incessant barking of dogs, the clamouring of geese and the distant cries of a cock carrying on a conversation with the next farmyard.

Most of the farms they passed were similar, grey stone buildings with byres, barns and larders all under one roof. There were a few jet-black cypress trees alongside. The living rooms were reached by a short flight of stone steps, with the pigsties and henhouses below.

A girl tripping down through the trees, driving a flock of sheep, greeted the two men as if she saw them every day and passed on.

Striding forward, FitzGerald and Goode heard explosions in the distance from time to time.

As they approached a river, they made the time of day with a peasant woman.

After perhaps a minute, they heard her call out to them, stopped and turned. 'Young men,' she said, 'if you are two of those, I would not cross. There is a patrol waiting on the other side.'

They both thanked her.

Goode: 'That was a close shave.'

FitzGerald nodded. He was thinking, *it isn't just the Riva girl and her relatives who help us. Even this stranger has. And you can't say it's just the women, because Zanoni... but then, did Zanoni really know what he was risking? Did he, just like his wife, think he might be getting help on the farm?*

Goode made a guarded criticism of his chief, 'It makes one wonder if we are not a bit crazy, Sir. Sometimes I ask myself what I'm doing walking on from day to day towards a front that will be almost impossible to get through.'

It had now been nine days since they had left PG500 and they had covered little ground, despite FitzGerald's efforts at speed. He had had to admit to himself that five miles was about the limit of his strength without a break, very different from the twenty-odd miles of which he had been capable before his capture. He knew that Goode pined to join the *bande* and was accompanying him only because he needed support. *The Italians are providing well, I must admit, making it feasible for me to go it alone. My calf is steadily strengthening; I can feel it. I can cope with his pack myself, so it's maybe time to let him go. Getting over the lines to our own people seems more and more difficult to achieve. I should have made for Switzerland. That means internment.* He shuddered at the thought. With the partisans, Goode might achieve more than trying and failing to get to the river.

As they plodded on, both were in a brown study, avoiding thinking about the pain under FitzGerald's armpits and the rubbing of the pack straps on his shoulders, or the ache in Goode's shins. As FitzGerald lifted up his eyes to the hills, now terraced in patches no larger than a small room, the image flashed before him of his father reading Psalm 121 in his sonorous voice. The staple crop here was the chestnut, for there was not sufficient land cleared to grow any quantity of wheat or potatoes.

They were both wrestling with where their duty and inclinations lay. Neither wanted to waste time. *Life is short. I must serve the purpose for which I exist. I must make my mark.* Both men had these thoughts, propelled by the androgen that determines a man's life, channelled by the biblical purposiveness with which both had been indoctrinated as children.

Ready to rest after five or more hours' walking, they found themselves beside a farmhouse yard. Two men were sitting in the sun in their underclothes, drinking wine of which there was a large fiasco on an upturned tea chest. Beside them, a housewife was mending socks. Other clothes were drying on a washing line. The wife looked up and smiled, unperturbed.

One of the men, who was swarthy and long-haired, cried out, 'More *Inglesi*!'

FitzGerald, offended by his inability to disguise himself, but smiling: 'Is it so obvious?'

They all laughed.

The other semi-naked man rose and put out his hand: 'I am Stavros, Greek. This Oleksiy, from Poland or Ukraine, he does not know! We both run from Todt. Oleksiy is bricklayer. I am worker. And you run out from camp?'

The wife addressed the newcomers. 'You must eat.' She rose. 'I'll get food.'

Stavros the Greek questioned, 'You hear explosions? Coming here?'

Goode was confident. 'It should be the Germans demolishing their magazines in retreat.'

Greek: 'No, they smash houses of the peasants. Here –' he pointed at the *fiasco* – 'drink, *Inglese*man.' He rinsed his own tumbler and that of the Pole, wiped them with a cloth napkin, filled them from the fiasco with red wine and presented one each to FitzGerald and Goode.

As the men sat and sipped the wine, the woman took down the dry clothes from the line and handed them over to the Greek and the Pole.

She remarked: 'Today everything dries in a few moments.'

Oleksiy had the leaf of a chestnut tree in his hand. To the two newcomers he announced: 'Welcome to the land of chestnuts.'

The woman looked up proudly, 'The chestnut orchards stretch for many *stari*.'

Goode was interested. 'Yes, I saw that, and that they seem ripe. When do you harvest them?'

'We will pick the chestnuts later this month.'

'For sale?'

No, we dry them and ground them into flour for bread, at home. A chestnut polenta is much richer than maize polenta. But today I make pasta.'

With that, she rose and beckoned Goode to follow her into the main room of the house. There she took a large board, covered it with flour and made a hole in the middle into which she broke three eggs. She then worked the flour into the eggs until she had made dough which she rolled out like a tablecloth. Folding the dough like corrugated paper, backwards and forwards, she cut it with a knife so that when it opened out, it formed thick strips and was ready to be put into a pot of *minestra* which simmered over the fire. Later they sat round slurping the soup.

FitzGerald asked, 'Where's your husband, *Signora*?'

'He was murdered three months ago today.'

Goode dropped his spoon into his bowl. 'What?'

Their host looked straight at them, 'With our three sons.'

The men all stopped eating and stared at her.

FitzGerald asked, 'What happened, how were they murdered?'

'They hid some foreigners up in the steading in the hill, where we keep our animals in summer. The devils came when they were all there, took away the foreigners and killed my men. I found them myself.'

She spoke matter-of-factly, as if discussing something over which she had no rights, power or feeling.

Goode was the only one who spoke, the other men glancing

at him as if appointing him their spokesman: 'And still you are helping these –' he pointed to the others – 'and us too?'

'My brother is in the east, and we have heard nothing of him for a year. They shot my husband and our sons. They have taken everything important from me already – what more do I have to fear?'

She stared straight at them, defiant.

Goode opened his mouth to speak but halted: he had nothing to say. He looked down into his bowl.

The woman picked up a wooden ladle with a long handle and stirred the *minestra*, gazing into it as if reading tealeaves. No-one spoke.

Once the meal was over, FitzGerald gestured to Goode and they picked up their kit.

'Thank you, *Signora*, we'll be on our way.'

The woman reacted straightaway: 'Wait to eat again! You are too undernourished to walk far.'

'No, no, we must be off. You've given us enough food.'

'Take some more.' She went into the back of the room and came out with a basket, handed them bread, onions and tomatoes. Seeing the Greek and Pole picking up their bags, she questioned, 'You are all going?'

Oleksiy now became the spokesman, 'Better together. And better for you. We go south too, *Mammina*, Little Mother.'

Goode wanted to show appreciation, 'Thanks to you we will have company!'

'Be careful!' Her eyes were sad.

FitzGerald, for an instant, questioned if they should stay. But the thought passed.

The Ukrainian kissed her hand, in a manner as stately as any Prince of Kyiv; the Greek hugged her. After a brief hesitation, FitzGerald copied the Ukrainian and lifted her hand to waft his lips over it. Goode shook the same hand.

Down the path, onto the road, here cobbled, they tramped. They met a dog, petted it; it followed them.

Goode held back for FitzGerald, but the other two pressed on. FitzGerald had to concentrate hard to negotiate the stony ground. His leg hurt more today and, regretfully, he called for a stop several times. Perhaps he did so, too, because he wanted to talk.

'You tell me, Goode, that these people see us as liberators, on the side of the people against the capitalists, but I don't think class conflict enters their minds.'

Goode sat, his elbows on knees, on a rock, gazing out into the valleys.

'That child who called you "Papa" exhibited an instinct that came from somewhere else. All these people, the Zanonis, that lady who fed us today, who has lost all her family...'

Goode did not reply and FitzGerald went silent. *What kind of man am I, beside these... heroes? These people that I despised are courageous and self-sacrificing in ways that I can hardly imagine of my own chaps. What does uniform do? It reminds us that we have chosen to conform, to do not as our hearts move us, but as the herd and its leaders want.* To his astonishment, he felt tears well up, though they didn't fall. He saw Goode looking at him as if trying to divine what was going on in the old fellow's mind.

'This is love, Goode; this is love for the world, for people, for all God's works. Based on a belief about what a human being should be, can be, if he or she is to claim as much.'

'Yes,' Goode looked faintly uncomfortable at the words coming from his chief, 'It seems that the poorer they are, the more decent they are.'

FitzGerald stood up, stiff and with his calf aching. *It'll get better as I move*, he consoled himself. Goode leapt up and threw his pack on his back before reaching out to steady FitzGerald who, seeming dazed, teetered. They set off, FitzGerald leading and Goode holding himself back and whistling half-remembered pibroch.

Dusk fell and they knew they must halt soon, before the pitch-black night obliged them to drop where they stood.

Tired, and just in time, they found what had been marked on

the map, a typical summer shelter about eight feet long and four broad with a sloping roof of trees, branches and clods of earth. There was no sign of Oleksiy and Stavros, but there had been an open fire on the floor that was still warm. It was ventilated by a small hole in the roof. They relit the fire and roasted their potatoes in the embers. As the night's chill came, they covered themselves with charcoal sacks.

They ate some medlars and then fell asleep immediately.

FitzGerald woke at about 2a.m. with the ache in his leg. As he lay pondering whether he could re-light the fire from the comfort of his blankets, he heard the soft tread of someone circling the shelter.

Immediately alert, he tapped Goode and sat up. Goode, too, was instantly awake and began to put on his boots. Then the pacing stopped in front of the door.

CANAPÉS IN CAFÉ ROSATI

By October 1943, via Tasso 145, Rome, had been transferred from the cultural department of the German Embassy to the Italian office of the s*icherheitspolizei*, secret police (SiPo), run by Herbert Kappler. Kappler had impressed his superiors with the success of his interrogations and had consequently been awarded the *SS-Ehrendegen*, or sword of honour, raising his status in the eyes of his colleagues, even Fröhlich's.

About ten days after the trouble in Ginestra, Fröhlich drove to Rome for a briefing from Kappler about the partisan situation and the escape lines being run for Allied prisoners by priests in the still-unoccupied Vatican City. In his turn, Fröhlich had to report that distractions requiring his attention had made it impossible to devote adequate resources to the escapers from PG500.

After that was over, Fröhlich was invited to join colleagues for a drink at Rosati's in Piazza del Popolo.

Fröhlich strolled down the Corso with a smile on his face, admiring the women and occasionally glancing into a shop window. The stylish bars, restaurants and sophisticated shops that he passed on his way to enjoy a vermouth with Reder, of the Panzergrenadier-Division „Reichsführer SS", and Priebke, Kappler's, number two, made a pleasant change from camp life.

Under a big pink umbrella on the pavement in front of Rosati, it was good to unwind. Although they had agreed not to talk shop, eventually the conversation drifted to the work in which they were all engaged, for which they all hoped they would become famous, or at least receive medals or even the sword of honour.

Priebke, on account of being able to speak Italian, was the main channel of communication with the OVRA, the fascist secret police. He had many entertaining stories to tell, which was why real soldiers, and his seniors, such as Reder and Fröhlich, were not too snobbish to sit down with Priebke, an ex-waiter of The Savoy Hotel in London. His imitations of the prisoners' excuses could be hilarious, as was his regaling them with the promises made, and revelations offered, by the desperate.

'Are there any good bookshops in Rome, Priebke?' Fröhlich asked once he had ordered a second round.

'I'm not much of a reading man, these days, Fröhlich.' Then he had a thought. 'See that priest over there?' Priebke pointed to a tall, well-built and fleshy man in a black soutane and biretta, talking with two young types wearing blue soutanes with the scarlet sash of the German College. The other two officers glanced over. 'He'll know.'

Priebke felt important, informing two real soldiers. 'That priest is a Croat. He was secretary to the queer who ran the pope's household not long ago. The queer was so flagrant with urchins that the pope had to get rid of him.'

Reder guffawed; Fröhlich looked disgusted. Priebke snapped his fingers and the priest started and looked towards them.

'Filipović! Come and join us! Have a beer!'

The man in the soutane, adjusting his moiré sash, lumbered up and approached the table with an ingratiating lowering of his head.

'In Rome lobbying to get your old job back?' Priebke cracked and was gratified to see by the priest blanche; he had probably hit the nail on the head. Without waiting for an answer, he went on: 'My colleague here wants to buy books in Rome. Where do you suggest? Sit down!'

Filipović obeyed the order and looked from one to the other. 'Gentlemen, good day. What kind of books?'

Fröhlich, unlike his colleagues at the table, who had been raised Catholics, had been brought up Lutheran. Although he was now a disciple of the Nazi religion, he nevertheless displayed a tinge of respect for the uniform of the clergy, that of an army that had survived longer than most. His politeness offset Priebke's lordly tone.

'Thank you, Father. I am looking for a copy of the Georgics – in Latin or English.'

Filipović looked relieved and forthwith offered to buy a copy and get it to him.

'Are you a classical scholar, Father?'

'My field is patristics, *Herr Sturmbannführer*.'

Reder, who had once considered a career in the priesthood, looked disgusted. 'So, you are studying all those old Jews?'

Filipović was about to reassure Reder but, concerned the discussion would get out of hand and become hifalutin talk about ideology and literature that might exclude him, Priebke quickly moved the conversation on.

'Do tell my colleagues, Filipović, about romance in the Vatican.'

Filipović looked embarrassed and clammed up.

'Does the pope screw boys too?' Priebke demanded.

Filipović found his voice and his reply was emphatic. 'Certainly not; the Holy Father would never countenance such a thing.'

Priebke sparred, 'He tolerates it as long as it doesn't become public. If it does, the perverts get the chop.'

'Please excuse me,' the priest rose, 'I must return to my flock.' He gestured towards the two German deacons. The three officers did not rise. Only Fröhlich nodded a kind of farewell.

They had all taken off their belts and caps, which were on the spare wicker chair. They sipped their vermouth. Fröhlich stabbed an olive with a toothpick that flew a little Nazi flag.

Priebke felt that not enough interest had been taken in his

insinuations, so he did not wait for the questions but instead volunteered information. 'The Croat's boss was sacked because he couldn't stop playing with boys. They say he was punished by giving him charge of an orphanage.' Priebke laughed loudly at his own story. 'The Croat himself was posted to some lucky parish further north.'

Priebke was reaching the limit of Fröhlich's amusement. As he had stated to the Irishman some weeks previously, Fröhlich was not in this for promotion, profit or pleasure. To achieve a better world, certain classes and races must be eliminated. *In any endeavour,* Fröhlich admitted to himself, *you have to have executives less committed to the cause, careerists and opportunists.* Nevertheless, men like Priebke irritated him.

Even Priebke could sense from the click of Fröhlich's tongue that he did not like this subject.

Reder wanted to clarify that it was not just gossip, and added: 'Celibacy, it's an open invitation to perverts. And perverts are very useful for intelligence gathering.'

Priebke laughed, though a little nervously. 'Indeed, we get most of our information from men dead scared of what we know about them.'

Fröhlich turned to look out onto the piazza.

Reder mentioned a name. 'Venturi?'

'Yes, the pope's emissary to the *Duce*. He's sound on the Jewish question, although he interferes on behalf of those yids who pretend to be Catholics.'

'What about the Irish priest who helps the fugitives?'

'Flaherty? We'll eliminate him soon; he's a nuisance. But there are useful priests. It's thanks to that Filipović that we know that the Umbria *bande* are in cahoots with another Irishman, a colonel who got six hundred out of PG 500 –' he was about to say "whom 1st Panzer let get away", but stopped himself – 'who tricked the Italian commandant.'

Fröhlich showed no reaction but was instantly vigilant at the mention of PG500.

Filipović and his two acolytes were just rising from their table. Priebke looked over at him.

'Hey, Filipović! Who do you think did it, managed to get the English away? You come from Ginestra, don't you?'

He looked unwilling but responded: 'I am acting priest in Ginestra, yes. They say it was all organised by the camp commandant working with left wingers, socialists.'

Fröhlich spoke. 'Do you know who and how?'

The priest nodded. 'There are some soldiers who have returned from the crusade in the east; some say they were involved.'

Fröhlich immediately recollected Foschini, but managed to appear detached, lest he be thought to be accepting responsibility for the monumental failure that had made him a laughingstock. "Six hundred?" he knew they had cackled at HQ. "Fröhlich missed six hundred! His eyesight must be going."

Fröhlich sounded nonchalant. 'It will be helpful to me if you can find out more about the Irishman and his local accomplices.'

Priebke was glad to be of service. 'Of course.'

The priest was hovering, ill at ease. Priebke turned to him like a lord to his scullion.

'That will be all for today.'

Father Filipović gave a half-bow and, indicating to his acolytes to follow him, left the café.

The vermouth made Reder peckish. 'Let's have some canapés.'

All growled agreement, so Priebke called over the waiter.

From the street, it was not only beggars that looked hungrily at the three big men in uniform. Well-dressed ladies with emaciated faces and elderly fathers in frock coats flapping on thin frames looked as if they were salivating as they passed Rosati and the plate of canapés.

Fröhlich soon took his leave of his brothers. The priest's revelations about FitzGerald had given Fröhlich pause for thought. As he strode away from Rosati, he was cudgelling his brain as to how he might get hold of that Irishman before he could cause real trouble.

DR SCOTTI

Meanwhile, well north of Rome, in the foothills of the Maiella National Park, both FitzGerald and Goode were hurriedly tying their bootlaces after hearing the stirring of leaves outside their bothy.

A voice, speaking English with an Italian accent, called to them through the door.

'Mr FitzGerald! Mr Goode! Do not shoot. I am Dr Scotti, a cousin of Riva Lucia's mother.'

When there was no immediate reply, he called: 'Can you hear me? I am the doctor. La Riva's cousin!'

The same thought crossed both minds: *how could anybody know where they were, unless they had been followed*? Yet the man Goode let in did not look like a fascist informer. A short, balding man with a large black moustache, natty in knickerbockers and an alpine jacket, bustled in, carrying a loaf of bread and a small churn.

He shot a cheery smile at the two suspicious men. That and the whiff of fresh bread, the sight of the milk in the opened churn and Dr Scotti's enthusiasm soon improved their responses and FitzGerald thanked him for producing breakfast.

The doctor explained that he had driven by car to the village below in order to pick them up and carry the injured colonel as far away from the devils as could be managed. They needed to get further into the mountains as all the communities of the foothills were being combed for supplies and young men; hundreds were being taken for labour.

'But how did you know where to find us?'.

The doctor gave an enigmatic smile but did not answer; he diverted their attention with more up-to-date information than they had had since leaving PG500. To the southwest of them, the devils were defending the Gustav Line below Monte Cassino, but that line was being thinned out as they prepared to retreat northwards. Where FitzGerald was aiming for, it was expected that, by the end of October, Montgomery's forces would be crossing the river.

It did not take many minutes for FitzGerald and Goode to swallow breakfast, pack up their few belongings and follow the doctor down the hillside in the direction of the village. At the junction in the road, at which the way to the village forked to the left and the continuing road south forked right, there was a motor car with a woman hovering impatiently about it.

FitzGerald recognised Lucia immediately, though she wore a nurse's outfit of blue and white that made her look almost metallic in the pale light of the moon. He wanted to ask her where they were heading, but this was not the right moment. They were exposed in the moonlight at a treeless crossroads, with a now-agitated Dr Scotti at his heels.

Lucia and FitzGerald hesitated for an instant, probably both wanting to ask questions, but the doctor, pointing at Goode, hovering behind them, directed, 'Get him inside, don't stand there.'

Lucia slipped round to the boot of the car, tugged it open to reveal a space made larger by excavating under the back seat, and gestured for Goode to climb in. Both he and FitzGerald noticed the pungent petrol fumes, but realised that it was no good worrying about poisoning if the alternative was capture.

As FitzGerald got into the back of the car, he realised for the first time that the door panel had a red cross painted on it. This partly explained how the doctor was able to drive about the countryside during curfew without being riddled with bullets. He gingerly put his weight on the one part that had not had its struts removed from underneath to make Goode's hidey-hole and tried to look relaxed.

The doctor drove fast on a narrow winding road, raised about the surrounding country on an embankment with deep ditches on either side. It was an eerie night. The moon, like a huge rusty coin, had barely risen above the level of the vines and long, tattered streams of mist floated about the fields. There was not a living soul to be seen. The blackout and the curfew had done their work well.

They crossed a little bridge over the stream that flowed between high, grass- covered embankments. A farm stood alone like a guardhouse on the far side of the bridge. They roared through a hamlet and then followed a winding road that eventually crossed another stream.

Fitzgerald calculated that they were heading almost due south now.

At a sharp bend in the road, they crossed an irrigation canal by a bridge, and after a while came to a junction with a signpost. They appeared to be near the main road because Fitzgerald could hear traffic and distinguish the peculiar whining sound that the treads of cross-country tyres of army vehicles make on a hard surface.

They must have covered many miles, still without seeing anybody, when they approached, from below, a township that looked about the same size as Ginestra, with a large castle and a church with the spire looming up in the middle of it.

'Fortress of the prince,' said the doctor in a relaxed tone that suddenly changed to urgent. '*Carabinieri*. Get down.'

There were two figures on the road ahead, and one of them was waving the car to a halt with a torch. The left passenger seat was occupied by the doctor's gladstone. The doctor turned round, took his hand from the steering wheel and lifted the leather bag with one hand. With the other, he stretched over, got hold of FitzGerald's head, forced it down and put the bag on top of him, while giving instructions to Lucia, who had seized the steering wheel. When the doctor resumed direction of his car, she unfolded a blanket over FitzGerald, just as the car came to a stop.

FitzGerald could hear the doctor cranking down the side window and could see the glare of the *carabiniere*'s torch through the blanket when he shot it into the car.

'Hello boys!' The doctor's tone was both authoritative and comradely.

The response was verging on being mistrusting. 'Doctor, where have you come from?'

'I've just had an emergency case. Pneumonia.'

'And now?'

'What do you think?' he said testily, 'I'm going home to bed.'

There was a pause. Fitzgerald wondered if the doctor had been believed. The *carabinieri* seemed to be walking round the car. He tensed, expecting to be exposed at any moment. Then he heard: 'Doctor, do you have a moment to look at my skin?'

'Why, of course. What's the trouble?'

FitzGerald heard the doctor get out of the car.

'I shall have to take off my breeches. Can we go into the shelter?'

At first Lucia sat tight in case the other *carabiniere* should saunter over to investigate the car. She saw that there was a shack built of wood, big enough for two to sit in. Then, remembering the gladstone, she got out, picked up the bag and took it to him.

'Doctor, your bag.'

As she knelt down and placed it beside him, partly to avoid looking at the sergeant's bare thighs, for he sat on the bench with his breeches and long johns pulled below his knees, covering his jackboots, she nevertheless glanced at his face. He was a strong-jawed man with a curling moustache over full lips. He had long eyelashes and thick eyebrows: a powerful-looking man. As she stared, he took off his bicorn and she saw a full head of dark, wavy hair. She thought he looked much as Domenico would have looked in another twenty years.

'*Signorina*, do you not recognise me?' As he asked, he reached for his cloak, which was scarlet-lined with a metal chain and clasps that jingled as he moved it, and laid it over his bare thighs. Dr Scotti, prevented from conducting his examination, looked up in surprise.

She had risen, concerned lest the man pay more attention to her than to his own illness, and retreated to the car. Now she turned back.

'Yes,' her heart pumped with the shock of realising that this man had been stationed at Ginestra. That he had probably seen her every day for years.

'You were with the Station Sergeant.'

The man smiled. 'I was a corporal then. I am now a sergeant.' Perhaps because he had remembered about her marriage and her husband's death, a shadow flitted over his face and he looked uncomfortable, tongue-tied.

'Congratulations.' She understood from his face that the recognition was not a disaster and relief poured over her. The discomfort – of both of them, though for different reasons – was ended by the doctor.

'Nurse, I need hot water.'

The sergeant had a nasty rash all up one leg, itchy and now bleeding from being scratched. It was an allergy with which the doctor was familiar, so he ordered Lucia to warm up some water on the tiny paraffin stove he carried to cauterise his instruments, had her bathe it and provided a soothing cream, telling the uncomfortable sergeant how to deal with it in the days ahead.

'Doctor, I am in your debt. *Bacia la mano*, I kiss your hand.' The sergeant kissed the doctor's hand several times as the nurse stowed away her equipment, returning to her seat beside the driver. Then, when Doctor Scotti was back before the wheel and had switched the lamps back on, the Sergeant looked over at Lucia, to whom it seemed as if his eyes were twinkling. 'Thank you nurse,' he called out, and put his hand on his heart.

Beyond the township the car left the main road, such as it was, and entered a labyrinth of small lanes, at which juncture FitzGerald was once more allowed to come to the surface. There were neither houses nor any other buildings to be seen. It was cooler and there was low-lying fog, dense in places.

They drove for some time along a road on top of a dyke, the biggest they had yet seen, high above the tops of the trees that grew in the low ground on either side. Then they turned off down a sort of ramp and followed a long, uphill ride through plantations of poplars which covered the foothills for some miles, until finally the car stopped in the middle of one of them and they heard what seemed to be a million frogs all croaking at once.

Lucia hurried round to the boot and rescued Goode, who came out stiff and cold; he jumped up and down to restore circulation and some warmth. The doctor handed them their packs. Silently, they all left the car and walked up a narrow track through the woods for about half an hour before arriving in a clearing.

There was a lean-to propped up against two of the larger trees, a place for temporary shelter from the elements for foresters and mushroom pickers. After the comfort, or at least warmth, of Zanoni's bed, it was disappointing.

Lucia explained. 'You won't have to stay in this place long. The house that will take you is quite near, but we think it would be better if you stayed here for a couple of nights in case the car was followed.'

The doctor added, with a self-deprecating smile, 'It's one thing to have you and me arrested, but quite another if they find you in the farmer's home and kill everybody.'

Without asking FitzGerald if he wanted advice, Dr Scotti told him to sit down on the bench under the lean-to, checked the colonel's plaster cast and demanded details of the break and what the hospital doctor had said. He told FitzGerald that if it were to heal permanently, he must rest it for another four to six weeks.

Lucia handed them each a small bottle of insect repellent. 'You may need this; there are many mosquitoes. Put it on your face and hands. At noon tomorrow a man will come here. He will whistle three times, as if he were whistling to his dog, like this.' At this point she gave a rather muted imitation of what it would sound like. The doctor took over from her and did the imitation better.

'Has he got a dog?' Goode asked.

'No!' Doctor Scotti glared at Goode. 'He is about 45 and he has a beard. You can call him Giovanni. If it is safe, he may take you to his house. There is enough food and water here to last you until he comes.'

Lucia went on with her instructions: 'Don't drink the water in the ditches. Don't use all your water and the food because he may not come. If not, another may come, or I. If anything happens to either of us, you will hear from others.'

About to get back into the car to leave, Scotti turned round again: 'If you can't get through to the River Sangro, we will get you to Switzerland.'

Neither man wanted that.

'We are going to the river,' said Goode, 'to the Biferno.'

The doctor ignored him, 'The nearest village is in that direction; don't go to it until we have made sure it is safe. Whatever you do, if we don't come back, don't try to go back down. Climb up. Make for the mountains.'

'If you don't come back?' Goode asked.

Lucia replied. 'If we don't come back, it is because they have taken us or killed us.'

FitzGerald looked at Lucia. Her tone was matter-of-fact, without a trace of that undisciplined emoting that he ascribed to Italians. *Yet*, he thought, *she knows what will happen to her if she's caught.* Looking at her, he, for the first time, told himself that she was both a beautiful woman and a brave woman. *It's the bravery that makes her beautiful, not merely lovely to look at. Oh, but stop it, FitzGerald!*

When you rely upon someone to convey or carry out orders, you need to be confident of the man's skills, not his personality or looks. These Italians are always going on about personality, relationships, that kind of stuff, which is probably why they are so bad at soldiering. Yet, this has its plus side. Had the Riva woman and her peasant people been more modern, conformed to rule by law rather than rule by personal feeling, they would never have stuck their necks out for us. Remember the little girl who called me "Papa" in the presence of the Huns. These people! So quick-witted, so brave!

They went down back to the car to see off the doctor and his nurse. FitzGerald saw that Lucia turned and glanced back at him as the car drive off. *I'd have liked to talk to her, understand what she's doing, so far from home.*

The moon was shining between the tree trunks. It was chilly and damp, because the area was irrigated by a network of shallow ditches, and incredibly noisy. By comparison, the croaking of the frogs outside the Zanonis' farm had been a mere gurgling, but even the racket these frogs made was not loud enough to drown out the noise of the gigantic mosquitoes, which, thirsting for human blood, dived on them.

Goode remarked laconically, 'It's like the Stukas when they used to come howling down to bomb the harbour at Tobruk.'

FitzGerald grunted. Returning to the lean-to, they laid out the blanket that the doctor had given them, got into their sleeping bags, rubbed their arms, hands and face with the ointment that Lucia had supplied, put their heads in their packs to shield themselves from mosquito attack and fell asleep. The last picture that came into FitzGerald's mind was of Lucia, turning her head to look at him, a slight smile on her lips.

THE FRIEND OF THE FRIENDS

Twenty-four hours later, nobody had arrived. They passed time by telling each other stories in Italian, acting out imagined conversations until drowsy.

On the second morning FitzGerald woke with the light. Goode was still asleep. FitzGerald put on his boots then, slowly lifting himself with his crutches, got himself upright. He would take his morning exercise. As he hobbled along, always keeping an eye on the topography so that he might find his way back to the shelter, a few drops of rain landed on him. *Refreshing*, he thought, lifting up his face for more. It was not yet hot and, he said to himself, *the sort of temperature in which we could march most comfortably, were it not for my infernal crutches.*

After half an hour or so he was about to turn back when he came to a mountain stream, with fresh water cascading over pebbles and grasses. As he knelt down to bathe his face in the cold flow and drink from it, he heard voices. He pulled himself up and walked downstream away from the shelter until he unexpectedly found himself next to a pool beside which five girls were scrubbing linen, pounding the washing against the rocks. Beside them were straw-plaited baskets.

Two of them were probably late teenagers, the others younger. They did not seem disturbed to see him, but giggled at his evident astonishment. A sixth, childlike, girl appeared from behind them and went up to FitzGerald: 'Are you a German?'

'No I am –' he hesitated for a minute – 'an American. Why?'

'Mamma says that the Germans will kill us. But I don't know why. Will you Americans kill us too?'

'No.'

'Then come and eat with my family.' She looked at his crutches with compassion. 'You must be tired.'

To FitzGerald's astonishment, she took him by the hand as if he, not she, were a child, and led him up a steep sloping path, a basket of damp laundry on her left shoulder, pausing each time he struggled to get his footing.

The rain pattered on the leaves. A few moments later, from above, from wherever they were heading, he could hear a song, shrill children's voices and, after a few minutes, as the music came closer and closer, they came across five little singers walking along the track and leading three pigs.

'*O campagnola bella,*
    [O lovely girl of the countryside,]
tu sei la reginella.
    [You are the queen.]
*Negli occhi tuoi c'e il sole c'e il colore delle viole, delle valli
    tutte in fior...*
    [In your eyes I see the sun, the violets and the valleys
    in bloom...']

The singing stopped and the children halted uncertainly, staring at FitzGerald.

One child, who was clearly scared, asked, 'Eh, Maria, have you found a German?'

'No, an American.'

A slightly older girl gave a laugh and called out: 'Ow! Maria has found America!'

His guide's warm, soft hand left his dangling beside his left crutch and he felt a sudden pitch of disappointment. The child putting her hand in his made him happy in a way he could not analyse. Instead, he thought about her name. *Another Maria. Is that because the real god of these peasants is Gaia, the earth mother of eons before Christ, who has to be wrapped in the swaddling clothes of the Virgin Mary in order to pass muster with the priests?* As this flitted through his mind, FitzGerald hoped he looked fatherly rather than military, and asked, 'Where are you going with the pigs?'

'To forage for acorns in the wood.' With that, the older child turned away from him, back to the business in hand. 'Come on everybody.' She marched to the front of her little team and led them past FitzGerald and the first Maria.

The children grinned up at him and put their hands out to tap FitzGerald as they passed, *perhaps to see if I am real*, he wondered.

His guide took his hand again as they continued up the track to a clearing where there was a farm, looking, to FitzGerald, even poorer than those before. As they approached, three naked infants rushed out. In the yard were pigs, a donkey, pens with pigeons, two dogs and a coop of chickens.

The infants stopped when they saw him and stared silently. FitzGerald understood that they were not afraid, just curious. Was it because they, so far from civilisation, had simply never come across a beast or man who threatened them?

Three women whom FitzGerald gauged were in their thirties appeared, stout and wearing shapeless dresses in a dark hue. They stared at him, saying nothing, until an older woman, her grey hair tied back in a bun, with an air of authority about her, came out, wiping her hands on her apron. Behind her tottered a very elderly man whom FitzGerald rightly guessed to be her father. She spoke: 'Welcome! Welcome to our home.'

Her father mumbled something into her ear but she overruled him.

'My father thinks you are a spy. But I say a man with a good face like yours cannot be a wicked spy. Come in.'

FitzGerald followed Maria into a cavernous living room. Everywhere there were sacks of grain and jars of preserved vegetables. There was a tiny charcoal fire around which the family had probably been sitting.

Framed on the wall were certificates of military service in "The Great War for Civilisation", yellowed by the cooking smoke. *Even these people, so far from the cities, had been corralled into our wars,* FitzGerald found himself thinking. He imagined some 18-year-old from this farm sloshing about in the muddy trenches of World War One, wounded, uncomprehending and lost. He suddenly felt pity, then anger, at the unjustness of war, how it destroys the little happiness that poor people can make for themselves. A glass-fronted cabinet had faded photographs, of couples in wedding day clothes, tucked into the edge of the glass panels.

'Sit,' the matriarch commanded him.

'I have a companion.'

'Bring him.' She addressed the Maria who had brought, as FitzGerald began to see it, this calamity upon them. 'Maria, go fetch the other guests.'

FitzGerald wished good morning to the old grandfather who was without teeth, wore a faded trilby and a patched waistcoat, but the old man merely nodded.

Outside the rain had whipped up, beating down on the roof and running down the wooden door.

The matriarch turned to her preparations, pouring maize flour into a great black cauldron of boiling water over the fire and stirring it with a wooden ladle until it formed a paste. Glancing at the watching FitzGerald, she explained the yellow flour by pointing to the maize cobs hanging in clusters from the roof. The smoke-blackened ceiling was covered with them. It was polenta once more.

After half and hour or so, while FitzGerald attempted to banter with the children who gathered round to stare at him, Goode was brought in by Maria, looking like a damp and dishevelled schoolboy. The matriarch eyed him, head to feet, as if assessing a farm animal at market. '*Ma che bel ragazzo!* What a handsome boy! Sit down.'

Then the door opened again and Oleksiy and the Greek stumbled in, dripping from the rain outside, and bowed to the women. They had been driven up by the doctor through the early hours, waved through the *carabinieri* post, left on the outskirts of Pozzo and told to go up a track to this house.

Oleksiy knew more than FitzGerald: 'We are on the outskirts of the village of Pozzo, which is the home of the nurse's grandparents.' They were just over a kilometre above Pozzo, at a farm approached only by a stony track from the village, up which Oleksiy and Stavros had climbed. FitzGerald and Hood had been housed a kilometre further west of the farm where they now were, not far from the road and from where Pozzo was invisible.

The matriarch sighed, looked them up and down. 'So many poor sparrows, far from home and mother. What a world! I shall wash you all now. Where have you been, so wet and dirty? Take off your clothes and let me dry them.'

When the men hesitated, she encouraged them with, 'Don't be shy! I wash my own menfolk!'

They stripped to their undershorts. With four clean linen cloths dipped in almost boiling water, the matriarch sluiced them all down and handed each one a cloth to deal with his more intimate ablutions. She then produced cloths for them to dry themselves. While this was going on, the father shuffled off and came back with four spanking new German greatcoats, which they tried on.

Goode fingered the insignia on his new greatcoat and beamed.

Once the men were wrapped in their stolen greatcoats, the steam from their own clothing rising around the stove and the water on the floor had been mopped away, the room started to fill up with women and children gazing in awe at the four big men. The matriarch turned the result of her labours with the maize flour out onto the table, where it lay for the moment in a great steaming mass before she cut it into strips with a piece of string.

After they had eaten, and when the singing had petered out, Goode turned to his haversack. He had a reserve of goodies assembled from Red Cross parcels, including chocolate and cigarettes, which he presented to the matriarch. There were gobstoppers, which he gave to the children. They unwrapped them in wonder, sucking them slowly and every few minutes taking them out of their mouths to gaze at them and see whether they were diminishing.

When the food had been cleared away, the old man took a jug of wine and poured each of the visitors a large beaker.

After asking his guests where Ireland was, about their parents and their wives, the old man complained about the lack of manpower and how useless women were at farm work.

Goode volunteered. 'Can we do something to assist you?'

The woman butted in. 'Yes. Go with my father.' As she spoke, the old man straightened himself in his chair. 'Work with him in the fields.'

Goode: 'We can, but not for long; we must leave you in peace.'

Before FitzGerald could intervene, she did. 'No. You stay now. Later, the call comes.'

FitzGerald: 'Call?'

'The friend of the friends knows that you are safe here. It will be dangerous for you to move too soon. The friend will come and get you.'

Perhaps it was the warm, heavy food, perhaps it was the wine, perhaps it was the sensation of being mothered, but FitzGerald did not want to argue back. He had somehow gradually accepted that he was no longer the authority, the decision maker. He felt a laziness encumbering his mind. A wistfulness about this beautiful landscape, with these protective women in their run-down homes, suffused him. Goode was about to remonstrate, perhaps to query who this "friend" might be, but FitzGerald gestured with his hand to stop him and concurred.

'Very well. Show us how to do what your men ought to be doing.' He trusted her, or else he just did not want to think any more, or make more calculations.

Goode looked at him as if he could not quite believe what his chief was saying.

'Tomorrow,' said the old man. 'Today is your feast of welcome.'

The next day, and over the following days, Goode, Oleksiy and Stavros went off to dig the fields high up, where it was too steep for the plough. They had two hoes between them, with blades a foot long. The first blow of the ground told Goode what the day would be like. The blade came out thick with clay, so that he had to clean the blade after every other stroke. And so on, all day. Goode shared the work with the Greek and the Ukrainian.

FitzGerald was given tasks that he could do sitting down. He sewed sacks and did repairs on wooden furniture under an awning in the yard. Sitting at a home-made table, he would rise every hour or so to lumber up and down for twenty minutes.

On the lower, easier slopes, the old man was ploughing. FitzGerald could see that ploughing was not easy. Was it the wrong time of year? The oxen stumbled in the clay. The cloven hooves sank deep and each step was an effort. The old man had to goad, feed and use pet names, as well as curses and yells of rage. If the storm of demands slackened, the ox ceased to pull. Sometimes the man was at the tail of the plough, leaning on the handles; sometimes he was at the beast's heads, tugging at their horn or nose ring, with his feet slipping and sliding in the mire. The oxen pawed the ground and blew huge puffs of steam.

At midday, the women came into the fields with a basket of hot, baked dough, a kind of pizza, wrapped in a cloth, a piece of cheese, and a bottle of thin wine.

As light faded, one of the younger women came to rescue them and they dragged their weary limbs back to the farm. Speechless with exhaustion, they ate in silence while the females chattered around them. The old man too was silent, slurping his polenta.

Once the polenta was all eaten, the men sipped their wine until the old man rose, went to a corner and came back with an accordion which he started to play. Little by little, first the adults and then the children began to sing.

'*Campanelle che ssuone mattutine (din don)*
 [The bells which sound in the morning (ding dong)]
S'arisbejje nghe ll'angele li cille (din don)
 [Wake with the angels and the birds (ding dong)]
Ma ci sta na fijole tante bbelle (din don)
 [But there's a girl so beautiful (ding dong)]
Chi jje piace lu suonne la matine. (din don)
 [Who loves the morning bells. (ding dong)]'

After a few songs, heads started to nod and the old man led them out to the byre to sleep with the oxen, who were white and long-horned with huge, liquid eyes and wet muzzles. The four companions lay on sacking in the straw, using their haversacks as pillows and the looted greatcoats to cover them. They fell asleep immediately.

FitzGerald woke often throughout the night and listened to the faint clunking of oxen, who had bells round their necks, pushing and shoving against each other and the chains from their stalls, then another kind of clomp, clomp as they chewed the cud. From their bellies came long rumbling belches as they digested the chopped fodder of leaves and grass. Their dung splashed on the floors and flecked the sleeping men.

I shall soon walk as well as before, FitzGerald thought. *I am well-fed, I am in the most beautiful landscape, and I am free of constraints and responsibilities. Why not stay in the hills, work for some of the peasants whose men are far away? Forget war, promotion, Ireland, the US. I could take a girl, a farmer's daughter, and settle down. My accumulated pay would buy us a farm easily.* As he imagined himself exploring female flesh, his thoughts turned to Lucia, wondering where she was and marvelling at her incessant activity on their behalf. Did she have to cajole their hosts, or was generosity just the way of life? Is this *xenia*, the sacredness of hospitality?

Then, irritation with her, a kind of resentment, banished his fantasies. *I am a soldier whose duty it is to return to lead my unit in the liberation of this benighted country and exterminate the oppressors.* He turned over and went back to sleep.

Every morning, the atmosphere was heavy with ammonia. As he stumbled out into the yard, his eyes would stream. A dash of cold water cleared his head. In the kitchen, the matriarch would be fanning a charcoal stove to boil a pan of thin milk. The children were running in and out, hungry, smelling of sleep, urine and unwashed clothes. The old man came in. As usual he said nothing, probably turning over in his mind the day's work. Breakfast was home-made bread, broken into a bowl of warm milk.

One day the matriarch said to FitzGerald: 'Now you will go to the empty farmhouse nearby.'

FitzGerald looked askance.

'It was a message from your friend.'

'Our friend?'

'*L'innominato*, the nameless one,' she laughed, but said no more.

Perhaps, thought FitzGerald, *we do too little useful work so we should be made to forage for ourselves. Or maybe they don't have enough food.*

The house to which they were taken, on the instructions of the "unnamed", had clearly been abandoned many years before. On the lower floor were chickens. A rope ladder that could be hauled up through a hole in the ceiling was how they would get to the upper floor, to sleep.

It was the sixth week on the run, 11th October, when FitzGerald cut off his plaster cast. He stood up, wobbling. Goode was watching him, ready to lunge forward and stop him toppling. Together, they walked out to find the matriarch hurrying towards them.

'Now we'll be off and out of your way soon,' Goode was satisfied. Their packs were ready for this moment. At last they'd be getting back into the fight.

The matriarch 'You cannot go alone; winter comes.' 'Stay, help us in the *vendemmia*, grape harvest! Everybody is happy at the *vendemmia*!'

'We need to get back to work,' Goode argued.

She tried another tack: 'Today the friend of the friends comes. If anyone knows the routes south that are free of enemy, it will be the unnamed,' she revealed with a surreptitious look.

FitzGerald only half believed her. *Where did they get this information from? Was it invented?*

Her daughter-in-law had come down to join the conversation. 'Signora Lucia is coming up the hill now. The signal came.'

Goode, 'Lucia Riva?'

'Yes.' The daughter-in-law was proud. 'She's the one who got all six hundred prisoners out of the camp at Ginestra. A miracle!'

'I know her. We come from Ginestra.'

FitzGerald and Goode, their packs loaded, went out into the yard and the women gathered around them to form a little crowd.

At that moment the dogs started barking, the infants started running and everybody turned to the yard entrance. There, walking in, was Lucia, at the head of a crowd of local women, holding by the hand a small boy dressed in a tattered smock.

FitzGerald stiffened and started forward as if to greet her but then pulled himself together.

Lucia looked through the others crowding around him, smiled. 'So, Colonel, you've not left us, gone back to war?'

'Impossible, Signora Riva. You have done so much.'

She ignored this compliment. 'Bregante Salvatore, the children and I are in a house near here. The Germans have given up their search. For the moment, we can relax.'

The boy pulled her arm and she glanced down at him. 'This, Colonel, is Enrico. We travel together.'

'So Mr Bregante has not returned with his family to Greppo?'

'No. The devils made the house uninhabitable. They smashed everything, even the cat's saucer.'

'Thank God you were all out of the way.'

'We weren't. Bisnonna stayed. They… I won't describe what they did to my husband's grandmother.' She swallowed and passed a hand over her eyes, as if to block out some terrible vision. 'Bisnonna died alone.'

Later, they sat together around the table in the old kitchen that served as FitzGerald's desk and the four men's dining table. For a long time, no-one spoke. Enrico squatted in a corner, his eyes fixed on the four men.

PEASANT LIFE

While FitzGerald and Goode had been absorbed into peasant life on the farm, waiting for FitzGerald's leg to heal, Lucia had, occasionally with the use of Dr Scotti's car, but usually by foot or donkey, been visiting the hamlets and isolated bothies where fugitives were holed up. She organised young boys to lead Jews, deserters, even two downed pilots, hated for their bombing raids, to hideouts whence they might set out for the coast. She found bicycles for them to ride, oxcarts in which to hide, clothing to disguise them. Through the grapevine, she learned that *Inglesi* commandos had already evacuated dozens from the east coast.

She herself had trudged down and up beaten tracks and goat paths, carrying soap and medicaments, spare clothing, candles and tobacco. She connected the men and their hosts, with the wider world; she was proof that they were not abandoned, and she passed on such news as she had of their fellows or of the war generally.

She wore out several pairs of shoes in the rain and slush. She learnt not to be afraid of the wild boars, but how to avoid their haunts. She repressed her dread of the eerie dark of the mountains and forests and ignore the constant sensation of ghouls and trolls peering out from among the chestnut trees.

In the towns, which she knew well, she always felt watched and was unsure whom, aside from the three older women, her own mother, the *dottoressa* and Donna Chiara, she should trust. Yet she felt confident among any of the country people and, in the hills, safe. *Why? I am not really one of them. Except that they, confronted with a choice, obey their instincts. As I suppose I did, though only after resisting them.*

Lucia shuddered. *I never need to go to the towns again. This is my life, for the war will go on. I must show these soldiers how to be real men. That colonel has already changed. I can tell, even if he cannot, that he is a different man. Not the young one, though; he is still a boy, like my Domenico. They are brainless when they are young.*

She was on her way back to Pozzo after a long day and was about a mile from the house when Enrico rushed out from behind a broken-down shrine and into her arms. As usual, he said nothing but clasped her hungrily.

'Oh, you naughty boy. Uncle Salvatore will be so worried about you. How long have you been here?'

He unclasped her and looked up into her face, his lip trembled a little. 'Morning.'

'You followed me this morning?'

He nodded slowly, his eyes still fixed on her.

'I'll always come back to you, Enrico; you don't need to worry. And next time I take the mule you can come with me.'

A great smile grew on his face and he stepped forward and once again put his arms around her thighs and clasped himself to her.

Looking out over the path she had just taken, Lucia began to talk.

'You know, Enrico, although we can't keep track of more than half of those who left Ginestra, I still haven't once heard of a recapture of any of them. Isn't that wonderful?'

The boy now walked beside her, a proud partner. She spoke to him as if he were her accomplice, whether he understood or not. 'The local people like to see me with you, Enrico; the forester chuckled you under the chin, the *Inglesi* used that old shoe to play football with you, the captain calls you my *copin,* my mate. You camouflage me, do you know what I mean? If I were without you, I'd not be respectable! Only a short time ago, if a man spoke with me, I would down my eyes and hurry past. Now they do what you and I want.' She stopped a moment and looked down into the child's face with something of the adoration of a mother for a son. 'Did you see, Enrico, how the elders of Pozzo, Dr Scotti, the Station Sergeant of *carabinieri,* all ask me, just an insignificant girl without a husband, what to do?'

The house to which they headed had been allocated to FitzGerald and his companions at a meeting of the local menfolk, who had listened to a respectful proposal from Riva Lucia. She had appealed to their charity and, most of all, she made them feel that when they held out an arm to the outcasts, they were chivalrous, *galantuomini.* She did not hide the risks involved from them.

What Lucia did not pass on to the elders was that Captain Foschini expected that this particular farmhouse would become a hub from which the fugitives of the area could be located, then reallocated when a host family could no longer cope, to those who needed a handy man or two. After she had helped with information gathering, Foschini intended to call upon the men she had identified to join the partisan operations, though he did not share this with Lucia.

Once they arrived, Enrico ate and slept while the adults talked for several hours. Goode at some point got up, unnoticed, and went outside. Then, there was a long silence, until suddenly broken by a crash as a group of small children in ragged clothes and dirty faces, flung open the door and rushed in, stopping before the big foreigner to gawp. The seriousness left Lucia's face and she looked down merrily at the children, beckoning them closer. They crowded in around her. Woken by the hubbub, Enrico got up and stood beside Lucia, as if claiming her as his. FitzGerald saw that as she continued to chat to the little visitors, her arm went around the child whom she had brought with her, and his cheek rested on her.

As he watched her, he turned over in his mind the obstacle that she had related to him and Goode earlier. Not many kilometres away from what had, in effect, become a headquarters, the factor of the Vacca estates had been round his peasants, demanding that they immediately expel any fugitives they were harbouring and warning them that the militia would be called in to punish anyone who did not do so. Goode wanted to kill the landlord; FitzGerald was beginning to think that he needed to pull together some of the fugitives into a *banda*, to make a show of force. Violence was on the cards.

NOBILITY

Perhaps Lucia's successes had fostered in her a sense of invincibility, because her plan, to confront the landowner, and convince the son of one fascist general and brother of another, that he should turn a blind eye to what was going on throughout his estates, was a tall order. To beard Vacca, she did understand that she needed to engage diverse skills and networks, in particular those of the Sanvitales.

Lucia made use of Dr Scotti's motor and Gino's cart to get back to Greppo. The burial of Bisnonna had been immediate, the neighbours had seen to that, so the obsequies had been performed and Bisnonna already rested in the family plot.

After finishing the cleaning of the house that the neighbours had commenced, Lucia set out for Ginestra, first calling upon the Croat priest to thank him and settle his fees.

She was not at ease with Father Filipović, nor, by the look of him, was he with her. The big, fleshy man with the ginger-blond hair stood in the vestry beside a polished table on which was a huge silver monstrance, a tin of silver cleaning paste and some gilt-edged books. He did not ask her to sit down, presumably, she surmised, because she was a woman. *Dear old Don Carmelo would never have been so cold*, she thought as she stood before his successor; the

Croat and the late Father Carmelo had been at daggers on account of the Croat's rigidity about obligations.

'Fortunately, I had been to Greppo only a week previously and taken the *signora's* confession,' he informed Lucia, 'you may take comfort from her sins having been remitted.'

Lucia just uttered an 'Ah' and lowered her eyes.

'My child, you must feel remorse at what you did, which brought about the dear *signora's* passing. In this moment of penitence, should you be ready to confess to our Lord, do allow me to help you.'

It was a blow to think that Bisnonna's death might be blamed on her siding with the prisoners. But Lucia was no longer the humble recipient of other people's judgments, nor was she going to allow the priest the satisfaction of seeing her writhe.

She managed to take her leave of the parish priest without showing that she understood his accusation and, even before seeing her mother or the *dottoressa*, went to the fortress to confer with her former employer. Donna Chiara was in the library where Lucia herself had, only a year or less before, spent many happy hours cataloguing the collections of several centuries of Sanvitale manuscripts and collating sources for Donna Chiara's study of the medieval merchants of Palma.

As the footman announced her, opening the door with a white-gloved hand, the countess rose from her boule desk with a warm smile, ran towards the younger woman and embraced her.

'These days you say farewell to someone and never know if you will ever see them again. The heart is a maw of fear and agitation. I am so happy to see you, my darling Lucia.'

At that moment, Don Maurizio ambled in and smiled at Lucia.

After curtseying, Lucia explained that Don Carlo Vacca had, some ten days after the *Inglesi* had escaped from PG500, been found to be threatening his peasants with losing their homes and livelihoods should they shelter fugitives, and that she hoped the Sanvitales would deal with this. The Sanvitales, with their many centuries of quarterings behind them, might not see the recently ennobled Vacca as on a par with them, but – perhaps just because of this – the Vacca family would respect their advice.

The American woman was alert to Lucia's assumptions and gave a ringing laugh. 'Oh, you understand the *nobiloni* very well.'

'Shall we appeal to their Christian feelings?' Lucia queried.

Donna Chiara chuckled. 'Coming from the *dottoressa*'s student, that's a bit rich.'

Her husband mused over the point: 'The marquis is a member of the Papal Guard and his uncle is a bishop, but the younger brother, Carlo, who lives on the estate, is just a playboy. You could get somewhere with him because he will certainly care more about the survival of the estate than about political commitments. Anyway, he is managed by his mother, who is pretty pragmatic.'

Don Maurizio was uncomfortable shopping his near neighbours and tried to exculpate them: 'They are not really fascists, just selfish.'

The countess laughed. 'To them you are a Christian if you go to Mass a few times a week, give lunch to the bishop three times a year and donate a chasuble to the church. We should appeal to their self-interest. The trouble is, since they know that Don Maurizio and I are out-and-out Anglophiles, we would not be very convincing to them.'

Disappointed, Lucia surmised that her friend did not want to draw the attention of the Vaccas to her own family or put themselves, or the refugees they protected, at risk of investigation and discovery. She had predicted this response but was determined to involve them.

'Will you ask Captain Foschini to talk to them? Perhaps to represent the greater interests of the upper classes? He is not noble, but is thought to be on the same side politically.'

Not long after agreeing to Lucia's proposal, Donna Chiara took action. Perhaps because she wanted to draw Foschini further into her web of rescuers, or maybe she wanted to put the two young people together, the countess was keen to get Foschini mobilised.

In two days' time, he would drive Lucia to the Palazzo Vacca, ex-Villa Carignani, in the Sanvitale's Daimler, the only such car in the vicinity and thus easily recognisable. The delay was to give time to find a respectable British officer to join the delegation.

Lucia decided that, despite the logistical hurdles to be overcome in bringing the *Inglesi* to join the party, they should be accompanied by FitzGerald. His presence would reassure the Vacca family that the fugitives to be succoured were not mere hoi polloi but gentlemen who might be influential with the Allied authorities, who were expected to be in power before long. Then they might as well add Goode to the party, not only because he spoke Italian, but also because of the air of menace that accompanied him. All this required some organisation but was judged by Alessandro and Lucia as well worth the effort if it not only frightened the Vacca family into playing ball, but served to demonstrate to all the local landowners that the tide was turning and that it would be more dangerous to remain loyal to the old regime than to help the coming one.

Thus, with FitzGerald and Goode now in suits from the wardrobe of Don Maurizio and Lucia wearing one of Donna Chiara's more formal dresses with matching hat, Alessandro drove the Daimler up the long approach to the villa on the slopes of the hill. From afar he saw a German jeep below the famous double external staircase leading to the front door, so he quickly made a U-turn and tucked the Daimler into a copse by a path that led to a little shrine in the woods. Asking his three passengers to stay in the car, he returned to the drive to remain unseen behind a hedge until its occupants, including a German officer, had been bid farewell on the steps of the villa by a man in blackshirt uniform, and the jeep left.

After a pause to ensure that the Germans really had left, he drove up before the great entrance where, a few minutes before, the Germans had parked. He led his team up the marble steps and tugged at the iron bell pull, waiting hardly a minute before a footman with a claret-coloured and frogged tailcoat answered. The footman's white-gloved hands directed them into an ante-room. His Excellency Don Carlo and Her Excellency Donna Maria Assunta would be informed of the arrival of Captain Foschini Alessandro, 3rd Alpine Division, and his friends. Neither Goode nor FitzGerald spoke in front of the servant.

They were begged to wait here in the Morning Room for "Their Excellencies".

The larger-than-life-size portrait of a man resplendent in the full gala outfit of His Holiness' noble guard loomed over them. Also set in an elaborate and massive gilded frame was a full-length painting of a younger man in the sable uniform of Mussolini's musketeer guard, his black gloved left hand on the pommel of his dagger, his right holding a standard modelled on those of the Roman legions of 2,000 years ago.

FitzGerald stared at the blackshirt's portrait with disgust: 'Foschini, these people are total fascists. I hope you know what you're doing here.'

'They are just timeservers. Don't worry, Colonel, this portrait will come down soon!'

At that moment, the musketeer himself, Don Carlo Vacca, was putting his breeches back on to meet the new visitors whom the butler had situated in the Morning Room. His mother, small, white-haired, wearing a tweed skirt, cashmere twinset and bulky pearls, stood holding his tunic. She was impatient: 'Darling, you should always wear the uniform, I don't know why you took it off.'

'I'll wear it as long as the Germans are around, but otherwise I'll wait and see.'

She gazed at him adoringly. 'In uniform you are so like dear General Starace, but even more handsome.'

'Oh, Mamma, Starace's infant granddaughter peed on the *Duce*. Stop talking about him.' He paused. 'But he dresses well.'

'A gentleman must have a fine uniform. I wish you too were a member of the pope's noble guard with that splendid outfit.'

'Why do these people come here unannounced, at the time of our *seconda colazione*? It's so rude, so not correct.'

'Never mind, dear,' hurried his mother, 'it may be very good for us that they come.'

'Do you think when I go to Sulmona I should wear a helmet with this uniform? Unione Militare has just delivered the lightweight, parade version of the musketeers' helmet to me, on time too. The peasants complain that deliveries of salt don't get through. What nonsense.'

'A helmet is too heavy. Stick with your fez.'

Ignoring her suggestions, the youngest son opened a round, purple box with the insignia of Unione Militare, the officers' tailors, on the top, and lifted out the black helmet, with the skull and crossbones of the musketeers on the front.

'It's very lightweight. Although not correct to wear it with militia uniform, it is more in-keeping with the military situation than the fez with its flashy gold-wire badges.'

'Oh well, if it is really lightweight!'

'Rommel is said to be in Sulmona, and as everybody knows, Rommel is a stickler for correct dress, so I must do things properly.'

As Vacca admired himself in the long glass in his dressing room, pulling in his tummy, he confided to his mother how irritating it was that he would have to wear "that ugly new uniform" when he went up to headquarters at Salò. 'It looks so left-wing.' His mother did not want him to go to Salò and instead encouraged him to think about meeting Rommel in Sulmona.

'I think I shall wear my Order of the Roman Eagle around the neck, in the manner that Germans wear their Knights' Crosses. Captain Foschini downstairs was awarded the Knight's Cross in Russia. It was in the paper. In *Il Popolo d'Italia*.'

It crossed his mother's mind that this Foschini had probably done some fighting to get his cross, but she did not mention this, lest she upset her son.

Donna Maria Assunta cajoled him. 'I shall invite them for

lunch. They can have the *colazione* that was prepared for that rude German. Don't you think?'

'Them? How many of them are there?'

'Captain Foschini, two officers in *borghese,* civvies, and a female whom Esposito says he recognises as the secretary to Countess Chiara. Not quite *tout Paris* but the best we can get these days. '

Her son grumbled. 'Such outdated expressions, Mamma, nowadays you say "*Le Gratin*".' When she apologised, he asked, 'The American woman? Why's she sent her secretary?'

'Oh, I expect Foschini is having her. Or the others are. Or all.' His mother grinned maliciously.

'Is she pretty?'

'In a common, low-class kind of way. You could have her if you want to. You are so handsome and have such charisma. But be careful. The Germans have raped so many girls that there is a lot of that terrible disease about.'

Downstairs, Foschini was explaining to FitzGerald, 'Carlo Vacca is the youngest son. The Vaccas were industrialists in this area for a few generations before they bought this house from the impoverished dukes of Carignani. His father was a general in the North African adventures, created Marquis of El Agheila for his campaigns.

'Carlo boasts that his uncle brought the media under control at the start of the regime. His maternal uncle, Scipione degli Scipioni, is Minister of Marine. His elder brother is that chap up there,' he pointed to the portrait of the man in a Napoleonic outfit, 'and the other is a bishop.'

The double doors of the morning room opened, the butler entered and announced in a voice like a trumpet:

'*Nobildonna* Maria Assunta Vacca Scipione dei Conti Scipione degli Scipioni, Marchesa of El Agheila and Dame of the Illustrious Royal Order of Saint Januarius, and *Nobil Homo* Don Carlo Vacca, dei Marchesi di El Agheila!'

FitzGerald, Goode and Foschini rose from their seats and, after a moment's hesitation, so did Lucia. The woman who greeted them was very short and dressed, Goode thought, like the wife of a Scots laird. Aside from a heavy pearl necklace she wore a large diamond-studded bracelet and matching pendant earrings. She emitted, despite being tiny, an air of intensity and authority.

The contrast with her son was great. He was large, handsome, clean-shaven and straight-backed; nevertheless, there was a simpering quality to his walk and petulance on his lips. To Lucia, who had been spending time with soldiers who looked like ragamuffins, he seemed something out of an opera, with gilded buttons, gleaming riding boots and a gold-wire belt, from which, knocking against his thigh, was a glittering dagger with an eagle's head pommel.

Donna Maria Assunta announced in the voice of a woman twice her size, 'My dear friends, do sit down, how wonderful to see you.' Casting a glance of admiration at Foschini, she went on: 'Our hero! Ah, how my breast heaves with emotion to see fine men! Admiration, but also consternation! Yet it is God's will! *La guerra è per l'uomo come la maternità è per la donna.* War is for men as motherhood is for women. Don't you think, dearest Captain Foschini?'

Foschini ignored the question, bowed, kissed her hand, thanked Donna Maria Assunta for finding time to see them and then introduced his companions. At the sound of the English names, Don Carlo started, but his attention was soon fixed on Lucia; his mother showed no emotion at the discovery that two of the enemy were in her morning room, but smoothly carried on as if this was exactly as anticipated: 'Oh, but it is you who have done us such honour, a hero of the terrible Slavic wars brings to us…' she hesitated for a moment as to how to refer to FitzGerald, then went on, 'a knight of the British Empire! The unity of all brave knights! You will lunch with us? Of course you will! I won't take a refusal! By wonderful coincidence we are to be joined by dearest Father Filipović from Ginestra. I have already ordered a simple repast. It will be ready in a few moments. Meanwhile, let me show you around the villa.'

Lucia started at the name of Father Filipović and glanced at Alessandro, whose face revealed nothing.

With that, Donna Maria Assunta turned swiftly to lead a tour of her husband's great house, her guests falling in behind. 'You have already enjoyed our entrance; it was designed in 1673 by the Dominican friar Cirrincione Andrea.'

She marched back into the entrance hall and stopped when her group had all assembled around her, with Lucia last among the guests and her son taking in Lucia's back. 'All the rooms of our *piano nobile* have their 18th century rustic coffered ceilings with decorative motifs perfectly preserved. Let me show you some of the friezes installed by the 17th century dukes of Carignani...'

At lunch, the youngest child of the family, Donna Ippolita, who was the same age as Lucia, also appeared, with Father Filipović behind her. After introductions, she was sat between Foschini and Goode. The absence of ancestors on the walls was made up for by huge landscapes with elaborate gilt frames on every wall, illustrating the charming ruins of Roman civilisation among the woods and hills of 18th century Lazio. The party did not sit at the dining table, which could hold seventy guests, but at the round, and thus more intimate, breakfast table.

Don Carlo had Goode on his left but seemed to prefer to talk with Lucia on his right. In the place of honour on Donna Maria Assunta's right was Foschini and on her left FitzGerald, on whose left was the priest and then Lucia. Goode spoke over Don Carlo to Lucia, which was a relief to her as she had no wish to speak with the priest. Father Filipović was ignored by his hostess, sat in silence with his head turned towards her, concentrating.

Opposite, Goode was discovering that Donna Ippolita's life was planned around appointments with her dressmaker, *La Sarta*. He learnt of little shops in Florence where they made beautiful lace and delicate undergarments for ladies, and Donna Ippolita offered to show him where he might buy something enchanting for his wife. Goode allowed her to imagine that he had a fiancée.

Once she had exhausted the subject of shopping, Donna Ippolita revealed her serious side: 'Would you allow your fiancée to dance with another man? Would you let your wife wear a low-necked evening dress? Would you let your wife go out by herself? Before being married, would you sit in the same room as your fiancée alone? Would it be refined to kiss her?' "Refined" was her most important word.

Goode attempted to move the conversation away from morality and get some idea of the current political situation and what these landowning people thought of it.

'Are you aware, Miss Ippolita, that Mr Mussolini is establishing a new government to rival that of Marshal Badoglio?'

'Oh yes!' Her eyes shone with enthusiasm. 'The *Duce* is the greatest human being ever. He will defend us. Is not Italy the most beautiful country in the world?'

FitzGerald overheard, thought of the hungry villages he and Goode had walked through, full of people that had barely enough food for themselves yet shared what they had with the runaways. He controlled his desire to wolf down the veal on his plate and to mop up every drop of the marsala sauce with bread. *Our hosts today want us to be charmed into thinking well of them. Perhaps that is all you can do, if you want to preserve your patrimony in wartime. Lucia's right to organise this theatre. Our hosts will attach themselves to the winner, as long as they can work out whom that might be; until that time, they must antagonise none. We have to make it easy for them to turn a blind eye to us.*

Goode pondered what Mussolini's comeback might mean for the men hiding out in the hills. Then he was dragged back into gossip by the shrill boast of Donna Ippolita as she called across the table to FitzGerald.

'Isn't Verdi the greatest composer who has ever lived?'

After telling FitzGerald about Italy's superiority, she turned to religion.

'You are not Christians.'

'Yes we are.'

Goode added that he had gone to Sunday School every week as a boy, instructed in the bible by the clergyman's wife.

'Your priests marry so they cannot be Christian.'

He demurred.

'Then what do they believe?'

Goode was keen to explain Presbyterianism.

'You mean you choose your own priest?'

'Something like that,' he said.

'Then he will go to hell. Isn't that true, Father?' She looked across at Father Filipović, who had remained quiet until now.

'Yes, Donna Ippolita, but you must pray for his immortal soul every morning.'

Donna Maria Assunta had just got wise to the nature of the conversation and leant over to admonish her daughter: 'Leave him alone. Maybe our guest is religious in his own way.'

Her mother addressed Goode. 'It is so sad that so many people are homeless at this time, often fine, upstanding gentlemen like you, Captain.'

Goode was vehement. 'It is much worse for others. As we speak, Jewish families with young children and elderly are struggling over the Alps to Switzerland, cold, hungry and afraid.'

'Oh, I know! The Alpine guides are making good money from them. And then they double their money by selling them to the Germans! 10,000 *lire* for every Jew, even children! It's disgraceful!'

Seeing the look on Goode's face, Donna Maria Assunta quickly added that she would never countenance such dishonest behaviour.

In disgust, FitzGerald turned away and caught the eye of the priest.

'Father,' he said, not remembering the man's name, 'If God loves suffering humanity, why doesn't he – instead of doing the odd miracle cure here and there – help out the Jews?'

Filipović affected a face of saintly resignation. Alessandro, listening from the other side of the table, pressed him, for he had been troubled again and again by the memory of the barbarities inflicted in Ukraine. 'Yes, how does the church manage to hold onto the idea that there is a God who cares about us when such a cruel fate is visited upon innocent women and children?'

There was silence over the breakfast table. Everybody was waiting for the priest's reply.

Filipović remained composed and answered in a sermonising tone: 'To suffer is to come closer to God, to know that you will have your reward in Heaven. Perhaps they are the lucky ones.'

There was a silence. Everybody appeared to be thinking hard.

Then Lucia exploded: 'Just for saying that, if there were a hell, you should rot in it! Join the lucky ones yourself!' She rose as if to leave the table, then, remembering her purpose here, sat down, looked away from the priest and her eyes landed on Foschini. The priest blanched and looked down, avoiding eye contact.

FitzGerald noted that. Foschini immediately turned to Don Carlo.

'The crimes of the Germans and those of our own people who have gone along with them must be paid for, sooner rather than later. So, you see Don Carlo, it is very risky for you to antagonise the *Inglesi*.'

Don Carlo blanched.

His mother leaned forward and butted in: 'When my son issued his suggestion to our peasants, he was thinking of wild creatures who might steal and attack our people and crops. He wanted to protect them.' She looked coquettishly at FitzGerald. 'We had no idea that those hiding up in the hills are gentlemen like dear Colonel FitzGerald! Now that we understand the real situation, our peasants will be told to give their best hospitality to the English gentlemen.'

FitzGerald bowed his head slightly, his serious demeanour hiding the scepticism within. To himself, he was sardonic at the part allotted to him by Lucia, that of the representative of the next set of rulers. Yet he was only too aware of the significance of their mission; nothing could be achieved by talking about atrocities that were unimaginable, even unbelievable, to most people. They must focus on getting the landowners to realise that their interests required them to disobey the occupiers. Lucia's machinations, and his own ability to suppress what he felt for their hosts, mattered to the safety of many hiding in the hills, to say nothing of the lives of those who hid them.

He looked over at the woman whom he had once dismissed as a "slip of a girl". Unwillingly, he had come to accept that, in the battles fought behind the lines, her leadership was superior. *We are her cyphers.*

Don Carlo took his cue from his mother. 'Naturally we will do everything in our power to help our friends.'

Foschini: 'You don't need to do anything beyond letting your peasants know that they can aid whomsoever they like, Don Carlo. As long as the Germans think you are on their side, then this area can be safe for the guests.' As he said this, he glanced at Father Filipović, who was looking straight at him.

Lucia watched Alessandro, FitzGerald and Goode at work. While they talked, she took in the silk wallpaper, the great gilded picture frames, the mighty table with its silver gilt centrepieces, the heavy silver cutlery with which she was eating and the crystal glasses out of which she sipped not an Italian, but a French, wine. She did not resent such wealth; it belonged to a different circle. She had, in the last few weeks, held a position of leadership in circles that she might never have touched upon had Domenico lived. Although her love for him was undimmed, she found herself pleased to be, at least for the moment, free of expectations, able to do what she thought needed doing rather than what a wife and daughter-in-law has always done. *Am I betraying my Domenico? I have become a different person in such a short time,* she mused. *Would I be doing these things now had Domenico lived? Heavens, he cared about the cattle and the ducks more than these devils care about the children of man. He would be doing what I am doing were he still with me. If the priests are right and he lives on in some heaven for those killed too young, he will be pleased with me.*

Lunch was completed with an enormous Mont Blanc cake of chestnut marmalade and whipped cream accompanied by peaches in liqueur. Foschini refused coffee in the Withdrawing Room and his little party was escorted back to the front door.

Mother, son and daughter stood under the portico with the priest and waved as the Daimler drove off.

The daughter said: 'That Riva is an immoral woman, going around with all these men.'

Father Filipović wanted to add something. 'You are so observant, Donna Ippolita. La Riva has been thought of as a loose woman. In Ginestra, I mean.'

'Do you confess her?' It was a naughty question.

'Oh no, I am sorry to say she rarely enters the church. I am afraid that she associates with communists.'

Donna Maria Assunta shuddered.

Don Carlo mused: 'Good figure. I have invited her to help me reorganise the library.'

Donna Ippolita sniffed but said nothing. She turned to her mother. 'Low-class women serve a purpose, but it is not very edifying.'

As they returned indoors, Don Carlo remarked: 'I think I won't wear my uniform around here anymore. When I go to Sulmona I'll take it in a suitcase and change at the palace before meeting Rommel.'

His mother agreed. 'Quite right, dearest. And when you're there, check that Calogero has stored all the good paintings and porcelain in the basement properly and that the gardeners have not got lazy in our absence. We can't have the palace falling to pieces just because there is a war on. '

THE GRAPE HARVEST

On a warm morning in mid-October, Foschini sent over a message to FitzGerald in Pozzo that Italy would declare war on Germany at any moment. Allied Command was instructing its personnel behind enemy lines to make contact with Committee of National Liberation (CLN) representatives and be ready for a call to action.

FitzGerald received the message with more pleasure than he wanted to admit to himself. Now that headquarters was, in effect, licensing him to remain, FitzGerald could forgo the shame he had felt at dragging his feet rather than making directly for the lines. He had been a week without his plaster cast, but he still needed crutches and to be careful not to put much weight on that leg. It had been only a matter of time before his excuse for being dilatory would have evaporated. Now he had another one.

Against FitzGerald's better judgment, Goode was already working with Foschini. FitzGerald could see little military value in the minor operations carried out behind German lines, and, influenced by Lucia, he considered that they rarely justified the escalating reprisals.

For the Germans were no longer hiding their savagery with the pretence of being allies. As units withdrew from the front line, they careered through towns and villages like the Tatar hordes of a thousand years before. The slightest suspicion that an Allied soldier had been harboured was excuse for destroying everything they could see, leaving wrecked homes without food, water or electricity. They sent out raiding parties that pillaged, gang raped, tormented and murdered.

When Goode returned from one of his forays with the partisans, FitzGerald's tone was acid, 'So, you can now come clean about joining the commies!' FitzGerald remarked to his subordinate.

'You can put it like that, Chief, or you can say that my plans are now legit: Italy has joined the democracies in the fight against the very fascism Italians invented.'

'Fascism is just a spinoff from communism,' FitzGerald cheerfully riled the younger man.

Goode didn't rise to the bait. *Probably*, thought FitzGerald, *he just puts down my views to my age and whatever class category he has put me into, associates me with the "former people"*. He sighed.

Goode sought to reassure him that they were not changing sides. 'I'm going to see if I can help Foschini and the local partisans to work together for the common cause,' he offered, 'maybe a foreigner has more chance of getting them to collaborate than an Italian.'

'Especially if you can provide them with supplies.' FitzGerald guessed that drops of arms and kit would be on their way if General Alexander were really serious about the war behind enemy lines.

He saw Goode off, watching his slight form stride away down the hill towards Pozzo, to meet his contacts.

Then, FitzGerald went to assure his hosts that he would indeed take part in the wine harvest while he awaited developments. He learnt that Vacca's tenants were no longer being bullied into rejecting fugitives. 'The hicks are being allowed to follow their altruistic instincts,' he said to himself with satisfaction.

Around Pozzo, there was no longer any pretence at ignorance of the hidden men. Gabriella, one of the older women, insisted on doing the colonel's laundry and sent up her daughter daily with food, despite Goode's protestations that they could be self-sufficient. Children crept up at all hours to look at the "soldiers" and the parish priest, a nervous and scholarly youth, visited, hoping to shrive them but instead lent them novels, plays and poems, especially those banned by the fascists.

When the day of the wine harvest arrived, one of the first vineyards to be dealt with was just below the village. Five or six families joined forces to pick the grapes. Some local men who had been hiding high up in the hills came back down to Pozzo along with assorted fugitives. FitzGerald and Goode greeted Stavros and Oleksiy and nodded at the two Kalmyk boys who were now dressed like poor shepherds, speaking some Italian and shyly imitating their hosts.

The women and girls were softly singing "*Alle Orte*", "To the Orchard", as they made preparations.

'*Ji vaj'all'orte a coje li rose,*
    [I go to the orchard to pick roses,]
scontre lu spose scontre lu spose,
    [I meet my sweetheart, I meet my sweetheart,]
Ji vaj'all'orte a coje li rose,
    [I go to the orchard to pick roses,]
scontre lu spose e mi mett'a parla.'
    [I meet my sweetheart and start talking.]

Each of the singers received a pair of clippers and a large basket. The vines were loaded with endless bunches of grapes and the snip-snip of the clippers never ceased, nor did the songs of the women, as bunch after bunch was dropped into baskets.

After a basket was filled, it was taken to the oxcart carrying much larger baskets, into which it was tipped. Once fully loaded, the cart went to the winepress and another cart took its place. The weather was sunny and everybody was happy, laughing and joking.

FitzGerald watched as Bregante taught Enrico and Ebbo to cut the grapes, and then showed them how to tread them. Standing near the winepress, Lucia looked amused. A South African, Uys Krige, was sitting with his diary on his knee, jotting down notes for the book he intended to write about Italian country life should he live.

Every so often, Bregante glanced at Lucia and smiled; she would lower her head and smile to herself. FitzGerald observed them, something scraping within.

Tables and benches were brought out and laid for lunch. Everybody sat down. Lucia was between Bregante and FitzGerald. He could tell that some of the women were whispering about Lucia, their smirking glances betraying them.

All were hungry and ate fast, except for the mothers of small children who expended their energies in bringing their offspring to the table, getting them to eat the best food before they rushed off to play catch around the yard. Catch turned into blind man's bluff, which evolved into hide and seek, with the little ones crouching under the table and crawling between the adults' legs. Every so often a parent would call out instructions to some boy or girl to stop being rough or to come and sit down and eat fruit, but no child paid attention and the parents would just resume chatting to their neighbours. Enrico remained close to Lucia, holding tight to her skirt.

Four men with accordion, tambourines and a drum started on "*Quant'è bello lu primm'ammore*", "How lovely is first love and then the second's better". A man or woman jumped up after every iteration of the chorus to provide a new verse, the racier the better, and everybody joined in the chorus, which got louder and louder. The laughter rose as the claims became ever more preposterous:

>'*La legge de natura è veramente esatta*
>   '[The law of nature is really fact]
>*Quan' lu marito è sicco la mugliera è chiatta*
>   [When the husband is dry the wife is flat]
>*Quant'è bello lu primm'ammore*

[How beautiful is first love]
Lu secondo è cchiù bello ancor
[The second even more]

'*E si' le corna tue fossero bandiere*
'[If your horns were flags to fly]
Sarebbe tutti i giorni festa nazionale
[It'd be national holiday every day]
Quant'è bello lu primm'ammore
[How beautiful is first love]
Lu secondo è cchiù bello ancor'
[The second even more]'

When Lucia rose to minister to a child who had fallen over and cut himself, FitzGerald got up to join her, as if to examine the boy's graze. After she had cleaned the scratch and released the child to his mates, they both strolled outside and stood by an old walnut tree, out of sight but overlooking the valley.

'You look too serious, Mr FitzGerald; how can you keep such a long face when we are all cheerful? Are you unhappy?'

He laughed at himself: 'I fear I am too happy. Instead of enjoying myself, I should be fighting. I came here to save civilisation and find myself in a village treading grapes!'

She mocked him: 'You are *in* civilisation. This is civilisation, not picture galleries and parliaments. Look around you at these families, communities, affections. Isn't this civilisation?'

FitzGerald was surprised into momentary silence. 'Well...' He stared at her and spoke as if repeating a rubric: 'I am here to defend freedom and democracy.'

She shrugged. 'For you city people, these things may matter. Rich people may want these lofty things, but we only want to be left alone. To live in our own way.'

'Perhaps you are right. But even if you're right, I shouldn't be enjoying you but helping you.'

'Of course I am right. I am a woman, and I don't have fantasies about saving the world! What gives you the right to remake us? Fascist, communists, liberals – they are all the same. Just men after power. I don't want to be rescued, saved. We want to be left alone to live and die as we want to live and die.'

For some reason that he could not identify, a picture came into his mind of his English teacher, standing before a blackboard, chalk in hand, declaiming "Dover Beach". How did it go? He was startled out of his reverie to see her staring at him like an officer assessing a recruit or a mother a possible son-in-law. 'I think you like it here. You are not as confident about saving civilisation as you were when we first met.'

'Here? It's different. You can almost forget the war.'

Her chin jerked up. 'Forget the war? How stupid are you, Colonel?' She spoke his rank with a kind of disgust. 'We're here – we have abandoned our homes – because of the war!'

'I'm sorry. I meant the front, where the fighting takes place. Here it can be very relaxed and beautiful.'

'Mr FitzGerald, though you are a big soldier, I think you still do not understand what war is. War is not what a soldier does, but what soldiers do to everyone else.'

There was a pause: neither appeared to know what to say. It crossed his mind that she was just a young girl, yet spoke down to him like a grandmother. As if they were moved by the same impetus, they started to walk away from the house, towards the orchard.

Lucia turned her face to glance out over the valley below: 'Ovid lived near here.'

He was glad at the change of topic. 'So he did. Sulmona is on the other side of the hills. Where Ovid was born. Dryden wrote: "Ovid, the soft philosopher of love. His love epistles for my friends I chose; For there I found the kindred of my woes."'

Lucia: '*Est deus in nobis, et sunt commercia caeli: sedibus aetheriis spiritus ille venit.*'

FitzGerald felt a great warmth suffuse him in an instant,

drawing him towards her. He checked himself and translated: 'There is a god within each of us; we negotiate with the heavens from which ethereal realms we take our inspiration.'

Lucia, with pleasure, as if seeing something in him for the first time, said, 'So you people know our poets?'

'Americans can have a classical education. My mother taught me Latin. Until I came here and met Italians, I rather suppressed what my mother taught me. You know the USA is very big on mannishness, we don't have much space for poetry – our ideal man is aggressive, assertive, makes a fortune, conquers enemies…'

'And masters women?'

After a pause, he said, 'I suppose we are not very subtle. Not many American men would admit to reading Ovid to understand women! Maybe Virgil is more appropriate here at this time. Didn't he write about people's endurance of violence as being like that of "some rock which stretches into the vast sea and which, exposed to the fury of the winds and beaten against by the waves, endures"?'

FitzGerald was astonished at himself; something was coming out of his past that he had almost forgotten existed. *I am thinking like my mother. What she taught me meshes with life here, where I am guest in a world so different from home, though linking me somehow with* Máthair's *sweetness.*

'When I look around me and see your people's stoicism, I think of Virgil. Was your husband a poetry lover?'

Lucia laughed. 'No! He only read the grain prices.' She smiled fondly. 'That was all the poetry he needed!'

They were silent, FitzGerald imagining that she was thinking of her husband, that he had no place to disturb her at such a moment. Then, she went on, in a manner so intimate that he was nonplussed:

'You would think him ill-educated, but he knew so much about the land, the animals, how to build houses and conserve food. The seasons and the habits of oxen. I admired his rootedness and his strength. His unlettered wisdom. He is… was part of the landscape. When he built a wall or planted a tree, he did it not just to earn his living, but for future generations.' She went to the present tense. 'He is an artisan who makes everything beautifully, to perfection, just as his father taught him.'

FitzGerald noted the tense and averted his eyes. When she stopped speaking, he looked again into her face and saw tears trickling down her cheeks like rain on a windowpane.

Before he could say anything, let alone move his arm to put it round her, as he found himself propelled to do, she moved away a pace, wiped her cheeks with her apron in one rapid movement and then turned back, staring defiantly at him: 'And that came from his grandfather before him.'

'Passed from parent to child, generation to generation,' was all that FitzGerald could say, looking into her eyes, so clear and, it struck him, so bright, glittering.

'Yes, he built upon the donations of the past, what he had learnt from his forbears about how to be a human being. Destruction and cruelty never entered his mind. Only creating and nurturing. What is this hatred of difference that you and these devils have? You can't rest until you have forced everyone else to be as you want. Why can't you leave others alone?'

She mused, as if to herself, 'I don't want to be a restless city person, with shallow associations and no purpose beyond amusement. Always excited by a new distraction – fascism, communism, revolution, war... or like that general's daughter, shopping...'

'How can a little village be enough for you?'

'When the Germans have gone, the life of which Virgil wrote will be resumed.'

'If the devils have not killed or enslaved you all.'

'Even the devils can't kill or enslave us all.'

'Tell that to the Poles.'

He looked at her directly, with feeling. They both sought the words under the words. She blushed and looked down.

Then, trying to change the topic, they glanced over at the crones who had tottered to within hearing distance and were staring at them.

FitzGerald asked, 'What are they saying?'

'They gossip. There are not many other pleasures. Except at harvest time, the festivals. We women at least have gossip.'

He wanted to say "about you and me?" but something held him back, so instead he asked, 'About you and Bregante?'

'Of course! We live in the same house now, so I can look after the children. They think this very exciting.'

'Do they think you should marry?'

'No. They think I should never talk to a man again, just wear black and look mournful forever. Probably they say that I am whoring with all you foreigners. But I don't care what they think.'

'Bregante is a good man. But not educated as you are.'

'What has education got to do with it?'

'You should marry someone…'

She cut him off: 'If I were to marry, I would marry someone who can harvest grapes. Come, Bregante will teach you all you need to know to impress a good girl!' Laughing, she ran back to Bregante and said something to him, pointing to FitzGerald. Bregante went up to FitzGerald with a smile and invited him to sit with the old ladies and cut grapes.

That afternoon, the men and boys trod the grapes in large, straight-sided barrels. They had rolled their trousers up high and hopped into those barrels, knee-deep in grapes, trampling them until every drop of juice was squeezed out. The singing of male voices echoed around the land and the women, down the hillside, would, every so often, halt their picking and listen to those deep chords. Some would find their eyes wet as they thought of their own men far way in places with bizarre names like Belorussia, Caucasus and Ukraine, wipe them with their sleeves and turn back to the vines.

Lucia sat to watch the treading and Enrico sidled up, as if he had been waiting for FitzGerald to go, and put his head on her knees. Her hand stroked his hair. *What am I doing, talking to this man so intimately? He is a married man, passing through our lives for an instant. The scent of my Domenico lingers everywhere and his arms are around me in my dreams. This* Inglese *is... not wanted, confusing. He will be gone soon. How can I forget his bullying manner and obvious contempt for all of us?* She glanced down at the boy who had stirred her that day on Via Mazzini. *He has closed his eyes as if he were asleep. Perhaps he is.*

FitzGerald went back to where Lucia and he had been talking. He noticed a little green and white purse on the ground and picked it up, turning it over to find it embroidered with white cranes. It must be hers. As he moved away to find her and return what she had dropped, it seemed to FitzGerald that their conversation had been like the culmination of a long track of discovery. The woman he had grown grudgingly to admire seemed very different from that with whom he had first crossed swords a few weeks ago. Her perspective might have changed but so, he uneasily felt, had his. She thanked him when he returned her purse, but gave her attention back to Enrico, so that he walked away.

Lucia spent the rest of the day with her brother-in-law; once FitzGerald had gone, she passed the place where he had been sitting and found that he had left his webbing belt behind. She picked it up and examined the brass clip, turning the belt over and over in her hands. Then she took the belt with her to her quarters. She did not return it to FitzGerald.

PART THREE

FITZGERALD TAKES COMMAND

GENERAL NERI'S REQUIREMENTS

The days passed quickly. Goode was out in the hills, organising, managing, conferring with the partisans. His equipment consisted of a pistol, submachine gun, ammunition, maps, a flashlight, sleeping bag, socks, first aid kit, toothbrush, soap and razor. The razor was only for returning to base; while in the hills, Goode let his stubble grow, darkening it and his hair with charcoal.

FitzGerald still held back from action, telling himself that he was biding his time until the situation was less confused. He reminded himself of Captain Foschini's description. 'There are loyal *bande* such as ours who fight for Italy under the king and don't want Mussolini back. There are communist *bande* who idolise the USSR and want to exterminate all who don't. There are gangsters masquerading as *bande* who just loot and rape. And there are Salò troops, regulars and irregulars, who are under German control. Each group has a different story to tell, belief to propagate…'

FitzGerald was quite clear that God was on the Allies' side. Thus, it was practicalities that held interest for him, rather than beliefs. He knew that, because the Allies recognised the CLN, groups recognised by CLN were supposed to get supplies in order actively to disrupt German communications and reinforcements.

As a British officer accessible to *bande* leaders, he was a valuable asset, since MI9 personnel would almost certainly use him to assess the reliability of *bande* requesting assistance through CLN.

Goode had been reporting Foschini's efforts to pull together a partisan force, in the face of competition from the communists. Foschini hoped to get recognition from the Committee. FitzGerald was chary of helping any of the "so-called Italian resistance", consistent with the general suspicion of the Anglo-Americans of Italians who claimed to have changed sides. Nevertheless, he kept in touch with Foschini and his unit.

Meanwhile, as Stavros and Oleksiy were working in the fields, he did light jobs around the farm, repairing sacks or feeding the chickens. He would swing down towards the village and go down the little road as far as the convent but no further. When he saw people he would avoid them, excepting the five old men who spent every afternoon dozing on benches in the *piazzetta*. To them he would nod and they, if not fast asleep, would doff their trilbies. Once he saw a young nun emerge from the convent and run down the road, away from the village, but no movement could be seen behind those high walls.

Lucia spent more and more time at what even the local Italians now called "Fizzi's HQ", which they pronounced "Akka-koo", or termed "*Stato Maggiore*", "General Staff", in comic deference. With Lucia's help, Goode gradually identified many potentially useful soldiers, though few were from PG500. Other British, Australians, New Zealanders or North Americans had evaded capture following a battle or had got out of those prison camps in which their officers had tried to hold them in, as commanded by the War Office. There were Russians, Muslims and persecuted minorities from the USSR who had been press-ganged by the Nazis and then managed to flee their masters. Georgians and Bohemians, compelled into the Waffen SS, had fled their units and sought protection, food and a way to survive. These were leery of the communist partisans because they universally hated the communist parties of their own countries and were more likely to be candidates for Foschini's lot, although they also feared being taken for Nazis by the Allies and handed over to the Russians for punishment. The nearest local *banda* was led by a general known as Passo di Lupo, and his commissar, Neri. Goode wanted FitzGerald to go to meet the general but was told that if the partisan wanted to meet him, he would have to visit Pozzo.

Goode, sometimes with Lucia, walked for miles across country to check on clandestines and brace them for the last weeks before the front, as it was assumed, would pass over them. The fugitives from Ginestra, those who had sought safety in the Abruzzi, were no longer the neat, energised evaders whom FitzGerald had spruced up in September, but often bearded, unwashed vagabonds, justifying their grub by doing heavy labour on the farms. Goode saw they needed organising, given some purpose, made to re-join the struggle. FitzGerald prevaricated both because of the complexity of the situation, with so many factions and interests jostling for attention, and because he was being urged by Lucia to do nothing that might attract the enemy's attention to Pozzo.

Their relative positions had changed. It was tacitly accepted by all that the young woman was no longer the leader. She might propose, but FitzGerald would dispose. She was one of the team, a specialist, certainly, with essential contacts and skills, but a subordinate. When she came back from her expeditions, before she had even taken off her clogs, she reported to him with shining eyes. He would be waiting for her and no sooner had she arrived than the seriousness that hung about him would evaporate and he would smile and laugh and make her join them in food and wine. Goode noticed.

At the abandoned farm, FitzGerald designated an empty outhouse as his office, in which he could talk quietly with Goode, Bregante and Lucia about what was going on and in which, at other times, Goode and Krige could jot down their notes for the books they were writing. One day Lucia brought a wireless, which she described as a gift from Captain Foschini. He, she said, was nearby, training up his small group of Italian deserters. FitzGerald accepted the wireless but avoided meeting Foschini and being put under more pressure to join forces.

One early evening, soon after they had returned with a couple of Tynesiders, canny and distrustful until Fitzgerald and Goode had led them in singing "The Blaydon Races", they were in the "office", in conference with Lucia, when Enrico opened the door and peered around it. He whispered:

'*Zia* Lucia, *Babbo* says the *banda* is coming.'

'What? Who?'

'The *banda*. He said not to say devils. Just *banda*.'

FitzGerald rose and strode to the door, with Lucia and Goode behind. As they emerged they could see six men walking slowly towards them a couple of hundred metres downhill. When FitzGerald realised that they were armed, he cursed to himself that he should be posting sentries.

The six were, to his mind, dressed like pirates in children's books: they wore bandoliers, carbines on their backs and pistols in belts, broad-brimmed hats and German issue boots. They reached the open patch of ground before the house and stood looking. FitzGerald waited. He guessed who they were. They would be from the so-called Hammer and Sickle Brigade, a group of ruffians camped in a deserted villa a few miles away.

After a few seconds of waiting, a young man with long hair in ringlets, a goatee beard and spectacles, with a beret like that of a left bank painter, stepped forward and spoke directly at FitzGerald.

'You are Colonel FitzGerald?'

'That's me. And who is it who is honouring me with a visit?'

The spokesman seemed rather nervous. 'I am Neri, Commissar of the Hammer and Sickle Brigade.'

'My dear General, how good of you to come. I have heard of your exploits.' Goode gave FitzGerald a startled look.

'Please, just call me Professor Neri. Or my battle name, the Crow. I am only the Commissar of the Brigade. I am not a hero as you are.' Neri paused as if to see whether his compliment had registered. 'Congratulations on your successful escape.'

Fitzgerald made a slight bow. 'Won't you come in and sit down, Professor, er, Crow?'

They entered. FitzGerald pointed to one of the three chairs and took another for himself. His two companions remained standing, as did the five pirates, who crowded into a corner.

Neri sat, shifting his holster, which had hung in front like a codpiece, to the side, and repositioning his bandoliers to a more comfortable position.

'Today is a great day,' Neri pronounced.

FitzGerald, thanks to Foschini's gift of the wireless, had heard the news, but waited to let the guerrilla commander speak further.

'This morning, Italy has declared war on Germany! We are allies!'

'Ah yes, splendid.'

Neri appeared not to notice the foreigner's nonchalance and began to discuss the strategy he felt should be taken by all the guerrilla forces. He was looking forward to the "United Nations forces", as he termed them, breaking the Gustav Line of German defences and his men and FitzGerald's hunting down Germans fleeing like rabbits.

FitzGerald was pondering what his duty now was. Rather than seek to penetrate the German line, at great risk of failure, trying to return to his troops, should he, as Goode constantly urged, team up with guerrillas and hit the Germans in the back? This was the most dutiful option; the most manly and exciting. But it was also the one that carried the most danger of collateral damage. Slaughtering of the innocents. This, not just the ambiguous political situation, was holding him back.

I have to make a choice, a decision. I must be a maker again, not a taker. Should I join Neri and co. and, as the experienced soldier, take them over, or do my own thing? Do I have to set up my own band, or join Foschini, if I am to have the heft to influence events?

He brought the commissar into focus and, to end the silence and create more thinking time, asked: 'What is your background, General?'

Neri frowned slightly at the word "general". 'I was a student at La Sapienza before this war. Then a professor in Moscow. Now I am Commissar the Brigade. We have very active and enthusiastic students and some former soldiers.'

'What is it that you profess, Professor?'

'I am a professor of Marxist Theory. Until Mussolini fell, I was in USSR. I came back to make a new Italy, a people's paradise like Russia!'

'Let's deal with the Germans first!'

Neri shrugged. 'They will be vanquished. Even they know that. A few months and we will be burning their villages.' He gave a broad grin at that thought. 'Now we are planning how to run our country when the Nazis are gone and the fascists dead.'

Goode was all attention. FitzGerald too found himself interested: 'And what are you planning?'

The professor drew himself up and began to declaim, as if he were at a rally. 'Italy will have a cleansing revolution. Everybody will live in a class-free equal society, ruled by the people. But first we have to smash the fascists. So, we are uniting all the different groups of resistance fighters.

'The Germans are being forced back from their line south of Rome, their *Winterstellung*. We must undermine them in the rear. Your comrades will not be able to get south and pass through the lines before snow falls in mid-November. It will be extremely cold. Like Russia. They will be much better employed working with us, rather than freezing to death on the way south.' He shuddered at the thought.

FitzGerald had also considered that: 'The Maiella is not impassable in November.'

'True. But a month later there is a big snow and you cannot move without skis. Except for the few who got through in the good weather, your men are trapped here. They can serve the cause best by staying, so it is best that you collaborate with us in liberating Italy.'

'You'll join forces with the other groups?'

Under the illusion that he was receiving a sympathetic hearing, Neri went on, 'They must come under our command, as we are the people. To have a future in New Italy, all anti-fascist forces must make a united front with us. In this area, we have many fighters. When you and your international regiment join us, you will be second-in-command.'

'But I don't have an international regiment.'

'You can form one in a matter of days. We know that you have located many fighters. Together, we are the nucleus of an army that will grow in numbers every day as the United Nations make their victorious advance. '

FitzGerald had given some thought to this possibility in his discussions with Goode. Many of the clandestines were leery of the undisciplined *bande* and would resist involvement with them. Anglos were suspicious of Italians with weapons, though most had been won over to the farmers by their generosity and friendship. A few of the ragbag of deserters and local boys fleeing the corvée, brutalised by their experiences, might be seduced by lust for females and loot, but these men would not make up a serious unit under the command of an inexperienced man such as Neri.

'We will take a long time to become a fighting force. And be of no use to you.'

'You are too modest! You are real soldiers, real British officers. Italian officers are no good; they are mostly liberals or monarchists, always ready to compromise. And the CLN has told us that your orders are to support us.'

'But General,' he brought to mind Goode's taxonomy of their weaponry of the day before, 'between us we have a few Italian submachineguns and some ancient revolvers, relics of the previous wars. Oh, one of us has a walking stick with a tiny pistol in the handle. Are we going to fight the Germans with these?!'

'Your air force will drop us weapons and ammunition as soon as they know you are in our high command!'

He'd said it. FitzGerald had suspected what Neri really wanted and now he had heard it from the man's mouth. So he revealed his own reasons for not going along with Neri. 'Then the Germans will slaughter not only our men but all the villagers round about.'

Neri sat back and contemplated FitzGerald. FitzGerald could see that he was sufficiently perceptive to understand that, for the moment, the foreign colonel was intent upon resisting his overtures. He would want to get something out of this encounter upon which he could build in future. *First, he will show me that he can operate without me if necessary. And second, he will try to compromise me.*

'You cannot make a revolution without breaking eggs, Colonel. I propose to destroy a German fuel dump about ten kilometres to the west. Your military knowledge will be vital to us. If we can set explosives, we will achieve much more. Some of your friends are explosives experts and have time pencils. Please lend us your experts.'

One of the men whom Goode had identified as potentially useful was an older Tatar, an explosives specialist trained in the Soviet Army who had twice changed sides, leaving it to join Vlasow's Russian Liberation Army and then deserting when transferred to the Waffen SS in Italy. He had shacked up with the daughter of one of the farmers but regularly declared that he would leave her if he could kill Germans under "the Irish colonel's command".

FitzGerald paused. He did not know the details of Neri's scheme but if he detonated a fuel dump without a time pencil there was little chance of anyone nearby surviving. *The pencil is essential to delay the detonation of explosives once in place. It saves lives.*

'I have already explained that we have no forces to unite. But you are right, we do have an explosives expert. If I agree to your using him, it is only on the condition that he is never traced to here. The Germans will extract a terrible revenge on these people.'

'Of course.' Neri shrugged. He had got something he wanted.

Probably he guessed that, while FitzGerald did not intend to work with him, he did not wish to be reported as uncooperative. FitzGerald knew that Neri would despise him for considering the peasants more than the need to attack Nazis. *To men like Neri, peasants are always counter-revolutionary. That's why Lenin had had to liquidate so many, usually by starving them to death, but also by mass executions.*

'The man you need is well qualified. He will help you if I command him.'

'Then command him, dear Colonel.'

Neri left, shown out by FitzGerald with cool courtesy.

FitzGerald and Goode accompanied him and his suite to the road and then returned to their lair without speaking.

When they were back inside, Goode opened up. 'Chief, we can expect trouble from Neri. He wants our men and he wants you so that he can say he fights with us. But what he really wants is supplies from our lot.'

FitzGerald stopped. 'Go on.'

'I'm told that it was half a dozen of his men who ransacked the villa of the poet Piccolo – only about twenty miles from here – last month and murdered his man. People say they raided the Hermitage of Carmine and stole all the silver.'

'I think what you're telling me is that we've got to get organised, isn't that so, Goode? We can't pick grapes any longer.'

'To set up a fighting force seems the only way to stop Passo di Lupo vying with Foschini's lot to be local hegemon. We'd better be the ones to receive supplies from Bari, not them.'

If Goode, usually sympathetic to the Communists, wanted Neri's gang confined, then FitzGerald was happy to comply. Matters were now clarified. He knew what he had to do.

WHO ARE THE COWARDS?

A week or so after the grape harvest, Lucia burst into FitzGerald's office, thrusting so hard that the door crashed back against the wall.

To his astonishment, she yelled at him. 'Why did I help you, you and your six hundred? Why did we people of Ginestra feed you and clothe you? Why did my neighbours in the hills take you in, give you beds and warmth, and...' she faltered, at a loss for other things to list. 'Why? So that you would live and no longer fight and kill! So that you would go back to your families and your sweethearts and your children and teach them peace...' She wiped her hand across her wet face and looked up at FitzGerald, clenching her teeth and with fury in her eyes. Gone was the acquiescence that he had recently sensed.

FitzGerald just looked at her, digesting her words. She went on, 'You think all Italians are cowards, but you are a coward!'

As she halted before his desk he rose and, in a faintly facetious tone, asked, 'Really, Why?'

'You are helping those bandits! Neri! That thug! You know that they will provoke the deaths of hundreds, but you are supporting them so as not to be thought afraid!' As she shouted, Lucia gripped the edge of his desk as if about to push it.

I've never liked whining females, he reminded himself, *I'm going to get angry. I must control myself.* He spoke evenly. 'Not so. They will go ahead anyway. I can't stop them. But I can give them expertise so that their action is not a total disaster.'

'Liar, it is because you are afraid of telling him no. You don't want him complaining to the politicians and the politicians reporting to your own generals.'

'Believe that if you wish.'

'I do. My husband was afraid of being called a coward, too. To me the biggest cowards are not the boys who run away – they have real courage – but those who hang on doing evil.'

FitzGerald thought himself very reasonable. 'That is not —'

She interrupted him. 'He who cannot tell right from wrong is not manly. Manliness is having the courage to do the right thing. The men and women – and children – who have risked their lives helping you and your six hundred – do you not think their courage is much greater than fighters?'

FitzGerald straightened himself, moved round the desk, thinking about her words. He felt at that instant that he had to acknowledge something that had been growing on him ever since leaving PG500 for the world of the farms. He looked straight at her: 'Yes.'

Lucia did not notice but continued. 'Look at your generals. They know that they are doing disgusting things and commanding others to do disgusting things, yet have not the courage to refuse orders. And because of you, there are many like me, women who grieve already, and women who know only that their husbands and sons and brothers are in the east, not whether they will ever return. Or whether they themselves and their children will be violated and murdered.'

Fitzgerald drew a line between his people and the Italians. 'Our soldiers don't do these things.'

'Who knows? But you respect these Germans, who do. I can still see you and that murderer befriending each other.' She was trembling now. Though her voice was loud and her words exasperating, he saw her, perhaps for the first time, as a young girl who had undergone terrible trials over mere weeks and who had never, until now, snapped.

He spoke calmly, more conscious than ever before of the gulf in age and experience between them. 'Since I came to live in your hills, I've seen things differently. I've understood that there is a higher kind of courage than that of soldiers. Your people are… how can I say it? You risk your lives and those of all you love to help strangers.'

She stood, slightly turned away from him, her head down gazing at something on the wainscoting. She was very still, as if waiting for something, or in a trance.

He approached, put his hand on her arm and looked at her face.

'Look at me.'

She looked into his face but made a gentle gesture of rejection, shaking his hand off her arm, saying, matter of factly, 'It seems to me that we only do what comes natural to us.'

'But why does it come naturally to you and not to others?'

'I don't know. I just know that I can't stand by and see others suffer.'

'I wish all felt as you do.'

He moved closer; he was about to touch her again.

She broke out of the semi-trance and rapidly walked away: 'I am not available to be a spoil of war!'

'Lucia,' he corrected himself, 'Mrs Riva, that's wrong! You know I—'

'I know that I am only the woman conveniently nearby.'

'There are many women here.'

'Then seduce them! Colonel, it is late. We have work to do tomorrow. And I have to think about my children.'

'Bregante's children.'

'I am their mother now. Because your American friends killed their own mother! Like you killed my Domenico… Oh for God's sake, go, FitzGerald. Leave us in peace, you and your armies and your purposes. Have you not done enough damage?'

Lucia left, slamming the door.

FitzGerald gazed at the door through which she had charged. 'And I thought she was playing broken wing,' he remarked to himself. He returned to his maps. *How stupid I am.*

Lucia was in turmoil, though she did not admit to herself why. As she fled from the hated soldier, the killer, the image of Domenico came back into her mind, his arm around her, laughing. She thought how, in their teens, he had followed her like a thirsty puppy; in their early years, she had taken control and told him what he could, should and would do, relishing her power over this beautiful male with his great fists and wide shoulders. Then, as their pathway grew clearer and both knew, though it was unspoken, that they would never part, that they would grow old together, she had ceded her authority to him. Of course, in private she always had her opinions and remonstrances, but once they had talked and his voice echoed through her like the tones of a violin on an enchanted evening, she felt herself subdued, overwhelmed and an obedient slave to the man who, just before, had been her naughty boy. In such ecstasy they made love. As she thought back to those moments, her heart cried out in longing for her man, for his sound, his smell, his body wrapped around her.

And then the thought of FitzGerald momentarily obliterated her memories and she was revolted by her treachery.

THE NUNNERY

The next day, FitzGerald was sitting at a table outside his HQ, studying Italian, shaded by vines on a simple frame. Lucia walked smartly up the hill, across the yard and stood in front of his table. 'Colonel FitzGerald, please act!'

FitzGerald rose: 'What is it, *Signora?*'

'Some of the clandestines are trying to break into the convent. They are drunk. They boast that they will ravage the sisters. The sisters must be very frightened. If someone calls the *carabinieri*, then all the clandestines in this area are in danger.'

'Fools.'

FitzGerald bellowed at Goode to come down off the flat roof from which he was checking the approaches through binoculars. Since the unannounced visit from Neri, they had stopped relying on the locals to warn them of approaching strangers and set up a rota of lookouts. Goode slid down the ladder and dived within to pick up his webbing belt and holster, which he clipped round his waist. As soon as he was out of the door, they strode off, with FitzGerald passing on Lucia's report.

It took barely ten minutes for them to arrive at the outskirts of Pozzo, in the centre of which, next to the church, was a medieval palace with iron cages on every window. Until the 19th century, it had been residence of the bishop who ran the area, then was later turned into a Dominican convent.

In the piazza, as they approached the steep walls of the convent, raucous singing came to their ears. They stopped for a moment and made out that the words were in English. The lead voice was one of the Tynesiders, and, judging from the accents of the others, men of several nationalities had all learnt the words:

'Three German officers crossed the Rhine, *parlez-vous*.
Three German officers crossed the Rhine, *parlez-vous*.
Three German officers crossed the Rhine, *parlez-vous*.
To shag the women and drink the wine,
Get in get out stop shaggin' about, wo-ho, wo-ho, wo-ho!

'They came to the door of a wayside inn, *parlez-vous*.
They came to the door of a wayside inn, *parlez-vous*...'

And on and on it went, detailing the well-known ordeal of the 'daughter fair' at the hands of those Huns.

FitzGerald scanned the *piazzetta*. All the villagers had fled; the Greek and the Pole were quietly playing *scopa* in the shade by the church and ignoring the gestures of the others to join in.

In front of the convent's massive doors, which had great iron enforcements and rusting studs, were eight or nine youths. A short, plump man in British battledress was conducting the singing with a bayonet for a baton, lurching from side to side.

Two youths were on a tall ladder, trying to chip away with chisels at the cement that held thick iron grills over the lowest window. So old and decayed was the brickwork that they had already made headway.

Others were lying on the flagstones, laughing and toasting the workers with red wine. They fell silent as FitzGerald stood near them, his hands on his hips.

The two on the ladder looked over and hesitated.

Goode went to a lean-to shading a big rainwater barrel. Seizing a bucket, he rapidly filled it, then roughly chucked its contents onto the conductor.

Flopping down onto his haunches, the conductor dropped his baton, which clanged on the cobbles. The choir stopped singing and their conductor turned and said venomously, towards Goode: 'Clear off, you bastard.'

He tried to get up but Goode moved fast, pushing him down easily and standing over him to ensure that he wouldn't move.

FitzGerald called out: 'Alright boys. That's enough. Do you want to go on one of these transports to Germany?' He saw that he had the attention of every man jack. 'If someone complains about you to the police, everybody here is off to a death camp or hard labour in the bauxite mines, same thing but more protracted.' He let that sink in.

'We are guests in this place and if the Huns find us they are going to kill our hosts. And probably burn down the whole village too.'

He paused like an orator.

'We are soldiers, supposed to be fighting the German devils, not frightening poor old women.'

A drunk shouted out, 'Some of them are young!'

An American voice added, 'Tight pussies!'

A strapping Tatar in his forties, wearing German breeches and a brown Soviet jacket, rose and swaggered forward like a gang boss. He was well known to FitzGerald and Goode as a man who itched to fight and kill. 'American, British, whatever you are, we are no you command. I command this company. House is full of fascists and first operation of my battalion is to clean it out. Ha ha!'

Goode shouted back: 'Where are your weapons? Where is your commission? If you assault this convent, you are just bandits.'

The Tatar eased a Luger pistol from his trousers. He glanced dismissively at Goode, then turned back to FitzGerald, at whom he pointed his Luger. 'I have been captain in Soviet Army and commanding artillery in German Army of Russia Liberation. Today, this,' he waved his pistol, 'is my commission. If you block way I will shoot you, American!'

Two of the other soldiers had weapons too, which they readied, sighting on FitzGerald. Behind the Tatar, the drunks leered at the two opponents.

FUEL DEPOT

At the very moment that FitzGerald and Goode were confronting the men, their would-be ally, Neri, was contemplating his target.

Beside a hamlet where peasants were still working the land, in a yard that might, from the air, be seen as an extension of a larger farm, supply trucks came and went, collecting petrol barrels from where thousands were secreted under canvas or stored in the peasants' barn. Sentries guarded the approach and patrolled the perimeter.

On a hill above, Neri and his group, concealed by shrubbery, looked down through binoculars.

One partisan, whose family hardware store had been torched by the Germans, growled to Neri, 'They don't even have a wire fence.'

'Because from the air, this just looks like another farm. If an aircraft comes, any truck hides under the trees and the guards disappear. Then all the airmen see is a few peasants.'

His deputy, a former teacher, added, 'The farmers are cover.'

A teenager who looked barely 12, wearing a helmet several sizes too large, asked, 'What happens at night?'

Neri deployed youngsters because they aroused less suspicion.

As long as they kept their cool and lied themselves out of trouble, they could avoid being shot if stopped by the enemy and so return with their reports. Adults, suspected of being partisans, would be killed on the spot, unless they were judged to be worth taking in for questioning under torture.

'They can't be busy at night because they're scared of putting on the lights.' Then Neri ordered, 'Let Fiore sneak around and find out how many guards there are.'

The former hardware store owner was in awe of the supplies he was threatening. 'That's a lot of fuel. Several thousand barrels. If we destroy that, we do a lot of damage. Shouldn't we just kill the guards and steal the stuff?'

'No. The only buyers on the black market are Nazis themselves. We'd make money but not weaken their war machine. We have to set it alight. The whole area will burn like an inferno.'

A plump boy called Rossi, whose mother thought he was hiding with cousins, suggested, 'We'd better warn the farmers. Their whole farm will be destroyed.'

'Rossi, Rossi! No! The Germans would know something is up. No-one must be warned.'

'But they'll burn alive!'

Neri took the boy by the lapel and stared into his eyes. 'We are willing to sacrifice our own lives for the cause, so why not these kulaks? Harden your heart, Rossi! Steel yourself not to weaken! You cannot make an omelette without breaking eggs! Be strong!'

Rossi hung his head, ashamed either of his soft-heartedness or his inability to counter his leader. He knew that if he were thought unreliable, he might not last long. He had seen others in this category go into the woods to gather firewood and noticed that their companions returned without them.

Not for the first time, Neri regretted the lack of discipline among the partisans. Seeing himself as an Italian version of Trotsky, the military commander, he wanted to lead men as iron-hard, as unquestioning, as brutal as had Trotsky in the glory days of the civil war, when hundreds of thousands of hindrances to the revolution had been eliminated and when Lenin could command the annihilation of whole districts. Instead, he had boys just out of their mothers' arms and men who were only with him to get fed and escape corvée. In the north, partisan groups consisting of Jews, social democrats and other persecuted people who were fighting for their lives, put up a much better show.

After several hours of reconnaissance and planning, Neri and his scouts slipped away.

SINGSONG

In front of the nunnery, FitzGerald was facing down men who would be welcome recruits to Neri's partisan battalion, as both he and Goode well knew.

Unfazed by their weaponry, Fitzgerald ignored the Tatar and looked towards the others. 'How many of you are Brits and Americans?'

Three put up their hands.

'And the rest of you?'

As he looked from face to face, they admitted their nationalities. Czech. Danish. French. Norwegian. Russian. Turkmen and other nations he had never heard of, desperate for liberation from the communist empire. *Truly, patriotism is what will save us from the monster ideologies*, he thought. *The country people may not know what Italy is, but they love their home and its own customs. All of which the Nazis and communists want to eliminate.*

'Oleksiy and Stavros I know well. They're here to defeat the Nazis. What are the rest of us here for?' He fixed a straight look at each in turn, inciting them to shout back. 'Just tell me!'

The Frenchman, swaying and shaking his fist in the air: 'Kill Germans!'

The Czech leapt up: 'Send the barbarians back where they belong!'

The Russian remained on the ground beside his bottle: 'Communist no! Socialism no! Liberation yes!'

From one of the men on the ladder came an American voice: 'Pulverise Germany!'

The Dane rose unsteadily, put his finger across his mouth in a parody of Hitler's moustache and spoke formally: 'Save the world from crazy Hitler.'

In comparison, the Norwegian beside him seemed quite sober: 'Down with imperialists!'

FitzGerald now addressed Goode. 'Mr Goode, look at these chaps. They are all real men who know why they are here. We must work together. Tomorrow morning, we start basic training. We are going to build an army to defend our Italian friends.'

He turned to the Tatar and used his name, speaking with both authority and respect, as one warrior to another. He was once again the leader who had led his six hundred out of captivity: 'Alim Galiev, you have a choice between being a bandit who will be hanged by any army – German, Italian or UN – which catches you, or being a wise peacemaker in the tradition of your great namesake.'

He looked round at the other men: 'Captain Galiev bears the surname of a great Tatar hero!' He fixed on the Tatar, who looked momentarily nonplussed, and lowered his weapon. 'You are a paladin, not a robber. We need you. Together we are going to build an international battalion to defend these good villagers from the Huns – that's the polite word for the Germans – and I need every man jack of you to join us in the fight. Shall we work together?'

The Tatar hesitated, then put his Luger back in his belt, advanced on FitzGerald, hugged him, then kissed him noisily on both cheeks.

Cries went up: 'Yes! We're with you, Sir!' There were shouts of: 'When can we get guns? I want to kill more Germans! Grenades!'

FitzGerald extracted himself from the Tatar's embrace but held onto his hand and called out, 'Boys, we're better than the Germans! Treat the Italians as you would treat your own mothers and sisters. And sing a better song.'

Galiev started singing the Russian soldier's song, "Katyusha", and the others joined in bit by bit.

THE CHESTNUT FESTIVAL

By day, fighter planes with US markings patrolled the country ways. They glinted as they slipped over the low hills, level with the ruined watchtowers. The noise of their cannons was like a pneumatic drill. They shot at any moving thing. Goode saw bullets raise the dust all around a peasant as he drove his ox and cart; the man flopped over and squeezed into a ditch, crawling out only after the sky was silent, to gaze at his dead beast and smashed cart. The fighters machine gunned down a truck loaded with contraband sugar. As soon as they had gone, the locals were on it like ants, staggering off on the hillside paths with hundredweight bags on their shoulders.

Late October was harvest time for the chestnuts. Large white sheets were spread on the ground around the tree trunks. Ladders were then placed to enable the men and boys, armed with long lengths of bamboo-like cane, to climb into the foliage high in the trees and flail the branches around them. Chestnuts were easily dislodged and fell into the sheets, whereupon they were gathered up. FitzGerald was now using a walking stick. His leg was almost back to normal, though he occasionally limped when a sharp pain would course through his calf after he'd put too much weight on it.

One of the white sheets was taken downhill to the last house in the village. The lookout would hang it out of the window if soldiers or police were seen coming up the road. 'That way,' said one of the old men to FitzGerald, 'we can relax.' FitzGerald was not so sure; if Neri's gang were operating in the neighbourhood, Pozzo would be targeted by the Huns. He wasn't so naïve as to think that the fascists or the Germans didn't know that there were clandestines here; what he hoped was that they did not know that he and the Bregantes were among them.

When rain fell, everybody sheltered in the village's large communal kitchen where a "*ballo*" was to take place. A ball. The kitchen was half as large again as any FitzGerald had ever seen and it looked even larger because, except for a long trestle table and stools, most of its furniture had been removed. The room was lit by a paraffin pressure lantern. There was no fire in the hearth; there was no need for one, due to the number of people in the room, and the lantern gave out an enormous glow, making it stiflingly hot.

The tablecloth was thick, home-made linen. The colonel sat on the right of the oldest man at the head of the table. Captain Foschini was at his left; the other males lined both sides. The only female sitting down was Riva Lucia. The local women began to serve what astonished FitzGerald and Goode, who had no idea that such fare could be secreted for a *festa*: huge mounds of pasta *asciutta*, boiled meat, boiled tongues, boiled chicken, roast meat, ricotta and other cheese, as well as bottle after bottle of wine. Children gaped from the door, waiting to snatch a half-gnawed bone or a chicken's foot. The cats snarled and spat among the debris beneath the table. There were speeches from the captain, from FitzGerald, and the elder, who was nominated as an unofficial mayor.

When the rain ceased for a while, the women cleared the dirty plates, then went to eat the remnants in the open. The main trestle was removed and stools collected at one end, where the old people gathered. Stories were told: stories about peasant cunning; about monstrous practical jokes; of the days when they were conscripts;

when they slept on grass mattresses on the tiered banks of grim barracks and got to know the brothels of the garrison towns.

The locals began to sing *stornelli*, two grandfathers accompanying the voices, one with a fiddle, another an accordion.

'*Vieni, c'è una strada nel bosco,*
 [Come, there's a path in the forest,]
Il suo nome conosco,
 [Its name I know,]
Vuoi conoscerlo tu?
 [Do you want to know it?]

'*Vieni, è la strada del cuore,*
 [Come, it's the path of the heart,]
Dove nasce l'amore,
 [Where love is born,]
Che non muore mai più.'
 [The love that never dies.]

After that, a couple of Russians pranced a Cossack routine and the two Kalmyks joined in. One Kalmyk sang a folksong; the other beat time.

A cloth was pulled away to reveal a harmonium and everybody cheered when a man in his forties marched up to the instrument, sat down and began to play. By that time, local girls were creeping in, all dressed up, and local boys, out of their hiding places, started to dance a rather ramshackle version of "*Lu saltarello*". The girls without male partners danced with one another. FitzGerald sat watching, his arms flung over the backs of chairs of two of the old men, laughing with them at their mutual incomprehension. Goode, nearby, sat stiff and uncomfortable, as if he thought he did not belong at a dance.

'Come on, Goode; don't disappoint the girls. It's you they've come to this shindig for.'

Goode blanched as if FitzGerald had thrown a paper dart at him, then reddened. FitzGerald needled him again: 'Into action, Goode; Scotland the Brave!'

Slowly and with apparent reluctance, not looking at his boss, Goode approached one of the girls who lived near their own farmhouse, gave a stiff bow and asked her to dance. FitzGerald's two old men were grinning, FitzGerald responded to their amusement: 'I thought he was windy for a moment, our Scots brave, but he's not let down the side after all!' Clapping each old man on the shoulder, he got up, looked over at Lucia, then strode over and stood before her.

'Mrs Riva, a dance?'

She accepted soundlessly and they danced until they tired of knocking into the rollicking youngsters and went out for fresh air. Under the eaves, several couples were locked in tight embraces, regardless of the drizzle.

They stood under a canvas awning, designed for keeping timber dry in the days when there had been timber.

'I haven't obeyed your instruction to leave.'

'So I see.' Her face was expressionless. 'I am glad you did not leave, and sorry I spoke as I did.'

'But you're right. I must go. I'll stay only until our commandos arrive to back up Foschini.' As he said this, FitzGerald felt himself a fraud. He recognised in himself that he wanted to stay and wanted the Italians to beg him to stay. He looked at Lucia, who then said what he had hoped she might say: 'Why go? You are safe here. And we need you.'

He was terribly happy. 'I am one of your charges and you want to keep on looking after us! Tell me, young lady, why do you do what you do for us lost men?'

'Because, old gentleman, I am a woman.'

'So?'

'We have to get through this world with as much happiness for ourselves and for others as we can make. Let men waste their lives piling up money, fighting or forming committees. We do the important things. Loving and nurturing, comforting and protecting.'

'Nurturing any dirty drunken soldier who begs for shelter?'

'We look after you poor creatures in the hope that someone will do the same for our men.'

'And what about the men here? Don't they resent your taking risks for strangers, strange men?'

'They had good mothers.'

'You make Ginestra sound like a matriarchy.'

'We are strong, but not in the way German women are strong. Donna Chiara tells me the Germans oblige their women to become men. Men who happen to be part-time breeding machines with nothing of Demeter, of real love. This is why their males are so driven and frustrated, lusting only for power and possession.'

FitzGerald did not react to her philosophical musings, it hardly mattered to him what she said, as long as she spoke with him. As she talked, they drew closer together and an observer might have imagined that they were about to kiss. Then they heard running steps coming closer and broke apart, immediately. As they looked round for the runner, a boy arrived panting before them. 'Devils! Fascists!'

Lucia grabbed his collar. 'What do you mean?'

The boy was panicking, his words tumbling out in a muddle. 'Blackshirts. And Germans. Now. Here. Coming up the hill.' Lucia glanced down the road and suddenly saw from the far house the white sheet of warning being lowered from a window.

She seized FitzGerald's arm urgently: 'Look – the sign. Go! Quickly back up the mountain. I will send the others. Let them not be drunk!'

He hesitated, but she goaded him on. 'No, you go!' Then she chose the right argument. 'Lead your boys out. Command them up the mountain! If you are found, they will kill everybody!'

Oleksiy and Stavros came out at that moment by chance.

'Quick, you two. Get the others out. The Germans are coming.'

There was chaos in the party room as every man sought to flee. The women remained behind, clearing the place up and trying to make as if they had been there on their own.

PREPARING FOR BATTLE

As they scrambled up the track in the direction of Santa Femi, there was no doubt that something strange was going on down below in the village and in some of the outlying farms. Light was pouring from unshuttered windows, which was unusual and probably illegal. Hoarse, outlandish cries could be heard and, along the path from the village to the house in which they had been dancing, torches were flashing; none of the locals possessed torches.

Goode led the clandestines in retreat. FitzGerald took up the rear, following ever further behind as he felt his way step by step while they rushed upwards. It was two hours before they arrived at the little hamlet that had long been prepared as a place of retreat and they collapsed onto the cold floor of an empty barn.

When FitzGerald finally arrived, he found only Goode awake, checking the approaches. He had lit a fire in the rusting brazier and covered each of the others with a blanket from the store. Goode had equipped this shelter with a few essentials only a week or so earlier, in case of a raid.

Goode made some acorn coffee on the paraffin stove and he and FitzGerald sat together beside the brazier, their hands around their tin mugs. The slight form of Lucia, still in her dance dress, slid through the doorway.

Both men rose to greet her and they could see her smile reassuringly in the flickering light.

She spoke first: 'It's alright. They're not following. I have a sentry posted overlooking the village – he's Signora Manca's youngest – who'll tell us if they move. But the devils are over the moon. They've stayed in the village hall, eating and drinking. Signora Manca invited them.' Lucia giggled unexpectedly, which made FitzGerald want to reach out and hug her. 'Some of the girls who just before were dancing with your lads are now dancing with the devils.'

FitzGerald: 'So what were they after?'

'They are after our boys. You know, quite a few are soldiers who ran away from the army after the 8th September. They were ordered to report weeks ago, but none of them did. The Germans search for them because they are afraid that they will start a *banda*. Luckily almost all of them were at the ball and –' she looked around at the prone bodies – 'you've got them with you here.'

So, this was neither reprisal, nor an attempt to get hold of him or other fugitives; just a pressgang raid. At least, FitzGerald hoped so.

By early the next morning, Goode had been down to the village, watched the Germans withdraw, talked with the villagers and returned. He found that Lucia had rustled up some breakfast – a slice of grey bread and lump of cheese for each man, washed down with acorn coffee – and that FitzGerald was handing out ammunition and checking that the weapons were usable.

FitzGerald decided to return to their HQ, which had been left alone. There would be two changes to their way of life. First, they would establish a rota of sentries on the approaches to Pozzo, not just the HQ. Second, they would carry arms in future. Pozzo being higher in the hills than regular German patrols came, there was little risk of bumping into unwelcome visitors; but, as last night showed, there might always be surprises.

They carried all the equipment and weaponry that had been unearthed from their hiding places, down to HQ. The lookout rota was set and the Pole and the Greek set off to establish the vantage points covering the approaches to Pozzo.

Once they had left, FitzGerald selected, from among the pistols that Goode laid out on the table after cleaning them and greasing the working parts, the smallest and cleanest. He turned the weapon over, admiring its lightness relative to the Luger he had in his own holster.

He saw Lucia staring at his hands and anticipated her question. 'It's a Walther PPK; German, of course. In your hands, it won't murder any more innocents.' He held it out to her, but Lucia did not move. He went on, 'The PP stands for "parabellum pistol". It refers to that Roman admonition that all soldiers know: "*Igitur qui desiderat pacem, praeparet bellum.*" "Let he who desires peace, prepare for war".'

Lucia refused the weapon and her tone was cold. 'That's the excuse you men use when building armies. But I believe the opposite. The more soldiers and weapons there are in the world, the more likely there is war. We must stop arming ourselves if we wish for peace.'

At that, FitzGerald gave a short laugh. Goode remained at the table, giving final checks to the weapons he had laid out for distribution. FitzGerald put the pistol he had proffered back down on the table and moved away.

'Should the Huns arrive here and we are disarmed, there won't be much point in our wishing for peace, Mrs Riva. But I realise that I cannot persuade you to think responsibly. Perhaps Mr Goode will be more successful.' He addressed him: 'Goode, you give the *signora* a weapon, if only so she can protect herself.'

Her intervention was sharp. 'No thank you, Colonel.'

Goode held out the pistol by its barrel. 'If we are attacked here, we will need everybody to fight.'

She responded, 'And you will also need someone to care for the wounded and shelter the children. That is I.'

'But Signora Riva, you can't rely on others to protect you if you are attacked.'

Lucia's anger showed in her whole body, which became instantly tense, and her face flushed. 'No! Never. I am a woman. I give life; I do not take life. I feed, I clothe, I wash the wounds. The vile things that men do I will never do.'

FitzGerald turned his back on her with a rapid movement, 'God! This bloody woman!'

Lucia gave him a look of loathing, said nothing and left.

Goode was amused by FitzGerald's irritation. He goaded him just a bit. 'We've got a man here like that, too. Kilby. He's a pacifist.'

FitzGerald's anger had another outlet. 'What! What the hell's a yellow belly doing here?'

'The War Office thought it would be fun to send him on a raid with the commandos as a medical orderly. Probably hoped he'd get killed. But he got captured. And escaped.'

'Pair him up with that woman. And let the Huns pacify them together!'

FitzGerald left the room to pace along the farm path. Already energised by danger, he was further roused by Lucia's insubordination. *What are you doing, FitzGerald?* He demanded of himself. *It's my duty to go south, but I'm prevaricating. I've been ensnared by the charm and generosity of these hosts. Weakened. They've no purpose in life beyond survival. Who among them would sacrifice themselves for the cause as we do? The clash with Lucia over the weapon was good. Now I see the great gulf in understanding that exists between us and them. They are the white man's burden. I almost went native; I have no right to do so.*

JUST ANOTHER VILLAGE

A few kilometres from Pozzo, Fröhlich's men were at work, administering justice. Down in the valley, they were herding all the inhabitants of a village into its cemetery and then torching the houses.

What FitzGerald had feared had come to pass, but he did not yet know it, because he was in the hills and preoccupied with the defence of his own encampment. The Hammer and Sickle Battalion, or elements of it under Neri's leadership, had totally destroyed the most important petrol dump in the vicinity, and with it four of Hammer and Sickle's youngest recruits, who had been burnt alive in the conflagration they had started, along with uncounted peasants and their children. The final cost in Italian lives, of this contribution to the democracies' "oil plan" to eviscerate Nazi fuel supplies, would be much greater.

In the first days of November, the two armies competing for Italy had checked each other on the Gustav Line. The democracies sought to tie down as many of the Nazi forces as possible; in turn, Hitler's men were preventing their enemies from getting near the resources of the Balkans and Austria. The looting of Italy was well under way. All military equipment seized from the demoralised

Italian armed forces, who had been abandoned by their generals, and as much food, vehicles, engineering works, minerals, gold reserves and even art treasures as could be loaded up, were being carted back to Germany.

The Salò government could do nothing to stop this, let alone the other two governments – the monarchy down in Brindisi and the CLN in Rome – who simply bickered. In central and northern Italy, partisans of the same stripe as Foschini's men, or else communists, were sabotaging German communications and seizing their supplies; Jews were hiding out in the wilderness, their young ones armed to repel the hounds of Himmler; brigands posing as partisan troupes, made up of desperate males of every nationality and background, roamed the hills, seizing food and hunting women.

Aside from looting, German units were holding down the population, punishing any resistance and making examples of those with the temerity to show charity to the outcasts.

After the petrol dump incident, and shortly before being transferred north to prepare for the killing fields of France, Field Marshall Rommel permitted the selection of villages for destruction at random. At one of these villages, Fröhlich drove up to check and found a medical corps colonel who had come to inspect the regiment's medical team.

The medic was complaining. 'In Russia we had flame throwers and it was much easier.'

'Brunner has put in for flame-throwers for months, but none have arrived.' Fröhlich was famous among his colleagues for achievements in Ukraine that had given his unit the sobriquet "Blowtorch Battalion", so he knew the value of that equipment. 'It seems all our flame-thrower production goes east!'

The medic was petulant. 'They put too much effort and resources into liquidating the population there. They could so easily just let them starve to death and leave us, who don't have that option, the resources.'

A little girl ran, crying, out of one of the houses, her hair on fire.

Fröhlich watched her being shot and shook his head sadly.

'They are just animals, really. No power of reason.'

'Like the Slavs,' was the medical officer's summation.

Far above, FitzGerald and Bregante were standing on the flat roof of his HQ, looking down into the valley below, where, spreading as far as the horizon of dark mountains, was a myriad of lights. Lights wavered and changed colour intermittently from bright orange to dull red. Hundreds of fires were burning, each of them representing the house of a peasant family.

FitzGerald spoke first, 'That is the New Order.'

Bregante was stricken. 'It is a pity that the world cannot see this; nobody in England or America could believe that such a thing could happen in a Christian country.'

Lucia came out to join them. When she saw what they were watching, tears started to course down her face. Bregante took her two hands in his and gazed intently at her: 'My dear, it will be over soon. The devils will go and –'

'They will all be dead.'

FitzGerald watched them, outwardly impassive. *Could I have organised resistance?* he thought, not for the first time. No: it would simply have stimulated greater repression, larger numbers of Germans. *But what I must do next time is remove the peasants, help them into the hills with us. Though God knows how we will feed the hundreds...*

FitzGerald was in command. The Italians, even the ever-resilient Lucia, seemed too overcome to know how to react. He ordered Goode to organise two teams to scour through the desecrated villages as soon as the Germans had withdrawn. They were to see who might have survived, aid them and report back to headquarters.

THE AUDIT

Two days later, FitzGerald sat at his table, compiling his report. As Foschini entered, dressed in a simple soldier's jacket and breeches without insignia, he looked up. 'Eight survivors found. We sent down a dozen men to the villages at dawn and they have all come back. They talked to witnesses and made notes on the spot. They buried many, but not all, bodies. This is what they tell me:'

Grief and anxiety were written on Foschini's face. He sat down heavily without speaking.

FitzGerald read out: 'Gessopalena. Half the village has been demolished by the Germans. They blew up over fifty houses at three in the morning while the inmates slept. A few of the bodies have been extricated and the stench of death is everywhere.

'Casoli. When the Germans came, they tied up the old men, raped the women and then killed everybody. One survivor.

'Village of La Fàrë. Completely destroyed by the Germans, who also demolished bridges and the viaduct.'

Lucia was outside the door, listening. Her hands were straight by her side, her fists clenching and unclenching, her face taught and staring. Tears rolled down her cheeks.

'Selva. All men killed immediately. Some of the women were

raped and killed on the spot. Otherwise, they were taken away, tied up and then, at the end of the afternoon's pillaging and burning, as the soldiers sat round a fire drinking, they were dragged out and raped by the men one or two at a time. Many were killed thereafter, although some were allowed to run away naked and bloody, and are wandering around in such a state of shock that they are unlikely to survive. Four died of exposure overnight, including two little girls and a grandmother.

'Civitella. Not a single building remains. The German method was to close all the doors and windows and then explode a mine inside each house. This blows down all the walls and the roof and usually sets fire to the ruins as well.'

FitzGerald looked up. 'This serves no military purpose whatsoever.'

Foschini made no reaction, just stared as if he was watching the killings before his eyes. FitzGerald looked down and continued reading.

'Santa Agata. The Germans rounded up all the families, locked them in the largest room and set fire to it. When they tried to escape, the Germans outside amused themselves by shooting to wound, sometimes only killing them after eight or nine shots.

'Pennadomo. Houses looted, all females tied up and raped. However, the Germans got so drunk that they left without burning the houses down.

'Chiesa. Burnt to the ground. Some of the sick from the hospital were found on the road outside the village and shot.

'Another village nearby, no name written down. After the German patrols destroyed the villages and blew up some of the houses, their blackshirt helpers entered the church where the old priest had remained with the elderly and infirm, dragged the priest outside and hung him. They then took petrol –'

Lucia burst in, her face wet with tears, her hands over her ears: 'Stop it! Stop it! I can't bear this anymore. How can you men do such things? How can you read such things?'

FitzGerald started up as Foschini seized her arm: 'Lucia!'

Lucia screamed, 'Why did you not stop them? What use are your soldiers and your guns if you cannot protect us against these beasts? I hate you, all of you!'

FitzGerald turned to Foschini. 'This might have happened even without Neri making the attack.'

Lucia broke loose from Foschini and shouted in FitzGerald's face. 'Lies! You failed to stop those so-called *bande*! You let them provoke the devils!'

Foschini called over to her, 'They must be punished. They can't get away with this. Tell FitzGerald he must fight, not just wait!'

'Yes, yes, anything to stop this. What are your men doing, FitzGerald, standing aside?'

Foschini looked at FitzGerald. 'Fight with us, Colonel. Listen to Riva Lucia.'

THE DROP

From Allied HQ, FitzGerald and Foschini requested weaponry with ammunition and essentials such as boots, first aid kits and communication equipment. A message came back naming a certain November night, and FitzGerald and Foschini combined forces to stake out the dropping zone, some thirty minutes' fast walk from HQ.

Reliable men were put in charge of the radio to receive the confirmation and runners stood by to alert the teams that would be needed to cart back supplies.

On the designated night and the next, no planes came. Everybody remained on standby, with Foschini sleeping in the farm near headquarters.

At 21:30 on the fourth night, a young Canadian came running in to HQ, gasping, his hair plastered with sweat. 'Sirs – *le sigarette sono arrivate*. The cigarettes have arrived.' It was the code. The signal. FitzGerald sent the runner off and rose immediately, slipping his Luger into its holster.

As he left HQ, he found Foschini arriving with Lucia. Together they made for the beacon on the track above the stream and found Goode and his team dragging faggots from out of the bushes.

In the moonlight, the dropping zone could be seen marked out on a wide grassy slope enclosed by two abutments of the mountain. Piles of brushwood had been distributed in the shape of a letter "H", to be lit when the plane was heard. On the edge of the field was a small stone *cascina*, steading, that served as a shelter in which to wait. A fire smouldered in one corner, emitting clouds of acrid smoke but little warmth. There was snow on the mountain summits and the sentries posted beside the signal fires shivered with cold.

When the sound of an aircraft was first heard, the time, on a luminous dial held by FitzGerald, read 23:00. 'Time over target,' was all he needed to say. At a command from Goode, the sentries lit the fires and the dry brushwood flared up and burned brightly, throwing grotesque shadows against the slopes at the edge of the dropping ground.

From the distant drone of airplane engines, there was more than one machine.

FitzGerald spoke. '*A posto, ragazzi*. All's well, lads. The light's good. Stand by the flags and keep them waving.'

The brigaders stared in silence at the planes, white under the eerie light of the moon. By the flicker of the flames, their expressions were a mix of bewilderment and hope. They might, if the drop equipped them as they hoped, be about to become real soldiers again. Their hearts pumped at the throbbing of the engines, jumped as a pilot flashed the recognition signal.

Twice the planes circled over the mountain.

Meanwhile some local people, the poorest peasants or *carboni*, who eke out a living on the higher slopes, had seen them and begun to collect on the edge of the field.

The letter H stood out against the mottled background of snow and dark earth. The leading airplane came towards them and passed overhead.

Brigaders pointed out to each other the openings in the fuselage and white parcels waiting to be thrown out.

Slowly a plane circled to the right, followed by the others, and passed overhead a second time. Foschini's men began to wave frantically, and, forgetting that they could not be heard, shouted encouragement to the pilots.

The leading aircraft approached a third time, gradually losing height as it did so. As it came over the drop area, the containers attached to the underside of the wings were cut loose. The same procedure was followed by the next plane and the next. Cargo cascaded down. Then, as the first plane came round once more, a figure could be seen to jump from the doorway; a silk parachute burst open above him and a murmur of surprise arose from the watching crowds.

'*Un uomo, e un uomo*! A man! It's a man!'

The peasants stood open-mouthed as the parachutist floated to earth, landing neatly in the centre of the field, and then became enveloped in the cords of his parachute, which crumpled to the ground beside him. Several ran forward to help him.

Eventually the arrival was untangled and he strode up to FitzGerald, his teeth shining white through his facepaint, in a broad smile.

'Colonel FitzGerald, I presume?'

He was a big man, not only tall but broad, and made massive by his huge backpack, ammunition pouches on his chest and round helmet with its leather protector covering the lower part of his face.

'Indeed. And of whom do I have the honour?'

'Rourke, 3 Commando, 2 SAS. Excuse me, Sir, but I had better give the others a signal so that they can join the party.'

He pulled a Very pistol from his pack, pointed it upwards and fired a green signal. It rose into the air in a wide arc, leaving a trail of white smoke behind it, and then fell into nearby trees.

On seeing the signal, the leading pilot dove his plane again. Six bundles shot into the sky and then more from the following aircraft, until the whole sky seemed full of moths.

FitzGerald looked upwards: 'How many are you? We expected only gubbins.'

'There are twenty of us. We were a bit puzzled – somebody has put out a lot of signals down there and we were about to drop on them when we caught sight of your two flags.'

'That's either the commies or the Huns...'

The wind had slackened and the parachutes were floating down very slowly. Some appeared to have floated far away and others were caught in the chestnut trees. Spectators ran off to find them.

For half an hour the planes continued to unload equipment, arms and rations. More than three hundred parachutes lay scattered around and the men were collecting the canisters, bringing what they could carry to a central dump for distribution under the eyes of Goode and Foschini.

The planes circled for the last time, dipped their wings in salute as they passed overhead and flew back south. FitzGerald allowed himself the thought that those pilots would be back among his kind for breakfast, whereas he...

The new troops formed up on the field and Rourke called a roll before being led to shelter by Foschini. Under Goode's command, men assembled the supplies and stored them swiftly in several different locations, with a responsible man in charge of each consignment. The women gathered up the parachutes to make clothing and bandages for the wounded.

In the packages dropped were German rifles – doubtless captured in North Africa – together with ammunition, grenades, boots, socks, cigarettes and chocolate. No light machine guns. No mortars. As Goode would report to FitzGerald next day, 'Nothing to make us into a real fighting force. Gadgets for sabotage, little anti-tank mines, explosive pencils, caltrops... Such as we used against you at Bannockburn.'

'Excuse me, Goode, but my ancestors were with Bruce at Bannockburn. They were Irish chieftains as well as Norman lords.'

Goode apologised and the younger and older man both smirked at each other.

FitzGerald laughed: 'Caltrops may not be over-useful. But at least they've sent a few rifles.'

Goode had worked hard to instil discipline into his mob of brigaders, but it had not been easy. He hoped that either the newly-arrived commandos would take over from the local *bande*, which might at least have the benefit of deflecting the attentions of the Germans from the villagers, or else they would absorb Goode's men, provide models of soldiering and lick the brigaders into shape. It soon dawned on him that neither would happen. The commandos melted away on their own, unilateral, mission. While Goode was frustrated, FitzGerald was glad that his men, rather than join an offensive, could do the work for which he had recruited them – defence of the local population against marauders, German or other.

PART FOUR

NORTH AND SOUTH

THE LEPIDOPTERIST

A week later, Lucia and Goode were talking to a grandmother beside her oven. The wizened old lady in black, with a black headscarf, was the decision-maker in a group of ragged children and two younger women. Her house was too near the road for her safety, but she wouldn't leave. 'Nobody ever comes up here; we are forgotten.'

'The road below is too crowded; they'll certainly be using this route too,' Lucia kept telling the incredulous old matriarch. 'Soon the devils will come up the track and stop at the farmhouse. They will drive off the oxen. What they can't take, they will smash. The people will be violated and probably killed – yes, even the children and you, in your eighties. So, *Nonna*, all the family must get away. Lock stock and barrel.'

Next day, the grandmother finally gave the order to her terrified family to evacuate. In two sluggish cartloads, they moved their belongings and the home was left empty. The family joined their neighbours in a trail of tears up the mountains, far from the helmeted hordes, spilling like larva along the lanes and gullies below.

On one of the many days that Lucia was trying to explain to frightened farmers that they should leave their houses, FitzGerald and Foschini were a few kilometres away, in a heavily wooded side of the hills, conferring beside a narrow road. Goode and a young Italian, Muro, Foschini's adjutant, made up Foschini's staff. A detachment of Foschini's, mainly consisting of bitter, fierce young Poles, sat around below, hidden by the scrub bordering the road itself.

FitzGerald was speaking. 'Rourke reports that my own outfit is fighting just over the river.'

Foschini, about to reply, was suddenly distracted. 'Look! Devils.'

A Mercedes-Benz staff car was driving slowly up the road. The four drew back into the trees; the others, further down the track, likewise melted away.

'What can it be doing here?' questioned Muro.

Goode replied. 'The roads below are chock-a-block with retreating vehicles and refugees. The car will be using the hill roads to make speed. Must be.' He looked at Foschini. 'Shall we take it, Sir?'

FitzGerald allowed no time for his Italian colleague to respond. 'No. There is no point of sheltering these poor people if we invite a roundup here.'

As they watched, the car stopped about three hundred metres from them and a very youthful, bespectacled officer got out, holding a butterfly net in his right hand, and strolled in their direction.

Startled, FitzGerald retreated further back. The other two followed him smartly.

'What the hell is he doing?'

From below, the other officer in the car could be heard calling out irritably, 'Don't be long, Krapf, be quick.'

'Wanting a crap' suggested Foschini, as the one with the butterfly net dived into the trees.

FitzGerald and Foschini both watched the car, from which they saw the second officer get out and stretch. The driver also left his place, fiddling with his breeches buttons, about to pee.

FitzGerald, Foschini and Muro were squatting in silence when the officer with the butterfly net almost fell over them. They started up and found before them a slim, gentle-looking youth with spectacles, rather bookish. He looked horrified at the sight of the three men.

In Italian, FitzGerald said, 'Good day, Lieutenant.'

After a moment's astonishment, he replied in English. 'You are English, are you not?'

'Very brave of you to say so.'

The German smiled a sweet smile, *like a chorister*, thought FitzGerald. He noticed that the German had a pistol holster but made no move to open it. Neither he, nor the two Italians with him, had reached for their weapons, so unthreatening was the apparition confronting them.

FitzGerald pointed to the butterfly net: 'Foraging for your troops' dinner?'

The boy laughed a merry, tinkling laugh. 'No, I am after a Clouded Yellow butterfly. *Colias croceus*. This area is famous for having Clouded Yellows in November.'

'And you are the official Wehrmacht butterfly collector?'

The German grinned, clearly liking the quip. 'No, entomology is my hobby. I am the education officer under Colonel Selmayer. When the war is over, I will be a schoolteacher again.'

'So, you teach the stormtroopers of the Third Reich about butterflies?'

'Oh no. My present job is to give lectures to the troops on Italian history and culture.'

Foschini broke in. 'So that they know what they are demolishing!'

Krapf looked down, pained. 'We have made a lot of destruction. I am sorry.'

Foschini was mocking, bitter. '*Es tut mir leid!* I'm sorry!'

FitzGerald was torn between eliminating the visitors and avoiding repercussions. 'You'd better clear off. There are many Italians who are not satisfied with "sorry". Selmayer, he's the local commander, isn't he? He has murdered their families.'

Instead of taking his cue and turning away, Krapf asked with youthful eagerness, 'Are you the famous Colonel FitzGerald?'

'Famous, I don't know. Why do you think that?'

'Oh, your picture is in our office. All the *wehrmachthelferinnen* – that's our lady auxiliaries – say you are very handsome.'

'I am honoured.' The idea that he was a pin-up for the enemy army was novel to FitzGerald.

'Fröhlich says you are the organiser of guerrilla raids here.'

'Thank you for the warning. SS Major Fröhlich?'

'He is promoted to *obersturmbannführer* – lieutenant colonel. But yes, it must be. I understand that you and six hundred others escaped his search at Ginestra. All Fröhlich's colleagues are laughing at him.'

'I am glad they laugh. Please take a seat, Lieutenant.' To himself: *If I am to send this kid back alive, I'd best see what we can find out first.*

Krapf squatted down on the grass.

'It's not true that I organise raids. In fact, I discourage them. I don't want to give Selmayer any excuses for killing more innocents.'

The German looked carefully at him. 'I believe you.'

FitzGerald said nothing. He and Foschini gazed at the young man, puzzling what to make of him.

Then Krapf, as if he had suddenly liberated himself from the shackles of convention, spoke with passion, 'Colonel FitzGerald, many of we Germans do not understand why we are still at war. We will soon be fighting in France as well as Italy.'

Goode noted that the German assumed that the Allies would be crossing the channel but said nothing. FitzGerald found himself both repelled by, and in admiration of, the boy's candour, putting it down to effeminacy.

Krapf continued. 'What is going on in Russia is more than flesh and blood can stand. We are on the retreat from Smolensk; we are retreating to the Dnieper. According to people who have just come from there, we are losing more men every day than we have lost here in Italy in an entire month. Nobody believes we will win: we only hope that we can stop the Russians getting into Germany.'

Foschini had met former allies who had said similar things to him in the hospital and convalescent home where they had shed their faith in the *Führer*. He felt sympathy, but FitzGerald had none. He greeted this confession with a wry glance, in which a certain triumph lingered on the corners of his mouth. The lepidopterist saw their reactions and lowered his eyes like a naughty schoolboy.

As they sat silently, there was a shout from the car. 'Come on, Krapf!'

'Colonel, I had best leave you. I will not speak of our encounter.'

'And I won't kill you. Just get away while you can.'

At that very instant, there were shots. A cry. Whoops of joy. Krapf sat as if petrified. FitzGerald and Foschini jumped up and started off down the slope towards the road, but Foschini remembered Krapf and detailed one of his men, an Italian, to stay with him. The young man had risen and was standing with his cap in one hand and his butterfly net held out in the other, like some curious mockery of an athlete's statue.

FitzGerald found that both the driver – a teenager, by the look of him, with soft down over his lip – and the middle-aged officer had been shot. Foschini's men were grinning and shouting with joy as they stripped the bodies of watches, rings, wallets and boots, bantering and bargaining about who was to get what.

FitzGerald turned to Foschini, indicating the triumphant Poles. 'Idiots.'

One of the Poles heard and shouted: 'Why? Two less Germans to rule the world and a lovely car for us!'

From the look of mortification on his face, Foschini understood FitzGerald immediately and answered the Pole: 'If the devils know this happened here, they will kill every man, woman and child for miles around and burn twenty villages!'

A truculent blond, a German cap perched on his head, shot back: 'But they don't know.'

FitzGerald, appalled at the indiscipline, was about to intervene when Foschini rose to the occasion. Instead of the unsure, reluctant rebel that he had seemed to FitzGerald before, he snapped back into his role of officer of *Alpini*. 'They will come looking. Get the car into the river with the bodies tied in so that they can't surface.'

Other men had congregated around and Foschini gave out orders.

'You, take the devils' uniforms, guns, wallets, everything, back to base.' The Poles looked sour as Foschini turned to his adjutant. 'Strip the car of anything useful.'

Foschini turned back to face FitzGerald. Before he could speak, FitzGerald said very quietly. 'I'd let them have the personal stuff if I were you. Or you'll have trouble. Just get hold of anything useful to operations.'

Goode, having just overturned the body of the dead German officer, raised his eyebrows in a way that FitzGerald interpreted as a private signal. He went over to Goode.

'Yes?'

Goode pointed down at the body, which had lost its trousers and boots.

FitzGerald looked at the dead man's jacket, the chest of which was torn and bloody, 'He's a full colonel.'

'See his gorgets, Sir. He's general staff.'

'Well done, Mr Goode. What on earth is he doing gallivanting around these back roads?'

'It could be a recce. It might be just that he wanted to make the butterfly lassie happy. Either way, we've caused ourselves trouble if his muckers knew he was coming this way.'

'As Foschini has already noted.'

While they talked, Muro was enthusiastically scavenging in the car. He called to his commander. 'Look, Sir, here's a briefcase! With documents!'

Foschini took it, glanced at the papers within, handed it to FitzGerald and returned to his original train of thought. 'And you two, I want this car pushed into the river at its deepest point, with the bodies strapped down. Do it! Fast!'

The Poles looked unhappy, even resentful, but went to the task of eliminating the evidence.

FitzGerald and Goode were sifting through the documents in the briefcase.

As they did so, Foschini's man appeared with the entomologist, who had been relieved of his belt and holster, his net trailing from his right hand.

Krapf, faced with the driver's body, cried, 'Oh poor Wallraff, poor Liesel!' Then he saw the body of the middle-aged colonel: 'Oh Colonel!' He looked round at nobody in particular. 'He has three children!'

Krapf knelt down beside the older man's body, just as one of the Poles was tugging off his socks. Krapf, seemingly unaware of what was being done, embraced him and placed a cheek next to his. Tears were coursing down his face.

Laughing, the Pole gave him such a kick that Krapf collapsed across the corpse. He righted himself, turned to look up at Foschini, who was nearest to him, and said, 'He came up this road to please me. Oh God.'

FitzGerald looked up from reading. 'Foschini, get one of your boys to look after this ...' he hesitated, then added 'this child. Not the Poles or Russians; they'll just cut bits off him.'

Foschini pulled Krapf up and away from the bodies. The German seemed stunned and let himself be pushed round then relinquished to two of the men. Foschini then came over to where FitzGerald was glancing at documents, produced by Goode from the German briefcase. He opened out some architectural plans and stared at them, along with Foschini. They looked tellingly at each other.

Speaking quietly, FitzGerald said, 'Foschini, we've got both the plan of fortifications for the next line of defence, and the order of battle, if I am not mistaken. A lot of stuff about the new defensive line.'

Foschini seized the papers and gazed at them. 'No!' He glanced down, rapidly, turning the pages over fast. 'My God, what treasure!' Foschini looked back up at FitzGerald, exhilarated. 'When they find out these plans are missing, they may change it all.'

FitzGerald countered. 'It wouldn't be easy.' He pointed at an elevation. 'They must've had thousands of slaves building that for months. Making changes takes a long time. Time enough to bomb.'

'And time for rear operations,' added Goode.

A shot rang out. Both men looked up.

'What did you say to your men about the butterfly lover?'

'I told them he is a prisoner to be treated according to the Geneva Convention.'

'Perhaps they haven't read the Geneva Convention.'

Both men started walking towards the sound of the shot, while Foschini still sifted through the documents. As they did so, the Polish boy who had answered back appeared carrying Krapf's clothing over his arm, boots in hand and cap on head.

'Here's the booty, Sirs. No holes or blood; he took it off before dying.'

Looking at his commanders' faces, he spoke to their unasked question, but with an ironical look on his face. 'Shot while trying to escape, Sir. Unfortunate. But think of the butterflies that will survive!'

FitzGerald turned away in irritation and spoke with Goode. 'The late entomologist told me our friend Fröhlich is looking for me around here. You'd better make sure there are none of us within ten miles, but also post a detail nearby so that if the Huns do start venting their fury on any remaining locals, we can distract them.'

'And you, Sir?'

'It's about time I'm off south. Now.' He waved the papers. 'With these, there's no choice but to hurry. If we're lucky we may have a few days before the Huns realise they are missing and a little longer before they can react.'

'So you really are leaving us?'

'Yes. You can take care of everything here. Cooperate with Captain Foschini, but keep our chaps separate.'

Foschini was astonished at his sudden decisiveness. 'But FitzGerald, you can send someone else with these papers. Your leadership is needed here.'

'No, I am not a good leader here; I'm thinking all the time about collateral damage or the whines of the women. I'm just holding Goode and you back. Your girlfriend has sewn so many doubts into my mind that I've seized up!'

'Not my girlfriend, FitzGerald. But I too will go, back home. Goode is a fine commander. With your SAS working behind the lines here, the main focus of partisan activity will be further north, maybe even around Ginestra. Also, I want to see what I can do for Ginestra as the devils retreat past it. My mother is there, and all my childhood friends. They may be in danger again.'

'And you'll take Lucia?'

'No, she'll stay here with Bregante's children until Ginestra is safe. Also, she is still the organiser, keeping hidden all your soldiers, along with many others.'

Behind their words were thoughts which had nothing to do with military dispositions. FitzGerald pretended to speak lightly, as if joking. 'I'd like to be the best man at your wedding!'

'She won't marry me, FitzGerald. Should she re-marry, it will be to Bregante.'

'Really?'

'How can you ask such a question? Do you know her so little?'

'Why should I know her? I am just one of the six hundred prisoners she helped.'

Foschini laughed. 'How modest you are. When I saw you two together, I was angry for Domenico. And galled for myself, as if she had passed me over yet again. But then I realised she won't have you; even if a decade goes by and her memory of him fades, she'll never leave Domenico's family. Her sense of responsibility may make her continue as your guide to the lines, but don't make the mistake of thinking that there is more to her feelings for you than responsibility. I've been in love with Lucia since she was a child and I know her every mood.'

FitzGerald did not want to hear these things, 'Really?'

'Yes, I used to take her fishing. And run up the hill with her on my shoulders.

When she was 13, my mother told me that I would marry her.'

'And why didn't you?'

'She never wanted me as anything more than an elder brother. I was into politics then, and soldiering. She disliked both. Quite unlike all the other girls who sought men who would leave for the cities, she had fallen for a farmer. But you know that.'

'She writes poetry and plays the piano…'

'And reads philosophy and loves art. Don't I know it? I thought that, if I downplayed politics and soldiering, I would get to her heart through Leopardi and Tasso, but she preferred a man who killed pigs for a living, for whom she would cook and sew and carry the bedpan for his mother.'

FitzGerald gave a sardonic smile. 'What a waste.' Foschini shot him a glance that said that, had he not needed the *Inglese*, he would have hit him.

FAREWELLS

Once he had made his decision, FitzGerald did not allow Lucia to cross his mind again. He moved fast. He went straight back to his HQ, packed his rucksack, and took off his uniform, folding it neatly and placing it on Goode's kit to indicate that it could be redistributed.

The next morning, two months since leaving PG500, he dressed once more in the civilian clothes he had worn on his flight from Ginestra, since cleaned and mended.

When he came out into the fresh, cool air, a group of brigaders and local peasants surrounded him.

FitzGerald, with Foschini by his side, chatted to the men by way of saying farewell. The family from the nearby farmhouse had come too and all embraced him, the females with tears in their eyes. Then came Bregante and his children.

One of the women called out, 'You cannot go on alone, it's winter soon.'

He responded, as was his wont, 'I must get back to my soldiers.'

'He is a good father to his soldiers,' he heard a voice say; they were murmuring, talking about him.

An old man called Giuseppe shuffled up. 'Be careful, very

careful, my boy, especially where you place your feet in the dark of the night. Trust every local you may meet on the mountains, in the fields, along the lonely paths or on the farms, as if he is your own brother. He will help you, show you the way, give you food and water. And he will ask nothing of you. Go into the villages if you must. There are good people there too. But avoid the towns like the plague. You see, my son, where there are many men together, God's air gets a little thin…'

FitzGerald gave a short bow, more of a nod, to the group. Then he steadied himself to do something that he found unnatural but that, in Italy at this moment, seemed necessary. He embraced Giuseppe and kissed him on both cheeks because it was the right thing to do.

'Gabriella and her family are coming up to see you!' someone called out, so FitzGerald went forward to meet the woman who had done his laundry and say goodbye to her and those who had brought him and his men food. Halfway down the slope, about twenty men, women and children were coming up, plus the priest. FitzGerald returned three Pirandello plays and a volume by Benedetto Croce that the priest had lent him. A lady whose name he had forgotten presented him with a pair of much-darned socks.

The priest advised him: 'If you find traces of the shepherds, follow in their tracks until you catch up with them. They are all good people.'

FitzGerald was soon on the way out. Foschini and three or four others took him to the main road. There, Foschini stopped and held both FitzGerald's hands in his. Even FitzGerald understood that this was a different Foschini from the jilted lover of the night before. Foschini, for a moment, looked into his face, then, releasing his hands, embraced FitzGerald, grazing his cheeks: 'God bless you, FitzGerald.'

FitzGerald forbore from making a witty remark when he saw that the captain's eyes were wet, and he understood from the inflection in his voice that he really was moved in a manner that FitzGerald was not.

As they stood there, Foschini struggling to suppress his feelings, FitzGerald wanting to leave this scene without offending the Italian, Bregante re-appeared with Lucia. He was wearing an Alpine hat, with a new, long feather. Holding his hand was Enrico, in a dark jersey and rather scuffed leather shorts. Lucia wore a long black coat and black headscarf and carried an Italian army backpack in her hand.

Foschini knew then that she would leave with FitzGerald and that Bregante could not stop her. He could see a new lustre in her face. How he hated the thought, but she looked as she had when courting with Domenico. It was unbearable, his chagrin was uncontrollable; he turned away to look elsewhere, anywhere but at her.

Lucia went up to FitzGerald, ignoring Foschini, and said in a soft voice, 'I will accompany you.'

When Lucia had understood that FitzGerald had reverted to plan and really did intend to leave Pozzo and risk the perilous journey, eventually through the lines, but first through the ranks of retreating devils, her first thought was to remonstrate with him. Had he not promised to protect her people? To reinforce Goode and carry out the policy of reacting rather than initiating? But she had heard that he now had an overriding reason for getting through and knew that he would claim that Goode would take over.

And then she thought, *why should I not go? My job is done. Goode is already the main connection between the fugitives and the locals. The landlords have been squared, the farmers advised.*

She was surprised at how easily Bregante had accepted her proposal. She knew that Salvatore could love her, would love her, and that she would, could, reciprocate his love. It would never be the kind of love that she had shared with his brother, though; she would be marrying him out of duty. Then there was Sandrino. He would always adore her, but her feelings for him would be compassionate and sisterly. She would be marrying him because she loved his mother and pitied him. As she thought these thoughts, she blushed hotly in shame. Padre *Carmelo would tell me Domenico is watching me and that I am committing adultery in my heart even to think like this. But only the priests believe the dead watch us. Consoling nonsense. Domenico lives on only in my heart and that of his mother and brother. For us he is immortal, but for no-one else, still less for a mythical God.*

In her imagination, she could see Enrico playing with Chiara and Ebbo in the farmyard a kilometre away. Signora Bregante was cooking and Bregante was bringing in the firewood. Enrico was happy with the animals, the other children. She smiled as she pictured Enrico carrying a newborn piglet in his arms to show to Bregante, who got down on his haunches to admire the piglet and congratulate Enrico in Italian. No, she had to admit it, she was no more needed by the children than by the fugitives. Not for now, anyway. They could do without her. *The only person who needs me now is FitzGerald.* She laughed at her own reasoning, unsure whether she deceived herself.

Lucia made it sound very simple. 'You mustn't go alone. I will accompany you.'

FitzGerald looked from Lucia to Bregante in astonishment. 'Unnecessary. I speak enough Italian to fool the Germans.'

Bregante showed that this though this might not be his idea, that he at least concurred. 'Never Italians. You will be picked up by the militia if you are alone. Lucia can be your niece. That's much safer. Germans will not recognise you as a foreigner – they can't see people, only categories – but every Italian will, and the nearer you get to Rome, the more fascists there are. She will teach you how to behave like an Italian and when it is safe or not safe to talk.'

FitzGerald did not know whether to show his delight or not. He suspected that Bregante was doing something very difficult and he wanted to tell him that he was grateful for his trust as much as for Lucia's help, but that would appear to be acknowledging that there was some rivalry between them over Lucia. It also might suggest that this was not Lucia's free choice, but Bregante's. So, instead, he ignored Lucia and asked, 'Are there still fascists?'

Everybody laughed. Then Bregante answered, 'A few. We have our zealots, too; otherwise how could we have had the Inquisition?'

Bregante embraced FitzGerald. He turned to look at Lucia with affection. FitzGerald watched him, a sensation of humility coming over him as he thought of the sacrifices that Bregante and all his friends and neighbours were making. And how were they being repaid? He knew that some of his men took what they could, slept with the daughters and were careless with their traces, no matter how much discipline Goode pumped into them.

What can I do to change men's behaviour? It was fixed long ago. Forget it, I must get those documents to HQ; that way, many lives might be saved. My getting back to the regiment does not matter to the winning of the war, but the documents might.

Lucia looked down, blushing as if she understood that the two men were thinking about her. FitzGerald stepped down the path, his stick gripped in his right hand. Lucia followed behind him. At first, they were watched by the crowd, the priest waving, his right hand clutching the Pirandello.

The last time they looked back, they saw only Bregante in the distance, conspicuous by his Alpine hat. He had been watching them as long as they were in vision; now he was a vague figure in the cold light, stooping to enter the house with Enrico holding his hand.

THE PRIEST AND THE CRUSADER

While FitzGerald and Lucia were striding south, Fröhlich, returning to Palma from anti-partisan operations further north, received a visit from the priest Filipović, whom he had met in Rome but who had slipped his mind while he busied himself with establishing order around Florence. His men had recently shot several parish priests of villages thought to be succouring partisans, so he was puzzled when his orderly announced, 'There is a priest asking for you, Sir; he speaks good German and says he knows you.'

'Knows me?'

'He claims that *Hauptsturmführer* Priebke introduced you at Security HQ in Rome.'

'Oh, him.' Fröhlich recollected the unpleasant sensations he had had during that conversation, feeling that there was something depraved about Priebke and his connections with the Roman priests. He hesitated a moment, then remembered that this man was from Ginestra and commanded the waiting orderly. 'Bring him in. And stay here.'

The priest's ginger-blond hair was topped by a moiré biretta. His well-tailored black cassock had a silk trim that denoted, Fröhlich guessed, rank of some kind. He gave an ingratiating smile to the immobile Fröhlich, who stood in front of his desk and clearly had no intention of smiling or shaking hands.

'Filipović of Ginestra, bringing the book you requested, *Herr Obersturmbannführer.*' He held out his left hand, in which was a grey paper package the shape of a book, tied with hempen string.

'Ah yes, of course.' Fröhlich relaxed slightly, though he had felt immediately repulsed by something inexplicably unmanly about the priest. Without touching them, he knew Filipović' palms would be soft. The word *fettsack* – tub of lard – came into his head, for this was not the self-flagellating kind of Roman priest, thought Fröhlich the lapsed Lutheran, but the confidence trickster who would moan on about miracles and souls in heaven.

He opened the parcel; it was Virgil's "Georgics", a good edition, buckram-bound and with the bookplate of some wealthy family – Abramowicz – inside the front cover, lined with ebru paper.

'Thank you...' he could not bring himself to say 'Father' to such a prissy *fettsack*, but, 'please take a seat.'

He looked up at his orderly. 'You may go, *parteigenosse.*' His orderly raised his arm in salute, turned one hundred and eighty degrees and marched out.

Filipović was pleased to hear Fröhlich refer to his inferior as "party comrade". This gave him confidence to broach the issue that currently agitated him most – the fact that Jews who had been converted to Catholicism were being arrested and deported just as if they were ordinary Jews. He started by assuring the German of his admiration for the *Führer*, his loyalty to the Salò administration and his antisemitism. Fröhlich did not much value declarations of loyalty, even from a Croat; they were two a penny. Nor did he think much of converts to Catholicism. His responses may have made this obvious, for the priest shifted the subject to Ginestra and Fröhlich began to pay close attention.

Filipović felt his way carefully, sensing a sharpening of interest when he mentioned the Irishman who had been in charge of the prisoners, when they had escaped under this officer's watch. He did not say that he had sat at lunch with FitzGerald, but he confirmed that the man was in the hills, organising resistance.

Fröhlich agreed that this might be a serious nuisance. Could the priest locate him? Possibly. The priest could give no guarantees, but as proof of his loyalty, could point the Germans in the direction of where remaining Jews were hidden around Palma. 'And Ginestra?' Fröhlich asked. 'What is there to know there?'

Filipović had been kept in the dark about goings-on at the fortress. Although he had his suspicions about the "refugees from the cities", he was not going to sell out the count and countess. The same did not apply to Alessandro Foschini. This was a bombshell and he kept it until last. 'Are you aware of where Captain Foschini is as we speak, *Obersturmbannführer*?'

'In Salò, on Graziani's staff.'

'Only in theory, *Herr Obersturmbannführer*. He's with the Irishman. And so's his mistress, the widow Bregante.'

Fröhlich did not then notice the reference to Lucia, so dumbfounded was he by the news of Foschini's perfidy. His mind flew to the front cover of "Signal" this month that bore a photo of the two smiling comrades, intertwined.

'Are you telling me, Priest, that Foschini has joined the communists?'

Stilled by the intensity of the German's expression, his eyes boring into him, Filipović indicated his reply only with a slight movement of the head.

Fröhlich sprung up in fury, strode over the room and back. 'Traitor!' he spat out. 'Traitor!' To himself he promised: *I shall kill him.*

ARRESTED!

As FitzGerald and Lucia approached a small village, halfway between the home they were leaving and the main road that would take them towards Sulmona and the front, they were met by a local man who would get them through it, a taciturn peasant wearing a mouldy, almost green, black suit and an *Alpini* hat from the Great War.

Although the *Alpino* was beside them, FitzGerald felt exposed as he walked through the village street. He saw the quick glance with which people took them in. Women drawing water at the fountain laid down their pitchers and stared without remark or expression. They turned a corner. A man was walking towards them in the field-grey uniform and black shirt of the militia. His carbine was slung.

Signalling to Lucia, FitzGerald turned and marched back round the corner with a clatter of boots on the cobbles. He stopped when out of sight. He could hear the *Alpino* laughing and walking back towards him. He had his arm round the militiaman's waist. FitzGerald stopped and let them come up.

The militiaman shuffled along with an embarrassed grin on his face. 'This is Dante,' said the *Alpino*. 'He's not a bad chap, guards the railway line.'

Lucia joined them, amused. They chatted for a few moments. Then the militiaman mumbled something into the *Alpino*'s ear, in dialect so thick that even Lucia couldn't understand.

'Ha! He says you are being followed by a spy.'

'Spy?!'

'A child. They use children, these fascists. I can see him now.' As he spoke, the *Alpino* strode over to the monument, calling out 'Come on boy! I can see you!' As he did so, a child darted from behind the monument, careered round the *Alpino* before he had time to fling out an arm and threw himself at Lucia.

'Enrico!'

FitzGerald and Lucia had walked for three hours since leaving Pozzo and apparently Enrico had too, in his case quite often running to keep up, but always hiding. The child was exhausted and FitzGerald watched gloomily as Lucia petted and scolded him.

'I suppose you want him to come with us?'

'We can't leave him here, nor let him go back alone, even if…' She left it unsaid.

The route FitzGerald and Lucia were to take required them to skirt the Gran Sasso, a massif of several of Italy's highest mountains. This was already daunting enough, reasoned FitzGerald, without a child that he was sure he would find himself carrying. Yet, after what he had seen of refugees and rescuers, of self-sacrifice and charity, how could he let Lucia imagine that he hated the very idea of having the child with them? He said no more but focussed on what had to be done.

They had a map provided by Alessandro and they knew where isolated farms would probably accommodate them. Unless they were to climb high and cross the great Campo Imperiale, they would need to follow the beaten track. Going off the roads was only a last resort, as winter in the mountains was to be avoided not only because of the cold and ice, but also the hungry wild boar and wolf packs, which were more dangerous even than the Germans. FitzGerald had a pistol but Lucia had again refused a weapon, saying she did not know how to use one and she did not wish to learn.

They were at the start of a three-day hike, unless they could find transport, which was unlikely, not only because there were no petrol supplies for anybody other than soldiers, police and medical personnel, but because the enemy had stolen every horse and mule and slaughtered every ox. The first two days, with nights spent with peasant families whose main mode of communication was to give food and smiles of welcome, they followed winding paths and minor roads but thereafter could not avoid the major road on the south of the massif. Sometimes Enrico would walk beside Lucia, holding her hand, but as he flagged, FitzGerald would hoist him astride his shoulders and march on.

They found themselves heading southeast on roads full of enemy traffic coming at them: horses, mules, bicycles and trucks with riflemen on the running boards, little horse-drawn carts, droves of looted cattle and oxen, men on foot in German uniform, armed and unarmed, and Hungarians and Rumanians from the Organisation Todt. On horseback were Kalmyks and Tatars in fleece hats and *cherkesska*s and with long sabres that slapped their ponies' flanks. Many foot soldiers, shabby and tired, squatted by the roadside under their section corporals, some bartering loot for food, most plodding on with vacant eyes. Once some brave heart started singing:

'*Auf der Heide blüht ein kleines Blümelein
und das heißt: Erika...*'
'[There is a little bloom on the heath
named Erika...]'

But nobody joined in and he gave up after the second verse.

Lucia's heart went out to the men who were grey with fatigue, their eyes red, mouths open as if gasping for air, some even barefoot, dragging their rifles behind them. FitzGerald's reaction was different. He remembered newsreels of the Nazi army goose-stepping into Paris, almighty and contemptuous. Now its remnants were unshaven, unkempt and in no military formation: they were just a horde of scared men. He saw some riding the few remaining oxen; others were crowded onto peasant carts, sleeping in each other's arms as they jolted along. There were wounded, screaming from the juddering as they lay on wagons stolen from street cleaning departments. This, though, was not the longed-for end: he could visualise fresh troops taking up new defensive positions. He was sure that Rommel's successor, Kesselring, would throw many more bodies onto the pyre to hold the next line.

The three of them walked behind families with bundles, themselves part of a throng of peasants heading home. Nobody took any notice of them.

A column of several hundred manacled prisoners stumbled by, stinking of sweat and urine. All the men, aged between sixteen and sixty, looked dirty and unkempt, with uncut hair and unshaven faces. Most wore clogs and elements of a dark, prison uniform, mixed with what had probably been their own civilian clothing. These were slaves, being transferring northwards to labour on the next set of fortifications. As he watched them, FitzGerald saw one older man point up into the sky and cry out. The prisoners around him shuffled to a halt and followed his pointing hand. The guards too paused and craned upwards. There, circling above them, not that high, was an enormous golden eagle, soaring and swooping over the column as if inspecting them. A cry of wonder went up from among the prisoners.

One of the guards raised his rifle. As the shot rang out, there was a collective whimper from hundreds of watchers. He was a poor shot and the eagle did not check its course, but soared upwards, majestic, until it became a mere dot in the sky. Then it disappeared among the clouds. Lucia said, 'There is a poem by Trilussa called "The Eagle". He depicts the eagle up in the sky, looking down on pompous men holding meetings, and seeing us for what we are in his perspective – silly, benighted, little things.'

Then there was a panicky movement ahead. There were shouts and people scrambled away from the procession as a motorcade rammed its way through the crowds, forcing everybody else – trucks, mules, bicycles, carts – off the road to let it through. The car commanders stood upright in the turrets, goggles and scarves covering their faces from the grime that flecked their black jackets and caps, making them look, to Lucia, like strange fiends of the underworld, riding on ghouls from the imagination of Hieronymus Bosch.

FitzGerald and Lucia stepped back and sat down beside the throng, trying to look disinterested, though Lucia felt temporarily hypnotised by the sheer proximity of the dark beasts in such strength and numbers. FitzGerald glanced at her taut face and nodded at the armoured cars. 'What a tourist trap! This place is swarming with Germans like it's Berlin.'

His nonchalance broke the spell that had momentarily numbed Lucia and she started to take out a meal of cold boiled potatoes, tomatoes, olives and grapes. Enrico tucked in first. They each got a swig from the *fiasco* that FitzGerald carried over his shoulder when Enrico was walking. He never complained, but FitzGerald knew when the child could go on no longer, because he would turn and look at FitzGerald with inquisitive eyes, whereupon FitzGerald would hand the *fiasco* to Lucia and lift him up.

Now before them, walking under SS guards mounted on horses and trying to keep up with the pace of the vehicles in the column, was a gaggle of twenty adults with several small children, some carrying suitcases and all splattered with mud. There were little ones being dragged along by the hand, mostly crying or else in some kind of catatonic trance, being pulled by their mothers who stumbled beside their men, carrying absurdly impractical suitcases meant for holidays.

FitzGerald watched Lucia staring at the prisoners and knew what she was thinking from the expression on her face.

'I suppose that these are resisters who have been hiding in the hills.'

As he spoke, two tears slid down her cheeks and her lip

trembled. 'Look. *Poveretti*. Why? Why do they do it?' Her glanced moved to FitzGerald. 'Why?

An intense desire came over him to run over to the column, spray the guards with bullets and rescue the persecuted, but reason intervened. Even the smallest gesture by him would condemn them both and save not a single prisoner. Afraid that she would be unable to resist her impulse to act, remembering the moment at the farm when she had risked instant death to shout, he put out his hand and took hers.

A moment later, he realised that he had made a move that he would never have dared a few hours ago. And then she responded in a manner that astonished him, though at the same time it seemed natural. She edged closer and laid her head on his upper arm.

At this moment, FitzGerald felt he knew her heart. There had been acrimony between them as he had scorned the peasant fatalism, and she had derided his mission and self-righteousness. Yet she had not practised that fatalism, but been more dynamic, shown more initiative, risked more, than any of the six hundred officers and gentlemen. *And I?* he demanded of himself, *have I not disavowed my claims of moral authority, my evangelism?*

The armoured cars inched by, in decent order compared to the other vehicles. The last vehicle was a jeep with one officer in the rear and two men in front. At the very moment that they drove past Lucia and FitzGerald, the officer removed his hat, goggles and scarf to wipe his brow and smooth back his hair.

Without gesturing or turning her head, Lucia said in a low voice, 'That is the one who was at Ginestra.'

It was indeed Fröhlich, his face haggard, his appearance dusty, stained and crumpled. His left hand was bandaged.

'Don't let's make a movement that might attract his attention.'

Both looked down. The trail of vehicles was slow; tense, they watched Fröhlich pass by. Only then did they get up to continue their walk.

'He has more important things to concern himself with than

us.' Although he spoke to reassure Lucia, he thought to himself that, even while running away, the devils – he more and more used the Italians' name for the enemy – still had time and energy to search for Jews. So maybe they had energy to search for them too.

They walked on.

As the retreating hordes passed, Italians peered out from caves and spinneys and thickets. Seeing the end in sight, they embraced each other and lifted children up high. They laughed, they cried tears of joy. 'We have survived!' 'We have survived!'

After three days, FitzGerald and Lucia reached the outskirts of Sulmona, perhaps two kilometres from the statue of Ovid that stands in the centre of the small country town and railway hub. Ahead they saw a German unit blocking the road as it refuelled from a roadside supply and the men relieving themselves against the walls of the houses. Rather than try to get through, they decided to wait for them to continue their journey and slipped into a *locanda* in which a few old codgers sat before demijohns of wine. There was no food.

Not until FitzGerald and Lucia had sat down at a table did they realise that, hidden from the entrance by a partition at the end of the room, were two *carabinieri* with two militiamen, playing *briscola*. Lucia had told FitzGerald before that she had little fear of *carabinieri*, who were almost all loyal to the king while seeking to reassure the Germans and their Black Brigade allies that they were impartially policing the country and threatened no-one except lawbreakers. A very few *carabinieri* might support the blackshirts and, as she saw one of them rise from his table and walk towards her and FitzGerald, the fear gripped her that this might be one of those.

It was a tall and wavy-haired sergeant who ambled over.

'Nurse?'

Startled, Lucia rose like a naughty schoolgirl brought to book by teacher and answered, 'Yes?'

'You remember how your Dr Scotti helped me?'

It came to Lucia that this was the man who had dropped his trousers to show Dr Scotti his sores.

'Of course! And you used to be in Ginestra with the Station Sergeant.' She gestured him to sit.

'The Station Sergeant was my teacher. A gallant gentleman.'

He glanced at Enrico and then turned to FitzGerald, who was pretending to be snoozing.

'My name is d'Apote. You're alone?'

'No, I am travelling with my uncle Carlo.'

The *carabiniere* glanced at FitzGerald, who continued to doze.

She looked at d'Apote steadily: 'Uncle Carlo is dumb.'

In turn, the *carabiniere* looked carefully at FitzGerald and smiled very slightly.

'Oh yes, of course, I remember it well.'

Before their conversation could take off, one of the two militiamen, a *capo squadra*, scraped back his chair. As he did so, Lucia realised that the whole room had gone silent. The old men no longer sipped their wine, the game of *briscola* was in limbo and even the proprietor behind his bar was immobile, watching. The *capo squadra* strode over, the metal heel tips of his German boots clinking on the flags, and stood beside the table, staring over them, his eyes fixed upon the girl even while he spoke to the sergeant.

'D'Apote, please don't keep this beauty all for yourself. Introduce me.'

'This young lady is the nurse of the finest physician in the area, Dr Scotti.'

The *capo squadra* leered. 'There is a shortage of beautiful young girls here, so you are most welcome.'

Lucia blushed.

The *carabiniere* sought to help her. 'She is married.'

'Excellent.' He laughed crudely. And stared at her, his eyes blazing with lust.

Lucia's colour rose. She stood. 'We must go.' She grasped

Enrico's hand and prodded FitzGerald, who appeared to wake. '*Zio, let's go.*'

The *capo squadra* demanded, 'Where are you off to?'

'Back to Dr Scotti's.'

The *capo squadra*, pointing at FitzGerald: 'And who is this?'

'My uncle.'

D'Apote: 'He's deaf and dumb.'

Capo squadra smirked and tapped the side of his nose. 'Franco, Franco! I have met too many *sordomuti*, deaf and dumb, recently. They each turned out to be either a deserter or a fugitive.'

FitzGerald rose and picked up his bag, moving after Lucia towards the door. As they reached it, the *carabiniere* sought to distract the militiaman: 'I always knew she had a deaf-mute uncle.'

Neither had noticed the other militiaman rise quietly, pick up his weapon and skirt the tables in the direction of the door.

The *capo squadra* still had his eyes fixed on Lucia. 'In the past, cripples did not have pretty nieces available to help them.'

Lucia and FitzGerald were at the door, but found their way blocked by the other militiaman.

The *locanda* was still as the grave. The *capo squadra* said, loudly, 'I don't believe this is the uncle.'

D'Apote: 'Well, it doesn't matter to us, does it?'

'We must do our duty, Sergeant. Either I take the girl in for thorough questioning –' he guffawed – 'or you arrest that deserter or whatever he is.'

The Sergeant in turn rose. 'Leave the girl alone. I will see what I can do.'

He strode over the room, heading for Lucia. The militiamen took up positions beside the door, their tommy guns raised.

D'Apote spoke in a low voice. '*Signora*, the *capo squadra* doesn't believe this man is your uncle. If I do not take him in for investigation, then he will take you both and also report me to the German authorities.'

'We'll get away now.'

D'Apote: 'I am sorry, but you can't.' He indicated the militiamen with his eyes who, at their position near the door, were stroking their weapons and scowling.

FitzGerald: 'Alright. I will be arrested. But Lucia, you and Enrico get out of this.'

'Yes. He's right. Go quickly, *Signora*, before the militia take you too.'

She hesitated. Looked at FitzGerald. Touched his sleeve: 'We will find you.'

As she left, Sergeant D'Apote called over to the *capo squadra*. 'I have arrested the uncle for questioning.'

He turned to FitzGerald, speaking with a low voice. 'Really, young man, you should have hidden among the Germans. They would never have realised that you are *Inglese*. We Italians notice everything about other people! And now I have to hand you over to the Germans. What a nuisance!'

'You could just forget me. I'll disappear.'

He raised his shoulders and opened his forearms in a gesture of fatalism. 'Unfortunately, that is not possible now that there are so many witnesses to your capture. It is my duty as a government servant to hand you over to our allies.'

FitzGerald's old disdain for the Italians was evident in his sardonic reply, 'Which government? Which allies?'

The *carabiniere* shrugged; the insult was like water off a duck's back. 'In this part of Italy, there is only one government. And here come our allies to take you away.'

That was true, too. Outside the door was a stamping of nailed boots on the cobbles; the door of the *locanda* was flung open and an NCO led in a detail of Germans.

Capo squadra: 'A successful day, *Herr Obergefreiter*?'

The NCO, a massive man with a crew cut and a neck like a bull's, known as Goliath to his squaddies, pushed past the two militiamen, not paying them any attention, and made for the bar. Without a word, the proprietor slid over a *brocca* of red wine and then provided the same for the other three. They stood silent until the *capo squadra* sidled up to Goliath and pointed out FitzGerald.

'We have a prisoner for you. For questioning. Probably an American.'

The German's glance at FitzGerald was fleeting; he turned back to the bar and knocked the side of his already empty *brocca* for more wine. Then, without facing the Italian, his eyes fixed ahead on his wine, he ordered: 'Bung him in the truck with the others.'

FitzGerald was hustled out by the two militiamen. He turned his head to see Lucia by the door of the *locanda*, listening to the *carabiniere*. Then he found himself at the rear of a truck of which a German guard was unchaining the tailboard. On the deck inside were three shabby men tied together.

As he was about to climb on board, the guard commanded him to remove his boots. FitzGerald's heart sank as he did so, handing them over to the guard, who then made him climb aboard. He would make no fuss, lest they search him and find the pistol. They had not yet demanded his watch, which had been provided for him from the drop. His original watch and ring had been taken long before, when he was first captured in North Africa. As he handed over his boots, he looked back to see Lucia and Enrico walking in the direction of the town, the *carabiniere* watching, until she disappeared into the distance. FitzGerald thanked God for the *carabiniere*. He had sensed the malevolence of the *militiamen* and seen it thwarted.

FitzGerald had one wrist clamped in a handcuff, chained to the struts that kept the canvas cover of the truck in place. The stink of urine was overpowering and the straw on the deck was filthy. Once the guard had climbed back down, FitzGerald said good day to the three men. One of them replied in a dialect that FitzGerald did not understand. The other prisoners were unshaven, unkept and bruised on their faces. FitzGerald surmised that they might be deserters, or suspected partisans. Yet there was nothing military about them. They remained wordless when two of the Germans from the *locanda* climbed in and others went to the cab. The two guards ignored the prisoners, talking about the price of tobacco, women and the lice that plagued them, for which they blamed "the filthy Italians". FitzGerald heard the cab doors crash closed and then the engine roared into life with a shudder and began to chug in the direction of Sulmona.

He knew that Lucia had a rendezvous to make with a guide and wondered what would happen to that if she distracted herself by trying to find him. Now he was in German hands, there was nothing she could do for him, he was sure. He had to get away himself with the papers intact. He had been surprised that the militiamen had not searched him, even for loot, and was hoping that by giving up his pistol easily, he would avoid a search that would reveal the documents stuck to his chest. On the other hand, his pistol, a Walther PPK, stuffed into his boot under his trousers, was a German's weapon and its discovery would lead to summary execution. He could not see himself remaining unsearched for long. He should abandon the PPK here in the truck beside him, where there was a pile of smelly sacking – an ideal place in which to hide it. Once found, it could be too late to know whence it had come. The truck had clearly not been cleaned for months; nobody would do it anytime soon.

He glanced over at his companions. The three Italians slept, sprawled over each other. The Germans sat by the tailboard, gazing down the road. FitzGerald used his unattached left hand to ease the pistol from his boot and make his trouser bottom free, so that all he had to do was slide the weapon from his trouser to the sacking.

Watching the backs of the Germans, FitzGerald reached over to take the pistol. No sooner he had put his left hand up his right trouser leg than one of the Germans, perhaps suddenly remembering that there were four captives behind him, looked round. His eyes landed, in that first instant, on the three Italians snoring on the floor. In that time, FitzGerald started to scratch his right calf violently, as if in agony of itching. As the German's inspection moved to the chained prisoner and he saw the contortion that FitzGerald had to go through to scratch, he gave a great bray of a laugh. FitzGerald smiled as if embarrassed, while praying to God that the pistol would not fall out of his trousers and clatter on the floor.

The cackling soldier shared this anecdote with his mate, who fortunately took no interest in seeing whatever was being related, so FitzGerald grabbed the pistol and slid it under the sacking.

SULMONA RAILWAY STATION

More men, roped in pairs, were picked up in three stops en route. FitzGerald had assumed that the truck would be driven directly to whatever assembly point was being used for prisoners and that he would be taken for questioning. He had not foreseen that the truck would weave around Sulmona to collection points where other men and boys, now recognisably forced labourers rather than possible partisans, were collected. As others were pushed into the truck in twos and threes, tied together rather than chained to the struts as he was, FitzGerald stuck to his place on top of the sacking that hid the pistol, refusing to budge lest some other captive find it and make a use of it that would condemn them all. He knew the Germans would have no compunction in machine-gunning everybody in the truck if one revealed himself as a threat. Less prisoners, less work.

Once the truck was so full that the two guards had themselves to squat, backs to the tailboard and rifles pointing at their charges, not one of whom evinced any energy for resistance, let alone escape, FitzGerald heard from shouted commands that they were to go to the *bahnhof*, railway station. At that point, progress became very slow, the wheels constantly dropping into ruts or climbing over debris. Eventually, the truck stopped with a jolt that flung the men against each other with much cursing and spite. The guards flung open the tailboard and started prodding the prisoners over the edge, where they arrived in heaps to the great amusement of the driver and others from the cab, who had come round to receive them and force them to their feet. FitzGerald was last out because the key to his handcuffs had to be found, and he was the only prisoner to jump down, rather than be pushed.

As soon as he did so, he realised that the truck had stopped because piles of smashed brickwork and tiles covering the road rendered it impassable. A shambolic crowd, they were urged like cattle through the largely bomb-destroyed streets, where huddles of dispossessed and emaciated people squatted on the piles of rubble that had been their homes, some scavenging to find blankets, kitchen implements or anything that might serve them in their new status as refugees. Allied aircraft had attempted to bomb the marshalling yards but succeeded only in wrecking homes.

The station, so far unscathed except for bullet holes, was a dignified 19th century building with a wide piazza around which were *palazzi* of the same era and one Palace of Youth, across the front of which was the slogan:

DUCE A NOI!
THE DUCE LEADS US!

The piazza in front was large and four streets led to it, the houses and shops of which appeared mostly gutted. There were several makeshift pens containing prisoners; guards walked around the pens and kept away the German soldiers milling around or squatting down on the square, presumably awaiting the next transport. FitzGerald thought it strange to see such chaos, odd that the men were not organised in units or under command. When he looked closer, he realised that he was looking at mainly wounded men and that all of them were dishevelled and filthy, as if pulled from combat and dumped here out of the way.

On the side of the station building was a stencilled head of Mussolini, in his helmet, with the slogan:

MOLTI NEMICI! MOLTO ONORE!
MANY ENEMIES! MUCH HONOUR!

Checking out anything that might be useful if he were to find an opportunity to scarper, FitzGerald saw that to get to the nearest platform, you had to go through the building, and to get to the platform on the other side of the two rail tracks, you needed to cross those tracks – or, as at this moment, go round the train that stood at the nearside platform.

His group was halted a few metres from the railway line and had a good view of the platform and a motionless train of wagons filled with German soldiers. Soldiers were on the roofs and running boards, too. The Italian engine driver and other operatives seemed to be struggling with the coal-fired engine and a worried transport officer appeared to be alternately demanding and begging that they get the train away.

Adding to the confusion, the platform nearest held several hundred civilians, crouching down with their bundles or even lying as if they had been there many hours or even days. Sentries were patrolling a slim space between the military train and the women, children and old people crowding the platform and the lines beyond the platform. If somebody inadvertently stepped over the invisible line, the guard jabbed at them with his rifle. The only non-soldiers allowed in the corridor were a couple of men with metal trays and aprons calling out again and again, '*cestini, cestini*', lunch boxes. The soldiers would shout at them to come up to their windows to sell them brown paper bags containing dough sticks, fruit, terracotta tubs of pasta, half-loaves of bread or bottles of wine.

Quite near to FitzGerald were three uniformed men talking

intensely in low voices, with drawn faces. FitzGerald saw, from his scarlet cap, that one was the station master, a stocky man with a look on his face as if he were facing the apocalypse. Then there was a German lieutenant, lean and bespectacled, holding a paper in his shaking hand and arguing fiercely with the third, a heavyset infantry major with a bushy moustache, whom FitzGerald surmised was the Commanding Officer of the entrained unit. From the lemon yellow on his shoulder straps, the lieutenant with the paper was a signals officer. His twitching frame and the urgency with which he shook the paper made him look insane; by contrast, the CO was inert, as if paralysed by panic.

FitzGerald guessed that the signals officer was predicting an attack. Why the CO was neither ordering an immediate departure nor detraining of the hundreds of men packing it, FitzGerald could not fathom. *The station master must be begging him to let all those people escape potential massacre. Given the armed sentries patrolling the platform edge, it would take just minutes to clear the platforms and then detrain the troops. Perhaps the CO thought he could get the train away fast enough, but the signals officer disagreed. Yes, maybe that was the argument.*

On the other line, a train shunted slowly past. It was packed, the roofs of the train covered with Italian families. The carriages were blue and FitzGerald could make out the name and logo on them: *Compagnie Internationale des Wagons-Lits.* Some of the hundreds of ragged people at the end of the platform were scampering beside them and trying to jump onto the running boards.

After forty minutes or so of hanging around, FitzGerald's guards handed over the men from the truck to two armed officials of the Organisation Todt. He tried to join them but was ordered to stay put. He thought that, as he had been detained by the militia there, he would be taken over by the militia here, but instead his German guards – who had perhaps forgotten, or just didn't care – marched him a few metres to a pen that appeared to hold about a hundred others, mainly in khaki uniforms. A group of about thirty Germans under guard were being put into the nextdoor pen; when they saw the khaki-clad prisoners, they yelled abuse and threatened them with being torn into pieces. What had brought these Germans into confinement? Not their ferocity, presumably. FitzGerald guessed black marketing, going AWOL or insulting their officers. They didn't look like conscientious objectors.

The hubbub from the crowds at the station, the yelling of the German detainees, the chugging of the train engine and the whistling of steam, the bellowing of orders, the intermittent bursts of machine-gun fire as the guards shot into the air to control their charges and the screams of women from the other side of the piazza… all made for an inferno such that FitzGerald had never encountered before.

Pushed into the pen, he found that he was in with Poles, recently captured. They welcomed him warily and invited him to squat down with them. Despite the howling chaos, they managed to tell FitzGerald of the heavy fighting south of Cassino. FitzGerald was astonished to hear of the casualties that the Germans had been prepared to take and had inflicted on the Poles.

In a contiguous pen they watched a Pole, carrying field glasses on a leather strap over his shoulder, being approached by a German who had entered the pen. Guards with machine guns at the ready covered him. In gestures watched by hundreds of soldiers in the other pens, the German demanded that he hand over the glasses. The Pole shook his head in refusal, whereupon the German drew his revolver and shot him in the chest. As he lay there, the German stooped down, took the glasses and swaggered away. After a brief pause, a roar of fury erupted from the hundreds of men in the pens nearby, almost drowning out the cheers of the small German contingent and the commands of the guards. A crowd of fellow prisoners gathered round the corpse. For a moment it looked as if a great wave of angry prisoners would launch themselves at the wire, but the guards shot hundreds of rounds over the heads of the crowd and the commotion did not last more than minutes.

The affair of the field glasses over, everybody seemed subdued. Hungry, tired and cowed, the prisoners reverted to lethargy, growling and complaining to each other. An American joined FitzGerald's group and told them, 'Yesterday that same German shot a Russian for smoking a cigarette.'

Somebody asked, 'For smoking a cigarette?'

'Sub-humans are not allowed luxuries. How dare a Russian smoke!'

'That's harsh.'

An Australian voice piped up that he had fled his prison camp and hidden out in the villages. 'A cobbler was repairing my boots in a village when I was recaptured. They beat him to death.'

Elderly women in overalls were ladling lurid, tomato-coloured pasta into the mess tins of the guards outside the wire. Seeing – or smelling – the grub, prisoners started to shout for food and water. A guard emptied his canteen of water onto the ground in front of some of the prisoners and amused himself by bellowing insults at them in English. 'Rich Americans!' 'Fat British capitalists!' FitzGerald heard him bellow. 'Hang you all.'

The American was laconic, 'They hate us because they think we are the ones on top. That's interesting.' The Poles, finding that they could not communicate with the English speakers beyond a few words, wandered off. The noise abated in the lull: FitzGerald remained on the edge of his pen nearest the road so that he could observe how things worked here, in case there was a chance of escape or even of being seen by Lucia, who he was sure would be looking for him. Behind, his companions mostly lay down in groups, closed their eyes. Through the wire he occasionally saw local people, mostly elderly peasants dressed in black, hurry by.

As he stared ahead through the wire, a child appeared, a girl of about six in a white dress, who gazed at the pens until her eyes met FitzGerald's. He smiled to see something so sweet in this sordid landscape. She turned away and went back to where an older woman now hove in sight, hobbling along with a big, covered basket that seemed heavy. She said something to the mother, then ran back to FitzGerald to press a huge autumn pear into his hand, before scampering away.

Instinctively hiding the pear, FitzGerald quickly looked at the guards in case they had seen the girl's act and would punish her for it, but they were busy gobbling their food. The couple were already nearly out of the piazza, the girl looking back at him with a jolly smile, made him think of family, friendships, the grape harvest and the cosseting in Pozzo, where he had felt so far from the world of men and war.

As he stared into the distance where the couple had disappeared, he became aware of a vehicle engine to his left and turned to see a jeep lifting itself over the broken masonry and smashed glass that scattered the road. He tensed, remembering the same vehicles driving along the road near PG500 and what he had hoped would be the last sight of *Sturmbannführer* Fröhlich.

PRISONERS IN SULMONA

Fröhlich had returned to Sulmona, summoned back for a commanders' conference. His jeep drove over rubble into the square, scattering the soldiers crowded at the mouth of the street. It contained a smartly-dressed Italian and the German, who jumped out of the front. Fröhlich looked as he had done on the road not long before, weary and dusty, with his left hand bandaged. He commanded his men to stop the German captives shouting abuse on pain of no food, then strode over to the next pen, his Italian companion, who had stepped out of the vehicle in a dignified manner and adjusted his tunic and the dagger at his belt, chatting beside him. FitzGerald recognised Consul Vacca; he was debonair compared to those around him.

A GNR officer from behind one of the compounds gave the fascist salute with gusto and reported to the visitors. As he spoke, Fröhlich scoured the piazza and let his eyes rest a moment on a priest kneeling beside a prone soldier. He sniffed the air and glanced at the nearest latrine trench. There was one dug inside each pen, giving off a stench almost unbearable even to the guards who could keep their distance. Fröhlich strode away to get to the next pen, leaving the GNR officer hurrying after him, reporting to his back.

Not until Fröhlich approached FitzGerald's pen did FitzGerald realise he was the very Fröhlich he had seen going northwards with his unit the previous day, his old acquaintance, and that the German had recognised him. The two top booted officers stopped abruptly by the wire.

'Colonel FitzGerald! What a beautiful surprise!'

FitzGerald faced his enemy and took in the sight of Vacca, with whom he had lunched last month. Would Vacca tell? No, of course not. *Is there any benefit to me to tell? No.* Vacca might be minded to let Foschini know of this prisoner, to curry favour with him. Vacca was staring at him, his eyes bulging, willing him not to talk. Meanwhile, Fröhlich asked, 'How about another lift in my car today, and maybe a meal?'

'No, thank you.'

'Another surprise!' Fröhlich laughed and the weariness left his face. 'I must say that although you caused me a lot of trouble, I admire you. How did you manage to get six hundred men away? It was a very impressive feat of organisation.'

'Thank you, Fröhlich. I just did what a soldier has to do.'

'Those Italians – that factor and his half-wit sister – made it possible, didn't they?'

'Do you think we British can't manage these things on our own? We don't need Italians!'

Although FitzGerald was vehement, Fröhlich narrowed his eyes, as if trying to compute whether he was telling the truth.

FitzGerald changed the subject. 'Congratulations on your promotion, Colonel.'

'It would have come faster had I been running the timetables for trains to Poland. Soldiers in the field like you and me always come second. As for you, I am sorry that now that you are back "in the bag", you will have missed your own promotion.'

He turned and ordered the GNR officer to take great care of this "naughty escaper". The GNR did not understand the order, so Consul Vacca translated into Italian.

Back to FitzGerald: 'Soon we will get you to Saxony and put you in a special castle with the incorrigibles. I will order that you be given a British uniform so as not be shot as a spy.'

'How very kind of you.'

'Kind? No, Colonel, I am professional, that is all. Kindness has no place where duty is concerned.' Then, Fröhlich laughed a boyish, bullying laugh: 'Perhaps I should have you shot as a traitor! I know that you are, in reality, Irish, so I do not understand why you are fighting for the imperialists. Your prime minister is a great admirer of our *Führer*.'

'Most of we Irish support Britain. I am merely one of hundreds of thousands.'

'Oh well! At least we have *you*! I am glad that you are a good loser. If you are not shot, when the war is over I will buy you a pint in St Stephen's Tavern! And perhaps we will go and watch the FA Cup together!'

FitzGerald gave a rueful smile. 'How kind.'

'I hope that we meet again in happier times.' The German was about to turn away, but instead asked: 'Your collaborator, the woman, what have you done with her?'

Vacca started, but FitzGerald was cool: 'I have no collaborators, Fröhlich, except my soldiers.'

Fröhlich looked as if he would prise more out of FitzGerald, but instead he desisted, turned on his heel and left, Vacca following him. FitzGerald found himself sweating. What did the Nazi know of Lucia, and how? And then he again looked around the pen, the piazza, at the guards. *Fröhlich will make damn sure I can't get away.* He felt the papers strapped to his chest under his shirt with his fingers. *What next?*

LUCIA IN SULMONA

Once she was out of sight of the blackshirts, Lucia pulled Enrico into a side street, turned corners and doubled back before resuming their walk towards what she thought would be the centre of Sulmona. Before long, she came to a *piazzetta* with a dried-up fountain and a chestnut tree offering some shade. Enrico, his eyes caught by a lizard, started to play in the dust. Lucia did not stop him. As she sat down on the only stone bench, the shock engulfed her. *I have lost FitzGerald. He has been taken away from me.* For the first time, she admitted to herself that a wanting to be near him gnawed at her. Her heart reached out to find him, to bring him back to her.

When she looked at Enrico, reason came back to her. *I can do this. Find the guide first, then seek the colonel.*

It was on the outskirts of Sulmona that they were to meet one of the guides who took fugitives around the massif and towards the battle lines. She headed for the rendezvous, under a bridge on the outskirts of the little town, and found the lad who was to lead them on the next, and final, leg of the journey. Nino was a cheerful, devil-may-care teenager with the confidence of an expert. He informed Lucia immediately of where prisoners were concentrated and agreed that they go to see whether they might find the *Inglese*.

An hour or so later, Lucia was looking over the ledge of a window giving onto Sulmona station, gazing at the crowds of penned men in cages, searching for FitzGerald's familiar face.

The windows of the buildings around the station were smashed. Only one building had collapsed totally, but it had fallen outward, blocking the street where it met the piazza. In a former bedroom of the house next to it, up whose stairs they had climbed, the floor scattered with rubble, Enrico sat on a twisted iron bedstead with buckled slats and watched Lucia spying on the men below. She saw a German NCO lead a column of Italian men of all ages and types – several in pyjamas, two or three in just underpants and vests, some with no shoes – towards the piazza. Behind them, occasionally snarled at by the guards, was a gaggle of women, also of all ages and classes, shouting instructions to escape at their men, cursing the guards, imploring them, weeping, praying. One or two of them were trying to pass articles of clothing to their menfolk. To see the faces of this group, and those in the pens, more clearly, Lucia climbed down to the first floor and found herself directly over the junction between the street and station perimeter, the site of the collapsed building, when the NCO halted his column and gave commands to the motley group, pointing at the rubble.

'Put this square in order – all the rubble must go to the edge so that the transport can pass. Get on with it! Hurry up, you lazy Italians!'

He was faced by a growl of grumbling voices as the Italians complained.

'I am a fascist, your ally, you made a mistake!'

'I have a medical certificate!'

'Let my son go, he is only ten years old!'

'I have no boots; how can I work?'

To shut them up, the NCO had his men guarding the soldiers train their machine guns on them, then shouted at them to work or be shot. The grumbling ceased. They started to pick up lumps of masonry, huge stones and roof tiles, splintering floorboards and all the other detritus of wrecked houses and pile them beside the road.

As she scanned their faces, Lucia's attention was deflected by some shouting and laughter from another pen. Looking towards it, she saw a few men in khaki uniforms being driven at gunpoint towards the clearance squad directly below.

As she stared, Lucia's heart jumped to see that among them was FitzGerald, who, when the detail was halted beside the biggest pile of rubble, went forward and started to help a very elderly man in pajamas shift a big lump of masonry.

Having learnt what she needed to know, Lucia left the window, turned back into the despoiled room to collect her silent companion, and headed for the stairs and back door.

THE BOMBING OF SULMONA

As they worked, FitzGerald was questioning the old man. 'How come you are here, Sir? Are you a Jew?'

'Not a bit. This morning the Germans arrived in our parish at first light and forced us out into a labour gang. They didn't give us a moment to eat or dress, nothing!'

'I am sorry.'

'Don't be. We're the lucky ones. Most of those taken this morning are on their way to Germany without clothes, food or water. At least I am at home. I still have hope!'

The old man looked at FitzGerald and smiled. FitzGerald looked doubtfully back at him.

The old man cocked his eyes and chuckled. 'I've always been a Dr Pangloss!'

FitzGerald laughed. 'How did you guess what I was thinking?'

Suddenly a voice from the prison cages cried out in English, 'Bombers, bombers!' Everybody, including the guards, looked up to see specks becoming larger until the same voice called out: 'They're ours! It's the Yanks!'

A cheer went up, with some of the boys jumping up and down in excitement. The work party just stared as if dazed, forgotten by the guards who were gazing upwards themselves.

Excitement quickly turned into terror as the planes swung lower and released their bombs over the railway line. The first fell well away, but the explosions created instant alarm. Prisoners looked desperately around for somewhere to hide but the guards snarled at them and made threatening gestures with their guns. One of them shot two prisoners in the chest as they attempted to climb the wire. They writhed on the ground, screaming.

In the background, FitzGerald recognised the heavy coughing of an Italian 90/53 anti-aircraft gun, but nothing seemed to hit their targets; possibly, he guessed, because they were manned by Germans unfamiliar with them.

Meanwhile, the troops on the train had realised that they were the target and were jumping, falling out of the wagons as from a sinking ship. Howls of fear came from the crowds on the platform who fled from the station, knocking each other over, trampling the slower underfoot and panicking the wounded in the piazza, many of whom were now limping or crawling away from the station.

The troop train had started moving off slowly, so it was still packed with soldiers when the planes returned for the second volley and scored a direct hit on the central carriage with an ear-splitting boom. FitzGerald and some of those around him were mesmerised by the sight of men covered in blood staggering from the train, two carriages of which were now just clumps of smoking steel barbs. In the pens, other prisoners shook the fencing and howled at the guards to let them out. More bombs destroyed the line at the head of the train or fell short onto the other side of the tracks, but none hit the pens of prisoners or the rubble working party.

As the planes turned away a second time, the piazza hushed, the quiet punctuated only by the shrieks of the wounded where there had just been wagons of soldiers. The old man looked up. 'Christ be blessed, we're not yet dead.'

On the platforms was all chaos and misery, with dead and dying soldiers flung everywhere. The prisoners in the pens and the working party for clearing rubble seemed suddenly as if turned to stone they stood or squatted dazed, seemingly oblivious to the screams of the victims and the crackle of flames.

'Don't speak so fast. They must have another load.'

And then the planes turned back.

The prisoners watched the planes coming round again, initially gazing with petrified awe. FitzGerald looked around carefully at his surroundings.

There was sporadic and pointless shooting at the planes by the guards. From the railway line and the burning train came more cries of pain and incoherent shouting.

There were no more bombs; the crews had another mission. They began to machine-gun the pens, finally breaking the resolve of many guards, who fled. In every pen, the prisoners hurled themselves at the wire fences, climbing on top of each other to get over, until the fences collapsed and a breach was made to enable the rest to run through.

A few remaining guards hesitated and raised their weapons, then gave up and took to their heels under the sleet of bullets from the planes. Men were dashing everywhere and being hit as they ran. FitzGerald saw his guards scampering down the street that their prisoners had been clearing. He climbed over the wrecked fencing, hurried over and slid into the empty doorway of a ruined house.

A few minutes later, as the planes flew over the station once more and rose in a great arc to return to base, a dishevelled Fröhlich and several SS men began searching among the survivors who had been rounded up in the square.

His sergeant major appeared, a bloody cut down his left cheek. 'I checked all the dead ones, Sir.'

'He's not among the living either!' Fröhlich bit his lip. 'Alright men, we'll not waste any more time on this.' He walked away, followed by his two men.

'Where's that Consul Vacca?'

'Dead, Sir.'

Fröhlich said nothing as he led his men out of the carnage.

Don Carlo's body was crumpled in a doorway round the corner from the square, the doorway of the only house not now burning noisily.

Breathing heavily, FitzGerald crawled into that very doorway. He was coated with white dust. His soles were bleeding and bruised. He turned and stared at the devastation behind him. In the smoke, soldiers appeared to be rounding up surviving prisoners. He took in the body of an Italian officer beside him, realising that he was more or less of the same height and build and started to unbutton the man's jacket, which was undamaged. In a few seconds he had replaced his own ragged jacket with the man's dust-coated but whole tunic and was tugging on his riding boots, which were mercifully the right size. It was then that he realised he was stripping the corpse of Consul Vacca, but he did not hesitate for a second.

He looked round for a hat and found the man's helmet beside the body, strangely lightweight and with a hole in it where a bullet had gone straight through. He ignored the blood and was about to put it on when he felt a hand seize his and he wheeled around in shock, ready to fight. A curly-headed boy of about 14, making FitzGerald immediately think of Caravaggio, was grinning at him.

'Got you, Colonel! Quick, come with me. We must get out while there is chaos.'

This was not a moment for questions. FitzGerald followed.

After a few hundred yards, they crouched in a doorway.

'You stand straight now. Put on the hat. You are in uniform, so if you just walk like an officer, no one will stop you.' He cackled. 'You are a blackshirt. How droll! Don't be too near to me, I'm a nothing.'

Fitzgerald seized his arm. 'Who are you?'

'Guide for *Signora* Lucia. Nino.'

Nino went ahead, bounding from door to door, checking round for Germans or militiamen as he went. He was agile as a flea; far too agile for FitzGerald at this moment, who was stumbling and still adapting to his new, stiff, boots.

The boy led him through deserted and rubble-strewn streets, hopping and skipping in front of him, and occasionally waiting for him to catch up in a way that he found rather galling, as if he were an aged relative taken out for an airing.

FitzGerald walked in a manner he hoped looked deliberate, always keeping an eye on Nino, but never looking as if he were following him. The few soldiers squatting beside the road took no notice. The shutters of the houses were all closed. In the distance he could hear the hubbub at the railway station but ahead was utter silence.

Finally, they reached the outskirts of the town and the bridge that he recognised from Lucia's description, as being their original destination. It was deserted. They climbed below it and he found Lucia cossetting a baby. Enrico lay asleep beside her on a piece of sacking.

FitzGerald was so overcome with relief and happiness at seeing her that he could not speak. He stood gazing at her until she turned her face from the baby and smiled.

'Well done,' he heard her say. Then she looked at the boy. 'Thank you, Nino.'

FitzGerald crouched down beside her. The baby whimpered. 'How did you manage all this?' he asked.

'When I found you at the collection point, I got hold of Nino,' gesturing at the boy, 'and told him to keep eyes on you.'

The boy saluted, mimicking a soldier, then, as if bored or perhaps wanting to leave them in peace, slid away.

'He is our guide whom we were to meet here.'

'And this baby?'

The baby was perhaps just a year old, with sparse brunette hair and large green eyes, dressed in what FitzGerald thought of as a kind of velvet jumpsuit. Beside Lucia was a pile of rather good-quality wrappings, including a piece of fur, and a leather handbag, open and showing a baby's bottle and rattle.

'I found him in a burning house. Everybody else is dead. His mother, or somebody, must have feared the worst, for he had been hidden in the latrine, together with these supplies,' she indicated the paraphernalia beside her. 'He was hard to wake, so I think they must have given him something to make him sleep tight.' She spoke matter-of-factly.

'My God. The bombers have much to answer for.'

'No, not the bombers. The place had been ransacked and the whole family killed in the kitchen. Perhaps his mother intended to hide with him, but did not do so in time. Praise God he is weaned. I have been able to feed him with what she left for him, but we need to get him to where he can be cared for. We'll go there now; Nino knows the way.'

'I must get over the lines. What I'm carrying could save many lives.'

'It could. But you can help me save one life for certain and still go on. Did they not take your information?'

'No, only my boots.'

He unbuttoned his looted jacket and raised his shirt to show the maps still pasted to his chest under his singlet.

'We are lucky. If they had found them, they would assume you killed those officers.'

'Quite. The Almighty has given me another chance to do something useful.'

Nino returned from reconnoitring.

'We're in the wrong place. The route's no good anymore. They have killed the guides and mined the paths. If we are to avoid the devils, it means going east into the mountains where neither they, nor the blackshirts, venture.'

FitzGerald turned to Lucia. 'Your role is to disguise me from the blackshirts, but in the mountains there won't be any. Your task is finished. Why don't you go back to Pozzo? I'll continue alone.'

Even as he said it, FitzGerald realised that he was asking Lucia a question other than the one on his lips. And it was the unspoken question to which she replied, with an answer which might or might not be true, 'I promised Captain Foschini that I would go with you all the way.'

Before either could continue, Nino butted in. 'Wherever Signora Lucia goes, she needs help to carry the baby. And there is her boy. Whether she go forward or back, *Signora* is in the mountains. Of course, she can carry the baby alone, but can she also find food and shelter? And can the boy protect her from wild men or boars or wolves or bears?'

FitzGerald felt relief to hear arguments for remaining with Lucia. He had seen, from the momentary flash of anxiety on her face as he had raised the matter, followed by the look of quiet satisfaction when Nino made his points, that Lucia was content to follow Alessandro's instructions, of which FitzGerald had just heard for the first time.

Nino explained that if Lucia wanted to find a home for the baby, they had better make for the hermitage 'where the brothers look after refugees, especially children. And there are ladies there, too.' Then, they could decide.

Before FitzGerald had a chance to ask, Nino interjected. 'From the hermitage there is a mountain route southeast that will take you to where the devils and *Inglesi* face each other and where the *Inglese* officer will guide you over the lines. To get to the hermitage, you will need help from the shepherds, shelter and food. I can take you as far as the shepherds, who will show you the goat tracks by which you can get out of the mountains.'

She held FitzGerald in her gaze as she said, 'With the baby to feed and keep warm, I will indeed need your help. Before, you needed me. Now, I need you.'

FitzGerald was battling to find his course of action. Time. Time. The idea that he might be losing time nagged at him. Was he risking his mission? Prolonging the war? He did a few calculations in his head and they always came out with the answer that he was wasting only one day.

'After the hermitage, I will need you again.' FitzGerald found it impossible to suppress the elation in his voice. The idea of leaving her, even as he had proposed it, had struck him as unthinkable. Now, they would be together until... until the end, whether that was death in the mountains or on the other side of the war. At that moment, all he cared about was that they would be together, that he would be near her. He could not admit it, even to himself. It was such a dereliction of duty. Any excuse would do. She was speaking, and Nino, but he hardly took in what they said.

'Nino says we could get to the hermitage in two days if we not dawdle.'

She had put down the baby, who lay asleep on a piece of tarpaulin, and taken up a haversack in her hands to sew something onto the straps. FitzGerald's expression made an unspoken enquiry.

'This is your pack. I know your shoulder blades were rubbed raw when you carried a pack before. So, I have some rubber to cushion between strap and shoulder.'

'Thank you, where on earth did the rubber come from?'

'Some of the devils' helmets have these things inside them. I just cut them out.'

FitzGerald did not have a chance to comment, for Nino was pointing up towards the mountains: 'Every October, the shepherds drive their flocks from Tuscany, all the way to Foggia, nearly three hundred miles away, to the snow-free pasture. We will catch them up.'

FitzGerald looked over his little team. 'Can we really do that? All of us?'

'There are few shelters and it's dangerous to health to sleep in the open, but the devils are below. We will find *carboni*, charcoal miner, shacks or shepherds' refuges.'

INTO THE MOUNTAINS

Step by painful step they climbed, up the steep slopes. Every now and again a pocket of mist closed in on them, blocking out the sun, the coldly glittering peaks and the softly gleaming valley.

Then, just as swiftly, they'd be out of the pocket of mist. They stopped, breathing heavily, gazing, with a feeling close to rapture, at all the silver beauty above and around and far, far below.

Before they left, Nino produced a well-used fleece-lined coat for Lucia, as well as thick trousers and leggings. The baby went inside her voluminous coat. There was a similar, shorter coat for FitzGerald, to go over his stolen jacket, and hat and gloves for both of them. Enrico was similarly equipped and kept taking off and putting on the sheepskin hat he had been given, admiring it.

Nino made FitzGerald promise to return their mountain gear for re-use at the end. He tut-tutted at the soft leather of the riding boots FitzGerald wore, but said that men would kill him to get footwear and he should never take them off in the mountains.

FitzGerald once again found himself follower, rather than leader. From the conversation, he realised that Lucia had organised these provisions, plus food and drink, during the few hours of his capture. They set off warm and loaded down with the weight of their clothing and, in FitzGerald's case, a rucksack of food. Water they would find from mountain streams.

Eventually they reached the pines, a still, black veil against the grey, jagged peaks beyond. There was moss under their feet again. They could no longer see the valley.

The grassy path curled in and out among the dark trees. They skirted a deep gulf, driven like a wedge into the mountain. The path broadened out, and in the middle of the sweeping curve it made to negotiate the gulf extremity, they found a waterfall.

Water fell straight down from a high rock with a melodious splash into a large natural basin. Lying on their stomachs, they drank the clear, pure water. It was icy cold, almost stinging the tip of their tongue at the first sip. They filled their water bottles. FitzGerald held the baby while Lucia fed him some of the *pappa* that she had prepared. He gurgled, smiled, slept again. Enrico put his little hand into the water again and again and then, when it was really very cold, took Lucia's hand and giggled when she said 'Ow!'

Then the climb began in earnest. Below was a chalky cliff or gorge, next a pine forest, and then beyond, much farther, they could just make out a hilltop town. Lucia bent down to point it out to Enrico. As usual, his face lit up but he remained silent. Although both adults addressed Enrico often, indicating pretty rocks or cloud formations, gnarled trees and a finch flitting by, he looked back at them, without speech. From time to time there was a monosyllable, but never a sentence. Lucia worried, but kept it to herself.

They were above the mist now, among the shining peaks, in the lofty, lucid world of silver and grey. They had long since risen above the forest. The universe was one of bare rock and bare earth. The ground, when their boots sank into it, was black loam, overgrown by moss or a sparse, sharp-edged grass. The rock was white or silvery grey wherever light touched it, and blacker even then the earth where it was sunk deep in shadow.

Every hour or so they sat down to have a few swigs of water and eat a mouthful of food. Then Lucia and FitzGerald looked at each other and at the view before them, with shining eyes, as if exhilarated by the effort or by the mountain air. Always their clothes were sodden with perspiration, and they found that they could not remain seated for more than a few minutes, lest they start to freeze up. Lucia checked the baby constantly but he was warm and, when awake, smiled. Lucia kissed him. 'My *passerotto*,' she cooed softly.

FitzGerald smiled to think that she used the same word to describe the baby as the rough fugitives. Little sparrow.

Much later, when they were already above the 6,000 feet mark, approaching the highest point on the Morrone range, he said, panting: 'The child must have a name.'

'*Passerotto* is his name for now,' she said.

Nino disagreed: 'He needs a real name. How about Sandrino? Alessandro? Then he will fight to avenge his family and defend our people.'

Lucia shuddered. She was thinking of Alessandro Foschini, but she said: 'I don't want him to be a soldier like the colonel. I want him to be a gentle person who loves and protects. Someone who pursues life, not death.'

'Vito,' said Nino, simply. And the baby became "life".

Nino and FitzGerald thereafter referred to the bundle as Vito, but Lucia always addressed him as her *passerotto*.

After some hours, their exaltation had dulled. It was getting too wearisome, this eternal toiling up one slope after another. Often there was no track at all, but Nino lead them through jumbles of huge rocks as if by instinct.

FitzGerald asked. 'How long to get to the top?'

Nino always laughed at his charges' questions: 'Oh, just a couple of hours more. You are tired, are you? Let me take Vito.' But Lucia would not let him take the baby.

They didn't speak again for a long time. Then Nino said, 'You know, my soldier friend, we *Abruzzesi* are always, at all times, a very courteous people. We never tell you the truth if we think it would depress or harm you. Say, for instance, there was another eight hours' march before you. Well then, we tell you it will take four hours, no more, just to encourage you, to keep you going...'

FitzGerald would once have bridled. Today he just smiled, suppressing a gasp at the pain he felt from time to time as his left foot touched the ground. He forced himself not to think how he was betraying his self-imposed mission, to deliver the intelligence he had so fortuitously found. He envisaged being interrogated by his superiors: 'Why did you take so long to get to us?'

'Well, you see there was a child, and a baby.'

The interrogator would be one of those jobsworths with a pencil moustache, plump belly and the ribbon of a long service medal.

'And a woman, I suppose?'

He wanted to hit the imaginary major with his cane. Instead, he glanced at Lucia admiringly. She never complained. She was so fast. He adjusted his pace to hers, as Nino always did. He marvelled at her.

Nino talked, helping the moments, the hours, go by. He told them that his parents had died a long time ago, before the war, so he had grown up with his grandparents. He seemed to FitzGerald more mature than any child of 14 he had ever met, given what he spoke about and the vocabulary he used, and this FitzGerald ascribed to his life with grandparents. Or maybe what he had witnessed in the short period of war had made him what he was. FitzGerald did not know.

Nino told them, 'I love these mountains. I could walk about here in the middle of winter blindfolded. Can you imagine the devils catching me here? What is more, do you think they can ever take these mountains from us? Even if they were to catch me by some trick and cast me into the deepest dungeon and put out my eyes, my empty sockets would still – yes, until I drew my last breath – hold the image of these peaks in my head.' He jabbed with his closed fists at his eyes.

At last, they came up on the first signs of human life – a little stone hut in the wilderness of white rock and black, flanked by a sheep corral that contained no sheep, but dung almost a foot deep. They pushed on. Half an hour later they came out on top.

The vast luminous world beneath was very grand: glittering peak upon glittering peak, rising out of a gaping abyss either brim-full of moonlight or covered by solid slabs of cold black shadow.

Nino announced, pointing into the distance, 'Below we are surrounded by roads and villages used by the devils. They often send patrols looking for escapers but never up this high, where there are no roads. On the lower slopes, the soil is poor and stony and little wheat is grown. Sheltering there are thousands of homeless people from the cities.'

They dropped rapidly from one level to the next along smooth grassy paths meandering among gigantic boulders scattered with snow over broad ridges that were mostly flat but at times resembled terraces. Then the barking of dogs drifted up to them through the frosty air.

Nino instructed them, 'It is the shepherds. Walk close behind me! When the dogs see me, they will recognise me as a friend. They are very fierce. If they don't like you, they will bite large pieces out of you.'

Enrico seized FitzGerald by the legs until he picked him up and planted him on his shoulders. A dozen large white Pyrenean sheepdogs, with thick and woolly long hair, charged up and frisked around Nino, jumping up against him and barking loudly. Nino bent down to give them each a playful clout against the head.

FitzGerald saw that to the left, not far from a precipice, stood a small stone building that was presumably their destination. It was a hut of limestone with a corrugated iron roof. There were sheep corralled into a pen built against one wall.

Outside, against the front wall and sheltered by a little rampart about two feet high, jutting out at a right angle from the house, sat four or five men, warming themselves around the fire of a few logs on which a stew was cooking.

Nino sat down between two of the men. Lucia and FitzGerald stood nearby, waiting. Nino spoke without preliminaries, 'Have the shepherds not left yet?'

A young man replied without looking up, 'No, they leave at dawn.'

After a while, one of the men, his hooked nose giving him a face like an eagle, invited the two strangers to join them.

'Come and sit down.' He had an extraordinarily deep voice, like the echo of a fathomless cave.

Lucia was shivering. FitzGerald stamped his feet and, taking her free hand, went to sit beside the fire.

Eagle Face ladled out a canteen of stew and passed it to Lucia.

'Chew it first until it is a mush, then give it to the baby,' he suggested. He thrust hunks of meat into FitzGerald's and Enrico's hands: '*Mangi! Mangi!* Eat! Eat!'

As they ate, the man questioned them.

'Where are you going?'

'Through the lines.'

Eagle Face looked grave. After a few minutes, in which he seemed to be trying to penetrate their minds, he spoke matter-of-factly. 'Avoid the road to Castel di Sangro because the Germans are defending Roccaraso, Rocca Pia, Castel di Sangro and Alfedena.'

'Thank you,' said FitzGerald. He wondered why Nino had not brought up how they were to pass the night. *I must get space inside for Lucia and the baby at least*, he thought. *We are supplicants.* He waited for Lucia or Nino to take the lead.

When they had finished their meal, Eagle Face spoke as if he were their host, or the landlord. 'You are cold, all of you. Go inside, you, your female and your little ones, find a spot to lie down.'

Lucia was dumb, perhaps cowed by tiredness. FitzGerald helped her up and together they went inside the mountain hut.

As Eagle Face held open the door, they perceived, dimly, bodies all over the floor. The walls were black and greasy, the smell of sweat was everywhere, punctuating the burning smell from a glowing brazier. Eventually they found a clear space and lay down together. Enrico held tight onto Lucia's back; Vito was against her breasts. A few moments later, somebody stepped over them and shoved a folded greatcoat under their heads. It was Eagle Face from outside.

They heard that deep voice again. 'Sleep now, I can see you are very tired.' Then he went, closing the door and immersing them in darkness.

Lucia, without looking at FitzGerald, curled up into his body, the baby now between them.

He could see that his coat was rough and scratchy to her cheek, so he pulled it away. As if in her sleep, she said 'the smell, the smell.' He was about to remove it entirely, when she said, 'so good.'

One arm around Vito, she slept. FitzGerald heard a gentle snore coming from Enrico, whose nose was pressed into Lucia's neck.

After an hour or so, he woke. Lucia and the baby were sleeping deeply, having detached themselves from his coat and curled up into a ball. FitzGerald, rising carefully so as not to disturb them, stepped over other sleepers and went outside to join the shadows before the fire. He looked for Eagle Face, but he was not present.

To the shadows in general, he asked, 'What has happened to the man with the hooked nose?' In the light of the flames, FitzGerald saw, from his sheepskin jacket, breeches and leggings, that the man to whom he had addressed himself was a shepherd.

'He's gone, over the mountains somewhere. He's a stranger; none of us know him. He arrived here at dusk last night.'

'Did he have an overcoat?'

'No, when he left he did not have his overcoat and I was surprised.'

After a little while, FitzGerald returned to the hut, where people were stirring. There was the scent of cooking, but Lucia and the children were still asleep. Eagle Face's overcoat was under her head. He lay back in his place beside them.

He looked up to a commotion, as some shepherds started

to bring in new-born lambs so that they would not die of cold. Illuminated by the brazier's flickering light, a young shepherd entered, his chubby cheeks red from the cold, carrying a lamb born just a few minutes before. He placed it gently on the ground, and on stiff, unsteady sticks of legs, the lamb took its first faltering steps and went sliding all over the place.

When it fell, it remained on the ground, lifted up its head awkwardly and looked about it with grey, vague eyes. It was blind. It got up again to flounder about helplessly for a few minutes, and then fell down once more. The lamb had a long, blood-stained strip of umbilical cord hanging from its stomach.

An old shepherd was looking at FitzGerald from a metre or so away. 'I see you cannot sleep, my friend; do not fear. It is only the mist creeping into a man's soul. Soon the mist will lift and all will be well. Then you will sleep. My name is Antônio. Consider me your friend.'

FitzGerald raised his palm in greeting. His eyes were now accustomed to the murk. He could make out more and more by the stuttering flames that he had not noticed when Lucia and he had stumbled in, exhausted.

Easing over sleeping bodies, he crouched down next to Antônio, who went on, 'I was a prisoner of the Austrians for fourteen months during the old war. For months, we had practically nothing to eat. But your plight is worse than ours ever was. It is a terrible thing to be an outcast, a fugitive. Is there anything more dreadful on earth than a manhunt?'

Now FitzGerald saw that a group of men and boys in heavy overcoats, lined on the outside with wool, from which the humidity was evaporating in slowly, curling wisps, were squatting before a steaming cauldron while large sheepdogs sprawled at their feet. The faces of both men and dogs were strangely blurred, scarcely visible through the smoke.

A sheep had been cut into small pieces and was now boiling in the large caldron. Their low, growling voices were punctuated by an occasional crackle from the fire. One of them was stirring the meat with a stick, another cutting notches in his crook, the third braiding a thong for his whip. Sometimes they were in shadow, sometimes the fire threw a ruddy glow that flickered over their faces.

FitzGerald could not make out who was saying what.

'In Teramo, the devils came across a peasant walking along a country lane with two prisoners and shot him on the spot.'

Another, illuminated, like the boy in "The Calling of St Matthew", thought FitzGerald, gestured in the direction of some sleeping forms: 'My brother was killed in Tunisia by the *Americani*. Why don't we take revenge? An eye for an eye and a tooth for a tooth.'

Another, older voice, remonstrated with St Matthew. 'But these men are unarmed, like hunted animals.'

FitzGerald recognised the voice of the man who had introduced himself as Antônio. 'You say "an eye for an eye and a tooth for a tooth", but we are a Christian people. We must love, not hate.'

St. Matthew spoke up again. '*They* don't think like that. As soon as they get the opportunity, they kill us.'

FitzGerald returned to his place beside Lucia and tried to sleep. He felt a lamb nudging him in the ribs with its head, bumping its firm little legs against his feet. He pushed it away gently with his hand or foot, but it kept coming back, trying repeatedly to climb on top of his outstretched body. Twice it passed water on him.

A few paces away, Antônio was still talking. 'I say we are a Christian people. If any of you were out in the mist and you found your neighbour's sheep or lamb dying of cold, what would you do? You wouldn't turn your back on it and leave it there to die, would you? You take it and feed it and return it to your neighbour when you see him again. That is what you do, is it not?'

There was a long silence. The shepherds moved their heads slowly as if doubtful. The silence was broken only by the splattering of the fire and the bubbling of the water in the pot.

FitzGerald slept. Lucia cuddled up to him, burying her head in his chest. FitzGerald woke when his face was being kissed, softly. He smiled. 'My love…' Then he opened his eyes and started to see that the kisses were from the lamb.

The shepherds were still talking. 'The devils have their hands too full to be bothered with the 3,000 sheep passing over the road in a valley between two mountain ranges.'

'Wrong. Sheep are just what they want. Their own country is starving, so they send our food back to devil-land.'

'If Pietro comes back with the news that the others have got over the valley, we will go. But if he says they will remain and not cross over because of the devils, it's no good going. We will just have to stay here.'

Lucia snuggled closer into FitzGerald's body.

In the morning, the bleary-eyed inmates of the shelter came stumbling out into the fresh air. A man in a worn British uniform and "South Africa" sewn onto his sleeve looked up cheerfully as FitzGerald came out.

'Good morning.' He had a strong Afrikaner accent. 'I'm Krige.'

'FitzGerald. You were at the wine harvest at Pozzo, making notes.'

'You're right. Come and eat. Going over the lines?'

'That's the plan.'

Krige the Afrikaaner and FitzGerald the American-Irishman found it easy to swap experiences. Perhaps, thought FitzGerald, because they were both foreigners twice over. Colonials, in some peoples' eyes, fighting for their oppressors.

FitzGerald told Krige of the flight of the six hundred and the way in which the peasants had helped them, then hidden them.

Krige had his own story. 'We were living in the house of a doctor who gave us his own clothes. Later we lived in a cave. The poverty of that village was something dreadful. There were no men, only a few women, all poor as church mice. Yet they were so hospitable. We were ashamed to take their food, but they didn't forget us; one of the women would bring soup or pasta to the cave, saying they wouldn't allow guests to starve. When the Germans came to the village, we got away but nobody else did. The devils killed anybody they found. And burnt the houses.'

Seeing FitzGerald's rapt face, he went on.

'We climbed up the Marrone and got lost in the mist. Then a shepherd came out of the mist, almost bumping into us, and saved us. He brought us here. We've been here for a while. I'm writing these peoples' story. It mustn't be forgotten.'

FitzGerald looked at him. 'I've come to understand how different they are from us. And how much there is to learn. Learn...' he paused as if trying to convince himself, 'about how to live.'

Krige looked at him with a smile as if he already knew all that. 'They are a different kind of human being from us. I hope future generations will understand. If I survive, I'll try to tell them.'

FitzGerald suddenly felt moved to be close to this man. He leant over to Krige, put out his hand and said, 'My first name is Gerald. It's not very different from my surname, but I'd like you to use it.'

Krige took his hand and responded with a slight smile. 'Uys. Well met.'

As a light spatter of rain fell, more men came out of the house. Uys Krige pointed them out: Russians, Slovenians, a Brazilian. And the shepherds.

The younger shepherds' ages ranged up from 10. They all wore leggings made of sheepskin, covering from below the knee to the ankle. Two had bagpipes. Clumsy shaggy sheepdogs settled at their feet whenever they squatted.

Krige and FitzGerald heard another shepherd talking. 'There are two hundred and thirty-five sheep missing. How on earth are we going to find them in this mist? And the ewes have begun to lamb. It may freeze later and what will happen to the lambs then? Oh, and I almost forgot. There are five more foreigners underneath the rock over there; bring them, they mustn't stay in the rain all day.'

FitzGerald checked through the door. Lucia and the children still slept.

When the drizzle stopped, a fire was lit on a stone. Broad strips of fat were thrown into three large frying pans, and when the fat became a sizzling liquid, the pans were withdrawn and all gathered round to dip their bread in the warm brown juice. FitzGerald put aside some soaked bread for when his little family might wake. After the meal, the men smoked. Antônio gave a tobacco leaf from his big brown wallet to each person. The recipients broke it up with their fingers and rolled it.

Krige pointed at two youths, well kitted-out, who were putting on their packs. 'Those are two students from the university in Rome who have brought drink and clothing and a packed meal. Most of us, like you and me, have only what the shepherds give us.'

The boys, realising they were being spoken about, came over.

Krige asked, 'Why are you here?'

The first student replied, 'To avoid forced labour.'

The second student went on, 'And because we want to fight with the *bande*. We have to get the Germans out.'

His companion did not want to have a political discussion. 'Come on, we're wasting time.'

'*Addio!*' They moved off.

Krige watched them go, 'They are in a hurry to get killed.'

FitzGerald: 'Boys will be boys.' Pointing to the younger shepherds, he added: 'They seem not so happy.'

'Who can blame the shepherds feeling unhappy? They are continually losing their sheep, the sheep are lambing, and many of the lambs will probably die tonight. What's more, they are saddled with twenty-one uninvited guests. You know some of them slept out in the open last night in their sheepskins to give us, recently their enemies, a roof over our heads?'

Nino, who had disappeared overnight to FitzGerald knew not where, reappeared. 'I have arranged with Antônio for you to go south towards the front with his guys. I shall leave you now.'

FitzGerald rose and clasped Nino's hand. 'Thank you, Nino. It ifficult without you.'

He grinned, 'You and *Signora* Riva together is not so bad.'

FitzGerald looked down in embarrassment and said, 'You have done another great service to the cause.'

Nino made an angry grimace. 'What cause? If we help you, it is because you are in trouble. That is all.' Then his mask of charm slid back on, 'Goodbye, *illustrissimo colonello*, illustrious colonel.'

FitzGerald accompanied him to the edge of the encampment; they shook hands wordlessly. As Nino left, FitzGerald spotted a small patch of mountain flowers and picked three good specimens.

He went in to Lucia, who was feeding the baby, and gave her the flowers. She smiled but did not speak.

He slept another hour. She and the baby ate again from the same pot. Then she woke him. 'We are to leave now.' Enrico was staring at him, bleary-eyed, as if trying to work out what dream he was in.

The mist had lifted, the rain had stopped, rays of sunshine shone through the clouds. Antônio called from the pack mules, 'We are off, we're off! Saddle up, saddle up!'

The dogs started barking. The shepherds set about the sheep pens, pulling up the poles and rolling up the long thin leather thongs stretched between them.

The sheep were herded into different groups; mules and the horses were brought, saddled and packed; and the shelter was cleared of its supplies.

Eventually the whole train set off. There was the clinking of bridle chains and stirrups, the clip-clop of horses' shoes. FitzGerald and Lucia had received shepherds' leggings and crooks and each was behind their own group of sheep.

They were learning a new trade from scratch and it was harder than FitzGerald had imagined possible. Some of his sheep caused confusion, straying into another group, until Antônio came running up and, with a slow shake of the head and a smile, sorted things out. FitzGerald found it difficult to move his sheep over the narrow spurs or through a defile, and again the shepherd came to his help.

'Why are they so naughty with me, but so calm with you?'

'They know I know what I am doing. They trust me to lead them right. It is not just you of whom they are suspicious. My son cannot manage them, because they sense he has no love for the mountains or them.'

'Your son?'

'Yes, he went to university and read a lot of books. He works for some party in Milan – communist or fascist, I can't remember which. Sitting at a desk, smoking and getting fat. He says we are backward and that the party will civilise us. After the war.'

They passed a tall wooden cross standing stark on the pinnacle above, climbed for an hour and then started going down, which only increased the difficulties with the sheep. Bareness. Dearth of foliage. Not a tree, not a shrub; only here and there a small, brittle shrivelled-up skeleton of a mountain thistle.

After his failure as a shepherd, FitzGerald was given a train of five pack mules, each attached to its predecessor by a thong. He guided the leader by pulling at a long halter on its neck. In the saddlebag of the lead mule were two lambs, their little white heads only just protruding from the bag. Enrico was lifted onto the second mule, his legs pressed against its flanks, his torso flat and his arms around the beast's neck. Lucia was told to put Vito into the saddlebag, and they walked one after the other beside their beasts.

It was Lucia who, after about an hour, glanced over and saw that FitzGerald's saddlebag was empty. 'Colonel, where are your lambs?'

FitzGerald called her to take his place so that he could go back to look for them. Vito was whimpering, so she lifted him out of his saddlebag and cuddled him. FitzGerald ran back to discover the lambs a few hundred yards away in the middle of the path, close to each other, still tied together by a piece of string which gave them a slack of about a foot. To unhook them, he stepped over them with great care.

Later when the caravan drew near to a flock, one of the lambs had no sooner bleated than a ewe rushed out from among the mass of sheep, bleating frantically and coming to a stop in front of the first mule. She continued bleating, her offspring adding their tremulous little voices.

Lucia lent down and cajoled her. 'Now come on, little mother, come on, you are not losing them, they'll be back with you tonight.'

The mist lifted, wheeling back not only from the pinnacle and its precipice, but uncovering the entire world below. It still hung, loosely draped, around the highest peaks, its greyness shot through with a luminescence as of glittering gauze. Down there, miles away, were little groups of brownish-white houses that denoted the scattered villages and hamlets perched against the flank of a mountain, standing out, clear-cut, on the top of a cliff or lying in the gentle fold of a green valley between hills.

The larger clusters far away were Chieti, Pescara and other towns. Still farther away was a blue strip of calm water with a fringe of foam where the sea touched the coast. Brown and white ribbons of road serpentined through an eternally undulating, chequered countryside. It was a world of mountain upon mountain, gradually decreasing in stature until the last flat level sank slowly into a quiet sea, under an immense sky that had been washed fresh and clean by the rain and was now limpid, from one horizon's rim to the other, with a soft, pale gold light.

As suddenly as it had gone, the mist fell once more. '*Che nebbia maledetta!* What hellish fog!' Somebody cursed. There was a dismal, persistent drizzle.

They came to a stop. The shepherds sat on their haunches. Someone started a fire to heat a cauldron of polenta.

FitzGerald stood by his lead mule, wet and dripping. When he had tethered him, he sought Antônio and found him talking to a shepherd whom he had not seen before, a small man dressed in black.

'This is Pietro, whom I sent out some days before to report on the situation. His report is not encouraging. Many shepherds and their flocks are massed around Giove. None are willing to move since the devils have seized several hundred sheep belonging to some shepherds who, three days ago, tried to slip across the valley after nightfall. He says it's impossible to get across.'

FitzGerald returned to Lucia, who was feeding Vito and Enrico. After a few moments, Antônio followed. 'I have decided to get away from here before the weather gets worse, while we can get to a lower level where it will be less cold for the lambs. We will have to risk meeting the devils. We lost fifty more sheep last night. You can come with us if you think the devils less dangerous than the weather.'

Lucia could see that Antônio was taking no account of the fact that being caught harbouring FitzGerald meant death to him and his entire team, not just the theft of his sheep. She knew that FitzGerald would opt to go with them, because he would get to the lines much quicker, were they to survive. To her, the lives of the shepherds were more important than FitzGerald's documents. 'Thank you, Don Antônio. We'll make for the hermitage.'

With a stub of a pencil, Antônio drew carefully on a piece of paper, torn from FitzGerald's diary, and pressed against a pannier, a map of the route they should follow across the mountains, valleys and the three rivers that lay between them and the hermitage.

'Your 8th army is already attacking here –' he pointed at a black dot – 'Campobasso, and that is your direction. Stick to the sheep tracks. As the winter rains haven't started yet, you won't have to swim through any streams. The water will probably be only up to your knees.'

He smiled as he glanced at their serious faces, following every word.

'Compared to the distances you have already travelled, what lies ahead is nothing; a day's walking to the hermitage and a day thereafter to get to the river. As long as you do not have to detour to avoid the devils.'

Antônio looked into FitzGerald's eyes. 'I pray that you can be united with your loved ones in the home your forebears made. So, take care and do not take risks, my son.'

After embracing FitzGerald, bowing gravely to Lucia and stroking Enrico's cheek for an instant, he sent them off towards the forest.

The Morrone, on their right, was now bathed in sunlight: the valley below was a single white pall. Beyond the valley, on their left, the mighty Maiella range towered out of the mist into a cloudless sky.

FitzGerald looked in wonder at the mountains ahead. 'The Maiella, more than 9,000 feet high, the second-highest mountain in Italy... and we have to get over it or round it.' He was holding Enrico's hand.

Lucia pointed up to the hills, then glanced down at Vito, who smiled and gurgled. 'Look: snow! We'd better move fast. The first snow. Snow means impassable tracks... and wolves.'

They entered the depths, dappled with sunlight, of a birch forest. The path, a mule track twisting in and out among the trees, lay buried under a mass of crimson, brown and gold leaves, many of which were still dry and into which their boots sank with a crackling sound.

The entire forest sparkled like a gigantic cobweb, weighed down with dew and caught in a ray of sunlight. They struck glades and dells, partly open to the sky, that had as glittering a beauty as that of polished, many-faceted jewels. Sometimes, as they came out into a wide clearing, they got glimpses of the valley as, far below, the mist folded back slowly on itself.

Arriving at one such clearing, they found a boy perched on top of a large, bony mule. They halted for breath and, after a fleeting appraisal, the boy wished them 'good day.'

As with any encounter, Lucia spoke before FitzGerald could give them away. 'God bless you and your travels. We are on our way to the hermitage,' she said unnecessarily, for it was likely that the boy came from that very place.

'Bless you too. I am taking supplies to the shepherds.' He bent down to open a saddlebag. 'Here, have some bread and cheese.'

'Thank you, but only a little. We have food.' Lucia gestured to FitzGerald to go forward and take what was offered. As he did so, the boy shot him a long glance and said, 'There are two hundred prisoners hiding around Campo di Giove. You are in good company!' FitzGerald laughed, though he felt humiliated by the ease with which the boy had divined what he was.

Once the boy had proceeded on his way and they had continued their climb, FitzGerald remarked, 'You say you don't believe in God or the church, yet always greet people with a blessing.'

Lucia's eyes sparkled. 'It's just the way of country folk. We love our superstitions; we always have. Before the Christians, we had gods popping up to heaven and miracle cures and virgins giving birth. Nothing wrong with that. It's when you start saying your god is the only one to count that the trouble starts, that and the pretence that rules made by men come from God. That's the road to perdition.'

FitzGerald was fascinated by Lucia. *She makes me question everything, even why I am fighting. I'm no longer even sure that God is on the side of the democracies, that I am part of a crusade to spread progress and freedom. I'm a man, shouldn't I resist? Shouldn't she cleave to me, like Ruth in the Bible, rather than I to her?*

THE HERMITAGE

They came to a desiccated landscape of pale, jagged rocks and long ridges bare of vegetation that sloped up to another summit, covered with white screes that dazzled in the strong sun. By this time, Lucia was leading the way. It was not that she was physically stronger than he. She was young woman, slight, with soft curves and youthful limbs. He had been trained in an all-boys' school to be hardy, drilled to be a sportsman and warrior, then stretched by long marches and combat exercises. Despite the occasional uncomfortable reminder of his leg's recent break, he loped forward with powerful strides, the boy's little legs around his neck and arms round his forehead. Beside or before him, what she lacked in physical power she made up with energy and sense of purpose. In awe at her willpower, he thought, *I tire sooner than she; she goes on and on and on.*

The baby was on her back. They had tried putting him on her front, but this dragged her down and her back ached. They found that when Vito woke while on her back, he was happy as long as he could see FitzGerald, who, when the little head was poking blinking around, pushed himself nearer so that the him and give one of his happy smiles.

How does she do it? He could not take his eyes off her. *She's never worked in the fields, let alone trained in mountain warfare, but I suppose she's the descendant of generations of peasants who pulled through due to their intelligence, sharpened in struggle, their transmitted habits of discipline and endurance. What's more, a determination to survive, breed and protect.*

I am not the reason for her exertions. All her attention is on the children now. Enrico inspires her. The tiny creature mobilises her. Vito, helpless and so demanding, fills her heart with such overwhelming love that she breaks the limits laid on her body by nature.

On they went, each propelled by an individual ardour, their limbs aching and too exhausted for conversation.

At last, in the far distance, stood the hermitage – a white blot on an isolated mountain of nearly fifteen hundred metres. They stopped to rest and sat for a few moments on rocks – not too long, lest Vito miss the regular movement of their walking. Enrico clambered off FitzGerald's aching shoulders.

Lucia gasped out her words, 'We'll be safe there for the night. They will care for the baby.'

He studied the landscape. 'Even though there is a road, the Huns won't come this high, its too out of their way.' He was wrong.

After a further two hours, they arrived at a massive door made of horizontal slabs of mighty, thick pieces of timber that had probably been split out of one of the giant chestnuts lining the approach, some of which must have been two or three hundred years old. It had a massive iron lock and a bell rope at which they tugged. It clanged persistently from deep within. Lucia handed the baby to him.

Some five minutes later, a grill at the side slid open and they knew they were being scrutinised. Then, hefty bolts were drawn back, the wicket opened and Lucia was pulled wordlessly inside by an arm encased in a monk's sleeve, Enrico scurrying behind. FitzGerald followed, holding Vito. As he stepped over the threshold, FitzGerald saw an iron key, over a foot long, sticking out of the lock.

The monk who admitted them was so much shorter than both of them that they looked down on his tonsured head. He said nothing, merely looked them up and down, then beckoned. Although the stone-flagged corridors down which they walked were silent, except for their own steps, when they passed a doorway, an opening onto marble stairs descending steeply below them, they could hear a rumbling sound as if from many people.

As they walked, monks in soft sandals passed them noiselessly, their eyes down, carrying flagons of water or bundles of clothing. Benedictines, they were dressed in long, woollen cream-coloured robes that protect them against the cold winter. Further on, they heard organ music coming from the chapel.

The three turned up porphyry stairs, wide enough for twelve men abreast, shiny from hundreds of years of use, onto a landing, and came to a heavy door on which their guide banged with his fist. He put his ear to the door to hear the command, 'Come!', whereupon he turned to FitzGerald and whispered 'Our father, the abbot'. Then he leant against the door and gestured them in.

The abbot stood at the end of a long room, a library with an upper gallery, behind a massive table bearing several piles of books. The walls were entirely covered in bookshelves, with the exception of one full-length portrait atop of whose elaborate gilded frame scraped the cornice. Reached by a rickety-looking ladder, the upper gallery of books also went up to the ceiling, only punctuated by that portrait, of a Dominican friar, which reminded FitzGerald of El Greco. On the desk were papers, ink bottle and quill pens.

Lucia heard the door close behind them and realised that their guide had left and that they were alone with the abbot, a large, plump man, a contrast to the ascetic guide. He came from behind his table as they entered and smiled.

'Well, my children! What do you need?' He touched Enrico's head lightly with the fingers of his left hand.

FitzGerald started as Lucia went on one knee and kissed the ring on the outstretched hand. He remained standing, holding Vito and with Enrico gripping his trouser leg, merely nodding at the abbot.

FitzGerald answered, 'A roof, sir. And a home for the baby.'

'Your baby?' He closed in on FitzGerald, peering at the little face in his arms. 'How lovely!'

Although the abbot had not addressed her, Lucia responded, 'No, Father. We found him abandoned. He is named Vito.'

The abbot's voice trembled, if only briefly. 'It's a good name.' He hesitated. 'How blessed he is to have a new family.' He scrutinised them as a group, as if trying to understand their relationship and intentions, but again directed his question at FitzGerald. 'I have a lady here who has lost both her children in the bombing. She might like to help you look after Vito.'

As she replied, Lucia looked over at the bundle at FitzGerald's chest. 'Yes, Father, please. We are going south from here and, with us, the baby will be in danger.'

The abbot glanced at Enrico but said nothing, still facing FitzGerald.

'An escaped prisoner, I suppose? You can stay, but our food resources are minimal. There are a great many mouths here needing fed, so we cannot offer you much. But we can certainly care for the children. We have a good room for a little family, which has just been vacated. Our best room, in fact,' the abbot laughed. 'In the past, reserved for popes and cardinals who came here to meditate on their sins.'

Lucia looked at FitzGerald. They thanked the abbot, who rang a brass bell.

Another monk arrived. He was a slight, dark figure, with an air of obedience.

'Take them to the Silk Room, Brother, and put back the ancient crib.'

'It was not removed, Father, when the foreign officers stayed there.'

'Good!' He spoke directly to Lucia for the first time. 'The crib is 15th century. They say that when Henry IV slept here, so did one of his children. I rather doubt it. Anyway, we have a crib as a consequence of that story. At Christmas we use it for the *presepio*, nativity.'

Lucia again kissed the abbot's ring, FitzGerald gave another of his nods, the pretence of a slight bow.

'Thank you, Father,' he said.

Without speaking, the guide led them down the corridors.

FitzGerald handed Vito to Lucia and talked to the monk: 'I seem to hear a lot of activity. Have you many refugees here?'

'A few! I will be bicycling round our flock tomorrow just to make sure they are all getting their food and are not ill.'

'Bicycling?'

'Only two hundred or so are in the main building. The men are outside, and the complete families. There used to be many hermits in the vicinity and so many of them are in the little rooms of the hermits. Each of my brothers looks after several.'

He was not taciturn like the first monk. 'Down below in the refectory are mainly the women and children without families. Those who are with parents are outside; they have only lost their homes, but these in the hermitage itself have often lost everything, even their names.

'You are lucky that I can give you a proper room to yourselves. It is our guest room, where the bishop used to stay and once a pope too. Until last night, there were eight men here in this room – British, American, Polish and Canadian. All important officers, generals and suchlike. But they have gone and the room has been cleaned.'

'Over the lines?'

'Who knows? We do not ask. The war is not our concern, only the suffering.'

The party turned down a dark passage and the monk picked up an oil lamp from a chest and lit it before continuing down to arrive at an enormous 18th century press, almost the remaining length of the corridor. He then opened a door in the wardrobe and moved aside some vestments to open rear panels. He stood back and beckoned them to step inside.

As they passed through, brushing aside chasubles, cassocks and other vestments, all bearing a heavy smell of mothballs, he pointed out features of the room.

'This is the original doorway; we had it hidden when the rounding-up of the Jews started so that we might have a secret room. You will find another, small, door in the servant's room attached to the main bedroom. The other side of that door is hidden by a portrait in the gallery of the library. I will return with food through that door later. But you should only use it in an emergency.

'And one more thing.' He now addressed Lucia. 'The window looks out over the main door of the hermitage, but it is better not to look out lest people ask where this room is. At night, keep the shutters closed. The gentleman is so obviously an *Inglese*... If it got around that we harboured soldiers as well as refugees, we might get a visit from the authorities. You understand?'

The monk left them with the oil lamp and showed them another one to light. With a marble floor and light coloured walls, the room into which they had stepped was a large guest chamber as in a medieval castle, with two doors off it; the open one showed a servant's room with a truckle, over which presided, on the wall, a majolica Virgin.

The walls were lined with cream silk moiré, scuffed and torn in places. There was a huge four-poster bed and a rocking cradle of ancient design, with faded silk hangings. A large renaissance ironbound chest of polished walnut lay against one wall; a chaise longue with velveteen upholstery was against another, under a large window, currently shuttered.

Lucia cuddled Vito whilst FitzGerald explored, opening the second small door, entering and rapidly coming out: 'There is even a bathroom with a bath!'

At that, Lucia hurried in to see the luxury, standing beside the enamel bathtub with amazement that turned into sheer joy as she saw that the boiler attached to the wall was hot and that, turning on a tap, there really was warm water.

Not long after, in the abbot's library, the same monk arrived, carrying a basket covered with a white cloth.

His lord looked up from the manuscript he was poring over. 'You are taking food to the latest arrivals?'

'Yes Father. But, Father, I do not believe they are married. A young Italian girl, a foreign officer, surely with a wife at home, is it right? They may both be married to other people! I should put the female with the other women!'

The abbot was much older than the monk. 'Let them be, Brother. Who knows what they have suffered, and how much they have yet to suffer? Let them be happy for a while if they can. Come, I shall open the door for you.'

The abbot climbed up the ladder towards the upper gallery of the library and the portrait. Touching a corner of the gilt frame, the abbot released it to swing open and reveal the servant's room attached to the Silk Room. He stood aside for the monk to clamber in and then closed the entrance behind him. Once inside, the monk knocked on the connecting door. FitzGerald called out for him to enter.

The monk noticed that Lucia was not present; she was presumably in the bathroom. The small boy was fast asleep on the chaise longue. FitzGerald was walking up and down the room, and continued chanting to the baby as the monk came in.

> 'The Lord's my shepherd, I'll not want;
> He makes me down to lie
> In pastures green; He leadeth me
> The quiet waters by.
> 'Goodness and mercy all my life
> Shall surely follow me,

And in God's house forevermore
My dwelling-place shall be.'

The monk waited until FitzGerald stopped, by which time Vito was asleep. Then he said, 'Here is food. You may keep the basket. It can be a container for the baby.' He left through the main door, which opened onto the press and its vestments.

Gently, FitzGerald settled Vito down into the cot. 'Sleep tight.'
Lucia came out of the bathroom, dressed only in a large towel.
'He's sleeping.'
'Well done!'
She was watching him.
His eyes faced the ground. 'I will take one of the pillows and make myself comfortable on the chaise longue'
She laughed. 'You and I have slept beside each other for many nights already. Are you going to reject me now that we have a decent bed?'
FitzGerald's head jerked up and he had a quizzical expression. 'Come here.'
It was her moment to look unsure. After hesitating, she came towards him.
'Closer.'
She moved closer.
FitzGerald put his arms around her.
'Lucia.'
Their eyes locked together. They kissed.
Eventually she said, 'I love you FitzGerald.'
'I thought I was just something you had to look after, nurture.'
'Oh yes, that too. But whereas when we first met, I thought you just a warmonger and a silly boy, now I can see that a soldier can be… lovable.' She laughed, he smiled.
He stroked her hair. 'What flattery! From someone who despises soldiers.'
'I don't despise anybody. But I pity them. Now, long since you

left the camp, you seem to understand us, our point of view. Now you treat us as human beings, even though you cannot be as warm as are we.'

She lifted her arms round his neck, and as she did so the towel dropped to the floor so that she was naked. His hands moved slowly from her shoulder blades down her back, over her hips. They looked into each other's eyes.

They kissed again.

'I love you.'

'No you don't. I just happen to be the only available girl.' She laughed. 'But I love *you* because that's what women do when they come across silly boys.'

Into his mind came the picture of a man he had never met, who had nevertheless populated his thoughts, he now realised, since he had first met Lucia. From the very first moment of speaking with her, he had realised the depth of her love for her Domenico. He remembered the ardour with which she had called her husband a fool when congratulated for his courage. FitzGerald had at that moment asked himself why he, FitzGerald, had never had a woman who felt so deeply about him, or who loved him so intensely.

Now he questioned how he, so unlike Domenico, had come to the verge of taking the younger man's place, in her arms if not her heart. Had she changed, as the betrayed sometimes change, jettisoning fealty in favour of casual indulgence? While still holding her around the waist, FitzGerald pulled back so that he might look into her face, from which the amused look of mockery drained, and something both softer and more longing replaced it. No, she had not done that. She was still the woman who had loved Domenico.

He had found, and she had revealed to him, something of her deep self. He, having been under her instruction for many weeks of tribulations and snatched joys, was now capable of recognising it. *I have graduated*, he thought, *and can now share her world*. In the seconds in which these droplets of comprehension fell upon him, she waited. When she saw from the flicker in his eyes that he was back with her, she put up her mouth to be kissed; he bent and united the two of them in a long embrace.

At this very moment, unbeknown to anybody in the hermitage, a German medical column was climbing slowly up the mountain towards them. The roads were icy and the lorries, the big red crosses on their roofs grimy with oil and dust, slipped from time to time and their tyres whirred, with a noise like flocks of flying dragons. As they stopped and started, the wounded and bandaged men within groaned and cursed. In the cabin, an NCO with a hacking cough and a surgeon, every few moments rubbing his spectacle lenses with a dirty handkerchief, pored over a map with nicotine yellowed fingers and growled comments to the driver. The driver sat straight, his gaunt face staring ahead, his thin, blueing hands grasping the steering wheel as if clutching the last lifebuoy in a tempest. Then, abruptly, he broke his trance and braked as he felt the front axle buckle and the lorry keeled sideways, throwing his two officers into a heap and bringing yells and screams from within. The lead truck had broken down.

THE SILK ROOM

They were in bed. Lucia kissed FitzGerald lightly on the neck, her hand stroking his hair; he caressed her hips. 'When did you decide you desired me?' she asked. 'It was not at the Rovacchia. You despised me then, as just another weak-minded Italian.'

'I never despised you, but I didn't have much regard for Italians. After all, I am a soldier and I have seen Italians in North Africa whom I could not respect.'

'You did not understand how much we hate war.'

'Now I understand. You and Bregante, you are truly brave. And so many other families have taken so many risks to help us.'

'We just do what seems natural to us.'

'And when we talked at the grape harvest, it hit me that you are not only the bravest but the most desirable woman I have ever known.'

She laughed at that: 'So why not show me?'

'You appeared to have made it clear that you were with Bregante.'

'I am.'

'And yet?'

'Bregante needs me for his children, his mother; his own support. But I want you. I want to look at you all day and to bury my head in your breast. I want to stroke your forearm and listen to your voice. I want your arms around me and your cheek touching mine.'

'Even though it's unshaven?'

She touched his cheeks, which were heavy with stubble: 'Especially because unshaven! Come on, Colonel FitzGerald, don't waste time talking. *Carpe diem*! Kiss!'

When, on the morning of 15th October, the monk who had brought them to the room entered with acorn coffee, grey bread, slivers of ham and milk for the children, Lucia hid in the bathroom and Enrico took her place on the bed. At waking, Enrico had taken great exception to finding Lucia and FitzGerald in each other's arms, climbed onto the bed and pushed himself between them, then put his arms around a now-laughing Lucia. FitzGerald had left the bed and crossed the floor to open the shutters so that light streamed in and the fug of last night's oil lamp was driven away by an icy blast of air.

Once FitzGerald had opened the door and politely wished the monk good morning, the monk placed the tray down in silence. Leaving, as he was about to shut the door behind him, he said, 'Father Wolfgang will be your guide.'

FitzGerald was shocked: 'A German?'

The monk stepped back into the room and gave a wry smile: 'Father Wolfgang is in more danger from the Germans than you are, for he was a chaplain in their army. He will show you the way. And the abbot has commanded that the widow Lanza help you with the baby.'

The monk left. The two lovers clasped each other under Enrico's disapproving eyes.

Lucia and FitzGerald revelled in washing. They played with Enrico and Vito, who gurgled happily after eating bread mashed in milk. Later in the morning, Lucia was called out to meet Signora Lanza, the widow who might care for Vito, whom she took with her. Enrico followed. FitzGerald remained in the room and slept some more. He woke, accusing himself of not doing his duty. He should leave immediately, alone if necessary. With his map and advice from the monks, surely he could get through the next few miles? Lucia and the children would be safe here.

He dressed, ready to tell Lucia his decision as soon as she returned. When she did so, Vito was asleep in her embrace. She put him in the cot and then, with Enrico still holding her hand, lay beside FitzGerald.

Later, leaving Vito asleep, they went out through the press and stepped down the deep stairs to the great hall, full of people of every age and description, many lying on camp beds or sat on stools around teachests, some of the women sewing, some breastfeeding, one knitting. Children played with playbricks or lead soldiers or dolls in the spaces between the beds.

Lucia pointed out to FitzGerald a fair-haired young priest, so Germanic in looks that he had to be Father Wolfgang, reading to a group of small children. Beside him sat a woman nursing a sleeping baby. FitzGerald and Lucia approached and waited respectfully while he finished the story. He looked up and she saw a serious, almost grief-stricken, young face, which nevertheless smiled at them.

His voice was enthusiastic.' *Grüß Gott*! *Salve!* You are Signora Riva? You are a brave woman. I know what you've been doing further north.'

'Not alone, Father. There were many doing the work.'

'Would there were more. Most people don't help.'

Lucia recognised something in Father Wolfgang that propelled her to ask, 'And those who do help, those few, why do they do it?'

The woman with the baby took her eyes off it and intervened. 'A Christian education.'

The priest turned to her. 'I regret to have to say it, but Christ does not make men good. Almost all our German soldiers were brought up in the faith, yet which of those has for a moment hesitated to harm? I have given the sacraments to General Lanz. General Lanz, who has slaughtered thousands of unarmed men on the Greek islands.'

Lucia: 'You, a priest, say that it is not Christ who makes people good?'

'Oh, he may affect a few. But those are Christians because they are good, not good because they are Christians.'

'So the good people deceive themselves when they ascribe their goodness to Christ and Mary?'

'Especially Mary. Their ideal of what a human being should be. Mary, the goddess mother, existed long before Christianity.' FitzGerald noticed that this Wolfgang looked uncomfortable, as if he were a student trying to persuade himself of his own advocacy. 'And she is the most inspiring to the peasants! Of course! She nurtures, she conserves, she loves nature, the world of which we are part.'

Having said that, he recovered that priestly style and intonation with which his kind guide their flocks.

'And this young man is…?'

'Enrico.'

Enrico's eyes were on Father Wolfgang as he was asked: '*Sprechts du Deutsch*? Do you speak German?' When there was no reply, he asked, '*Verstehst du*? Do you understand?'

The silent boy slowly moved his head up and down in assent and the priest smiled. 'I have another boy who speaks our language here –' he pointed to a boy in lederhosen, who was standing a few yards away, watching them – 'would you like to play with him?' Enrico took in the other boy, then again moved his head up and down. The priest got up. 'Come, I'll take you to Fredi.' To Lucia's surprise, Enrico left her side and took the priest's outstretched hand. To her he said: 'Go back and rest now. I know you want to leave soon. I must go tomorrow morning and you can travel with me. For now, the boy can play with Fredi.'

FitzGerald had the decision taken out of his hands. He was a follower, once again, he said to himself, but he did not complain. The priest added, nodding, 'I shall come to you after lauds.'

When FitzGerald took Lucia's hand, his heart soared and Lucia turned dreamy eyes to him. Returning to their room, they played with Vito, placing him on the bed between them. He was made happy by their happiness, embraced by their embraces, kissed as partner in a conspiracy of affection.

Later, with Vito back in the cot, the lovers luxuriated in each other's bodies. Meanwhile, below, in the refectory, people of all ages were tossing and turning. Children were wailing. Father Wolfgang and the monks went from child to child with kind words and prayers. Enrico and Fredi chased each other around the big refectory and annoyed everybody before settling down to a game of drafts. Father Wolfgang stood over them, holding a distraught toddler in his arms and singing a lullaby until it slept. The widow Lanza knelt by her truckle and begged God to give her strength to be a mother to Vito.

RED CROSS COLUMN

The medical column arrived at the hermitage at around five in the morning.

An NCO jumped out and banged on the gates with an entrenching tool that he carried on his broad leather belt which sported a rectangular white metal buckle and the motto *Gott mit uns*. God with us.

FitzGerald and Lucia were asleep in each other's arms. They were abruptly woken by a knocking from within the press. FitzGerald opened the door and Father Wolfgang stepped in, dressed as a countryman, with a shoulder bag and crook.

'Look out of the window. Be careful not to be seen.'

FitzGerald opened the shutter a crack and peered down while Wolfgang waited by the door. In the courtyard he saw field ambulances and several trucks. German medical orderlies were carrying stretchers from them and into the hermitage. Others were carrying in equipment and medical supplies.

The priest sounded calm. 'A *feld lazarett*, field hospital, is being set up here. I suppose it is safe from bombardment. And they need heating and water.'

Lucia, from the bed, called quietly, 'We'd better go.' Then she sat up, holding the blankets over her. 'But my *passerotto*?' She meant Enrico.

Wolfgang looked at FitzGerald, avoiding her gaze. 'He's with widow Lanza. Safe, out of the way. The first place they emptied was the refectory. Everybody is outside, somewhere.'

'But Enrico! Where is he?'

'Signora Lanza and Sister Annunziata took both boys into the woods. They will be safe there; there are warm places. They got through before the soldiers put a cordon around us; the only direction we can go now is down the road.'

FitzGerald: 'Lucia, we must get out quickly before they find us.'

Father Wolfgang's voice was soothing. 'Don't worry. They are far too busy to notice you. They just want everybody out so that they can set up operating theatres and wards.'

'But my *passerotto*, I can't leave him. Take me to him. He needs me.'

'You can't get to him now. He will be very safe. Lanza is a very good woman.'

Lucia was standing beside the cot, looking down at the sleeping Vito. 'We can stay here, hidden.'

'No. You have no food. And you can't go out.'

'We can creep out at night…'

FitzGerald's heart was churning as he saw Lucia's agony, but he knew they couldn't. 'No, Lucia, we can't wait. Neither of us is German and every other Italian is being expelled…'

Father Wolfgang again spoke to them both. 'I promise you that once I have set you on your way, I shall go back to Enrico and look after him.'

Lucia's head dropped; she looked vanquished. 'Yes, yes, tell him I shall come back for him in a few days, I shall, I shall.'

Father Wolfgang went out into the corridor to wait for them.

Downstairs, monks steered the remaining children out of the building. Some of the little ones were screaming, some were silent, blank, gripping dolls or cushion as if they were mother. Women with messy hair and hastily pulled-on overclothes had a child in each hand. Others carried string bags bulging with clothes or pans and ladles strung together round their necks. There was a stink of sweat and garlic. Beside the throng, the stream of misery, the surgeon was instructing two monks on the supplies he needed for the operating theatres. Men on stretchers were being carried in, bloody and partially bandaged.

Soon FitzGerald and Lucia were pressing themselves against the corridor walls as more stretchers passed by them: now an overwhelming odour of disinfectant and iodine filled the passageway. Then came a stink like mulch, a rot of compost after a heavy rain. He saw her sniffing.

'It's gangrene,' he whispered. 'Rotting flesh.'

Exhausted, unshaven drivers had demanded hot drinks of the monks, who were now pushing through the corridors, providing acorn coffee and hot water for their new masters. They paid no attention to FitzGerald or Lucia with their baby as they joined the throng being pushed out.

An NCO, with a gaunt face and staring, insane eyes, impatiently twitching and slashing a cane across his own leg, stood by the door. He started to shout, '*Raus! Raus!* Get out! Get out!' Children cried and scampered away from him, though the women tried to calm them and called out not to run away.

Out in the woods, the shuffling of many feet, the occasional child's cry and the songs of birds seemed like paradise after the hubbub of the expulsion. The refugees were all doubling up in the hermit caves; at least, that was what Father Wolfgang said was happening. FitzGerald, Lucia and he walked together downhill. Vito was in a sling tied round her neck, his weight being taken by her cradling him in her arms. As they walked, they talked. The priest wanted to discuss again the horrors his country's armies were inflicting upon the world.

FitzGerald suggested that, 'Our soldiers don't behave like that. However flawed, our democracy teaches respect.'

'The English have laws to make them good. The Italians have instincts. My people had reason, but have abandoned it for a modern superstition.'

Father Wolfgang seemed desperate to offload his ideas. 'I have talked to Polish priests about this and others who have seen what is happening in the east. The people who turn a blind eye have no feeling for others. There is something wrong with how they are raised by their parents. The mothers lack love, or fear to express it. My mother is Italian. When I was small, she was always criticised by our German neighbours because she was not harsh with me.' He slowed his pace for a moment to let Lucia get ahead and look into Vito's sling, smiling and receiving a smile in return.

'Children treated harshly grow up hard on others. If your mother loves you, if you develop attachment to that person who is the source of life, you will behave with sympathy and respect others. It is not nationality, religion or wealth that determines how we behave with others, but mother love. And there is a lot of that in Italy, though never enough.' As he spoke, he looked at Vito, whose eyelashes were already long, whose lips now smiled in sleep.

Lucia doubted this. She knew some of the mothers of her schoolfriends were full of affection for their own children but amoral, ruthless and avaricious outside their family. She let Father Wolfgang be, because, as she said to herself, *he is a good man, trying to understand life without recourse to the usual priestly platitudes.*

Ever since he had fully comprehended the risk that the Bregantes and their fellows were taking in helping him and his kind, FitzGerald had been asking himself why they did it. This German was looking for an answer. A month before, if you had asked FitzGerald to address a priest as "Father", he would rather have bitten off his tongue, but today he started, 'Tell me, Father,' Wolfgang returned a quizzical smile, 'why do these peasants seem to think it a matter of course to give us hospitality, even at the risk of their own lives and that of their families?' He was going to add, surely not because of the Virgin Mary, but held back.

Father Wolfgang did not seem to reply precisely to FitzGerald's question.

'Look around you. You see a way of life that took thousands of years to make. Once the battle for survival was won, brutishness was no longer necessary; their ancestors gradually realised how men and women should behave towards each other. They developed the skills to feed and clothe themselves, and also to make art, to celebrate the beauty of the earth and all within it. This short life became precious. They discovered that making happiness brings meaning to their lives. In other words, they created civilisation, cultivating generous instincts rather than the aggressive. But later, the cities, for all their advances in thought and production, cultivated another kind of barbarian; he who seeks to enslave. You outlaws are benefitting from the humane instincts of the old culture. As you can see, it takes just a few hours to destroy it and replace it by the blind despotism of modernising men.'

As the sun rose higher, a fortified village slipped into sight. It stood on a rise; there was a solid-looking church with a spire on the perimeter. The walls of the houses were brown and gold, the village small and compact, and it looked old, substantial and gracious in the soft sunlight. To the left of them, against the mountain, they saw in a clearing the wreck of an aeroplane lying at a slant, an uptilted broken cross.

When they entered the village, FitzGerald and Lucia sat down on a wall to rest. There was at once a crowd around them, composed mostly of little boys. Father Wolfgang, some metres away, was in conversation with a farmer when someone called in a fierce voice from nearby, 'Devils coming. Stay where you are, don't run.'

Preceded by its roar, a lorry drew up in the square and several soldiers jumped out. Two of them made for the nearest house and came out with bread, wine and salami. Watched by a group of urchins, they handed their finds up to their mates and hauled themselves back in. Then the motor started up, the driver accelerated and the truck rattled past, kicking dust onto them.

The urchins scrambled away from the truck and their attention returned to the couple with the baby. FitzGerald and Lucia rose, looking round for Father Wolfgang, but he had disappeared. A plump woman in an apron and carrying a cloth bag approached them, declaring, '*Scampato per un pelo!* That was a close shave.'

'We are not staying.'

'But you had best have food. Here, eat.' She delved in her bag to hand over four round loaves of fresh brown bread, along with cheese and salami. 'Don't worry, the devils only found the old stuff. Yours is fresh, we hid it.'

They thanked her and the old lags who had remained in the square and turned south. As they set off, the rain began again.

FitzGerald now carried the baby. He looked into its little face and recited, 'I will lift up mine eyes unto the hills whence cometh my help.' As he did so, he glanced up at the majestic tor above. He sang to him as they walked down into the valley near the main Roman road, where they found destroyed houses, refugees in tents made of sticks and tarpaulins, and hungry people.

Lucia stopped beside a group of ragged children sitting in a circle on the ground. She bent low to speak with to one of them, a boy with brown hair and a dirty face. He was dressed in a man's jacket, too big by far but held in by a tight piece of rope.

'Where are your parents?'

'I have no parents.'

Lucia gave each of the children a biscuit, using up all those from the hermitage bar one, which she would mash for Vito.

Dusk fell. They walked through an undamaged village of seven or eight houses. A peasant looked over a fence, stared for a moment as if trying to understand who they were, then made a sign to be quiet. They went on in silence, except that not far away was the clatter of mules' hooves on cobbles and the squeak of saddlery. There were sentries under tarpaulins, but they were asleep.

THE VALLEY OF THE SHADOW

That night was the worst. For seven hours they walked. The moon gave a rare light for a few moments, then vanished behind swirling clouds, reappearing and disappearing intermittently. There was a constant drizzle. On their left was a steep mountain, its pitch-black bulk more menacing because the base was festooned with bright, shifting loops of light as trucks moved continually up and down the winding road.

They passed a group of Germans round a campfire singing "Lili Marleen" to an accordion. Once they had been left behind, Lucia broke their silence: 'That's a sad song.' FitzGerald grunted. He was holding the map close to his eyes.

Although there were lights in the distance, they became lost in a labyrinth of gullies where they were enveloped in darkness. Eventually, as they groped their way forward, they heard a hiss from the side of the road. They stopped, Vito jolting against Lucia's breast. Then an English voice called out softly, 'Over here.'

They could see only dark bushes outlined by moonlight, but they aimed for where the whisper came from. After a second's pause, a tall black shape appeared before them, put out a hand and took FitzGerald's.

'Welcome, FitzGerald.'

'Good God, that's Sam Perry's voice. What –'

In a low voice, 'Not now. Come with me.'

Lucia put out her hand and touched FitzGerald, who replied, 'It's alright.'

The drizzling rain ceased but their coats dripped and weighed them down. In one of the moments of light, FitzGerald realised that Perry was dry; he must have set out after the rain had stopped. He was wearing British uniform! *Have we already crossed the lines?* he asked himself. But he did not speak. Perry was walking slowly and gingerly, taking care not to make more than the tiniest rustle as his boots touched the damp soil. It seemed that wherever they were, it was not far from peril. Lucia and FitzGerald took their cue from him, praying that Vito would not wake and give them away to whatever lurking force Perry was avoiding.

They heard some chatting to their left. Just as FitzGerald realised the voices were speaking German, Perry stopped and turned to face them. He pointed to their right, where stood a white house showing a little light. He whispered, 'That's the house we make for. Cesare's.'

As they approached the house, they had to skirt a bomb crater. To either side of them they could see the outline of anti-aircraft guns and hear German voices grumbling or laughing, and the clink of KFS, cutlery, on metal canteens.

Before Perry could knock, the door opened and a woman stood framed in yellow light. 'Come in, come in. I am Cesare's wife.'

Cesare's home was the last stop for those going through the lines in this area. He was one of the few farmers who had remained right on the front, to protect his smallholding and prove to himself that he and his were indestructible, no matter what barbarians came.

In the room lit with the ochre glow of an oil lamp, Perry looked natty in a British officer's uniform. It was incongruous beside the plain peasant black-brown of the woman and the shabby shepherd coats and leggings of FitzGerald and Lucia.

The door was shut. The room was very warm. The woman,

without a word, took Vito from Lucia and laid him on the table. Seeing him smile, she beamed in response. '*Che bello, che bello,*' she crooned, over and over again.

'Well, well Colonel Fitz, you brought your whole family over!' Perry affected amusement at the sight of the baby. 'We're lucky your infant didn't give us away. Stuffed with laudanum, is it?'

FitzGerald just smiled; he knew that Perry would not join the dots, so he did not bother to reply. Instead, he explained to Lucia, although most of her attention was on Vito:

'Major Perry and I were in PG21 – he ran the escape committee – before I got transferred to PG500.' Then he added to Perry, 'So your escape plans worked, Sam? You got away. Did everybody?'

'No, that clever SBO kept most of us under wraps. Soon after I'd got into the hills, the Germans came and carted them all off to jolly Prussia. '

FitzGerald gave a brief account of the breakout from Ginestra, then, pointing at Perry's uniform, asked, 'Why?'

'I'm a feardy. My Italian's terrible, so I can't pretend. If I'm caught in mufti, I'll be shot as a spy. The Jerries are quite rule-bound. If I'm in uniform they probably won't shoot me.'

Perry told FitzGerald that he worked with the Irish priest, who was known for smuggling ex-prisoners, Jews and anti-fascists into hiding. They were often hidden in corners of the vast palaces of the Roman nobility, who were supplying them not only with accommodation, but also food, ration cards, forged documents and disguises. The pope's palatine guard had numbered four hundred in 1942 but now marshalled over 4,000, the new members being either Jewish or escaped prisoners.

Cesare's wife brought milk and bread for the child. Lucia she told to go upstairs. Then, without a word of explanation, she started to undress FitzGerald, who allowed her to pull off his clothes and boots and push him, covered with a large wool blanket, into a chair. A plate of steaming pasta, garnished with tomato, ricotta and a dash of olive oil, was put into his hands.

'The woman and baby are upstairs sleeping. You sleep here.'

No sooner had he eaten the pasta, washed down with an ochre-coloured wine as pungent as any red, than FitzGerald slept.

When he woke from a dream of patrols and guards, he saw Cesare's wife playing with a giggling, gurgling Vito by the fire. Perry was in a nearby rocking chair, reading what looked like "Blackwood's Magazine" and sucking on a briar pipe, a paraffin lamp casting its blue-yellow light over his face, hands and the volume. FitzGerald spoke to the woman:

'You are right next to German positions, *Signora*. How do you manage to stay here?'

'We have to. It's either that or abandoning the farm.'

'Don't the Germans force you out?'

'They all know us. They greet my husband. They are not as dangerous as you are!'

FitzGerald raised his eyebrows.

'Your people bombed us. Did you see the holes?'

'Yes. I'm sorry. I saw a big crater.'

'Don't worry, American. We welcome your bombers because they kill Germans. My brother was a slave in Germany for three years. He was the only one who got away; all our friends are dead. We'll do anything to help their enemies.'

As the reality of their proximity to Germans dawned on him, FitzGerald's concern rose. 'Perry, we should go. We endanger these good people and we'd better carry on and get over while it's dark.'

Perry lowered his reading matter, rocked his chair in a tranquil rhythm a few times before speaking. 'It's best to leave at first light, when the peasants would go into the fields. That's the excuse. The sentries are most tired then too, but you still need to know where they are. When Cesare gets back, he'll tell you about pickets, machine gun nests and so on. That's what he does. He's taken loads over the lines already.'

Cesare's wife grinned at FitzGerald. '*Chi va piano va sicuro e lontano*. He who does not chafe goes far and safe!'

As she spoke, there was a boom of artillery fire from the emplacement nearby.

Lucia came downstairs, having heard their conversation on the way. 'We need her husband for the last few steps.'

As she finished speaking, they heard a stamping of boots outside the door and then there entered Cesare, another squat peasant with muscled arms and huge rough hands, carrying a large sausage. Perry rose and shook one of those big hands. FitzGerald followed suit. Lucia lowered her eyes.

Cesare spoke first. 'So, Major Sam, what have we got here?'

'Father Wolfgang sent them.'

'Him. The only good German. Because his mother was one of us.'

All his movements were fast, jerky. He beckoned to FitzGerald, ignoring Lucia. When he had come over, Cesare re-opened the door and pointed outside.

'You see those mounds in the garden? I shot and buried a German patrol last week. If you occupy my country, I will do the same to you.' He pointed his finger at FitzGerald's chest as if it were a pistol barrel, 'Bang, bang.'

Lucia stared at Cesare. FitzGerald, unsure as to whether this man was comic or serious, asked, 'Don't they come for you, the devils?'

'They think I am a mere humble peasant, doffing my cap, offering them wine.

If you crawl to them, they are happy. They are having a wonderful time. Power, money and status. Especially the officers. They would be elementary teachers or bank clerks, railway porters or deodorant salesmen if they were not covered in silver braid with guns on the belt.'

Despite having witnessed the pain inflicted by the Germans, FitzGerald did not like to hear warriors diminished. He preferred to attribute the massacres to politics. 'They also risk their lives and fight hard. The Germans are good fighters.'

Cesare snorted in disgust, then took a swig of the yellow wine before opining. 'Men get sick of civilisation. They want to break rules, crack open the heads of better men, shag their teenage daughters and smash their pretty homes. Suddenly they can't bear to be told off by their wives for farting or to have to go shopping with them. They want to be ape men. Wolf warriors. That's why we have wars.'

Cesare did not wait for a response. Sam Perry was beaming as if he were attending a repeat performance of his favourite theatrical. FitzGerald had by now got used to the philosophising of his Italian hosts and did not answer back with his theories about democracy.

Cesare smiled at himself. 'Enough talk. I will take you now.' He had not sat even for a moment, nor greeted his wife. The sharp-eyed, angry peasant seemed all energy, resolution and even ferocity. It was difficult to imagine disobeying him.

While FitzGerald and Lucia replaced their now dry clothes, Cesare played with the baby.

His wife said: 'We have kept him awake so that he may sleep on the journey.'

FitzGerald realised that they had thought this through, whereas neither he nor Lucia had considered about how to deal with Vito on the last lap, when his silence would be essential.

As if divining his thoughts, Lucia turned to FitzGerald. 'Vito and I will go back. You don't need me anymore. I must find Enrico.'

FitzGerald hesitated, glancing at the others, listening for his reply. 'But I thought you were coming with me?' It had never been clear, neither to him himself nor, perhaps, to her, whether he thought she would complete the journey with him or just accompany him to the crossing, providing cover. In his heart he had made himself believe, at least since the hermitage, that they would be together always.

'I must care for Bregante and his children. And Enrico. Now, there is Vito too. And the children on the streets. Someone must help them.' Was she really going to leave him? Was everything she had said in the Silk Room just the heat of the moment?

FitzGerald felt that Cesare, his wife and Perry were all assessing him; that they had divined that there was more to Lucia's presence than her role as guide and camouflage. He spoke stiffly.

'But you may not make it back. And there are many desperate people on the other side that you can help.'

Cesare intervened, impatient and perhaps divining that this was mummery. 'The woman and baby will be valuable cover until we get to the river. After that, we won't meet any devils. It will be the British you have to convince.' He turned to Lucia: 'Come, in case there are new roadblocks. Then, when we get to the river, you can make your decision.'

Lucia, who had taken up the baby as she spoke, made as if to return Vito to Cesare's wife. Cesare interrupted that.

'Keep the baby. But not on your chest. Put him on your back like the local women. It is almost time to set off for the far fields, so we are going to work.'

Seeing her hesitate, he guessed her concern. 'There are no mines. And it is rare that they spray gunfire willy-nilly, since they might kill each other. If they were to take us, we would be transferred to the rear. The baby is safe.'

With that, he picked up two hoes and passed one to each.

FitzGerald took the longest hoe, its staff worn smooth from many hands. Had Lucia been concerned about the baby rather than wanting to leave him? *Now that Vito is coming with us, surely she'll stay rather than risk a return journey. Thank God for Cesare.*

It was very dark when they stepped out of the light, each carrying a hoe and in single file. As FitzGerald was about to leave, Perry stopped him. 'Good luck, old man. Take this.' He put a waterproof bundle into his hand. 'If Jerries come near, let them find this so they think they've got treasure. It's just a little distraction for them.' FitzGerald understood that Perry knew what he carried strapped to his chest, nodded and went on.

Major Perry watched them go, his unlit pipe in his mouth.

TO THE RIVER

They had not gone more than a hundred metres into the scrub when they heard ahead the sound of tramping boots and the clink of metal buckles that told them they were about to run into a patrol.

Cesare pushed FitzGerald down a bank and rolled down after him. Barely two minutes later, a file of six men halted and Lucia stopped to greet the Germans, showing them Vito's little head and wide eyes. As she did so, Cesare came up behind her, buttoning up his trousers, and hailed the soldiers, who recognised him. With sallies bellowed out and grins, the troops plodded onwards. FitzGerald re-joined the party.

There was little light from the stars: this time its absence would not be a handicap, but an advantage. Now there would be no danger of the moonlight revealing them to the enemy and they had a surer lamp for their feet than the moon: Cesare.

The track, snaking down the hill, was a ghostly white in the murk. There were farmhouses close by but neither Lucia nor FitzGerald thought about them, since their whole being was concentrated only on the river below and the supreme necessity of making as a little noise as possible. The path was flanked by stone hedges and FitzGerald noticed two weird fig trees, stripped of leaves, leaning over the right-hand hedge. Their branches scraped against its broken surface in the slight wind, resembling skeletons swaying on a gibbet.

Cesare called a halt, gesturing that there was to be not a sound. There was a stillness everywhere. The only noise was the occasional rattle of a stone or the clinking of FitzGerald's water bottle against his belt, the creaking of boots.

At length, they reached a tributary of the river. It was shallow. A part of its bed of shale and river pebbles was exposed. They took off their boots and walked through, the icy cold water never reaching above their knees. Slowly, their bare feet felt their way through another broad shoal; once, Lucia struck a depression and almost keeled over, only saving herself by digging in her hoe until she could right herself. Then they came out and found they had crossed, without mishap, the first water barrier. The next river would be the one that divided the two armies.

They came out on an island with clumps of reeds nodding gently in the breeze and about fifty yards of pebbles and shale. Cesare left them to reconnoitre, directing, 'Sit down here for a few minutes while I go to that farmhouse over there. Its owner is another stayer. He'll tell me exactly what the devils did in the neighbourhood late this afternoon.'

As they sat, in the distance a dog barked sharply.

When he returned, Cesare said: 'We'll have to go very carefully now: there is a machine-gun post over there.' He pointed to a dark wooded ridge dominating the river 1,000 yards to the right. They left the island and crossed to the other bank without incident.

Lucia's eyes seemed to be becoming accustomed to the dark, for she found she could make out more. Floundering through olive groves and fields that had been ploughed so thoroughly that each farrow was at least a foot deep, and with large square sods everywhere, they faltered again and again. Staggering along, FitzGerald tried anxiously to keep near Lucia lest she fall, and the child along with her. So far, his leg had held up, but it pained him and he set his teeth, determined it should not give out and buckle beneath him.

Stopping them, Cesare commanded again, 'We're going to stay here a while, so sleep. You need all your energy for the forest. In the last two hours of darkness, we'll get past any patrols that might still be knocking about. Your people –' he gestured at FitzGerald – 'might shoot us if they were to see or hear us moving about in the dark. You know yourself a man's finger gets itchy on the trigger when he's on guard at night, so we must time it to be near your side at first light. You'd best sleep.'

It seemed to FitzGerald, in his dulled state, that the hiss of 'Wake up, wake up, it's time to go!' came the moment his head touched the haversack that served as pillow. He sat up with a feeling of wonder, staring out at the sky now brittle with stars. Lucia, he saw, was feeding Vito.

They had not gone more than a half a mile further when they entered the forest and struck deeper and deeper into it. It was a broad winding path they were proceeding along and an almost flat surface. The going was good. Sometimes the tall tree foliage would completely shut out the sky, but it was impossible to stray off that even track, since the black splotch made by Cesare in front was always plainly visible.

If the Huns are here, he thought, *they'll shoot us. If the Allies are here, they too will shoot us. And if they're both here, they'll both shoot us and then probably each another.*

The trees were beginning to thin out when they passed a house. It had a dilapidated air, having long since lost its roof, and stood in a small clearing fifty yards from the track. There was a big tree in front of it, and as the tree's crown moved in the wind, a single large black shadow shifted backwards and forwards over the wall.

Then there were no more trees. The forest was a single black mass behind them. They had come out on the long, flat ridge of which Cesare had spoken. There grew a bright glow in the east. The light seemed to be pulsing in slow, even throbs. Lucia got the impression that now the darkness was rolling back from the face of the earth in slow heavy undulations.

Suddenly Cesare stopped dead and gestured them to halt.

'Listen, this is where I have to do something. This is where we are in vision. I'll run up the rise at its top end there. They will see me and that will give you the chance to slip into the brush by the river.'

'No, Cesare. They might hit you.'

'Don't worry, I've done this many times... Be quiet now.'

Cesare strode off up the slope. When he was about halfway up, somebody opened fire.

FitzGerald grasped Lucia's hand and pulled her across the unploughed, flat ground without one bullet being directed at them. When they arrived at the copse, he threw his arms around her and Vito and pulled them to earth, behind a bush. He was breathing heavily, looking anxiously into her face in case he had hurt her. She looked up from Vito, whom she had transferred to her chest, and smiled at the man, such that happiness welled up in him and dispelled the ache in his limbs and the pain in his knee, which had just hit something hard as it met the ground. He looked down at Vito and kissed the top of his head. The baby had not cried out.

Lucia put her hand in his and allowed FitzGerald to help her rise. There was a path through the thickets that they followed until they arrived at the riverbank. She turned her head and gave FitzGerald a smile.

'To the river,' was all she said, and all he replied was 'yes'. As they stood there, looking at the sluggish water through the reeds, Cesare suddenly appeared from the other direction, having gone round the outpost. They each released the other's hand and faced him.

'You deserve a medal, Cesare!'

'Bah! It was still devils. Your people have not advanced beyond this stream – not here, anyway. Now you are on your own. Your friends are on the other side. You can just swim over.' He looked at them both quizzically, as if wondering what they had decided.

Lucia was anxious, but not for herself. 'Will those on the other side shoot at him?'

Cesare grinned. FitzGerald could see that Cesare divined that she had made her decision to go back with him. 'Not here; they are used to us coming over. And the devils have very few troops left; they've mostly been moved elsewhere, so the last thing they want is to provoke a firefight that might bring superior numbers across the river. But there's always the possibility of some vindictive sentry wanting to target practise on you, so don't attract his attention.

'And for the *Inglese*'s question,' he was making fun of FitzGerald, 'you need not worry, I'll take care of the lady and her baby.'

His tone changed back to being business-like. 'Now say farewell, *Signora*. I will wait for you down there.' He pointed down from where they had come.

'You, *Inglese*, give me the hoe. Someone else will need it tomorrow.'

Cesare left, carrying two hoes.

Lucia made as if to take Vito off her back and FitzGerald helped her. She held him to her chest, looked up at FitzGerald, implored, 'Kiss him.' FitzGerald bent down and kissed the little forehead. Then he saw the wet on her cheeks. They stood before each other without touching. His heart was heaving and there was a sharp pain in his chest.

'Please come.'

'No. Don't try to move me. It is what I have to do.'

'You are obeying a rule, like the soldiers you deprecate. Be yourself.'

'No. For Domenico's sake, for my dead husband's sake, I must care for Salvatore's children. Otherwise, how can I think that I loved him?' She paused, then continued. 'And then there is Enrico. Now Vito.'

FitzGerald was instantly bitter, selfish. 'You never intended to come with me. I was just part of your ambition to persuade more men not to fight. You said you loved me, but you lied to me and made me go out of my way, you made me divert from my object.'

'Perhaps. But if I misled you it is because I love you, FitzGerald.' As she said that, tears coursed down her cheeks and she dropped into his now outstretched arms, which wrapped around her and pulled his little family tight into him. FitzGerald's fervour changed again, his anger dissipated and he felt intense contentment, even as he knew she would not join him.

'The Germans are withdrawing. We will be coming north. You can come with us.'

She was sobbing. 'Who knows? We are in the hands of generals and politicians.'

FitzGerald held her and looked out beyond her, along the path down which they had come. He, in this instant, understood that he was about to lose touch with someone who had changed him forever. He could never go back to being his former self, now that he had grappled Lucia into his heart with hoops of steel.

It was inconvenient to hold her in his arms with the big lump of baby against her breasts, but he bent over Vito and kissed the wet on her face and then their lips met and his hands caressed the coat that covered her waist.

She might never make it back. I might never find her again, in this god forsaken country, where ignorant armies clash by night. All these thoughts and many images of Lucia shimmered in his brain: their angry words in the Rovacchia; her striding over the fields to get away from the bothy; her appearance at that farm, a vision of youth and beauty among those knobbly faces and gouty old crocks; her looking into his eyes in the hermitage, as he slowly lifted his hand to touch her cheek. *I have to say it. I have to tell her. Even though she won't stay. Even though she won't stay with me. I have to keep a thread joining us.*

'I love you, Lucia.'

Lucia looked back at the soldier who used to wear a contemptuous expression, as leader of the six hundred prisoners, and in whom she now found the earnestness of a lovestruck teenager. It was her Domenico that FitzGerald brought to mind. As she stared at Domenico, the other man went on:

'Tell me you believe me.'

Lucia closed her picture of Domenico but remained wistful, resisting too: 'I believe you.'

FitzGerald laughed for joy. 'The first moment I saw you I wanted you.'

'You found me infuriating. You did not desire me until much later, you told me yourself.'

He gave a short laugh. 'Two different kinds of wanting. The second time it was the philosopher I wanted, not just the woman.'

'Because you saw meaning in my words.'

'Because you follow your heart, your good heart, and are as brave as the bravest soldier.'

'Only that?' She took his hand and pressed it against her lips, before turning away.

What could he reply? Nothing. He could not even touch her again, because she broke away and walked back down the track to where Cesare stood, leaning on two hoes, one in each hand. FitzGerald's eyes followed her. Tears were running down his cheeks. When she arrived beside the old farmer, she looked back and raised her hand.

Not until she had taken a few paces beside Cesare did it come over Lucia, the magnitude of what she had done. She did not look back, but she wanted to look back. She felt that she would never see him again, and the mere thought of it encumbered her feet. Cesare slowed his pace to match hers. After a while, she heard the voice of little Vito whimpering. It startled her out of her trance so that she quickened her pace. But still she asked herself: why, why? Why did I leave him?

FitzGerald stood watching until she had disappeared; once she was out of sight, he continued to stare after her for a few moments before his left hand picked up his haversack. Grudgingly, he turned, took the few steps to the bank and slipped into the river.

QUEEN OF HEAVEN

By the time Cesare and Lucia arrived back at the farmhouse, Vito was wailing and inconsolable. Lucia blamed herself, guessing that the child detected her agitation. Cesare had been entirely gentle, cooing at the child, letting Vito suck his little finger and holding onto her, probably unnecessarily, to keep her balance as they recrossed the streams. At the house he told his wife the young mother must be fed and made to sleep, that he would care for Vito while the girl was being looked after.

Lucia slept not only the rest of that day, but the whole night following. Vito, once he had been changed, had cried and eaten, eaten and cried, slept too. Both were worn out. Cesare's wife sat in the rocking chair beside the crib she had brought down from the roof, padded with a quilt and blanket. She dug out a dummy, boiled it and placed it in the baby's mouth. The slow rhythm of the cot as she rocked it, together with the sucking of the dummy, worked their magic and the swaddled babe slept.

At daybreak, twenty-four hours since FitzGerald had slipped into the river, Lucia woke from a dream that contrasted fearsome visions of the Styx with images of FitzGerald being pulled out of the river of life by monsters in uniform. To flee her nightmares,

Lucia left the bed, tidied her clothing and went downstairs to find Cesare in conversation with a German soldier while his wife fed Vito. Told that Lucia was their daughter-in-law, the soldier looked surprised but bowed to her and asked no more. He was here to swap some rations for home-made bread, and to have a banter with the farmer that he and his comrades thought their friend. He, too, was a country boy and felt safe with people much like his own.

After mother and child had both been fed well, Cesare walked with her towards Sulmona, on the conventional route rather than that for the clandestines. He apologised for not taking the cart, saying that as soon as the withdrawing troops saw a horse and cart, they would seize it. He hoped to hang onto his property until "the peace" came. On the outskirts of Sulmona, Cesare left her in the hands of a confederate, a widow who was caring for a wounded Australian in his sixties and an American aircrewman with a smashed leg. This was a mistake, because there was no need for Lucia to associate with clandestines or those who supported them. Alone with Vito, she could pass as just another refugee.

Unknown to either Cesare or the widow, the Australian was actually a general who had escaped from Villa Orsini, near Sulmona, a prison for senior officers, and been injured before he could leave the area. A tall 62-year-old with an eye patch, Carton was easily describable and one of the widow's neighbours had gossiped about him. The news that this famous prisoner – he had made multiple escape attempts since capture a year earlier – was holed up nearby got to Major Reder, who was quartered in a requisitioned house a few hundred yards from the widow's. When the presence of the eccentric general was reported to Reder, he was in conference with Fröhlich and, to amuse themselves, the two SS commanders broke up their meeting and, accompanying the detail that Reder ordered to arrest the general, made for the house.

Once the house was covered from all angles by his soldiers, Reder knocked on the door and told the terrified woman that if there were no resistance, nobody would be hurt. She should bring her guests down to the kitchen while his men checked the perimeter. Carton was not the kind of man to sacrifice the lives of others in a display of derring-do, and limped downstairs to salute the admiring and respectful Germans. Two of Reder's men helped the airman down while their comrades ransacked every room. In the kitchen, Fröhlich and Reder stood talking with Carton, while Lucia and her host huddled in a corner with Vito.

Lucia looked up from time to time at the men with their heavy boots, leather belts and pistol holsters. In Carton, who stood straight and whose bearing was as commanding as that of the devils, but without the menace of their accoutrements, she saw something of the man she had just left. The widow had told her of the old general's reputation for evading his captors. She guessed he would soon be taken away but willed herself to believe that this daredevil old man might be more able to communicate with FitzGerald than she. She longed to speak to him, to tell him about FitzGerald, for him to give a message to her man. Without forethought, she handed Vito to the widow, rose and went towards the officers. The two devils had their backs to her and were facing Carter, who saw her between their shoulders. As she approached and stood behind them, Carton smiled at her; Reder and Fröhlich each turned in astonishment as Lucia, afraid that she had only seconds to get the old man's attention, forced herself to speak.

'Sir General,' she said in a choking voice, 'when you escape next time, please take a message to Colonel Gerald FitzGerald.'

The general masked his surprise in that look of polite imperturbability that is a stock skill of the English gentleman.

'Of course, Madam, it will be a pleasure.' He spoke as if at a garden party, but his glance went to the baby behind her.

Lucia did not know what more to say. Reder and Fröhlich stared as she took from her pocket a little green purse embroidered with white cranes and held it out to the general. Before he could take it, Reder woke up and snatched the purse, opening it and looking inside. There was nothing there. He felt along the seams and pressed the embroidered cranes as the general looked on, amused, and Lucia looked on, anxious.

'Just a love token, don't you know!' General Carton held out his hand. Reder hesitated and then put it into his prisoner's palm.

Carton turned to Lucia with a fatherly smile. 'Dear lady, do not fear, I shall give Gerald your token, though it may take me a little time.' Lucia felt that in her silent reply and intense look, she communicated her message, so torrid that even the old general – perhaps especially the old general – would know what to say.

Fröhlich might not have discerned that the young mother cuddling her baby in the widow's kitchen was the woman Bregante, had a flicker of recognition and revulsion not passed over her eyes as they met his. Fröhlich had not forgotten the woman who had shouted at him and been defended, in front of all his men, by that Irish bastard. The Irish bastard had been in his thoughts often since the miracle of finding him at Sulmona; losing him thanks to the air strike had been the devil's own luck. Everybody associated with the Irishman and his exploits, with Foschini, with the factor, with this factor's sister or whatever she was, all these traitors had come to loom large in his imagination. *Getting hold of the woman is better than nothing.*

The widow and Lucia and the two officers were put onto two separate trucks. The Italian females might be shot out of hand, but the English had to be handed over to the authorities responsible. Although Reder was already famous for massacres and Fröhlich for exacting punishment without remorse, neither wanted the English to witness their implementation of law. Reder told Fröhlich he must deal with the women. The men were to go back to Villa Orsini.

Once in possession of the Bregante woman, Fröhlich did not know what to do with her. Handing her over to Priebke did not appeal; the man was squalid. He had a pretty good idea of what leaving her in the hands of the militia would amount to, and, while he fully expected her to be shot, he did not want to encourage the illegal and undisciplined vices of those people who sullied the great cause to which he had devoted his life.

Although he did not acknowledge it to himself, there was another factor. Those he had condemned to death up till now were mere cyphers, numbers. Even the children had no human form, were just crumbs to be brushed away, thought of as blocks to progress. This woman was very real, had a personality. She had castigated him in public in front of one English officer and appealed to the old English general in his presence. Was she just to be eliminated like the grains of sand in their thousands? Didn't she need a trial? How could he dispose of her?

Quite soon, an answer was provided for him by Consul Vacca's brother, who had hot-footed it to Sulmona as soon as he had heard of the death of his valiant sibling, looking for Fröhlich to verify and explain the sacrifice and expecting to collect his corpse for burial in the family plot.

The Vacca brother and the second son of the hero of El Agheila was a bishop, but when he tracked down Fröhlich, he wore the garb of a simple priest. This, and the evident sadness of the man, moved Fröhlich to behave in a subdued and respectful manner, despite his distaste for the morally corrupt allies whom he was obliged by his superiors to endure. Foschini's treachery had hardened him towards all Italians.

He tolerated Vacca for a full hour, in the course of which he learnt that the bishop, thanks to the kindness of prison director Carretta, regularly attended Rome's Queen of Heaven prison to wrestle with condemned political prisoners for their immortal souls. Fröhlich, who considered torture, at least of women, to be counterproductive, speculated that this might be a more efficacious way of learning more about the Irishman and his networks than Priebke's bloody methods.

Having decided, Fröhlich acted. He despatched both woman and baby to the Queen of Heaven, with an injunction that she was to be shriven by Bishop Vacca.

PART FIVE

MATTERS UNRESOLVED

CAFÉ ROSATI, *APERITIFS*

FitzGerald arrived at allied headquarters in the Palace of Caserta near Naples, two days before the 8th Army began the offensive that was, eventually, to break the German line on the Sangro River.

It had taken him six days since finding the German staff officer's papers to reach headquarters. He had, though, with Foschini's help and before setting out, taken the precaution of extracting some key information from the documents and, after encryption, sent it back by radio.

By January 1944, New Zealand troops were in position at Cassino, which would soon become a notorious battleground. In mid-January, the US army attacked along the Gustav Line. With Operation Shingle, British Admiral Troubridge landed forces at the port of Anzio, behind the Germans, on 22nd January. By the middle of February, there was fierce fighting around Anzio and Cassino. The Maoris advanced on Cassino but were forced to withdraw; it was Polish troops who finally captured Cassino, on 18th May. On 5th June, the pipes and drums of Scotland's Gordon Highlanders paraded in St. Peter's Square, Rome.

On that very day, at the Arco delle Campane, Arch of the Bells, the entrance to St. Peters, beside a Pontifical Swiss Guard in morion and breastplate, his tasselled halberd at arms, stood Gerald FitzGerald. He was in a new uniform, made bespoke for him by a tailor who had a short while earlier been making them for Germans. During fitting, he had booked the tailor to make a winter coat for Lucia as soon as he could get her to Rome; the tailor had recommended Rocchi, the jeweller in a nearby alleyway, so that he had ordered her a gold bracelet too.

FitzGerald gazed across the piazza towards a white line painted on the ground, linking the two arms of Bernini's colonnades. Only hours before, German troops had patrolled the other side of that line, preventing anyone from crossing it onto papal territory. Where FitzGerald now stood had often waited Monsignor O'Flaherty, Sam Perry's partner in their massive escape operation.

Half a year before, FitzGerald had been debriefed, reprimanded for disobeying orders by organising the flight of prisoners from Ginestra, denied return to his unit and posted to command the Allied Protection Commission (APC) for liaison with the Italian resistance. He was phlegmatic about his own fate but exasperated by his inability to find out anything about Lucia. Secretly, he starved for some token of her, especially at night, when he ached for the warmth of her beside him, the touch of her hand.

FitzGerald's operatives in the APC were very well-informed on the activities of partisans and Special Operations agents. FitzGerald was in regular contact with Foschini and had sent supplies to Bregante via Goode, who was now with a group of leftist partisans that coordinated with both Foschini's King and Country and Neri's Hammer and Sickle brigades. Yet no word had come of Lucia. She had not arrived in Pozzo and Ginestra was still occupied by German units. The death of Cesare in an airstrike as he returned to his farmhouse cut FitzGerald off from further intelligence. Lucia had simply disappeared.

Once the Germans had fled the, now starving, Rome, the APC was busy trying to feed the fugitives who had come out of hiding, and the families who had cared for them. FitzGerald and his team worked every hour of the day and much of the night to support their dependents.

FitzGerald was stirred by the beauty of Rome but, in his first busy days, had barely appreciated the mighty palaces, elegant piazza and pretty churches, let alone the ruins of the forum and colosseum. Now he allowed himself a circuitous route from St. Peter's. He had plenty of time before meeting Father O'Flaherty. Under a bright sun, he strolled through the Pincio gardens, passed Villa Medici and stepped down to Piazza di Spagna, stopping for a moment among the jostling Anglo-American youths, with their khaki shorts and box cameras, to take in the Keats-Shelley House on one side and Babington's Tea Room on the other. At the bottom of the steps, he first turned left to admire the palaces and avoid the fountain, which was cluttered with squaddies with their arms round local girls, throwing ten-lira pieces into the water.

What a fine building, to harbour such a vile organisation, he said to himself in front of the Ministry of Propaganda. *Here, the inquisition and religious wars were inspired, brainwashing and torture employed.* His thoughts flew to the Queen of Heaven, which he and his team had investigated as soon as they arrived. *Is my Lucia imprisoned?* The idea was too terrible. He saw her as she had been in the Hermitage. In his fantasy, they were back there together. She combed out her hair. She slowly lowered her towel. He touched her. He smelt their lovemaking. He heard her voice, but could not make out her words.

And then she was gone. The tall soldier, with an air of loneliness about him, turned away down Via del Babuino to Piazza del Popolo. There he found the pretty café, Rosati, where he was to meet the priest.

It was a disappointment. O'Flaherty knew nothing about Lucia, though he had requested information of all his contacts. At the end of their meeting, he did offer a slither of hope. 'There's an escape line in the north, run by an Italian, helped by anti-Nazi German officers. Prisoners of war, refugees, anybody who needs to get away – they help.' Yet FitzGerald was sure that Lucia would never willingly have gone north. The answer to the mystery lay between here and Ginestra, he was sure. He had to get to Ginestra.

Though they abandoned Rome, the German commanders made several attempts to hold fast as they retreated north. They found the Allied advance unstoppable and it would prove to be so until they blocked it at the Gothic Line, north of Florence. In this situation, FitzGerald, as he sat in Rosati's, after Monsignor O'Flaherty had left him, determined that he would head for Ginestra under cover of the advancing armies. The priest had left one olive in the dish. FitzGerald stabbed it with a toothpick that flew a little Union Jack. *I must find out where Lucia is, I must; I will not give up.*

As he rose to leave, picking up his cap and swagger stick, a familiar figure strolled in, accompanied by two other officers. The man with the eyepatch instantly recognised FitzGerald and called out.

'My dear boy, I've been meaning to get hold of you for days.'

'Glad to hear you got away again Sir, congratulations.' Carton's final escape was the talk of every mess.

'Same to you, Fitz, with brass knobs on for leaving a trail of broken hearts.' As he spoke, General Carton had his fingers in the pocket of his bush shirt, trying to claw something out.

As Fitzgerald looked askance, the General pulled out from his pocket a little green silk purse, looked at it and handed it over.

'Embroidered cranes, very pretty. A young lady I met on my travels asked me to give it to you. I wish I were young – ' He was about to make some comment about womanising when he saw FitzGerald's face, suddenly tense.

'Where, when?'

The general turned to his two companions. 'Gentlemen, I'll just have a private word with Colonel FitzGerald here, will join you in a jiffy.' They headed for the bar.

If anything, the general's revelations made the situation worse. In any event, it did not change FitzGerald's determination. He would go to Ginestra.

FAREWELL FROM MAJOR FRÖHLICH

Donna Chiara had been warned by members of the ladies' committee who were in contact with the *bande* hovering in the hills, waiting for the departure of the devils, that chaos might ensue once the devils started pulling out of the Ginestra area. Anticipating the anger of retreating troops and exhilaration of their replacements, she was preparing to join her husband in one of their tenant's houses, outside the town, until normality might be restored.

Fröhlich's unit had continued anti-partisan operations in central Italy, their base remaining near Ginestra. On a warm July morning, the main column was revving up on the outskirts of Ginestra, ready to start on the journey north.

In the piazza, two armoured reconnaissance vehicles were placed strategically as protection for Fröhlich as he leapt from his jeep and strode over the drawbridge of the castle.

Ignoring the *carabiniere* on guard outside the mayor's office, Fröhlich marched into the office of the Countess of Ginestra, who was at her desk with her assistant.

Donna Chiara looked up, her eyebrows raised, remained seated: 'You have come to say farewell, Major Fröhlich?' There was a touch of irony in her voice, though not enough to rile a man for whom English was his second language.

The German gave his Prussian bow, clicking his heels, 'That woman who organised the escapes from PG500 is in our hands. When we cleaned out Queen of Heaven, my colleague Rauff took her to Milan.'

Donna Chiara knew all about Queen of Heaven, the notorious prison in central Rome in which the party had imprisoned its critics.

'Who is it you mean?'

'Your factor's woman. Your factor, Bregante. Who will be shot before we leave.'

Donna Chiara stared at him for a few seconds as if she barely understood, or perhaps was trying to work out how to respond, before speaking.

'Jochen Fröhlich.' She used his full name, perhaps to suggest that he was a human being before he was a soldier. 'Why? The war is passing by Ginestra. What benefit can there be to kill a family man?'

'He disobeyed. His punishment must be an example to others.'

'Major Fröhlich, isn't this pointless? Is the war not finishing already?'

He looked angry at the suggestion that circumstances might change his resolve and his tone was cold and hard: 'No matter the situation, justice must be done.'

Donna Chiara bit her lip in frustration. 'I beseech you, in the bowels of Christ, think it possible you may be mistaken,' she said, the words of Cromwell coming out unconsciously.

Fröhlich stared at her uncomprehendingly.

As she stared at the angry man before her, it grew on her that nothing she could say or do would make him deviate from the rules he had chosen to follow. What was it these men had inscribed on their belt buckles? Father Filipović had told her, in admiration: "*Meine Ehre heißt Treue*", my honour is loyalty. They took pride in blind faith, just like the communist trades unionist, whom she had hidden in the cellars of the fortress from men as pig-headed as he himself. *Of course, Fröhlich won't have a clue what I'm saying.*

'Madame?'

'I just want to ask you, as a powerful man, to be magnanimous. After all, apart from the fact that executing Bregante will make no contribution to the war effort, hounding him down may even be a distraction from your busy schedule.'

'Thank you, Madame, for your consideration.'

'And as you know, Mr Fröhlich,' she went on, 'these people who help the afflicted, those in trouble, are the same good Samaritans who will help you in your hour of need.'

Something like disgust passed over the man's face. He abruptly raised his chin.

'Countess, I will say farewell.' He had started to turn when Donna Chiara suddenly thought of Fröhlich's reference to "the woman". 'By "woman", do you mean my assistant, Bregante's brother's widow?'

He stopped. A slight smile played over his mouth. 'Correct, Madame.'

She stared at him. The thought of Lucia in the hands of these men took all her heart for speech. She willed him to say something, anything, and he did, in a very business-like tone.

'It is possible to release her. The partisans have taken prisoner my colleague *Hauptsturmführer* Priebke. I propose an exchange.'

Donna Chiara knew nothing of this Priebke, but here was a lifeline. 'Will you…?'

'No. Talk to your priest here. Filipović. He can fix it with our police chief in Milan, Rauff, who holds the woman. Also, the *Alpini* captain…' a look of distaste spoiled his features, 'your confederate Foschini, will tell the priest how to find Priebke.'

'Father Filipović?'

'Yes.'

Fröhlich saluted, with the fascist arm raise and a '*Heil* Hitler'. He turned on his heel and left. As he did so, Donna Chiara saw that, although his riding boots were gleaming, the heels were worn right down. 'He needs a cobbler,' she murmured to herself, as she turned her eyes to the crucifix on the wall and then shook her head in wonder at this ugly encounter. At that moment, her husband looked in.

'Has that awful Nazi gone?'

'Yes, we must be off. But first we must warn Bregante. And find Father Filipović.'

THE PROFESSOR'S TRIUMPH

As the occupying troops pulled out of Palma, within the town, creeping round the corners to make sure the devils had left, appeared the Hammer and Sickle Brigade with their commissar, Professor Neri. They took over the office of the *podestà*, ran up the red flag and, in groups, started to search houses for alleged fascists. When they found such men, they tormented and beat them. If they were not dead after that, they would be shot. Their women were repeatedly raped before their heads were shaved and they were driven naked around the town. Once the commissars had decided to put an end to these proceedings, they had the bodies picked up and dumped in the river. The records of the local party committee had been burnt before the reds could get to them and you could not help crunching underfoot enamel party badges and brooches bearing Mussolini's head, that had just days before been worn with pride, now flung out of windows. There were not that many passers-by, however; a few young men stayed on the streets to laud the new powers and assist them in their decontamination operations, particularly where this involved breaking open shops or forcing their way into the better houses.

Professor Neri and his band were a fraction of the partisan group that was attempting to assert control over the area; rather than remain in a subordinate position in Palma, Passo di Lupo decided to carry out retribution against the fascists in Ginestra. He and his immediate entourage, including Commissar Neri, drove up one mid-morning, leaping off their trucks in happy anticipation of the the work to come.

The communists took over the mayor's office, ran up the red flag. At first, the main body marched and saluted with clenched fists, singing "Bandiera Rossa" and "The Internationale". Then, groups of them started to search houses. The Station Sergeant and his little team bided their time, hoping only to stop the most egregious acts of disorder and avoid being murdered themselves.

The professor had his men put up in the main square a "WANTED FOR TREACHERY" notice, with a photograph of Foschini, his German medals prominent, fraternising with Fröhlich. Nobody dared to stand out and tell the reds that Foschini had worked against the Nazis, if they had even known. Some may have thought he played a double game, because information about his activities in Abruzzo had not percolated through. Neri knew the situation, but now that the Nazis were on the run, he viewed Foschini's King and Country unit as class enemies, obstacles to the revolution to come, capitalists.

Some of the *banda* smashed open the door of the Foschini home. Inside, they ran amok, kicking in the furniture and clubbing the pictures on the walls, throwing books out of the window. Dottoressa Foschini at first sat rigid in her wheelchair until she was seized by the arm and pulled downstairs.

A long-haired man with a beret and bandoliers, unrecognised by anyone of Ginestra, kicked her with his German boots: 'Fascist scum. She ran the *Fascist Youth* And her son is a Nazi lover! Kill them all!'

Nobody knew where the son was to be found so they had to make do with the mother. Several of them dragged her outside onto the street, where fifteen or twenty boys – teenagers and younger in stolen German helmets and with bayonets and rifles – had surrounded two alleged militiamen and were pulverising them.

Neri had the priest brought before him. Filipović appeared to fighting men as effeminate, but he was not afraid. He stood up to Neri's offensive questioning, referring to Our Lord's sympathy for the poor and the church's siding with the oppressed. He quoted an encyclical of Pope Pius in which he had called for solidarity with the persecuted, implicitly criticising Nazism. And, finally, he told Neri where he could find Captain Alessandro Foschini, the "notorious fascist", who had returned to the area days before. For Neri, that clinched the priest's innocence. While the priest was still present, Neri despatched a team to the pharmacist's villa, where Foschini was said to be hiding, to arrest him. He gave strict instructions not to interfere with the pharmacist, whose mysterious ability to find medical supplies unavailable from any other source was legendary.

Just as Neri had shaken hands with Father Filipović and let him go, even accompanying him to the door, some nifty lad was hanging wire from the balcony of the palace that had been the party headquarters. A helpful passer-by quickly made it into a noose. *Dottoressa* Foschini, now only half-conscious, had the noose placed around her ankles and was flung over. As a crowd of men and boys gathered, there was much laughter at her undergarments. Some cheered wildly as the lads on the balcony pulled her up to dangle well above the ground, a target for stones and whatever rubbish might be to hand for chucking. Somebody ripped off her long skirt so that her face and upper body were not hidden from them. Afterwards, when inquiries were made, nobody could recollect how long it took her to die.

DEMOCRACY'S ADVANCE

Beside a main road a few kilometres south of Ginestra stood FitzGerald, watching Allied tanks and trucks rumbling gradually northwards. Columns of infantry were spaced in between. The Germans had no aircraft, so the forces of democracy could march like their ancestors, paying no attention to the skies.

The jeep beside him contained his driver, his head on the wheel, kipping, and his intelligence officer, a young captain, Lucy Addey. Her CO had just ordered her to desist from handing out army biscuits and even her compo rations to beggars on the road. For, returning north were carts with families, gaunt and with strained mouths and furtive eyes, their few possessions piled up. Many were on foot: all were hungry.

A few metres away stood a British armoured personnel carrier containing Captain Lange, who had arrived back with his unit after climbing over the Monte Moro to Switzerland, repatriation, then despatch to the APC.

Above the tramping of hundreds of feet, howling of babies and occasional bursts of song from the crowds on the road, Lange could hear louder voices as people shouted over the hubbub:

'Where are you heading?'

'We're going home. If there is still a home. We've been away eight months.'

By the road, some squatted, exhausted. Children ran up to the soldiers to beg for food. Several armoured cars crawled up to a deserted village and stopped.

Soldiers dropped off the vehicles and went into the abandoned gardens to defecate. The infantry following on received their command to break ranks and rest. A sergeant could be heard bellowing, 'Don't go into the houses, you animals! The Huns have passed through here. They may be booby-trapped.'

FitzGerald, once more suave and commanding, turned to speak with the female captain who had got out of the jeep. Her tight skirt and army shirt were set off by the holster hanging from her webbing belt.

'Two weeks ago you were listening to Tito Gobbi singing in the Grand Hotel in Rome...' Addey nodded. 'By the end of the year, you will see Toscanini in La Scala.'

'You think we'll have persuaded the Huns to leave by then, Sir?'

'Even if not, I'll take you there anyway.' FitzGerald gave one of his famous smiles, then, seeing a man appear from the bushes, turned to greet Goode.

In response to FitzGerald's message, Goode and Albion had arranged to meet FitzGerald here and now. Goode had arrived, looking like a brigand. He was bearded, dressed in leather breeches, a worn tunic from some unknown army, leather cross belts and an alpine hat without a feather. Following him were two even more piratical Italian guerrillas; one carried a cutlass in addition to his rifle and the other had two pistols protruding from his belt, which FitzGerald noticed was German.

After six months back with his own kind, exercising his profession, participating in the crusade in which he believed, FitzGerald had reverted to the identity that the boys had welcomed when he rode into PG500 carrying his guard's rifle that September long ago. Or not. His outward appearance was once again that of a man both decisive and supercilious, confident of the rightness of his cause, the superiority of his civilisation and of his own place of command. Yet the time spent among very different people, whose moral authority he had come to acknowledge, had both introduced doubts into his mind and reduced the rigidity of his self-control. He might still not show his emotions, but now he allowed himself to feel them.

So, when he saw the younger man, with whom he had disagreed profoundly over politics but who had recognised the moral grandeur of their rescuers sooner than had he, his heart heaved, and he barely restrained himself from enfolding Goode in his arms. Instead, he said:

'Well met, Goode. All in one piece?'

The bandit before him spoke with a familiar Scots lilt, 'Aye, thank you, Sir. You look well, Sir.'

'I am. What do you report?'

'The French 4th Tabor is about to descend on Ginestra. I suppose that's why you've come?'

'Yes. I don't want to leave Ginestra to them. The French have done the most filthy things around Naples.'

'Right, Sir.' Always the strategist, alert to the politics of the war, Goode went on: 'I don't know why we call them allies. In France itself they've mostly collaborated with their occupiers and the small number fighting with us are as barbaric as the Germans.'

'Napoleon must have killed off the chivalric gene.' FitzGerald moved towards the jeep in which his female intelligence officer sat staring at Goode as if struggling to see, in his outlandish outfit, an ally. 'Let me introduce you. This is Captain Addey, who has just been transferred from interrogating Nazi captives in Rome and recording their atrocities. Speaks Italian as well as you do. German and French as well. She is tasked with helping us find those of our people who escaped the Huns but who haven't reappeared. And making contact with the escape lines.'

As he saw Captain Addey's astonishment, he explained, 'Mr

Goode and I left PG500 together and spent some time in the hills. It'll be easier to believe he's one of us when we get him back into his kilt.'

FitzGerald had had a message sent to Goode, asking him to rendezvous and back him up for a task that he had now revealed as getting to Ginestra before their allies. Goode had suspected as much, and was concerned that the French might already be there.

It was at that moment that Albion walked out of the spinney.

'So you got my message,' was all FitzGerald said by way of greeting.

Albion was dressed as a peasant. 'Yes, Bregante is running the escape lines still. We got his message.'

It was Goode who asked the question that was on FitzGerald's lips: 'And his sister-in-law? The widow?'

FitzGerald spoke matter-of-factly, to hide his anguish. 'She stayed further south, didn't manage to connect with Sam Perry and the priest, O'Flaherty, who looks after people in Rome. There was a rumour that she was taken by the Huns, but it's not confirmed.'

Lange had been staring at Goode with an amused look and called out from the vehicle: 'You look bloody dangerous, Goode, I'd have shot you at first sight if you weren't talking to the colonel.'

'You wouldn't have had a chance. These two lads,' Goode pointed at the two Italian pirates, 'are very handy. They have a lot of scalps.'

The two Italians grinned and toted their tommy guns.

FitzGerald brought the interlude to a close: 'You done, lads? Okay, let Captain Addey sit in the front. You and I, Goode, will sit behind and jar.'

Albion jumped into Lange's vehicle, as did the two Italians.

Once the driver had negotiated his way back into the throng, FitzGerald had to bellow to be heard. 'I have taken French leave, if I can use that expression in current circumstances. I have warned Captain Addey that in accompanying me she is disobeying orders not to push so far north.'

Goode grinned and shouted back. 'It won't be the first time you have disobeyed orders, Sir.'

The colonel ignored the remark, so Goode leant forward and addressed Addey, shouting over the engine. 'We are not far from PG500. We're told it's now being used to hold fascists.' She nodded but did not try to yell back.

From then on, they gave up trying to talk, precluded by the roar of the engine, the clamour from the crowds and the honking of horns.

LIBERATION, FRENCH STYLE

Nearer to Ginestra was a bizarre caravan, led by a mounted Frenchman with an auburn moustache on his tanned face. While his sky-blue kepi was conventionally French, the rest of his costume was not. Over his uniform he wore a djellaba, the rough, homespun cloak of the Moroccan mountaineer, striped in black, brown and white. It contrasted with his business-like pistol, map case and field glasses, which were strapped across these exotic robes, and the military boots, not quite concealed beneath it.

Riding directly behind the French captain was his guidon bearer, a bearded, hawk- nosed Moroccan in turban and djellaba. Only it wasn't an ordinary guidon he carried, for the staff was topped not by the typical spearhead device, but by a shiny brass crescent of Islam; flowing from it was a long white horsetail, waving in the breeze. Marching in sandalled feet behind the guidon were about two hundred chanting Moroccan tribesmen, all bearded and steely-eyed and wearing striped cloaks. This was the pride of the French army, the goumiers of the 4th Tabor.

Barely a mile away, in the piazzetta of Ginestra, bodies were hanging from the balcony post upside down. There were other dead bodies scattered on the ground nearby. In front of the castle, a podium had been erected, with red flags and a long banner with the words:

VIVA LA GRANDE, INVINCIBLE BANDIERA DI MARX, ENGELS E LENIN!
LONG LIVE THE GREAT, INVINCIBLE BANNER OF MARX, ENGELS AND LENIN!

A small man in white overalls, atop a tall ladder, had whitewashed over some of the fascist slogans and was putting the finishing touches to the stencilled exhortation:

STALIN È SEMPRE CON NOI!
STALIN IS ALWAYS WITH US!

People were shouting: 'The Allies are coming! The Allies are coming!' Many were relieved that another army was on its way, after the two days of chaos under the reds, who had been entrenching themselves in order to present their government of the town as a *fait accompli* when the Allies arrived. In more fortunate towns, the British had appointed town majors to run them; while this was usually rather good for the apolitical citizens, the communists found themselves marginalised and, sometimes, criminalised. Comparing the town majors' attempts at fair governance, with German rule and communist power grab, the citizens had swiftly idealised the Allies and assumed they would bring utopia with them. Ginestra's citizens were running around in great excitement. When the 4th Tabor troops marched into the square, people poured out onto the streets and the crowds gasped to see black men for the first time, but nevertheless cheered and cheered.

Another, junior, French officer cantered up from the rear of the unit to the commanding officer for his orders. The latter pointed to the cheering crowds and gave a cynical laugh to his lieutenant as he rode up.

'*Ils le regretteront!* They will regret this!'

At their leader's command, the goumiers spaced themselves around the square, pointing their rifles with an air of menace.

A deputation of communists in red scarves, with pistols in belts and an occasional submachine gun, was assembling on the podium. As they prepared to greet the liberators with formal speeches of welcome, they found themselves surrounded by contemptuous goumiers.

The lieutenant bawled at the men on the podium. 'Throw down your weapons!'

The new mayor, his chest decorated with a scarlet sash, announced, 'We are the government of Ginestra!'

The lieutenant appeared to disagree. 'Not today you are not! For all I know, you are fascists. Put down your weapons or I will shoot you all.'

The men on the podium hesitated, then handed their weapons to a smirking goumier.

The French commander looked impatient and addressed the now-silent crowd. 'Is there a gaol in this hole?'

An onlooker cried out, 'In the castle.'

The Frenchman made a sign with his head to call up the NCO who stood in the ranks behind: 'Raqib Awwal, find the prison, lock them in.'

Protests from the communists were silenced when a goumier kicked one of them in the crotch. He writhed on the ground in agony. The other members of the provisional government were forced to pick up their comrade and enter the castle at gunpoint.

The French captain turned away from this theatre. He commanded: 'My group stay here. The rest can go searching for fascists.' He paused and leered. 'The convent is for officers.'

The third French officer, a mere aspirant, flushed and with an arrogant cast to his handsome olive skin and well-cut features, had by this time ridden up to hear his captain addressing his juniors. 'The nuns should be clean.' He looked at the youngest officer. 'Bring a couple of tasty ones back here for me and Monsieur de Brinon. We will make our HQ in the bar –' he pointed out the *locanda* opposite – 'for the next couple of hours.'

The captain and lieutenant turned their horses towards the *locanda* and dismounted, flinging their reins to a goumier, who tethered them to the iron rings in the wall.

On the other side of the square, a goumier caught sight of a young girl in the crowd, made for her, grabbed her and flung her over his shoulder. She screamed and the piazza fell silent. Many people stood, transfixed, staring in the direction of the screams; some fled. Other goumiers started seizing women and some smashed into a shop. At that, howls of terror erupted and the piazza emptied quickly.

The citizens' jubilation went from dismay to panic as the goumiers began to ravish the town. A short time later, at the convent, the aspirant and four goumiers had shot through the door and rushed in.

The Mother Superior stood before them and tried to speak but was felled. There were screams from nuns who were grabbed, their habits torn off them, and raped on the spot by the goumiers, while others chased round the building for the rest. They laughed and called out to each other, showing off their conquests as they dragged the now-naked nuns along by their arm or hair or leg. The aspirant relieved his men of three of the youngest nuns before they could be used and had them tied up in readiness for taking to the *locanda*. They knelt together, shuddering, weeping and jabbering prayers. The young officer laughed to see such fun.

At the other side of town was the *liceo* where several teenage girls were running up a line of men who pawed and clutched at them; the more the girls were terrified, the more gleeful were the men. A goumier sergeant entered, pulling beside him a naked boy who had blood streaming down his legs. He threw him over a school desk, laughing at the child's shrieks.

In the town, general looting was taking place. A man tried to defend his wife and daughters and was shot. The woman was raped on her bed while her daughters were being raped on the floor. Once they had beaten or killed the men and ravaged the females, the goumiers looted their homes of jewellery, silver or anything that seemed to them both valuable and portable.

Meanwhile, on the road into Ginestra from the south, FitzGerald's jeep drove into the outskirts of the town. As they rode down the street, they saw goumiers flitting in and out of houses. A naked woman was thrown out of the top floor of a house.

FitzGerald called, 'Stop!'

Goode jumped out and went over to the woman.

'She's dead.' He pointed to her wounds. 'She was probably already dead when they threw her out.'

Captain Addey paled. 'What's happening?'

'It's the French. They have been doing this up all Italy. The bastards gave in to the Nazis in their own country and are now they behaving like Nazis here. We'll find their officers.'

The British drove into the square, parked and immediately saw dead bodies and heard howls and pistol shots from the houses. In the *locanda*, FitzGerald found the French captain and his lieutenant and demanded that they stop the ransack of the town.

The Frenchman was nonchalant. 'Why? This is my men's reward for their efforts. How can I stop them after such a war?'

FitzGerald turned his weapon on the Frenchman, as did Goode. 'Captain, stand up. Hands up. Captain Addey, take his pistol.'

Slowly, both Frenchmen rose with hands in the air and Captain Addey tugged their pistols out of their holsters.

'Lieutenant. You go and tell the men that if they do not cease this behaviour immediately, I will shoot you all, starting with your commanding officer.'

'You wouldn't dare!'

FitzGerald did not grace the Frenchman with another word. He pointed his pistol to the floor and shot into the floorboards within a centimetre of the man's boot. The man jumped back, horrified.

The captain was laconic. 'Go on, de Brinon. The Englishman is mad. Humour him.'

With a sour expression on his face, the lieutenant left the *locanda*.

The French CO being cared for by Goode, and Addey remaining in the safety of the *locanda*, FitzGerald emerged into the square and looked around. There were shouts and bangings as doors were smashed, as well as screams and cries, but the only people he could see at that moment were the four corpses hanging from the balcony of what had been the party HQ. He walked towards them, stepping over broken earthenware, abandoned bags and bits of clothing. The female was upside down; her face disfigured into a repulsive balloon. The other three were men and one of them had only one arm, the stump of the other sticking out like an extension to the shoulder. With a start, he realised that it was Foschini. His bruised torso, with read weals across it, was streaked with dirt. His head hung down over his chest, still handsome despite the bloody gash in his cheek where an old wound had opened up.

FitzGerald was transfixed before the body of the man who had been his enemy, his rival, his comrade and, he now saw, his friend. How had it come to this? *Who had sought out Alessandro Foschini for punishment and death? And why? How Lucia will grieve.* Once upon a time, he would have gnashed his teeth and vowed revenge. Now, he recalled some lines that Lucia had taught him, from the poet of despair, Leopardi:

Dimmi, o luna: a che vale
    [So, O Moon, tell me what value]
Al pastor la sua vita,
    [Is the shepherd's life to him,]
La vostra vita a voi?
    [your life to you?]
dimmi: ove tende
    [Tell me: where is it leading]

Questo vagar mio breve,
    [My short street]
Il tuo corso immortale?
    [And your eternal road?]

Taking his pistol out of its holster, FitzGerald entered the open and empty palace, stepping over smashed furniture and files, climbing up the marble staircase, noted in the guidebooks as of exceptional beauty, to the *piano nobile*. Undisturbed, he untied and lowered the Captain's battered body onto the street below. Once downstairs again, he picked it up and carted it over to his jeep, laying it over the back seat just as some goumiers were being herded back into the piazza by their leaders.

It had not been easy to rein in the French troops in the middle of the best fun they had had for several days. But they were quick workers and had each already relieved themselves with at least one body and picked up whatever valuables were easily to hand. The lieutenant instructed the NCOs – and goumier NCOs are always obeyed. Receiving their orders, each man gave a final clout to the body he had last enjoyed, slung his plunder and made for the square and assembly.

As they formed up, one had a trombone and another a fur coat. A tall man with a big beard had a small girl over his shoulder and tried to join the ranks with his burden but his NCO gave him a great belt with his swagger stick so that he dropped her on the cobbles, from where she crawled beneath the legs of the guffawing men until out of the ranks. She picked herself up with the agonised efforts of a geriatric, streaming with blood, and slunk away.

It took less than an hour, a tribute to the efficiency of the NCOs, for the goumiers to be collected back into their ranks, their spoils piled onto commandeered trucks.

FitzGerald watched the French lope off, followed by their loot. No locals ventured into the square.

Both *carabinieri* and militia posts were empty. As he wondered what had become of them, a motorbike roared into the piazza, driven by a youth in partisan outfit, another boy pillion. The boy jumped off and sidled up to him, and after a moment's thought he recognised this as Aldo, the child who had guided him to his first hiding place months ago.

'Hello Aldo!'

'*Signor Colonello*,' the boy was urgent. 'You must go to Greppo. Now. For your friends' lives. Quickly.'

'Greppo? Near the camp? Why?'

When the child explained that Neri and a few of his men had disappeared in the direction of Greppo, shortly before the arrival of the French, and what was their probable intention, FitzGerald was electrified. It had not occurred to him that Bregante might be thought of as a collaborator by the communists because he had once distributed German leaflets. He wasted not a minute to purloin the startled partisan's motorbike. When remonstrated with by the partisan, FitzGerald shut him up by pointing out that he was wearing a British belt and holster, which could take some explaining in the coming order.

This silenced the partisan, who let Aldo remove his British booty, together with some ammunition clips, under the steady eyes of FitzGerald. Then FitzGerald lifted a bren and ammo from his jeep, shoved them into the excited Aldo's hands and directing him to climb up behind him on the bike, pumped the engine.

He yelled at Goode: 'When you're sure the frogs have gone, follow me. Leave Lange to run the town.' Goode waved in salute.

AT HOME

The families of Greppo had crept back little by little, always keeping a lookout in case of bandits or Germans, ready to flee at any time. They had not been troubled, and neighbours, led by the mothers, had joined together to restore Greppo to rights.

Once the message came that the last German convoys were to move out of Ginestra, Bregante and his children returned from Abruzzo. Not, alas, his mother, for she had died far from home during their fugitive life. A German priest had come out of nowhere with little Enrico, who now, his origins and old name forgotten, was an equal member of the Bregante family, all of whom missed a mother. The pain of Lucia's absence was felt by them all; hearing nothing from her, Bregante feared the worst.

Thanks to his neighbours, when Bregante arrived, his home had been cleaned, the rubbish had been removed and the flagstones were scrubbed white; he could begin to resume something of his old life.

It was mere hours after the German rear guard had withdrawn north that the three children were back playing with their neighbours. Bregante set up his workbench in the space in front of his home and set about repairing some window frames while chatting with old Giuseppe, who had remained as custodian throughout the period when the women and children of Greppo had hidden in the woods.

At about the same time as Bregante sat down to his carpenter's bench, Professor Neri and a trusty band of five braves had commandeered a rubbish truck from the local depot and driven in the direction of Greppo. They stopped off at PG500, which was now being used to incarcerate capitalists, whom the partisan guards would daily interrogate. Shopkeepers and clerks, housewives and lovers of those deemed fascist, even the women who had staffed the German military brothel that had been set up in a pretty 18th century villa, the owners of which had fled months before, were brought out for beatings and ritual humiliation. Among them were two deserters from the Nazis, Kalmyks whom Bregante pretended were shepherds, according to the camp commandant. They were now tied together and, their naked bodies bloody from beatings, lay where some months before, Colonel Vicere had taken the salute. Neri had them flung onto the truck going to Greppo.

After a coffee with the new camp commandant, an old friend from student days, Neri returned to his transport and gave the command to drive to Greppo.

When the elders of Greppo saw the truck lurching up the hillside towards Greppo, they had no intimation of what might follow. Had the enemy not been vanquished? Or at least fled? Were all Italians not now on the same side?

The truck screeched to a halt, slamming the five braves against each other so that they bellowed and cursed. Mothers looked out of windows and Bregante looked up from his woodwork.

'Hey, Bregante!'

He came out from behind the bench, watched by his neighbours. The two Kalmyk boys were pushed down over the tailgate to sprawl on the ground.

'Hey, Bregante! Look what we've found!'

Bregante walked over and looked into the boys' damaged, cowering faces.

Unsure of what was going on, but feeling no fear for himself, Bregante said, 'Two deserters. A long time they've been helping around the farms. Good boys. Why treat them so badly?'

'They are German soldiers, no? Russians who changed sides to save their skins?'

'Asians. Press-ganged. I found them some months ago. You shouldn't treat them like this; they are good boys.'

'Spies. And you helped them, giving them a home in the hills.'

'Yes, of course I helped them. Otherwise, the fascists or devils would have shot them. They are just children. Who are you, anyway, to pass judgment on them?'

Neri stood in an assertive pose, his legs apart, his hands on his hips, his chin uplifted as he spat out, 'I am in charge of the liberation here. And you are a criminal. Speaking for the Nazis. Helping traitors to the people. You deserve to be shot yourself!'

His men moved their guns menacingly. Bregante looked back at him, astonishment and disgust mingling in his glance.

Neri went on, 'I will not shoot you here. The people must see justice done. In Ginestra!' He turned to his men: 'Bind him. He has even admitted his guilt! Collaborator!'

FACE OFF

FitzGerald, with Aldo riding pillion, was bumping over the rough roads, jerking from side to side as he tried to avoid the worst potholes. Clouds of dust billowed up around them.

The boy had his arms tightly round FitzGerald. The bren was across his back and it knocked hard into his skin, but he didn't care because it made him feel like a warrior. Up and down, as if on a bucking horse, his light body jumped. Round his waist he had a webbing belt, too loose for him; ammo pouches bounced up and down, scraping against his bare thigh.

At the foot of the hill, where the climb to Greppo commenced, FitzGerald parked the bike and found the path that twisted round the hill and led to the postern. The little gate was open and, cautiously, FitzGerald looked through.

Greppo seemed deserted except for the corner near the Bregante house. Bregante was tied to the tailgate of a rubbish truck. Neri's men were sitting smoking on the ground. Three children were in the doorway, weeping desperately, being held back and comforted by an elderly woman. FitzGerald watched as Neri himself strolled round to the cab, then back to stand over his comrades; he was smoking a pipe.

FitzGerald had not been sizing up the scene for more than a minute when gunfire startled him and crows shot up from the trees with the velocity of lightning. The professor wobbled, tottered, fell; all in an instant. For an iota, the comrades were turned to stone, but as two machine guns opened up on them, they scrambled to their feet, only to be hit in the back, buttocks and shoulder. Not one was left unhurt; those standing were felled first.

The woman yanked the children back into the house.

Every time a partisan moved, tried to crawl away or get up, a new volley rang out and they subsided. Finally, there was silence from Neri's men; only the sound of wailing children could be heard from within the house. There was not a living soul in sight, except Bregante, tied to the tailgate, who struggled to sit up and look around.

Taking advantage of the postern being hidden by Bregante's lean-to, FitzGerald and Aldo climbed in the back window of the ground floor of Bregante's house. FitzGerald eased himself downstairs, putting his pistol back in its holster. The woman and children were cowering upstairs. As soon as he saw them, he put his finger on his lips. The woman looked wide-eyed with horror but Enrico recognised FitzGerald. The boy, who rarely spoke, whispered: '*Il Colonello!*'

FitzGerald murmured, 'Be quiet. Aldo will help you out at the back. Then run away as fast as you can, into the riverbed; hide in the bushes.'

FitzGerald relieved Aldo of the Bren and set it up on the tripod, its muzzle hidden by a swinging shutter of the first floor, ready for more partisans. But it was not they who arrived.

To FitzGerald's amazement, slowly, carefully, from behind one of the houses, walked Fröhlich, carrying a Schmeisser machine pistol. Three of his soldiers, each from a different point and all with machine guns at the ready, stepped cautiously forward into the open.

Fröhlich, looking around and seeing Bregante, said, 'How extraordinary. The communists wanted you too!'

FitzGerald readied the Bren and took up a position from which he could see through the open door and had a good view of Fröhlich standing over Bregante.

Meanwhile, Aldo helped the last child over the windowsill, down to the woman, who picked up her dress as they ran away from the house. As they ran, the girl stumbled over her dress and cried out.

One of the German soldiers shouted, 'People behind the house!'

Fröhlich shouted, 'Get them!'

Bregante pleaded. 'It's my children! Please, *Herr* Fröhlich!'

Fröhlich turned towards Bregante and spoke deliberately. 'You know the rule. All members of the family will be punished!'

'No! Please!'

Fröhlich turned to his men, 'You two go and find the brats and kill them. No, bring them back and we'll hang them all together. This will teach him.'

When Aldo returned, FitzGerald passed him his own tommy gun and whispered, 'OK, you get him into your sights from upstairs. But make sure you're not seen. I'm going to tell him where I am. You be ready to cover me.'

'Sir!'

FitzGerald remained hidden but shouted, 'No you don't, Fröhlich. You touch one hair of these people and you and yours are all dead.'

Fröhlich was for an instant stunned to hear that familiar voice. Then he put on a show. 'FitzGerald! How wonderful! At last, we meet again!'

'You are surrounded, Fröhlich. Get out quickly while you can.'

The German soldier told off to grab the children was quietly creeping round the back and making for the window through which Aldo and FitzGerald had entered earlier, and from which the children had escaped. Aldo, prowling between windows on the upper floor, saw him making his quiet, slow way round.

'I don't believe you, FitzGerald. You are alone. Otherwise, you would have shot us already. And I won't turn up this opportunity...'

As Aldo's target climbed up onto the windowsill, he fixed on him and fired. The soldier collapsed backwards out of the window. The noise galvanised Fröhlich, who turned to escape from FitzGerald's vision, but the bren was trained on him. FitzGerald pulled the trigger. Fröhlich shuddered and fell backwards as a bullet tore into his shoulder. From behind the well, another of Fröhlich's men tugged his chief almost out of FitzGerald's sight, leaving only the soles of his boots showing. Aldo stayed kneeling by the window, trembling, amazed at the body of the first man whom he had ever fired on.

The German next to Fröhlich was briefly visible. FitzGerald shot at him but missed.

As he scanned for movement FitzGerald heard the rumble of a heavy vehicle scrambling up the slope towards Greppo. *Is it possible that Fröhlich would have reinforcements for this? It should be Goode, following on.* The engine sound was killed a hundred metres or so from the great gate – the driver had heard the shots – and the three men and one woman in it jumped out and skirted round, making for the postern.

Goode made short work of the second of the three men who had accompanied Fröhlich and who was found by the postern, aiming for FitzGerald. Distracted by a child's cry from the copse nearby, he had not heard Goode's party approaching, so Goode got a clear shot. As the woman seized the child to pull it back, she saw Goode's target lying, bloody, below, and her hand went up to her mouth.

Without lifting his eyes or aim from Fröhlich, FitzGerald shouted back to Goode. 'There's one more at large, Mr Goode. Behind the well. I'm covering the officer.'

When Goode circled round behind the well, he found Fröhlich alone, where his last comrade had dragged him. Fröhlich's jacket was soaked in blood and he was unable to lift a limb. His weapon was nowhere to be seen. FitzGerald handed his bren to Lange and walked over to Fröhlich, standing over him.

'This was quite unnecessary, Fröhlich. Had you left Bregante alone, you would now be on your way at the head of your men. You waste your energies, and now your life, doing such pointless acts of savagery. You're not a soldier, you are a zealot.'

Goode untied Bregante, who stood up with difficulty, stretching and rubbing his limbs. He looked at Fröhlich with a combination of disgust and pity.

Fröhlich spoke slowly, his voice husky. 'You won. Except for the woman.'

FitzGerald stiffened and stared at him.

Fröhlich whispered, 'His sister. No, sister-in-law.'

'You mean Lucia Riva?'

Bregante started, moved a slight pace towards the inert German, crouched down beside him, listening.

Fröhlich made a grimace, intended perhaps to be a smile.

FitzGerald, 'What have you done with her?'

'Ask Kappler.'

'Kappler?'

'Our man in Rome. Cleaned out the gaol. Ten for every German.'

FitzGerald was as if paralysed. Bregante was the first to react; from crouching he toppled onto his knees and, in a strangled voice, 'No! The Fosse Ardeatine! No!'

Fröhlich's voice was slurred. 'Yes. Yes. Yes. They broke the law.'

FitzGerald, 'What is this?'

Bregante knew. 'On 24th March, three hundred were taken from the Queen of Heaven and butchered in the Fosse Ardeatine.. Reprisals. He says Lucia was one of them.'

'How does he know? Do you know if this is true?'

Bregante was looking up at FitzGerald, who stared down at him. 'It is possible. It was said that she had been taken to Rome.'

FitzGerald felt a chill run through him; he was heavy, as if his body had become a great sack of stone that he could barely hold up. To Fröhlich: 'Is this is what you did to her?'

Fröhlich was gazing up, wide-eyed, not looking at them, as if he were struggling to rise out of his body. He was trembling, his left hand shook and Bregante took and held it in both his, as if he were a mother with her child.

FitzGerald suddenly found his voice. Anger burst from him, his hands clenched. 'What do you mean? Talk! Damn it, tell me!'

But Fröhlich no longer spoke. FitzGerald put his hand under the man's nostrils and found that he was just breathing. He looked round wildly. Turned back to Bregante:

'Is it true?'

'It was said that she was in the Queen of Heaven prison from which Kappler took his victims.'

FitzGerald did not want to believe that Lucia might be dead. He pulled himself together.

'Not until I have evidence will I believe it.' With that, he strode to the jeep, then, as if bewildered by his own actions, returned to seize Bregante's arm and raise him, pulling him away from the wounded man.

The children came out of the house with the woman, who shuddered when she saw the dead bodies and crossed herself.

Albion approached, his pistol covering the last German, who looked about 15, his hands in the air, shaking, his face a mask of terror. Albion forced his prisoner's hands behind his back and tied them.

Lange and Albion made a pile of the weapons dropped by both dead *banda* members and Germans.

Fröhlich groaned; FitzGerald glanced at him. Then he said, 'Bregante, you shoot him. The right is yours.'

'No.'

'Shall I?' FitzGerald now knew his man, guessed the answer, but wanted to hear it.

'No. Poor sparrow.'

FitzGerald doubted this. *Pacifism, he thought, is not possible when you confront zealots, any more than is reason.* 'Then leave this babyface to look after him. You'd best not hang around here until the Germans and the French are both far away. We've cleared Ginestra. I'll take you and the children there. One of these vehicles will work.'

FitzGerald drove the *banda*'s truck, with Bregante beside him. The woman and the children were cargo. Aldo was allowed to drive the motorbike back, with Goode riding pillion to control his excitement.

FitzGerald did not linger in Ginestra. He made sure that Bregante and the children could be secreted in old Signora Riva's tiny home, refused a meal and agreed that they would say nothing about Lucia, particularly to Enrico.

'I must return to my outfit forthwith. But there is one reckoning I must have. That priest. I must know what part he played in this.'

He looked at Bregante, thinking that the Italian was so composed. For one who had just escaped a violent death by a hairsbreadth, his serenity was unexpected.

'He's no longer here. Father Filipović has been ordered to Rome to be secretary to Bishop Hudal. Forget him, FitzGerald; the war will soon be over and we must try to live together again. Germans and Italians, you and he, we are all born of woman.'

FitzGerald suppressed an angry retort, put his hand up and removed his hat, slapping his thigh with it as if swatting a mosquito. He could not bring himself to accept that, so he changed the subject.

'My unit is being posted to France. We will be fighting our way into Germany. The Huns never accept that they are defeated; will never accept it, until they have seen their own country destroyed.'

Bregante gave a sad smile. 'It is not because they are Germans, but because they are men.'

FitzGerald heard an echo of Lucia in the factor's voice but did not utter this thought. He embraced Bregante in the Italian fashion, even lingering for a moment with his arms around the man's shoulders.

'Signor Bregante, I have often been insulting of Italians.' He paused and swallowed. 'Please forgive me.' Bregante replied only with a slight smile. FitzGerald went on, 'You peoples' courage and humanity puts me to shame. Not just me, my boys too. You are our heroes.'

Bregante shrugged. 'We only know what we must do, if we are to claim to be men.' Then, as an afterthought, he added, ' And women.'

They shook hands.

As Bregante waited to wave him off, FitzGerald thanked and dismissed his lieutenants. Goode he commanded to take charge in Ginestra until the troops arrived. The others he ordered to hurry back to their units. He himself, with his driver and Captain Addey, made directly for the south.

Passing the cemetery, the place at which he had first seen the widow Lucia, nine months before, FitzGerald had the driver stop for a moment. He got out, entered the open gates and found the shrine to Lucia's husband. As he stood before it, he became aware of being watched and reached for his pistol. There was a scraping on the gravel, and from behind one of the bigger tombs walked Donna Chiara. They had never spoken, but each knew the other by sight.

FitzGerald put back his pistol and gave a motion of the head, rather like a bow: 'Countess.'

'Mr FitzGerald.' She paused as he remained silent. 'We have a lot to answer for, you and I.'

'You mean?'

'But for us, several people we cared for might be alive.'

'Don't blame yourself for surviving, Countess. It's fate.'

'The good die young and the bad die old. Isn't that what we Americans say?'

'All deaths diminish us, Countess. Thank you for the good you've done, you and your helpers. The country people. The doctors.'

She smiled and he gave his bow again, deeper this time, before turning on his heel, making for the jeep with a grim, set expression on his face. Captain Addey did not speak, nor did the driver. They returned through burnt and ravished countryside. FitzGerald sat beside his driver and gazed upon the charred remains of homes, smashed jeeps, scrawny waifs, holding out their hands for food; old men with their arms around their ragged granddaughters and wasted youths in dirty uniforms and bandages. Many abandoned, part-burnt vehicles decorated the roadside and a gagging stink rose from the unburied bodies around them. *I don't share the triumph of the Roman who has seen the barbarians scatter before him. I see what Lucia sees, weeping families for whom there is no victory. She would have an apt quotation from the classics to describe my transformation, but I'm bereft.* He searched his mind for some words of Virgil that he might recite to her when next they met. *We must meet – yet were she alive, Bregante would surely know. She would never abandon Bregante, Enrico, her Domenico's family.* Grief enveloped him, separated him. Neither Addey nor the driver spoke a word.

And yet, even if they have killed her body, she lives on, in me; in all those she changed. He looked out, over the detritus, up to the hills, and spoke aloud, but to himself. 'Now do I know where love comes from. *Nunc scio quid sit amor.* Now I know what love is.'

ACKNOWLEDGEMENTS

This is a work of fiction, though drawing upon many accounts of altruism in Italy 1943-4 and upon what certain fugitives learnt from their experiences. I have, with permission, used the words of Uys Krige, Stuart Hood and Eric Newby, all fine writers whom I could never emulate. I thank the heirs to their estates, Brenda Heinrich (Krige: *The Way Out*), Svetlana Hood (Hood: *Carlino*) and Sonia Ashmore, as well as Harper Collins (Newby: *Love and War in the Apennines*). More details of this book's debt to them and to others are provided on my website http://hugodeburgh.com/

I also thank Sir Max Hastings, for providing the afterword, and friends at the Monte San Martino Trust, who have kept vivid in the collective memory many stories of rescue in wartime Italy.

To the River is dedicated to the memory of the good people who saved so many lives. We know about them because of those who remembered, the writers Eric Newby, Stuart Hood and Uys Krige among them, as well as the former fugitives who invited me to their annual commemorations half a century ago: Anthony Laing, Ian English, Peter Langrishe and Maurice Goddard.

Any profit from this book will go to the Monte San Martino Trust, charity no. 1113897.

THE SECOND WORLD WAR IN ITALY
AFTERWORD BY SIR MAX HASTINGS

Many 21st century people who are not Italian merely have a vague notion of Mussolini's Italy during the war as a fascist state, which was a bungling accessory to Hitler's tyranny. In truth, as historians know, the principal victims of Mussolini's grotesque political and imperialistic pretensions were his own people. If he had preserved Italian neutrality in 1940, instead of plunging into war in hopes of a share of Nazi booty, I believe that he might have sustained his dictatorship for many years in the same fashion as General Franco of Spain, who presided over more mass murders than the *Duce*, yet was eventually welcomed into membership of NATO. It is unlikely that Hitler would have invaded Italy merely because Mussolini clung to non-belligerent status; the country had nothing Nazi Germany valued. As it was, however, between 1940 and 1945, the catastrophic consequences of adherence to the Axis were visited upon Italy. What I mostly want to do here is offer a brief narrative of what ordinary Italian people suffered in the war, especially during its last two years.

Italy's surrender in 1943 precipitated a mass migration of British prisoners of war, set free from camps in the north to undertake treks down the Apennines towards the Allied lines. A defining characteristic of such odysseys, many of which lasted months, was the succour such men received. Peasant kindness was prompted by an instinctive human sympathy, rather than by any great ideological enthusiasm for the Allied cause, and it deeply moved its beneficiaries. The Germans punished civilians who assisted escapers by the destruction of their homes, and often by death. Yet sanctions proved ineffectual: thousands of British soldiers were sheltered by tens of thousands of Italian country folk, whose courage and charity represented, I suggest, the noblest aspect of Italy's unhappy role in the war. A young Canadian soldier, Farley Mowat, arrived in the country with a contempt for its people. But he changed his mind after living among them. Mowat wrote home from a foxhole below Monte Cassino: 'It turns out they're the ones who are really the salt of the earth. The ordinary folk, that is. They have to work so hard to stay alive, it's a wonder they aren't as sour as green lemons, but instead they're full of fun and laughter. They're also tough as hell… They ought to hate our guts as much as Jerries', but the only ones I wouldn't trust are the priests and lawyers.'

For many months, even before Marshal Badoglio's government surrendered to the Allies, his fellow countrymen saw themselves not as belligerents, but instead helpless victims. The American-born writer Iris Origo, living in a *castello* in Tuscany with her Italian husband, wrote in her diary: 'It is necessary to realise how widespread the conviction among Italians is that the war was a calamity imposed upon them by German forces – in no sense the will of the Italian people, and therefore something for which they cannot be held responsible.'

The Italians' overthrow of Mussolini and declaration of war on Germany in October 1943, far from bringing a cessation of bloodshed and freeing their country to embrace the Allies, exposed it to devastation at the hands of both warring armies. The view of many Italians about their nation's change of allegiance, and about the Germans, was expressed in a letter one man wrote two days later: 'I won't fight on their side – nor against them, although I think them disgusting.' Iris Origo noted: 'The great mass of Italians "*tira a campare*" – just rub along.' Emanuele Artom, a member of a Torinese Jewish intellectual resistance group, wrote: 'Half Italy is German, half is English, and there is no longer an Italian Italy. There are those who have taken off their uniforms to flee the Germans; there are those who are worried about how they will support themselves; and finally, there are those who announce that now is the moment of choice, to go to war against a new enemy.' Artom himself was captured, tortured and executed the following year.

Nazi repression and fear of being deported to Germany for forced labour provoked a dramatic growth of partisan activity, especially in the north of Italy. Young men took to the mountains and pursued lives of semi-banditry: by the war's end, at least 150,000 Italians were under arms as guerrillas. Political divisions caused factional warfare in many areas, notably between royalists and communists. Some fascists continued to fight alongside the Germans, while the Allies raised their own Italian units to reinforce the overstretched Anglo-American armies. Italians were united only in their desperate desire for all the belligerents to quit their shores.

Instead, their agony persisted and deepened. In June 1944, amid the euphoria of the Allied armies' advance on Rome, the commander-in-chief General Sir Harold Alexander made a gravely ill-judged radio broadcast appeal to Italy's partisans, calling on them to rise in arms against the Germans. Many communities consequently suffered savage repression when the Allied breakthrough proved inconclusive. After the war, Italians compared Anglo-American incitement to a partisan revolt, followed by the subsequent abandonment of the population to retribution, with the Russians' failure to succour Warsaw during its equally disastrous Warsaw Rising in the autumn of 1944. The lesson was indeed the same: Allied commanders who promoted guerrilla warfare behind

Axis lines accepted a heavy moral responsibility for the horrors that followed.

The Germans, having previously regarded the Italians merely as feeble allies, now viewed them as traitors. An Italian officer, Lt Pedro Ferreira, wrote: 'We are poor wretches, poor beings left to the mercy of events, without homeland, without law or sense of honour.' He was serving in Yugoslavia, where many of his comrades were shot by the Germans after the armistice. The Nazi general Albert Kesselring ruled Italy with a ruthlessness vividly documented in his order of 17th June 1944: 'The fight against the partisans must be conducted with all means at our disposal and with utmost severity. I will protect any commander who exceeds our usual restraint in the choice and severity of the methods he adopts against partisans. In this connection, the principle holds good that a mistake in the choice of methods in executing one's orders is better than failure or neglect to act.' He added on 1 July: 'Wherever there is evidence of considerable numbers of partisan groups, a proportion of the male population will be shot.'

The most notorious massacre of innocents was carried out at Hitler's behest, with Kesselring's endorsement, under the direction of Rome's Gestapo chief. On 23rd March 1944, partisans attacked a marching column of German troops in Via Rasella. Gunfire and explosives killed thirty-three Germans and ten civilians. In reprisal, Hitler demanded the deaths of ten Italians for each German. Next afternoon, three hundred and thirty-five prisoners were taken from the Regina Coeli prison to the Ardeatine Caves. They were a random miscellany of actors, lawyers, doctors, shopkeepers, cabinet-makers, an opera singer and a priest. Some were communists, and seventy-five were Jews. Two hundred of them had been seized in the streets near Via Rasella following the partisan attack, though none was involved in it. In batches of five, they were led into the caves and executed, the bodies left where they fell. The Germans used explosives to close a shaft in a half-hearted attempt to conceal the massacre. The Caves became a place of pilgrimage and tears.

There were a handful of survivors of another massacre in the churchyard at Marzabotto, a picturesque little town at the foot of the Apennines, where in September 1944 Waffen SS troops exacted a terrible revenge from the civilian population for local partisan activity and assistance given to Allied prisoners. 'All the children were killed in their mothers' arms,' wrote a woman who miraculously lived. Though herself badly hit, she lay motionless under the dead: 'Above and beside me were the bodies of my cousins and of my mother. I lay motionless all that night, through next day and the night following, in rain and a sea of blood. I almost stopped breathing.' At dawn on the second day, she and four other wounded women crawled out from beneath the heaped corpses. Of her own family, five had been killed. In all, one hundred and forty-seven people died at the church, including the priests who had been officiating when the SS arrived; twenty-eight families were wiped out. At nearby Casolari, a further two hundred and eighty-two victims perished, including thirty-eight children and two nuns. The final local civilian toll was 1,830, which moved Mussolini to make a vain protest to Hitler. This was the sort of price many Italian communities paid for resisting Nazism, and which contributed heavily to the country's wartime civilian death toll of 153,000, three times that of Britain. Three-quarters of that number perished after the Italian armistice.

If the Allied invaders never matched the sort of horrors the Nazis inflicted on Italians, they were parties to lesser crimes: French colonial troops, especially, committed large-scale atrocities. 'Whenever they take a town or a village, a wholesale rape of the population takes place,' wrote a British NCO, Norman Lewis. 'Recently all females in the villages of Patricia, Pofi, Supino and Morolo were violated. In Lenola, fifty women were raped, but – as these were not enough to go round – children and even old men were violated. Today I went to Santa Maria a Vico to see a girl said to have been driven insane as the result of an attack by a large party of Moors... She was unable to walk... At last, one had faced the flesh-and-blood reality of the kind of horror that drove the whole female population of Macedonian villages two centuries ago to throw themselves from the cliffs rather than fall into the hands of the advancing Turks.'

Such Allied excesses, matched by the effects of air and artillery bombardment through the long struggle up the peninsula, ensured that few Italians gained much joy from their "deliverance". Two soldiers of 4th Indian Division were chasing a chicken around a farmyard when a window of the adjoining house was thrown open: 'A woman's head appeared, and a totally unexpected English voice called out "F*** off and leave my f***ing 'ens alone. We don't need no liberation 'ere."'

The wild Italian countryside and hospitable customs of its inhabitants prompted desertions from the Allied armies on a scale greater than in any other theatre. The rear areas teemed with military fugitives, men "on the trot" – overwhelmingly infantry, because they recognised their own poor prospects of survival at the front. 30,000 British deserters were estimated by some informed senior officers to be at liberty in Italy in 1944/45 – the equivalent of two divisions – and around half that number of Americans.

Both the Germans and Allies distributed broadsheets to the population, making competing demands for their aid. Iris Origo wrote: 'The peasants read these leaflets with bewildered anxiety as to their own fate, and complete indifference (in most cases) to the main issue: *Che sara di noi*? What will become of us? All that they want is peace- to get back to their land – and to save their sons. They live in a state of chronic uncertainty about what to expect from the arrival of soldiers of any nationality. They might bring food or massacre, liberation or pillage.' On the afternoon of 12th June 1944, Origo was in the garden of her *castello*, rehearsing "Sleeping Beauty" with her resident complement of refugee children, when a party of heavily armed German troops descended from a truck. Full of terror, she asked what they wanted, to receive a wholly unexpected answer: 'Please – wouldn't the children sing for us?' The children sing "O Tannenbaum" and "Stille Nacht" (which they learned last Christmas) – and tears came into the men's eyes. "*Die heimat* – it takes us back to *die heimat!*" So they climbed into their lorry and drove away.' Less than two weeks later, the area was occupied by French colonial troops. Here were the alleged liberators, yet Origo wrote bitterly: 'The Goums have completed what the Germans begun. They regard loot and rape as the just reward for battle, and have indulged freely in both. Not only girls and young women, but even an old woman of eighty has been raped. Such has been Val d'Orcia's first introduction to Allied rule – so long and so eagerly awaited!'

Allied forces sustained a sluggish advance up the peninsula, but from the summer of 1944 onwards, it was a source of dismay to Alexander's soldiers that Mediterranean operations and sacrifices commanded diminishing attention at home. 'We are the D-Day dodgers in sunny Italee,' they sang, in irony, 'always on the vino, always on the spree.' So they were regarded by some foolish people. They knew nothing of the reality of the mud, blood and misery in which the rival armies, and the Italian people, existed for most of the war years. The condition of the civilians was far worse in the last years of the war as they suffered from desperate hunger, indeed in some cases starvation.

For Italians, hunger was a persistent reality from the moment the country became a battlefield in 1943: 'My father had no steady income,' recalled the daughter of a rich Rome publisher. 'Our savings were spent, we were many in the house, including two brothers in hiding. I went with my father to the [public] soup kitchen because my mother was ashamed to do so. We made our own soup from broad bean skins. We had no olive oil… A flask of oil cost 2,000 lire when our entire house had cost only 70,000. We bought whatever was available on the black market, bartering with silver, sheets, embroidered linen. Silver was worth less than flour; even our daughters' dowries were exchanged for meat or eggs. Then in November, with the cold weather, we had to exchange goods for coal: the longest queues formed at the coal merchants. We carried the sacks back on our own, because it was better that no man showed his face [lest he should be conscripted for forced labour].'

The Allies who were supposedly liberating Italy treated the country with remarkable callousness. In December 1944, when there was hunger verging upon starvation in Italy, a British embassy official in Washington visited Assistant Secretary of War John J McCloy to protest against the policy of shipping extravagant quantities of supplies to US forces overseas, while Italian civilians were in desperate straits. 'In order to win the war,' he demanded of McCloy, 'are we not imperilling the political and social fabric of European civilisation on which the future peace of the world depends?' This drew from Mr McCloy the immediate rejoinder that it was a British interest to remember that, as a result of the complete change in the economic and financial position of the British Commonwealth that the war had brought about, we, in the U.K., depended at least as much upon the U.S. as we did upon Europe. Was it wise to risk losing the support of the U.S. in seeking the support of Western Europe? This was what was involved.'

The shocked British official persisted in pressing the case for feeding Europe's civilians. McCloy stuck to his guns, asserting that it would be fatal for Britain 'to argue that the war in the Pacific should be retarded in order that the civilian population of Europe should be fed.' The Foreign Office in London professed acute dismay on receiving the minutes of this meeting, but British impotence in the face of U.S. dominance remained a towering reality. That only a relatively small number of Italians died of starvation between 1943 and 1945 was due first to the illicit diversion of vast quantities of American rations to the black market, and thereafter to the people – much to the private enrichment of some U.S. service personnel, and to the political influence of Italian-Americans at home, which belatedly persuaded Washington of the case for averting mass starvation.

So there it is – just a few vignettes that I hope help to illustrate the nature of the tragic experience that the Italian people endured in the Second World War. It is because, as a historian, I know more than most people about the story, and about the noble part played by some of its humblest people, that I am so happy to support the work of the Monte San Martino Trust. It strives to keep alive an understanding of what we, the British, owed to many fine Italians; to show our recognition of that old debt of our fathers and grandfathers; and to renew the bond. It is sometimes said that in Britain, we remain in the 21st century too preoccupied, even obsessed, with the Second World War. But there are some aspects of the legacy that richly deserve to be kept alive, and indeed to be renewed, in the fashion the Trust aspires to do.

ABOUT THE AUTHOR

Hugo 'Huge' de Burgh is the author or co-author of thirteen books on investigative journalism, environment reporting and contemporary China. Of Irish origin, he spent much of his early life in Italy and Scotland. Since working as a social activist and journalist in Scotland, he has been a professor of media in Nottingham and London and Walt Disney Chair of Media and Communication at Schwarzmann College of International Relations in Tsinghua University. This is his first novel.

This book is printed on paper from sustainable sources managed under the Forest Stewardship Council (FSC) scheme.

It has been printed in the UK to reduce transportation miles and their impact upon the environment.

For every new title that Troubador publishes, we plant a tree to offset CO_2, partnering with the More Trees scheme.

MORE TREES
LET'S PLANT A BILLION TREES

For more about how Troubador offsets its environmental impact, see www.troubador.co.uk/sustainability-and-community